A M R *i i* K A

BOOKS BY M. G. VASSANJI

The Gunny Sack (1989)
No New Land (1991)
Uhuru Street (short stories, 1992)
The Book of Secrets (1994)
Amriika (1999)

AMR*ii*KA

M. G. VASSANJI

M&S

Cloth edition published 1999
First paperback edition published 2000

National Library of Canada Cataloguing in Publication Data

Vassanji, M. G.
    Amriika

ISBN 0-7710-8725-X

I. Title.

PS8593.A87A7   2001   C813'.54   C99-931343-6
PR9199.3.V27A87   2001

We acknowledge the financial support of the Government of Canada through the
Book Publishing Industry Development Program for our publishing activities. We
further acknowledge the support of the Canada Council for the Arts and the
Ontario Arts Council for our publishing program.

The epigraph on page 267 is taken from the Constance Garnett
translation of Fyodor Dostoevsky's *The Possessed*.

Text design by Kong Njo
Typeset in Bembo by M&S, Toronto
Printed in Canada

McClelland & Stewart Ltd.
The Canadian Publishers
481 University Avenue
Toronto, Ontario
M5G 2E9
www.mcclelland.com

2 3 4 5   03 02 01

For Nurjehan
The last train on Sunday
always left too soon.

Facing west from California's shores,

. . . .

I, a child, very old, over waves, towards the house of
    maternity, the land of migrations, look afar,
Look off the shores of my Western sea, the circle almost
    circled;

. . . .

Now I face home again, very pleas'd and joyous,
(But where is what I started for so long ago?
And why is it yet unfound?)

– WALT WHITMAN
"Facing West from California's Shores"

*W*e come from a small people, though we did not think of ourselves as such.

Aeons ago, or so it seems now, it was circles of time and recur-
ring rebirths that gave meaning to my innocent world; as did an
unknowable but ever-present God who could at once take on
friendly, familiar shapes – a fish, say, or a tortoise, or a prince out in
the jungle in the company of a woman and a band of monkeys –
and at other times be an irascible, possessive father. This was a time
when invocations worked miracles, angels kept watch over us, and
djinns lurked in the grey shadows of the sunset. Everything was
for the better, though, and because of our basic goodness it could
only improve.

But all this I left behind, having cut loose on a tangent one day
and escaped into come-what-may. And here I stand, after so many
years; and perceived from this, its westernmost rim, the earth *is* flat.
And my destiny ends here – a dive in the sand. There is no going
back, of course; just as surely there's no going on and around to
where I began. I've arrived here shorn of places and ready-made
truths. In this bewildered state in which I now find myself, following the recent event that gained me (if you recall) an instant of
notoriety and media spotlight, as I await my beloved without too
large a hope and chase shadows of vanished omens for meaning, I
sometimes indulge in beginnings. I try to imagine some starting

point in the past when that destiny began, that movement to reach out for a larger world. The furthest back I can go is to a medieval time, a tumultuous epoch in which I see a mystic mendicant who left a Persia ravaged by the Mongol Khans and sought refuge in the rich and chaotic soil of Hindustan – the larger India, today's South Asia – and found the people of my race and whispered to them of better worlds.

I write this account not without encouragement – to imagine beginnings, yes, and more, to sustain them and guide them to my present condition, here in the obscurity of these rented rooms near a beach. Thus, I've been told with compassion, will I heal my wounds, and (in admonishment) even save my soul from endless torments. As I write these memoirs, I must admit to this too: the probing attentions of a certain representative of the law. He does not interfere as yet but hovers just beyond the edge of my narrative.

Three kids, college age, are among my visitors here. They come because, so they say, of the funky beach around here; but also, I believe, out of sympathy and concern for someone they call "Uncle" simply because I belong to their parents' generation. Their burdens are of a different order: they discuss sex and AIDS, religion and intermarriage, the hangups of their immigrant parents; and their own impending futures. But I suspect they too are sometimes drawn to beginnings. And do I delude myself into thinking there's a certain wariness too, and awe, at some challenge from the past I may represent? Their names are Leila, Hanif, and Lata. Whatever their reasons for coming, their age and innocence do take me back to a more historical beginning.

My mind often returns to the same point, if not an actual then a constructed origin: a short stout old woman in a soft long dress, with greying hair somewhat loose and wavy in front but tied behind in a small bun, who –

Grandma was a singer, and a healer. I don't know which first. She never sang when she healed but she muttered strange prayers, using mysterious powers she claimed were her birthright. But when she sang, she opened curiosity and old cupboards and strange premonitions and desires, even the desire to get away, leave everything behind.

Translating an old folk hymn is like transporting a village house to a city avenue, it loses vitality, colour, significance – but here goes: one of the verses she used to sing went, "Higher and higher I climb / waiting for my Swamiji – Lord – to arrive . . ."

I would then imagine Grandma sitting high up on some tree branch, gazing out westwards towards the horizon in anticipation of that Swamiji, that Lord, who would come on a white horse in the company of princes riding elephants and amid the sounds of trumpets and tambourines to take her away to a promised land.

Our ancestors were Hindus who were converted to a sect of Islam, and told by that refugee from the Mongols to await the final avatar of their god Vishnu. In Grandma's words, the sun would arise that day from the west. How far was this west? Where did it begin?

My people sought it first in Africa, an ocean away, where they settled more than a hundred years ago. But in time this west moved further, and became – America; or, as Grandma said it: Amriika.

When I departed for that Eldorado she came to see me off at the Dar es Salaam airport, taking a ride from the local coal seller who lived across the street. The three of us sitting in the front of the pickup, my vinyl suitcase in the coaldust at the back, collecting black ugly smudges which eventually faded into a residual grey that I would treasure for years. The weekly flight to London left late at night. The airport was crowded with passengers, relatives, and those who had driven over just to have a look-see at a plane taking off into the dark, with people flying away perhaps never again to be seen. Sona, my classmate who was going with me, was of course there, having arrived before me. And also in that small throng there was Darcy, the awesome intellectual and Grandma's patient, who had come to know her quite well in the past few years. I remember going through the immigration checkpoint and turning around for one last look at Grandma: standing stiffly among the crowd, feigning sternness for grief, her right arm still raised in the goodbye she'd said minutes before, the hand closing and opening as if mechanically in one endless farewell.

I never saw her again. And Darcy, her friend who had now come to stand beside her? I saw the old magus years later when I'd almost forgotten he existed, and he offered a magic potion, a going home of sorts . . . but I'm getting ahead of myself, there's so much in the middle.

It was August 1968; a young man, about the same age as my three young visitors, left home.

I

SCHRÖDINGER'S CAT

(1968–70)

"I remember my youth and the feeling that
will never come back any more – the feeling that I
could last for ever, outlast the sea, the earth, and all men;
the deceitful feeling that lures us on to perils,
to love, to vain effort . . ."

– JOSEPH CONRAD
Youth

1

"*T*he pigs charged and we threw rocks at 'em –"

"Right *on*, man!"

Amriika. America.

Sirens hooting in the night, so demoniacally urgent, so persistent, sending chills up his spine where he lay wide-eyed in his bed, grappling with a world that had just cracked open. And he thought, What satanic crime is being committed somewhere? . . .

All around him a soft penumbral darkness, a stillness scored by the straight lines of dormitory bunk beds, spooky four-legged skeletons of iron standing upright in rows. On the brick wall behind him, some feet away, a barred frosted-paned window admitted muted, fitful versions of the frantic streetlife outside. The hum and grind of vehicles behind the wall, and a few human sounds: footsteps; discarded, disposable fragments of conversation. Headlight beams through the window, and flashing blue police lights, and the deafening sirens, behind him now, his heart pounding. *Here?* The sounds, the flashing lights, went away, disappeared into distance, anonymity.

". . . goddamn fascist pigs – it's a fuckin' fascist country, that's what –"

"Right *on* . . ."

Is that all he can say? The second voice, deep and gravelly, belonged to a black guy with an Afro hairstyle. I know what they're talking about . . .

The other voice, thin and whining and anxious, came from the bunk above his. The guy who occupied it was white, with a beard and long hair down to his shoulders, who'd stared at him in disbelief earlier as he came back from the bathroom changed into his brand-new striped pyjama suit.

The Afro, who was in the adjacent upper bed, was now saying, "Malcolm says we landed on no fuckin' Plymouth rock, this fuckin' rock landed on us, man . . . we gonna push it right back on their ass. . . . Yeah, man . . ."

That was quite a mouthful, coming from him; it reverberated like controlled thunder. The swearing made Ramji flinch. He wasn't used to it in English, this way, up close.

"You'll be there at the Commons tomorrow?" the white guy asked.

"You bet."

"Night."

"Night."

America.

Elvis. Yes, that was the first revelation from an alien world, before there was even a picture of America in the head. "Jailhouse Rock," and parents complaining of uncontrollable kids jumping on beds and chairs when it was played on the weekly request program

in Dar es Salaam; and they had it banned! "Can't Help Falling In
Love," that beautiful ballad sung to a music box in Hawaii, and I so
much wanted to be in love. But more than that, more than Elvis –
Kennedy. Ich bin ein Berliner, we all knew that much German; and
America was saving the world from godlessness. Then Kennedy
shot dead. Just that, a giant newspaper headline glimpsed in a
vendor's hand, and it seemed a little more charm was gone from
our world. And beautiful Jackie – why did she have to go and
remarry. Soviet premier Khrushchev banging his shoe at the UN,
the U-2 spy plane shot down over Russia, the Cuban crisis. Perry
Mason the lawyer-detective and Della Street his secretary having
coffee and doughnuts in some café in Los Angeles, discussing a
murder case. Pat Boone and Rock Hudson were the girls' heart-
throbs. And then the ugly side, the frightening America: dangerous
streets, sex, drugs. Blackboard jungle, cement jungle, neon jungle
. . . and the death's head of technology: ICBMs and MIRVs, marvellous and terrifying. As a teenager, he would wake up frightened by
nightmares about the coming Third World War. Two years before,
his class essay on the destruction of the world was read aloud in
admiration by the teacher. But there was also the thrilling moon-
landing. The fundis – tailors – outside Grandma's house were all of
the opinion that the Americans had the world fooled. "Éti, how
can anyone go to the moon – it's so small and comes out at night
and roams the seven heavens." Above all, Americans were friendly
people who said things like "ain't" and whose "can't" was so hard
to distinguish from their "can." And they had great universities
with towering columns and domes, where all the awesome modern
research was done, and to one of which he, Ramji, had been
admitted – the Tech. Some of the astronauts had actually studied
there; and also giants like Feynman, and Gell-Mann. . . . *Time* had

reported that even at the Tech and Harvard, students had come out in protest against that war in Vietnam. And now at this Youth Hostel on Harvard Square –

Suddenly, the bed heaved, tilted perilously on two legs for an instant – giving Ramji a tremendous fright – then came down safely back on all fours; the sagging weight on the upper bunk had rolled over to the edge.

"By the way, the name's Russell." The long-haired one to the Afro, across the aisle.

"George," came the reply.

Are they really shaking hands now, after all this? Only in. . . . He smiled, relieved, his heart yet to recover from the ordeal.

"Hey, pleased to meet you," said Russell.

"Same here."

"I say power to the people and down with the military-industrial complex!"

"Night again . . ."

Wait till I tell Sona about these two characters.

Sona, his classmate, had arrived with him from Dar, and was sleeping a few bunks away. What was *he* thinking?

It was Sona who first brought up the idea of actually going to America, when those who could get away had always gone to England. "I'm applying to go to America – Boston," he said excitedly one day to Ramji on their way home from school. "Why don't you apply too, we can go together!"

"Yeah, let's go to America!" Ramji had said. But when he thought about it, as the weeks wore on, he wasn't really sure he wanted to go. How could he leave Grandma alone? It wasn't such a small step, going so far away. And then, one evening –

"Mr. Kennedy . . ."

"Yes?"

"Mr. Kennedy, may I have the honour of shaking your hand?"
Pandemonium. Laughter. Disbelief.

"Of course, come forward and I'll be glad to."

And he had gone forward and shaken Bobby's hand to great
cheering. Except that it wasn't he who'd shaken Bobby's hand
but that nutty cricket captain of the school, who'd dropped out
soon afterwards. Still, it was as if everybody present there had
shaken Bobby Kennedy's hand, at the Diamond Jubilee Hall in
Dar es Salaam.

It was a thrilling, an inspiring evening. And it seemed to him
that it was only for him – that slim handsome American, with the
nonplussed look, the open mouth, the white teeth – that he would
go to America. Everything else, all the other attractions seemed
secondary, only that face which he had seen in the flesh drew him
on. The casually friendly face of America.

And then Bobby was shot dead. Did you hear it, Ramji? It was
Sona, late in the evening, standing at the door. What? Ramji asked,
What happened? Bobby Kennedy is dead – shot! Ramji just
couldn't believe it, but the local news had said it, the BBC had said
it. The two of them had tried tuning in to the Voice of America for
confirmation, but they couldn't hear anything through the static.
Afterwards they sat outside Ramji's house and chatted late into the
night, discussing this and the other assassinations. First JFK and then
Martin Luther King, now Bobby Kennedy. What an amazing
country America was. The next morning Ramji – his departure
only a few weeks away – said, I'm not going to this place that kills
its own just like that. His friend Sona had begged him, Ramji, you

can't do this now! His teachers too had begged him: Go. And Grandmother, sorely tempted to keep him home beside her, now that he wanted that too, nevertheless sent him to see Mr. Darcy. That intellectual who had been a grateful patient of hers, who knew a thing or two about the world out there. Go, Mr. Darcy said, there's nothing more important than your education. And so Mr. Darcy broke the jinx, his last-minute jitters, and here he was.

Sona, are you awake? . . . In the upper bunk Russell and George seemed finally to have fallen asleep. Tomorrow . . . he thought, tomorrow begins my first real day here . . .

He and Sona had been picked up at the airport by a rather nice and chatty couple from the American Host Program, called the Campbells ("a name that's been made famous by a certain soup company!"). It was warm and drizzly outside, and as they drove into Cambridge the city lights looked glorious, reflected in the rain. The Campbells drove Ramji and Sona along Memorial Drive by the Charles River, past the breathtakingly imposing lighted dome of the Tech, before depositing them at the hostel. They were simply the "picker-uppers," they said. Having given Ramji and Sona the separate particulars about their host families, where they would be staying for the couple of weeks before classes started, and brief instructions on how to survive in America, they disappeared into the wet night.

His "family" were John and Ginnie Morris of Runymede, New Jersey, and he'd called them collect, as instructed.

Mr. Morris, sounding ever so informal, almost jovial, said he had been waiting all day for Ramji's call. He had been informed of his visitor and expected him to arrive in New York. Never mind. Would Ramji fly in to New York? No, Ramji would take a Greyhound bus – at about eleven next morning after meeting the foreign student adviser on campus.

"See you in New York, then. We're all anxious to meet you."

The lunar astronauts, even while making the giant leap for mankind, were at least in constant touch with planet Earth, to which they would eventually return. When would *he* return? Someday. Meanwhile here he was, plucked out from his old life and suspended . . . in this silence, in this darkness, in this alien air, with the alien smell of the pillow and feel of the mattress, the cold tiled touch of the floor below him when he dropped his hand and let his fingers run over it. Perhaps he was dreaming . . . or had died and, now a disembodied spirit, was looking down on himself as he lay on the lower bunk, eyes fixed at the sagging shape of long-haired radical Russell above him . . .

Back in another world the sun is rising, the street beginning to stir, the day's impending heat a friendly suggestion in the warm air, the bright sky. The old woman in a loose frock, her face age-lined into a perpetual look of pain as if she's swallowed bitter medicine, is up and about in her home, having returned from mosque. She is humming, perhaps her monkey song about the transience of the world. The servant will arrive, the rooms will be swept; morning tea is on the stove. Soon she'll set off on some service or another – sweeping the mosque, preparing a corpse for last rites and the funeral, cooking for a festival. Outside, the radio at the Arab restaurant blares out the latest news in Swahili. Ah, that sound, the booming voice over the aromas of red-brown fried maandazi and the tinkle of teacups. Soon boys and girls in uniforms will set off for school. Shops will open. The street will be all a-bustle, and the sun bright and hot.

The tall leather boots of Russell expelled a pong close by and Ramji turned away to sleep.

The next morning the sky was clear; lugging suitcases, stopping to ask for directions, they lurched to the Square (the thought of the fare in shillings rendering a taxi unthinkable) and from there they took the Dudley bus to the Tech. The amiable yet patronizing letters of the Foreign Student Adviser had guided their applications over the previous twelve months and finally admitted them to the temple of learning, so it was natural in their minds to present themselves to him first. The lanky Mr. Neville was as friendly and easy as they expected. He gave them coffee and doughnuts, introduced them to his assistants, and assured them all was okay and it was best for them now to head for their respective host families, and see you on registration day.

The bus terminal was next to the Arlington subway station. The name rang a bell in their minds: Wasn't "Arlington" the name of that famous cemetery? It would be a wonderful thing, they decided, to see JFK's and Bobby's graves and the Eternal Flame on this, their first day. But nothing like a cemetery was in sight.

"Yes, this is Arlington," said the man at the ticket counter. The traveller's cheques had put him in a sour mood. "You ain't got no American money?"

"The cemetery," Sona said to him, a little too cockily.

The man looked up, examined Sona, chewing his gum vigorously, then spat it out into a trash basket. "Come again?"

"Arlington National Cemetery. We'd like a quick look."

"Hey Jack-o, come over here," called the man, to the porter standing nearby. "Take a look at this pair."

The porter came over, a stooping, elderly black man wearing a cap.

"Know where Arlington Cemetery is around here?" asked the ticket clerk. "Guys here want to go visit."

The porter looked astonished. "What −?" he began, but saw the smirk on the clerk's face. "Ah!" he said. "Arlington National Cemetery is in Washington, D.C. Yes sir. Washington Express − Gate Seven." He pointed.

"I'm going to New York," Ramji said sheepishly.

"Departing from Gate Twelve," the porter said.

"Westport," said Sona.

"For Westport, change at Hartford. Gate Six. But you ain't goin' to find Arlington National Cemetery where you's goin'. No sir." And he headed off, shaking his head.

"New York?" Ramji leaned towards the man across the aisle from him.

"It's New York City all right," said the man indulgently and smiled at him.

Of course, *of course*, this was New York, finally . . . his heart thudding inside him, his face glued to the window. Several times on the way he thought they had arrived, as they approached what looked like a big city, only to speed by it, and he had sat back.

There was no mistaking where he was now, what he was looking at. The sheer bigness, the busyness . . . this endless maze of streets, its thick and crawling traffic, blaring store signs, littered sidewalks . . . awash with people, droves of them rushing from place to place, crowding at the intersections . . . or standing idly or doing their jobs selling, unloading, washing windows. . . . And the Empire State Building, the skyscrapers, where? – Only when they were suddenly cruising through sunless streets did he realize that they were right in the midst of them, in between the tallest buildings in the world.

They entered an underground garage of buses and stopped at a numbered bay.

A metal-framed glass door led into the terminal, which he entered following other passengers, his blue vinyl suitcase in one hand, airline slingbag over his shoulder. Almost immediately, having taken a hesitant step or two, and a desperate sweeping look for his host, whom he didn't know by sight, he was caught in the tide of people heading towards the stairway. At the top, after two flights of stairs, he picked a spot to stand, set the suitcase down, and slowly took in the scene. Ahead of him, in the distance, doors opened into a busy street. Behind him, far away, the same. All around him a tumult. Long rows of busy ticket counters; a restaurant and newsstand, a picket line, demonstrators. How would Mr. John Morris pick him out from among this multitude . . .

A boy roughly his age catches his eye, starts walking towards him. Friendly purposeful look on the face, but rather unkempt with long hair and torn jeans and a half-open red shirt. . . . Two other similar-looking characters also converge upon him from opposite sides. Peace, man, says one, another one nods and gives a V-sign, they start talking of war and the military, and companies that make weapons, and he's caught in a barrage of words, a confounding jumble of expressions and ideas. You can be sure it's Buttonhouse . . . the friendly company that makes the refrigerators that keep your orange juice cool also makes your friendly missiles . . . you know what a cluster bomb looks like . . . sharp metal pieces flying in all directions embedding into innocent baby flesh . . . or how napalm scorches the skin? . . . He's staring at a picture: a horribly emaciated girl running stark naked, face contorted in pain. . . . There's more – take them. Flyers. What? he asks helplessly, recoiling a little. Peace, man, take care, they depart gravely, heading in the direction they came from. Why take care, are they warning me? . . . He looks quickly through a flyer. Namasté, a girl's voice close to him – he's surrounded, enveloped in swirling swathes of wildly bright colours, red and orange and blue. Namasté. This book contains the teachings of Lord Krishna . . . God, the speaker is incredibly beautiful, like a dream girl, blue eyes, long brown hair, tall, and she is dressed like an Indian, in a sari! Do you know of the Bhagavad Gita, she asks. He has the book in his hands, looking at blue Krishna with a flute and the sign of Om . . . and all around him a circle of close-cropped guys and angelic long-haired girls in orange robes and saris singing Hare Rama, Hare Krishna . . . and the deafening jangle of tambourines . . . and the pretty girl is saying . . . what? Krishna teaches the yoga of devotion. . . . What? With a beaming look, The donation is five dollars. . . . Reluctantly he puts a hand in his pocket . . . the cause is good, but this money is supposed to go a long away . . .

"No, we don't want the book," said a voice firmly beside him. "Mr. Ramji, I presume?"

"How about incense from Benares?"

"No, we don't want that either, thank you."

A round-faced man in glasses, grey suit, medium height. Ramji nodded to him, immensely relieved. "Mr. . . ."

"John Morris. John. Am I glad to see you."

Ramji had expected a taller American, a big man, if only from the voice on the phone last night. Lyndon Johnson–like.

They shook hands.

"Didn't know which gate your bus was arriving at, or which stairs you'd take." Mr. Morris paused, added: "I guess you found out there's at least a couple of buses leaving Boston every hour for New York."

"Yes. I didn't realize that the station would be so . . . big," Ramji said sheepishly.

"Glad you made it."

"How did you find me?" Ramji asked.

"Luck. Also there's not many people with your features in this place, and looking utterly lost." John Morris looked at him and grinned. "Good thing, though, you stayed close to those stairs."

He picked up the shoulder bag and showed Ramji where to throw the flyers he still clutched in his hands, after which they set off towards the Seventh Avenue exit.

They crossed two noisy intersections bustling with crowds of people before arriving at a sleek black car in a parking lot.

"The Grand Prix is Ginnie's. I drive a smaller vehicle. But I don't bring the car to work, today being exceptional. The commuter train's more convenient from Runymede."

John and Ginnie Morris. He repeated the names in his mind, recalling the letter he'd received from them only a couple of days before he left Dar. Their sons, John, whom they called Junior, and Chris, eighteen and fifteen years old. He couldn't remember what it was that Mr. Morris did . . .

Everything was America now, everything would be America. You could say that word, Amriika, a hundred times without repeating it once, each time would be different, that was the wonder of it. Where did it begin, this place, it simply happened all around him. He couldn't follow his host's remarks, the observations and explanations as they drove on the noisy New Jersey Turnpike, the world's busiest highway, busier than usual today at this hour and hot for the August weather, its toll booths where you flung money into baskets before you could pass, the enigmatic yet chummy billboards, the exits into Hoboken, Passaic, Teaneck, Montclair. Once as a boy he'd read an account in the Sunday papers about the famous Greyhound bus that covered every little corner of America; little did he know that one day he would take a ride on just such a bus and emerge in New York.

Mrs. Morris – Ginnie – was a big vivacious blonde, with shoulder-length hair, in a shimmering bottle-green form-fitting dress; she had a great wide smile for him as she opened the door, and gushed forth, "Oh, we've been so excited this past week – haven't we, boys – ever since we were told you were coming." Beside her stood a lanky long-faced youth in jeans, long straight hair covering the ears, a stray front lock across the forehead: Chris; and, on the other side of her, shorter and a little stocky, clean-cut and with glasses, his brother John Junior.

Ramji shook hands with all three, taken aback by the reception, and coming out a little too shifty with, "I've been looking forward too, to meeting you . . ."

"You must be jet-lagged," said Chris.

"I beg your pardon?"

"The time difference between your country and New Jersey —"

"Oh yes. It's eight hours."

"Past your bedtime then."

"I don't know what time you're used to eating dinner, but we eat early. I hope that's not inconvenient for you," said Mr. Morris.

"Oh no. It's fine."

They went straight to the dining room. Ramji was shown his place, beside Chris, opposite Ginnie and Junior. At the head sat Mr. Morris, who, when they'd settled, looked around and said, "Ready?"

They were all watching Ramji. He looked down and stared at his fork and knife, grateful there was no fish today to confuse matters with a fish knife and extra fork. Then he looked up and realized they were holding hands, waiting for him. Mr. Morris took his right hand and Chris took his left, and Mr. Morris said, "We thank thee, Lord, for this food, and bless Ginnie, Junior, Chris, John, and Ramji."

"Amen," they all said, each in his own fashion and time, and looked up.

"Is, er . . . isn't Ramji his last name?" Junior asked with a twinkle in his eye.

"Oh, in school everybody called me Ramji, it's almost like a first name now — you can call me that!"

"Let's start, everybody," Ginnie said, as the boys popped open cans of Fresca and Coke. He could have Dr Pepper if he wanted, she told him. He thought he'd try the Fresca, which was her choice too.

"And — Ramji, you can use your hands for the chicken, we all do."

Mr. Morris beamed across the table, benevolent and happy, the guest delivered into Ginnie's hands.

Besides the fried chicken, there was a potato casserole, broccoli, corn on the cob, and soft bread rolls they called biscuits; he was famished and did not hesitate over possible gaffes in his eating habits. Along with the boys he accepted seconds.

The cherrywood table, deep red tablecloth, high-backed chairs, floral placemats, sparkling chandelier; Ramji was overwhelmed by it all. The entire house looked beautiful and expensive; he would have to tread gingerly, try not to look an utter savage, or break things or slip somewhere, or whatever.

What do you say to them, who've got it all? That there is greater moral fibre and spirituality where you come from – as he'd been taught – and less materialism? That we don't go searching for useless causes and new faiths as Americans do, we know exactly who we are? That we have the secret gnosis that is the key to the universe . . . ?

Chris told him he'd joined the Buddhist faith. Junior, their mother said, was studying to become a Mormon minister; but he had a Catholic girlfriend with Catholic inhibitions. She smiled mischievously and Junior protested with "Mother!" The Morrises were Episcopalian. Chris went to military academy, which he hated; his brother had graduated from it and was attending college in Baltimore.

"It must be beautiful, where you come from," Ginnie said.

"Yes," he grasped the line gratefully. She was very kind and motherly.

"I saw a TV show about animals once – elephants," she said.

"Some years ago an Englishwoman was mending a puncture outside Dar and an elephant came by and stood to watch her!"

"I'd be scared out of my wits! And lions? And leopards? I bet you must have them practically strolling through your living rooms –"

"Mother!"

"Only in national parks," said Ramji, smiling at her, not a bit offended.

After dessert, which was apple pie, they all went and sat in the den, Ramji and John and Ginnie with their coffee, and John narrated to everyone's amusement how he had come upon a bewildered and besieged Ramji at the bus terminal. Then Ramji went to his luggage, lying at the foot of the stairs, and brought out his gift for the family: a wood carving. It looked so modest here, he thought, so rough. But serious carvers in Tanzania did not paint or polish their work, arguing for a primitive, uncommercial look. It was an expensive piece, though, of dark brown wood, the kind only tourists could afford. But Grandma had somehow brought it on his last day and told him to take it for his hosts. He presented it to Ginnie now, saying with a shy smile, "There are also monkeys in Africa."

"Is this a monkey – wait a minute, I must have it the wrong way up –" She turned it around a couple of times in her hands. "Oops!" It almost fell from her hands.

"It's a Makonde carving," he explained. "It's an abstract monkey, or monkeys – you can see the arms and legs, too many for one monkey . . . and an eye, an ear, and a mouth –"

They were all staring at him as he explained.

"It does look complicated . . . ," Ginnie said.

"The motif is the well-known saying, See no evil, hear no evil, speak no evil," Ramji concluded.

"And do no evil, I bet! Well, it's beautiful, it will go right up on the mantelpiece here!"

She liked it for his sake, but he hoped she would grow to really like it.

"Well, we should call it a day, I think," Mr. Morris said. He had been quiet for the past little while.

"You must be tired," Ginnie said to Ramji; and to her husband, "You too, dear."

Ramji nodded.

Mr. Morris gave Ginnie a peck on the cheek, wished all a good night, and went upstairs.

Ramji was shown his room. It was in the attic, to which narrow carpeted stairs led from the second floor where the couple and the boys had rooms. He was to have his own bathroom, a luxury that would save much embarrassment. It had no shower, if he needed to use one, though, he could use the boys' bathroom, he was advised. He didn't think that would be necessary. And if he felt hot up there, he could turn on the air conditioner. Finally, if he got hungry, he could run down for a late snack.

He quickly said his prayers, sitting up in bed. And then as he lay down to sleep, he thought the bed was so soft, and the linen so wonderfully crisp and fresh, he had never smelt anything as sweet before.

Sona loved writing letters.

". . . Have they shown off their automatic garage doors, and can opener and fancy phone with push buttons and the garbage disposal, and car windows that go up and down with the push of a switch?! Have they taught you the arcane secrets of their football, and that game of rounders that's as awkward as an itch and called baseball? . . ."

"Yes, yes, yes," Ramji wrote back. "They have shown me all those things you mention, and more – I have seen the gadgets and the gizmos (how I love that word!). And I'm *immersed* in television. Gomer Pyle has me in stitches, and I *love* Lucy and Dick Van Dyke, and Jeannie and McHale – and I could sing you the Gilligan theme song . . . and much more. I know about baseball now, but this is not the football season, you should know that! But no hippies here. No 'radicals.' Once, while watching the 'tube' with the family, there appeared a really offensive wild-haired man on it, wearing an Indian kurta and muttering 'Om, Om.' And he was all for drugs and free sex! 'Let me assure you he doesn't represent even one per cent of America,' Mr. Morris assured me. Mr. Morris was in the Second World War and he has a letter from President Truman, which he has framed and hung in his study.

"Next week Mr. Morris and I go to Washington. It will be Arlington *Cemetery* this time. (Yes, sir!)"

He could have said they patronized him, he had prescience enough for that. Yet there was a kindness and generosity, though they could undoubtedly afford what they gave him. There was a little bit of flaunting, too, as when he had accompanied Ginnie on a shopping trip, and a two-inch-thick meat sandwich was put before him and she watched him first gape then have a go at it. "We don't always eat like this, of course," she told him with a smile, "and I simply have to watch what I eat, so I'm afraid I can't help you finish it."

"You're so good," she said, still watching him, "so contented."

"I would say it's you who are good," he said, deeply moved, and thinking, After all, you hardly know me, and here I am sitting with you, your cherished guest.

In the three weeks he stayed with the Morrises, the boys were away visiting friends and relatives. Ramji would come down late in the morning, having stayed up to watch the late show on television, then to read, and he would often find her at the kitchen table sipping coffee, perusing a magazine or the newspaper. She asked him many questions about his life and once she wrote a letter to his grandmother. And so he grew quite fond of her.

One weekend John drove him to Baltimore and Washington. They stopped at Fort McHenry in Baltimore, over which a lawyer named Francis Scott Key had seen the Star-spangled Banner still flying, after bombardment by the British from Chesapeake Bay and the burning of Washington, and was moved to write the famous words that became the national anthem. "It's not that I fancy my own voice or anything like that," said John apologetically, singing a few lines for Ramji, "it's only to show you the tune."

They were at the parking lot viewing the flag atop the fort. A few people stopped to watch them, and John, after hesitating, was compelled to finish the anthem. The bystanders clapped.

"Well, I haven't sung for an audience in a long time," John said, his face cherry red.

"You sang very well," Ramji said. "And thank you."

"Tell you what — let's keep this little episode between ourselves, or I'll never hear the end of it."

As he prepared to leave Runymede to go to Boston and begin university, he realized that now he had crossed a threshold. He was simmering with excitement and was impatient to start his new life, yet he felt apprehensive about what lay ahead. He did not know what would become of him, what he would turn into. But he had come with a vow of constancy against temptation, a promise to uphold his identity and faith. That was the promise all the young people left with, when they departed for Europe or America: to return intact. John took him to Newark Airport to dispatch him on the Boston shuttle; before that, as Ramji said goodbye to her at the house, Ginnie gave him a peck on the lips and he blushed.

2

*A*mid the clamorous modernist echoes of Hindemith and Buxtehude and Berg from LPs around us, we sit cross-legged on the floor of the music library singing hymns to the Indian god Vishnu – whose other name is Allah, so our ancestors were taught several hundred years ago. Fearing persecution, they were secret worshippers, "guptis," who met in private with members of their new sect, the Shamsis. One of them would act as a sentry at the door; they even had a password. Where did *they* meet? Some shopfront perhaps, with grain and spices and all sorts of smells instead of a library with records and music. There's no persecution here, but still we feel a sense of oddness, of smallness, of . . . insignificance? We too are guptis, then; no one except the librarian and janitor knows we are here, every Friday night when the campus is so quiet and deserted that even the most diligent nerd is relaxing somewhere in the Student Center over root beer and a Reuben grill.

We come endowed with a key to that inner truth, the secret answer to all questions and desires. Humbly worshipping our God, following the path of our ancestors, we will obtain salvation, escape the endless cycle of rebirth; so we've been taught. Let the others outside hustle and bustle around, wasting their precious births, pursuing illusion, maya.

In front, facing everyone else – ten people on a good day – sits Sona, the mukhi: presider. It's a family tradition, he says, his grandfather was a mukhi too. There is a mukhi in every town, village, and city in the world where there is a Shamsi; he is an honorary consul, so to speak, an American Express office, traveller's aid, keeper of the flame.

Within a week of his arrival from Connecticut, at the beginning of the term, Sona had managed to contact community members at two nearby universities, Smith and Brandeis, and in Worcester, Amherst, even Hartford and Nashua: there's a mosque in New England, come when you can. And they came, lonely souls, grateful someone had taken the initiative. Besides students, there was an engineer and a doctor, and a divorced woman with a child. Sona had obtained permission from the Humanities department to use the music library; and so every Friday in a dense, carpeted area of the library he produced from his royal blue airline bag a white sheet, a bottle of holy water, a port glass, a small bowl, incense sticks, and matches, and conjured up a mosque for his congregation. They called it their "musical mosque."

Outside in the courtyard the trees swish in the wind that blows up from the Charles River, through the corridor between the Humanities building and Rogers Dining Hall, and creates – say the experts – a Bernoulli effect. A tall black iron sculpture, called "Futile" and looking like a scarecrow in agony, its arms and legs curving off in four directions, supposedly checks the force of that wind, though if you walk by it you couldn't tell it was doing its job. Bernoulli, eh?

It was a marketplace of ideas they were in, a veritable souk, this city of colleges, Cambridge, Mass., founded by another persecuted people three hundred years before. It was a home for heresies, where the intellect found a place to be and become, find its rhythm from a multitude of beats, sample from dozens of tastes. Flyers everywhere – on public walls, on lampposts, on notice boards, or handed out enthusiastically in the corridors, on sidewalks, at building entrances – shrieked out their messages like hawkers peddling their wares. What have we here? What do *you* bring with you? Weigh in your truth against ours, try our truth, and see its glory; or, if you happen to be lost, bring us your homeless tortured spirit, let us comfort your loneliness and doubts, choose this path already picked by a thousand others just like you. Everywhere, gurus, pirs, psychologists, zealots of every stripe were fishing for disciples.

And there were those who, Krishna-like, offered you the path of action. The activists, the radicals. Do your duty, look into your conscience, and act: Strike, teach, come out for the Movement, for the People, for Peace; sit in, join a rally, occupy a building; raise your voice and your fist. Bring the war home from Indochina. Bring the *wars* home from the Third World. Expose the Mammon behind the friendly mask – sponsor of the war in Vietnam and investor in apartheid, supplier to Salazar in Angola and Mozambique and to tyrants and torturers the world over: the Military-Industrial Complex. And its brains: the Dr. Strangeloves in the burrows of this hallowed university that's given you your treasured scholarship . . .

And you, Ramji, ask yourself, Where do *I* come in, dare I show this little secret I've brought with me – shabby and incomplete, like the sculpture I gave Ginnie, unsophisticated – this little truth that does not possess even a proper educated tongue to talk about it? And a little voice inside you says, Fear not, you don't have to show it yet, but you have the truth, as you have been taught; one day your truth will be known and appreciated.

The truth? God? The greatest achievement of evolution is that matter in the form of mankind begins to understand itself, as we sit here, you and I, discussing. So said the great Peter Bowra in his introductory lecture to freshmen. You have come to this institution with dreams – to demolish the theories of Einstein, Heisenberg, Dirac – and to build new edifices of understanding; but most – all? – of you will settle for more modest goals. What God, then? The equation of the universe, that's the new God, it explains everything, including you and me as we sit here. The Schrödinger equation of everything there is. There would be many debates those Fridays after the ceremonies at the "musical mosque" on that equation of state: who wrote it, and what was *his* equation, and so on ad infinitum. But before that, Sona presides: the hymn is sung, the prayers are said; then, gravely, he pours the holy water from the bottle into some tap water in the bowl, and each one present, in turn, takes with both hands the little port glass he hands them, and swallows a shot of the diluted holy water. Sona replenishes his bottle with the remainder from the bowl, and screws on the cap. We have brought the holy Ganges with us.

There must be some truth preserved in this ritual, a deep universal truth contained in its simple form, for didn't even Einstein say that beauty lay in simplicity, and that simplicity was a prerequisite of truth?

His roommate in Rutherford House was Shawn Hennessy, tireless worker in the radical cause, the first sight of whom had sunk all Ramji's enthusiasm at moving into a place of his own for the first time in his life. Ramji had just fitted his newly acquired key into the door and swung it open. The song to Mrs. Robinson, on his lips, picked up from somewhere during the day's registration travails, froze in an instant, for there stood in the middle of the room, somewhat startled, what could only be the co-owner of the room, looking back at Ramji's curious, anxious stare. What have I got myself into, Ramji thought, is this a student at Tech or a bum? The guy could only be described as slovenly, in dirty, worn-out denim cut-offs, unbuttoned red and black checkered shirt, and old sneakers. He was broad, perhaps an inch or two shorter than the gaunt Ramji, with curly overgrown brown hair and a light, virgin beard on his angular face. He grinned, came forward, and the two shook hands.

"Which do you fancy," said Shawn, "the window or the phone?"

The room had prominent bunk beds and two desks with chairs against the far wall that looked down from its fifth floor window onto the yard between the two parallel wings of the House. It was small and spare, and the walls were cold brick, but it had one item in it suggestive of pure luxury to Ramji: the black telephone. He was thrilled by it. In Dar, the whole street on which he lived had two or three telephones, and you had to go and beg a shopkeeper, money in hand, to be able to use one. Ramji quickly picked for himself the desk on which the phone stood, not caring that he would lose the window view. He got to take the lower bed, to their mutual satisfaction, and use the two lowest drawers of the dresser as added compensation for the phone on his desk. Thus they rapidly apportioned the room between them.

A red-and-black poster, two feet by three, of the revolutionary Che Guevara in beret and beard was Shawn's contribution to the decor of their room. Ramji stared at it awhile and nodded yes, he approved. It was somewhat stark but not unattractive, with a suggestion of daring and enigma. After some hesitation he brought out a khanga as his offering: it was a bright printed cotton cloth with a central motif of orange and green pineapples on a white background, surrounded by a green and brown border. A boxed message in black ran across it, saying, "Wayfarer, look back" in Swahili. It covered a good portion of the bare wall facing the beds, where he hung it with Shawn's help. Shawn looked rather pleased with the effect. "Authentic Third World in Rutherford House," he said, glowingly satisfied.

Having finished their decoration, they sat down in their arm-chairs facing each other. Through the open window came the shouts of guys playing ball downstairs, the enticing smell of a barbecue, the heady sounds of rock music playing on a stereo somewhere. Shawn launched into politics.

The War. Vietnam. What was in everybody's mind here, it was there wherever you turned. David and Goliath. Villages destroyed, children napalmed . . .

"You can work against it, you know," Shawn said, gauging him. Ramji was a little dumbfounded by the barrage of words, the artic-ulation, the certainty. "There's a demonstration tomorrow at noon, why don't you come? It's organized by the SDS – Students for a Democratic Society – we have thousands of members across the country, we are in schools and we are going to the factories. The young people of this country are against the war and we're going to stop it. You should join."

"But – aren't they the ones – I mean –" who also demonstrate in the streets and throw stones at the police, Ramji wanted to say. "No – thanks . . ."

"Why not?"

They are not my idea of America, for one thing, he thought; they are not the Morrises and Runymede . . . if you don't count the kids at the shopping centre. Instead of that, he declared, flatly: "I support the Americans in Vietnam."

"Why?" Shawn leaned forward in his chair now, so Ramji had to pull back nervously. He looked intense, expectant, as though he was about to learn something important.

Ramji explained. If Vietnam goes, then Cambodia follows, and Laos, and slowly Thailand, Malaysia, and so on, until the whole of Asia becomes one massive godless communist block under China. The domino theory.

"Where did you hear that?"

"It's obvious, isn't it? Even *Time* says so." Simple as ABC.

Shawn emitted a not convincing laugh, then stopped. "Wait a minute, wait a minute. Do you know what *Time* is?" he exclaimed, then stopped. He was stumped. "All right, all right – forget it. You going to the mixer?"

Neither was in the mood for the mixer that evening in the social lounge, so they shot some pool in the basement and then went out for a stroll on Mass Ave towards Boston.

It was a pleasant Saturday night, a little past sunset, a cooling breeze gusting along the avenue. Winter will come early, Shawn pronounced, sniffing the air a few times, and Ramji wondered whether to believe him. There were not many people around. Rush week was just over; this was carousing time. Classes began Monday. As they crossed the Harvard Bridge high over the Charles, sounds from a party came to tease them, laughter rippling merrily across the water. They could hear playful, spirited male and female voices; mouth-watering frolicking in a boathouse. They exchanged looks, and Ramji wondered why Shawn was alone with him tonight. Whatever the reason, he was thankful for the company. Straight ahead loomed the tall Prudential Building, a towering glass column glowing in the night. Across the bridge, they stopped for pepper steak subs and milkshakes. The diner was a dingy place, its walls covered entirely with autographed black and white pictures; yes, Shawn said, they most likely had all visited here – actors, politicians, and athletes. Shawn was from the Boston area, and his father owned O'Henry's Pub in Harvard Square, known for the best hamburgers in town. But the two of them didn't get along.

"He's a racist and a reactionary. He's refused to pay my fees."

He had a younger sister, and an older brother, who was in Vietnam.

"He's fighting in the war and you're against it?"

"Uh-huh. I can't wait for him to get back. You know there's already an antiwar movement among the soldiers in Vietnam? But I guess Pat can't write all that, the letters are censored."

Shawn spoke earnestly but without raising his voice or losing his cool, undeterred by Ramji's views. Spring had been just great for the antiwar campaign, he said, too bad Ramji missed it. Why do you think Johnson's not running for president? . . .

Ramji said he was against the communists because they were atheists. He explained to Shawn an ancient prophecy he'd heard many times back home: Satan would arise in the east, with a massive army of millions, and proceed to conquer the forces of good in the west. Who had such power in the east except China and Russia? But ultimately, the good would win, the West would triumph . . .

Shawn nodded.

They had been walking heedlessly ever since leaving the diner, the foreigner in the hands of the local. Suddenly, instinctively, Ramji grew alarmed; his steps faltered, he let his voice peter out into silence. The scene around them had transformed into one of an eerie dinginess. Shawn too had observed this and began to look about nervously. They were in a grim, dilapidated area of town, marked by age, debris, and trash; the street was dimly lighted, almost deserted. The buildings were low, making the sky large and expansive. It was overcast. There was a tavern at the end of the block, with a red neon sign outside over the doorway. Ramji guessed that this was a ghetto. He must have seen scenes like this in movies, he'd read about the poverty of such neighbourhoods.

"Where are we?" he asked. "Feels frightening."

"Don't know . . . ," Shawn said, and they crossed the road, to walk back in the direction they'd come from.

Two black women waiting under a streetlamp blocked their path.

"How about a good time, boys?"

"Uh –" Shawn paused, turned to look at Ramji. "Do you –"

"What?" Ramji asked, and one of the women made a go for his crotch – "You like this?" – and he moved back with a start, and Shawn said, "Let's go." They started walking away hastily.

"Fags!" called the women after them.

"I don't know, did you want to . . . ?" Shawn asked.

"No," said Ramji. Should they have? He didn't even quite realize the two women were prostitutes, he'd been so terrified.

"Let's run," Shawn said. "Can you run?" And they ran for several blocks until a police car stopped and gave them a ride. They were Campus Police; the Tech wasn't going to let its foreign student disappear inside a ghetto.

In Dar, not rich ourselves, we lived next door to Africans and were not terrified. The neighbours were Grandma's friends and gave me that khanga as a going-away present. Here even a simple street scene has an aura that frightens – why? I can't even recall what the women looked like . . . I only saw a red miniskirt and black thighs. And so you remain a virgin, because that faith of yours does not tell you how to cope with that insistent sexuality. The only time he visited a prostitute he had also returned empty-handed, so to speak. It was while on a school trip to Mombasa, when an audacious fellow among them did not want to return home to Dar without screwing an Arab prostitute. And so a few of the boys had gone along. But where to find an Arab prostitute? They went around the shabbier streets, inquiring discreetly, shook off a gang of Arab youths on the way, knocked on a few doors, were chased off, and finally found an African-style shared abode where in one of the rooms surrounding the courtyard a woman provided the services. She was Arab, as required, and asked ten shillings, which was steep. First Mehboob went, the instigator and horniest. He asked for soap and water to take with him and had also brought along a tube of antiseptic ointment. Then someone else went. Then Ramji, but he balked at seeing the woman nonchalantly naked in bed, except for a khanga covering, and somewhat piously, as he later described it, placed five shillings on the plate on the side table, murmured something, and left.

The first physics lecture was delivered by a donkey; a mechanical one. A crude-looking contraption of wood and metal, its voice coming from a tape recorder, this donkey wrote the formulas and drew diagrams on the blackboard using its tail. The writing was somewhat shaky; and the donkey could not cover the entire board, which had to be raised or lowered for it, using the electrical switch (and at times it had to be pushed closer or farther from the board). The effect, after the initial titters, was awe-inspiring, and the students sat enthralled by the contraption.

The author of this lecture was no less than Peter Bowra, who came speeding on his wheelchair to the stage area, when the donkey had finished its duty, midway into the lesson. Students loved him because he entertained as he taught; he once deduced the sizes of a marble, an apple, and the sun using the same principles, in plain English and without resorting to a single mathematical formula. As a student of Oppenheimer, he had worked on the Manhattan Project, which had made the world's first atom bomb in Los Alamos. There, as he put it, he not only jointly gave birth to the doomsday gizmo, he was also the one who babysat it as it was being delivered to the test site. His calculations of its effects on a typical modern city had made him famous; but they had also turned him against the bomb.

"Actually," said the professor, pausing a moment, "actually, the prototype for this machine is much smaller, and was designed to *transport* entire lectures — to the handicapped, to other countries, and so on. But one of my graduate students, as a bet, took on the project this past summer to build a large-scale version for class lectures. Admittedly it's crude, but it's no worse than a professor in a wheelchair with an extreme case of Parkinson's disease. And so: Bowra's donkey, as my students call it."

The class applauded wildly.

And for the coup de grâce, he related the story of Schrödinger's cat.

Consider, he said, this *gedunken* (thought) experiment: Imagine a cat inside a closed black box together with a contraption that, when turned on, has a fifty per cent chance of giving off a radiation, which would trigger the release of a poison gas and kill the cat. We turn the contraption on through some remote means. After a given time — let's say half an hour — would you think the cat was alive or dead? What is the state of the cat? The question was only partly rhetorical, but there were no takers: even if you knew the answer, you did not have sufficient backup to take on the challenge. Well, the answer was this: As long as you haven't looked inside the box, the cat is a Schrödinger wave, the dead cat and the living cat smeared out in equal proportions.

"Think about that. Any questions."

Laughter; after all, what could you ask? The story was told to impress upon you what exciting adventures in knowledge lay ahead during your stay at the Tech. But Ramji raised a timid hand.

"What does the cat think inside the box," he asked. "I mean, what happens to its thoughts, are they fifty per cent . . ."

There was laughter, Bowra was happy, and he answered, "Ah, a metaphysician. Well, it depends upon whether the cat is one of Minsky's artificial creatures or God's."

Did I expect an answer, Ramji thought afterwards, do I know what exactly I meant? It just seemed like the right sort of question . . . and anyway, I can say one day that I asked this question of the great Peter Bowra. Even though I may have made an ass of myself.

But the lecture that day had given him what he considered a more accurate, and scary, image of himself. He realized that to his grandmother back home, who could have no idea as to what exactly was happening to him, he would be very much like a Schrödinger's cat.

3

*T*he boy was always reserved, withdrawn, a resource unto himself. All the other children he knew had a mother and father and a few siblings, but he had only his Ma. At some point, when Ramji was not yet six, he asked her, Where is Bapa, and she said, With God. Is that Bapa? Yes. A man wearing a black fez hat; the photo was of him alone, head and shoulders, but he was the same man as in that other photo, with her, where they were standing side by side in some sort of yard. Why did others have younger mas and bapas, or mummies and daddies? He didn't yet know of death, to guess and understand the answer to his question, but he was lonely and confused, harbouring this little grudge against his fate.

Unlike other houses, theirs was not filled with the laughter and play and shrill voices of children, did not reverberate with their running footsteps, echo piteously with their wailings when they were hurt or punished. There were no quarrels with neighbours, no fights between sisters-in-law, between man and wife. During Eid no uncles and aunts came around for a family feast and to present to a row of anxious children fifty-cent thumuni coins or shillings; before Eid there was no last-minute excitement about whether the moon would be sighted or not. Yes, neighbours would call out Eid Mubarak! or Idi Baraka! on the morning of the festival, and sometimes a distant relation would show up, shake hands, press a coin into his hand, and depart. In the evening, when the Eid drums beat at the Mnazi Moja grounds, he went with his Ma to the mosque to pray.

Unlike other homes, which had a busy shop in the front part of the house, or on the ground floor of a modern two-storey building, theirs did not. So there were no crowds of noisy haggling customers to engage with, no month-end sales to anticipate or the jangling of a busy cash box, no exciting stories to tell about thieves and shoplifters. Though sometimes when the neighbourhood shops stayed open late in the evening before Eid or during month-end, Ma would keep the front entrance to their house partly open and bring out a chair to sit on the sidewalk and chat with people.

Every morning at a little before four, Ma would wake up, get dressed, and leave the house. She would knock at a neighbour's, where another woman would be ready and waiting. At this still hour then, the two would trek off to the mosque, walking in the middle of the street. At designated points on the street they would pick up other women who were likewise inclined towards meditation on the holy names at this spiritual hour, so as to attain enlightenment and freedom from worldly entanglements. Sometimes, if a companion failed to appear as they arrived, the women on the street would call out to her; for instance: Dolu Bai! Are you coming? And Dolu Bai would reply with a muffled shout: Yes! One minute! Or: Not today, Babu is unwell – I can't come! And then the women would wait, or shuffle off. They were not fast walkers, these women in their fifties; they walked in their slippers, with a

characteristically rolling gait, talking in murmurs which nevertheless could be heard for several blocks in the otherwise dead silence.

If Ramji woke up with her, he would join her in the march,
dragging behind with the few other sleepy-eyed boys who had
also decided to brave this hour; otherwise she simply let him sleep,
and if he woke up when she was away, he would be frightened in
the dark.

Ma was renowned in the community, and even outside it, for
her power of healing. She treated cases in which doctors had failed
or were not trusted. There would be one or two real patients a day,
appointments having been made the previous evening in mosque;
but there were always people who stopped by at any hour if the
door was open, to discuss minor problems. Her tools included a set
of rudimentary utensils: a brass bowl, needles, a brass tumbler; and
water; and, most important, her two small hands. The boy had
watched her treat jaundice, the patient almost comatose on the bed
(in such cases she did home visits), the woman running the needles
along the sick limbs while muttering her prayers, then dropping
them in the water. The needles, the water, would turn yellow over
a few days, as the sickness and its telltale colour were drawn out of
the body. Often, at home, a child or woman would be brought in
with a chronic stomach ache or loss of appetite, the result of a
"jealous eye," and receive a massage or rub. Back troubles were
healed by her stepping in a prescribed manner on the patient's back
and reciting a formula. Then there were the potions for all kinds of
troubles that went beyond the boy's privilege of listening in on. He
would come to know, later, that these were often marital problems,
in which a "he" was the source of all the trouble.

With all her religious communal involvement, she carried a
certain moral authority. She sometimes looked stern, but she was

in fact positively light-hearted. She loved to sing hymns and folk songs, she sang in mosque and at home. Her voice had a scratchy quality to it, an old woman's raspy voice painfully struggling through musical modulations. In the boy's experience, though, she always came through, successfully negotiating the musical highs and lows; if you listened carefully you realized there was an authenticity to the singing voice, only it was remarkably eccentric, unlike anything else heard in the mosque. And so he had to watch members of the congregation hold their sides in silent laughter, and wipe their tears, unable to control their mirth. Perhaps she knew this, for she was no fool. The boy once asked her, Why do you sing in public? She, breaking off her humming, replied with a smile he swore was cunning in its look: Why, to praise my Lord!

He was eight years old.

It was four o'clock in the afternoon, the long bell signalling the end of school had rung, and the rest of the boys in his class had rushed out for home. Ramji was putting his things away in his bag. He had been delayed because of a bathroom break, which the teacher had allowed only after intense pleading. Now she was waiting for him at the door and chatting with another teacher. Mrs. Nanji was saying, while looking at her pupil, "He lives with his grandmother – all alone, poor child, his mother and father died –" She broke off when she met his eyes.

As he walked past the two teachers and on homeward, by himself since he had been delayed, he could barely contain his excitement. He realized that he had the answer to the mystery of his life. Ma was his grandmother. This made sense. And his mummy and daddy? They must be that couple in that other picture on the wall, the "auntie and uncle." They were young and hand-some. The man wore a white suit, dark shirt, and cravat, he had slick wavy hair, and he was smiling; she was in a Western dress, hair done up behind her, in a bun, and was also smiling though not as broadly. They stood side by side, close, he turned at a slight angle towards her, hands brought together lightly in front of him at the chest. The background behind them was a plain dark grey, it was a studio pose. That photo had always had a certain magnetism for him. A few times when he stood under it, staring at the couple, Ma had come and stood behind him.

When he reached home, as she laid the bread and butter on the table and joined him for tea, he said to her, "Ma — I know. That auntie and uncle in that photo over there are my mummy and daddy!" Her face crumpled, and two tears rolled down her cheeks, one of them dropping into her tea.

"They are with God," she said, wiping her eyes, "and they are watching over you." He watched her as she picked up her cup and took a sip.

Since then, Ma always let him hold the plate of sweet vermi-celli, which they took to mosque on the morning of every Eid to say special prayers for the dead.

One day, she explained to him the meaning of a song that she often sang. Come let's go to Sister Hare's wedding, it went. Sister Hare goes shopping for a sari, the mouse scurries off with invita-tions, and the cat tries out her new dress. And so the animals lose themselves in preparation. Finally, dancing and singing, the monkeys playing flutes, drums, and tambourines, the wedding party sets off for the groom's house. But on the way they pass a leopard who lurks up a tree. The happy procession proceeds, obliv-ious; the leopard pounces; and the victims lie torn limb from limb, their possessions scattered in the forest. Whose wedding is it? — reflect on that, cautions Khoja Bhagat, the mystic author of the song, in his last verse; this life is one such wedding procession; it will come to naught.

Ma the mystic. On festival nights, as the band played and men and women danced the stick-dance dandia or the circular garba, she would request permission to sing, and in that voice edged with the years she would sing this wedding song, its sound drowning in the tumultuous noise of celebration.

As the boy grew older he retained much of the reserve that had been the strength of his childhood. Tall and dark, with a slight stoop forward, he could be seen returning from school or the library, his books clutched under one arm; and more often alone than with a casual companion. Gradually he was also drawn out by his classmates, who found out that beneath the surface calm and tranquillity was a person who could laugh, if somewhat sardonically, and become excited and passionate, if not habitually. He would play cricket and football with them, but as the years passed, sports became less important and weightier matters occupied their minds, such as their futures, and the grades that could help secure them.

For Ramji, adolescence was a time of excitement and fear. What he had were books, knowledge in its abstract form, but the keys to the universe lay outside his world. Even as he lay in his bed in the dark night, the buttons that could end his existence were somewhere far from him, where two powerful adversaries stood poised with their weapons of destruction. These weapons held a morbid fascination for him — from the rockets of Peenemunde aimed at London in the Second World War to the mighty Saturn and Soyuz rockets waiting silently in their silos with their payloads of nuclear and hydrogen bombs.

In contrast to that distant world which threatened dazzling death, glorious destruction followed by an endless doomsday of radiation tortures, his small world offered inner peace, a tranquillity that ultimately encompassed all existence. All the attractions and terrors of modern science were an illusion. This was what he had been brought up to believe.

One day, in his last year at school, he went and heard an American politician, and the charm and mystery of that world outside finally won over his resistance to leave. With his classmate Sona from down the road he applied to go to the United States, and within months they were ready to leave. On the eve of his departure, all the African women who lived in a community behind their house brought delicacies for him, whom they had always loved as a "noble soul" for his quietness and his success in school. Of course the food could not be taken with him, but the women presented him with another gift, which he put in his bag; a khanga, which had a message printed on it: "Wayfarer, keep looking back."

4

Christmas was when I committed evil, he thought, yet I cannot make myself regret it. In such a case the ritual of asking forgiveness is meaningless – or is it?

"The disciple has sinned, may those present forgive, may the Lord forgive . . ."

Kneeling, leaning forward in urgent supplication, hands joined before him, the sinner repeated the formula three times; the mukhi, his friend Sona, met his look eye to solemn eye, heard him out, said three times, "The Lord forgives," then dipped two fingers in a bowl of water and sprinkled it on the sinner.

Everybody underwent this monthly purification, stepping up to and kneeling before the mukhi, one by one; finally Sona too knelt, before a member of the congregation designated as deputy for the occasion, and asked forgiveness. This was the last ceremony of the Friday closest to the new moon. The prerequisite for forgiveness was repentance.

"For a moment there, you actually looked sinful, Ramji," Sona said with humour when it was over.

"Yeah, and I thought you were going to pour a bowlful of that water on me."

Why do we need these ancient rituals in the first place, asked someone, more for the sake of argument than anything, and sure enough a passionate one began, everyone joining in. A question like that, well timed with mischievous intent, never failed to kindle fireworks of endless argument, which was so much a part of the fun of these Friday nights.

But the last word on the subject was Sona's, and everyone stopped to listen. He gave a calm disquisition on ritual as poetry and the need to retain mystery, and Ramji looked at him admiringly.

"So, what sins did you commit during Christmas?" Sona asked when they were alone later, and Ramji simply shook his head. Not to deny sin, no, but to deny confession.

April is the cruellest month, yes, but for sheer doomsday bleakness, for gut-wrenching, soul-searing emptiness, you can't surpass Christmas. Ask your resident aliens.

Get away for Christmas, his Ethiopian friends told him; unless you want to risk jumping down from the fifth floor into that ultimate abyss. It is the worst time in America — if you don't have anyone. Last year it was Rich Corey, and he belonged here. Richard Corey? You're having me on — isn't he the fellow in the Simon and Garfunkel song? Same name, same fate; only, this Corey jumped. Why? Loneliness, perhaps; LSD; couldn't make the grade — who knows, could be a combination of all three. This first

Christmas, get away to your host family. Phone them, they'll invite you. They always invite you. Americans are kind.

The fifth floor had three Ethiopians, all bright, among the cream of their poor country's student crop, all waiting for the downfall of their diminutive but unshakeable emperor Haile Selassie. Ebrahim, Marek, and Tekle, of whom the first was tall with a halo-like Afro haircut, and an admirer of Dostoevsky's *Crime and Punishment*, a constant drinker of sweetened black tea, and a teller of Haile Selassie jokes. He and Ramji had developed a warm friendship, though they had yet to become close. Marek had a quiet, mousy American girl spending nights with him, and Tekle, as tiny as his emperor, was at his books day and night.

Hey Ramji, have you heard the one about Ethiopia's space flight to the sun?

To the sun?

You haven't heard it then.

No, tell me. And I'll tell you the one about Nehru and Nyerere stealing flatware at Buckingham Palace.

Listen, says Ebrahim. You know that Haile Selassie always says, For everything we do, we think twice – that's the royal "we." Well, last year UNESCO held a space conference for the benefit of Third World countries. Okay, you didn't hear about it, but it's true. Each leader was asked: Where, in the future, would you like to send your spaceships?

Yes?

Well, some said Mars, some Venus, many said the moon. When it was the turn of the King of Kings, the Lion of Judah, he said, We would like to send our men to the sun.

UNESCO thought these Ethiopians must have some ancient

scientific wisdom they hadn't revealed to the world. The Americans and Russians were curious. "Tell us," they said, "how you can send astronauts to the sun when advanced countries like ours can't. Do you know how hot the sun is?"

Haile Selassie smiled. He said, "For everything we do, we think twice. We will send a rocket to the sun at night!"

And now, tell me about Nehru and Nyerere.

Later, said Ramji. But tell me, how come you're not going to *your* host family?

Ebrahim's smile was part sheepish, part defiant. It turned out that on his first visit there he'd been accused of making a pass at one of the two daughters of the family.

Shame on you, said Ramji, how *could* you? And then: Did you do it? How old was she?

A tight-lipped silence. I don't have to tell you, the expression on Ebrahim's face seemed to say, I know what I know. And that's what stood between them, Ramji thought, what couldn't draw the bonds of Africa any closer: the feeling of black anger and the defiance that was an expression of "black power."

And so he was going to spend his very first Christmas at the Morrises. It was going to snow, it would be a white Christmas, the forecast said so. He had known Christmases only through storybooks – images of stockings, Father Christmas, and snow. Back in Dar, a shop not far from where he lived had stuck a cotton-wool beard on a roly-poly red doll to improvise a Santa Claus for its display window, in a background of cotton-wool snow and matchbox houses and a zebra-drawn carriage to make a Christmas scene that had drawn large crowds of viewers.

How do you behave at Christmas? He hadn't an inkling. Do you go around shaking hands, the way you did on Eid, and saying "Merry Christmas"? Shawn had coached him on what to expect, though Shawn had only contempt for the bourgeois likes of John Morris.

Ramji had practically begged for the invitation, hand outstretched. John had picked up the phone when Ramji last called, and when Ramji said he had no plans for Christmas, John had said: "You're welcome to spend it with us." And Ramji, demurring only a little, had accepted. He was ashamed, and a little angry at himself for his cravenness. But the alternative was to spend a week totally alone. Sona would spend the Christmas with a professor from Harvard who had befriended him, and the Ethiopians would be up to something or other together. Still, he vacillated over whether or not to go; then Ginnie called to make sure he was coming. We thought you had made other plans – so good you called, we all look forward to seeing you again.

On the morning of the twenty-fourth he took a ride with two graduate students, a small, wiry girl with short blonde hair called Gudrun and her equally small but dark and long-haired Pakistani boyfriend, Sam, who wouldn't tell Ramji his real name. Ramji paid six dollars to be dropped at Newark's train station, and there was a possibility of a return ride on New Year's Day.

"Ramji, you've let your hair grow!" Ginnie said when he arrived.

"More convenient," he said, a little embarrassed.

"You look wonderful. It's nice to see you." She gave him a peck on the cheek.

They tried to treat him as matter-of-factly as they could. Over dinner the boys talked about their visit to New York that day, and Ramji told them all about his ride from Cambridge. Chris asked, "Is the antiwar movement strong on campus?" and Junior burst out, "If I hear another word about those jerks —" while Ramji replied, "Yes — it's all over the place. My roommate's an SDS guy — you don't get to pick roommates . . . ," and Ginnie smiled indulgently.

After dinner the boys brought out their wrapped presents and placed them under the large brightly lit Christmas tree, which dominated one corner of the rarely used living room. Ramji said he had brought a few things along — could he also place them under the tree? Then, after coffee and pie, he sat up with Chris to watch "The Dick Cavett Show." "Is there an antiwar movement in *your* school?" he asked, in a bid to continue their previous conversation.

"Some," Chris said. "A few of us get together and talk about it. But it's a military school — a fascist place. I'm getting out of it."

Ramji realized he was treading dangerous waters and decided not to pursue the subject further.

He woke up in the middle of the night, his eyes fixed on the small attic window of his room, with the strange feeling that someone had been peeping in and had just then ducked out of sight. He shook himself out of the weird thought. It was simply the effect produced by the sudden sight of the glow outside. Something's lighting up the world at night, and I know what it is. He tiptoed to the window and looked out, his forehead pressed against the cold glass. Soft white snow clung to bending, pliable tree branches, there was snow on the rooftops and the ground everywhere, gleaming under streetlamps, porch lights, Christmas lights, imparting a quiet, heavenly beauty to the world. I wish I could tell someone about this; someone from *there*, who would understand what I mean. It's unfair to see and not be able to tell! Grandma with your ancient medicines, and your rejection of the world, what would you make of all this glory?

He hardly slept, couldn't help pondering: what combination of fate, circumstance, and divine purpose had brought him here? Why *you*, here, somewhere beyond the wildest dreams of your past?

The next morning he went down late, purposely, so as to be the least imposing on the family on this special day. Does breakfast come first or do they open presents? Am I dressed properly? . . .

They were all waiting for him as he arrived downstairs, turned beaming smiles upon him – Chris and Junior on the floor, John on an antique wingback chair, Ginnie hovering in the middle, a tray of glasses in her hands. The Christmas tree sparkled in its corner; the fireplace was crackling.

"Merry Christmas," he said shyly.

He was overwhelmed with presents, showered with beautiful things. A sweater from Scotland, a silver pen set, a pocket radio, things he would treasure for years; and socks, a diary, an alarm clock; anti-dandruff shampoo. In his turn he gave John a biography of Eisenhower, Chris a book on Eastern religions, Junior a calender, and Ginnie a bottle of perfume. All inappropriate, perhaps, but he hadn't known how to shop for Christmas presents. Shawn, ever contemptuous of imperialist pigs, had been no help here: take them Abbie Hoffman's *Steal this Book*, was his suggestion; he himself had given his Catholic father the radical priest Daniel Berrigan's memoir. And so Ramji had come with his meagre offerings, and was swept away by an avalanche of goodies, all thoughtfully chosen.

That week he learned about football and its pageantry, watched all the Bowls on television. Midweek, Gudrun called from Philadelphia and said she could pick him up on the first of January if he wanted. Apparently she was short of riders, and she sounded keen. Without thinking, he said all right. He gave her the address and she told him what time to expect her. No sooner had he made this arrangement than he found out about the family's plans, mentioned rather casually to him. Chris and Junior were on their way to spend the rest of their holidays with a cousin in Annapolis. John announced he would go to Baltimore later in the week to spend some days with his mother; Ginnie said she would join him on the first.

"I didn't mean to inconvenience you," Ramji said rather guiltily. Christmas over, he wished he hadn't come. It wouldn't have been so bad, had he stayed on campus, the days would have passed. He'd given the Morrises such short notice, they must have scrambled around looking for presents for him. It was clear now why he hadn't been invited at first. Perhaps he should have planned to return immediately, the day after Christmas . . . but wouldn't that have looked awkward, as if he'd come only for the loot?

"Nonsense," Ginnie told him. "You're one of the boys. You come whenever you feel like it, just as they do. John's mother needs him around this time of the year, and he has to go. She's a darling, but deaf as a doorpost, so it's hard for me to visit for long. I'd much rather prefer your company instead!"

John left on the early morning of the thirtieth. That day and the following Ramji spent with Ginnie as she went about in her Grand Prix running errands for the home. The first day she took him skating, at which he proved a disaster, though he enjoyed the experience. The next day they went to her club for lunch, where she showed him off to a gaggle of women – all in some ways reminding him of her and all extremely nice to him – and introduced him to their art teacher, Pierre. They all took a class from him at the Runymede Community College. "He's a riot," she said, when they'd sat down to lunch by themselves, then whispered, "There's more than one husband ready to shoot the guy. You know what I mean? And I don't think he's even French." Pierre was a few tables away, sipping wine with dessert in the company of a young woman.

"This chicken we're having is cooked in a smidgin of red wine – I hope that doesn't bother you," she said blithely.

He laughed. "I guess not, if it's cooked. A smidgin would evaporate."

Ginnie's friends came over in ones and twos for brief chats and New Year's wishes, beaming large flashy smiles at him, which he amply returned.

"Don't be too flattered by their attention," she told him. "They're predators."

"Really," he said, a little too seriously, and they laughed.

"I've warned you."

On New Year's Eve night he sat in the den and watched on TV the celebrations going on in New York. Guy Lombardo led his band in the Waldorf-Astoria ballroom, while out in Times Square the great suspended ball of lights slowly edged its way downwards, indicating the minutes left in the old year to the gaze of thronging crowds. Ginnie came and sat on the arm of the couch and watched with him. "Let's celebrate together," she said suddenly, "and to hell with the rest of the world. Right?"

"Right," he replied, unsure of himself. She got up and brought two glasses of wine. "No," Ramji said, "please – I can't have wine."

"Not even to celebrate? Not even a smidgin with me?"

"No," he said, "I can't . . ." He looked at her pleadingly. He wished he could oblige her, but how could he?

"Never mind," she said, "you can have some ginger ale. Surely that's allowed?"

"Yes, that's fine." He felt relieved.

"You are very observant, aren't you. I mean you –"

"Yes . . . that's how I was brought up. That's how everybody was. It's a matter of faith."

"Do you pray? I'm being nosy, aren't I? John always tells me I'm nosy . . ."

"Yes." He looked up at her. "I pray regularly."

"Every day? Before you go to bed?"

"Every morning when I wake up, and at night before going to bed. Actually the times are dawn and dusk . . . but that's not convenient here . . ."

"What do you pray?"

"Well . . . ," he began but didn't quite know how to answer her.

"I'm prying, I know. You're so nice and good natured."

Meanwhile on the TV the final countdown had begun, "Nine . . . eight . . . seven . . . ," chanted the crowd, and at the stroke of midnight the ball of lights touched bottom as the Lombardo band began the first strains of "Auld Lang Syne."

Ginnie sang along and said "Happy New Year!" and gave Ramji a hug and they too kissed as did the crowds at Times Square amidst much honking of cars and wild cheering.

"Happy New Year," he said to her, extremely moved by the moment. "You're one of the nicest people I've ever known!"

"Oooh, thank you. . . ." She wiped tears from her eyes. "I feel so sad this time of the year. . . ." They hugged again. "My makeup's running. . . . When is your ride coming – it's Gudrun, is it?"

"Yes, at noon. Is that late for you?"

"A little. I'll leave at eleven and you can go whenever the ride comes. Just make sure the lock catches when you close the door – you'll have to pull it tight. Will you remember to do that?" She sniffed, smiled.

"Yes, I think so."

"I'm sure you will."

"Good night. And thank you for everything."

"You are most welcome. But I'll see you before I leave. Good night."

In his attic room he looked out the window at the trees now bereft of snow, ghostly and barren, though the roofs were still covered white. A solitary figure, huddled in a coat, had appeared on the street, mesmerizing in its singularity and the distant regular sound of footfalls. Most likely someone returning from a party; and so the Christmas season's over – all that anticipation, the festivities and lights. . . . The phone rang somewhere in the house. A little later it rang again. Both times he heard Ginnie's voice, caught snatches of conversation. John and the boys calling to wish her a happy new year.

Inside the soft fresh-smelling bedcovers – the temperature in the room, aided by an electric heater, just warm enough for him – he was somewhat annoyed at himself when he realized he had an

erection. Doesn't know night from day, he mused, recalling an adolescent joke, a statement originally about the suddenness of death,
its disregard of time and place, applied to youthful tumescence.

There were steps coming up.

She knocked delicately. "Are you awake?"

"Yes," he said, then louder, "Yes!"

"I heard you," she said, coming in. "I couldn't sleep either. John
called. Wishes you a happy new year. The boys too. They called."

"I hope you wished them the same for me."

"I did. . . . Are you hungry? You shouldn't feel shy, you know.
You haven't had a bite since dinner, and that was seven hours ago."

"It's late now," he said. "Soon it'll be morning." Actually he was
quite hungry.

"What fortitude. . . ." She sat on the bed, close to his feet, and
she gave him a fond look as he tried to raise himself and balance
on his elbows.

"What do you think about when you can't get to sleep?" she
asked.

"I don't know . . . all kinds of things, I suppose." He felt awkward
leaning back on his elbows, and began to sit up some more.

"It's all right," she said, "don't get up. Sorry I disturbed you.
Well, good night." She moved closer and gave him a peck.

How nice she smells, her family shouldn't have abandoned her
at this moment . . .

"Why, you're inhaling me," she said, lingering over him.

He looked at her, blushing deeply.

She put a hand on his crotch, over the quilt. "My my, who's
going to take care of this little – not so little – problem. Not by
yourself . . ."

He tried hard to swallow.

Deftly she had found his crotch under the bedcovers, over his pyjamas.

He was flat on his back now and staring at her face, at her eyes, anxiously, breathlessly, almost tearfully.

"You should let go a little. . . . Nothing's that serious . . . nothing's worth holding on to so badly. . . . It's no sin to love a woman. . . ." She was on him, and he felt grateful, immensely, and they were kissing, and he didn't quite know if he was crying or simply moaning with happiness. His knowledge of such moments was almost nonexistent, he knew he had to do something with his lips, his tongue. Her mouth was large and wet and tasty. He wanted to eat her. "Life's not so evil," she said, pulling back.

He felt a pain, somewhere deep inside him; he couldn't breathe as he looked at her smiling face. He could see a faint down of blonde hair above her lip. There was a thin line, of age, he thought, forming at the corners. Her hair was glorious. She must have been gorgeous ten years ago. He took her hand and kissed her fingers just as she was drawing away, then moved it to his crotch. She pulled down his pyjama with that hand, bent and caressed him with her mouth. "Nice," she said. "Full blown and ready to burst." She sat up. "Wait, hold on, think of anything else, the lions on the Serengeti. You have to come properly." Quickly she had pulled down her panties – he assumed – from under her robe and had climbed on the bed and was wet and sticky on him, and Ramji was enclosed by her and sliding, helpless and joyful, grateful to that loving face above him, and all he could do was grab her buttocks with his hands and move, watching that face contort with pleasure and utter sounds akin to his, say to himself,

I am doing it, I am doing it, I am doing it to her. Thank you, God. Thank you, Ginnie.

"I had it all planned out, you know," she said.

"I am glad you did."

He was trying to be in command, pushing her down on the bed and mounting her, murmuring endearments.

"I don't do this all the time with any guest, you should know that," she said firmly but tenderly, and pushed him away to sit up.

"I know, I know . . . but I love you."

Suddenly she shrank back from him and he gaped at her as he beheld before him a stark-bald Ginnie! Her face looked puffed up, the makeup had smudged; and she was holding her blonde hair, a wig, in her hand. She could have been a clown.

"Ta-raaa!"

"What . . . what –" he said in utter confusion.

"Do you love me now?"

"Yes I do." Forcefully. How could he not? But what was the meaning of this?

"Aw," she cried, wiping her eyes. "Even if you don't mean it, thank you."

"But I do mean it," he said, staring at her baldness, then her face, still glorious. "Put it back."

"Better?" she asked, putting the wig back on her head. He didn't reply. "It's from my chemotherapy treatment – I've got cancer in my abdomen."

Stunned, all of a sudden his heart in his stomach, he choked back the words in his mouth, then recovered and said, "It's not bad? This chemotherapy – it works?"

She nodded.

"They say it does, but who knows. I lost my hair and my face is pudgy."

"It doesn't look pudgy."

What a time for her family to abandon her.

They lay side by side and she talked. "I want to tell you about myself."

"Please do, that would be lovely. I've often wondered. . . . I'm very curious."

He imagined, with her dreamy prompting, a modest American family in Florida. She was one of three sisters and a brother, Chris, who had been killed in the war. It took a moment to realize she meant World War II. Where, he asked. I don't know, she replied. He meant: against the Japanese or the Germans, in Asia or in Europe. (The war evoked images of heroism in him, he had known it only from the movies.) But he didn't persist. Her father had worked at an ice cream factory and would bring home buckets of the stuff ("that's why we're all so creamy and soft"); weekends he moonlighted at the Post Office. She herself finished high school and went to work at Woolworths. "Never was good at school," she said. "Not like you – I bet you topped everything." He turned to look at her: "But that's not everything, is it." "No," she said, showing surprise at his comment, "I guess it isn't." One summer in '49, she and her two sisters took off for Baltimore and Washington. With no intention of returning. "Why? Oh, Dad was sick and had retired, Mother never recovered from Chris's death, she drank. It had become a miserable house and we wanted fun." Fun they had, three beautiful blondes. Her sister Pat, who was the youngest of them, found a boy on the train up and married him in September – "she pretty much had to the way they went on. Never thought my shy sister capable of so much reckless passion. She's a widow now, in Annapolis, but with a brilliant son in the navy – like his father – did I tell you he was in the navy?"

"And you – how did you –"

"I stayed with Pat and learned to type, and then one day Frank – Pat's husband – brought home this serious specimen on a blind date and I gasped. What's that? I asked Frank. So that's how I met John. He was at Johns Hopkins on a veteran's scholarship. He took me to meet his mother, who took one look at me and said to him: Are you sure? You'll have to put a leash on her. Oh, we got along from day one, his mom and I."

And her older sister Sharon became a nurse and married – or just cohabited with – a rich old man. She knew how to take care of herself. She was a professional golfer now. "You should meet her – she'll sweep you off your feet."

She left him with a kiss. Yes, she loved him, she said. Would there be other moments like this, he was afraid to ask her.

"Call me," he begged.

"Of course I will," she said. "We'll meet again, silly. Remember what I said, you come whenever you feel like it, and call collect."

And the sin he'd just committed, the guilty secret. . . . He didn't think about it, not then, this was one glorious night without darkness, and he slept hugging his pillow.

"Nice little bourgeois retreat you've got yourself here," Gudrun said, as he opened the front door for her. She had on a striking new-looking red angora sweater over the patched worn-out blue jeans he recognized from the trip down. "I bet these people vote Nixon." She walked past him, asked to use a bathroom.

"There's a powder room just there," he indicated.

She ran in, and when she came out she insisted on a tour of the house, at least the main floor.

"So this is how the rich live," she said later, archly eyeing him from John's wingback chair, a can of Fresca in one hand.

"Didn't Sam come?" he asked as they drove out of Runymede.

"No, the jerk. You know what? He says he has to go home to visit, and guess what he'll bring back with him when he returns – a nice little Pakistani wife. Are you also like that – like to screw white women but end up marrying a nice little obedient Indian wife?"

He ignored the question. And she went on and on about Sam. "The asshole, didn't let on he was a Muslim – a fucking Muslim – and he came with me to meet Guru Maharaj-ji –"

"Who?"

"Guru Maharaj-ji –"

"Oh . . . oh, the –"

"Yes, the fourteen-year-old, but don't be fooled by that, it's only his physical age in *this* birth. We're all thousands of years old, don't you know – you're an Indian. You should come to Guru Maharaj-ji Center – it's on Boylston Street. Nothing will matter about this . . . this . . . material world any more . . ."

She was not a bad sort, just angry, mostly at Sam, whose real name she told him was Shamsul. The sweater, she admitted, was a present from her folks.

It was not an unpleasant drive. As they approached Boston that night, she asked him if he wanted to come home with her, she could take him to the Center the next morning. He said no, he'd rather be back in his room. She dropped him off at the front steps of the Tech, on Mass Ave, and drove away.

5

Spring brings forth protests on campus – loud reckless rebellion against that war in Vietnam, daredevil bone-risking defiance of authority and its policemen – as stereos blare out rock 'n' roll's homages to the sun; and for the new student, with a nagging conscience and in search of a cause, there is no more effective and poignant a call to the plight of the world's wretched than the movie *The Battle of Algiers*.

For many, their first viewing of the gripping tale (pitting coloured natives against a powerful European army) in a heady political climate is a first step towards radicalism, before they too come out shrieking slogans against colonialism and imperialism, chanting "Ho Ho Ho Chi Minh, Viet Cong is gonna win!" in the streets against their own government's policies.

Algiers a decade ago: on one side the native quarter, the casbah, the jumble of dusty, narrow, close-packed streets and mud houses and barefoot Arabs; on the other side, the spick-and-span whites-only European quarter where even children come out wearing socks and shoes, women shop in supermarkets, and teenagers dance gaily in cafés. It does not take much more to remind you where *you* came from, your Kariakoo in Dar es Salaam was the casbah. In the movie, a colonel of the French paratroopers, fresh from the campaign in Indo-China – tall, handsome, commanding, wearing crisp army camouflage, shades, and a beret – gives the order, and a guerilla hideout in the casbah, including women and children, is blown up. As the colonel says to the newspaper reporters, today an insurgency in Algeria, tomorrow where? And you realize the answer is probably: Vietnam.

And you, Ramji, are coming to realize that there *is* a different way to view the world than the one you were used to.

Of course, it's not just the movie that's told you this, it's the whole political scene around you, the flyers and protests, the special lectures, the debates on television, your peers, your roommate Shawn Hennessy. And it seems impossible now, it seems crass, to come from a country small like Vietnam, and also a colony of Europe once, and not feel a tug of sympathy for it. You wish you could turn away from the issue – but it's all around you – and think of the generous people and the scholarship, the wonderful things and great opportunities in this land of the free.

The big issue this spring was military research on campus. Could a university maintain its freedom and yet remain tied to directed research for the military? Did it befit a university's free spirit to be involved in the design of weapons, in methods of destruction of human life and habitats, as was going on even now in Vietnam?

On a Tuesday in April a large, noisy rally set off at noontime on Mass Ave to seek entry to and otherwise confront the Tech's Lorentz Labs, which were actively involved in the development of weapons systems – MIRV missiles, helicopter gunships, and much else that maimed and killed. The rally was given a rousing send-off on the front steps of the Tech by none other than the resident genius, Peter Bowra, speaking from his wheelchair in his trademark hoarse voice, appearing fresh from another awe-inspiring lecture to the freshmen on the wonders of the universe that were matched only by the wonders of the human mind. And so, encouraged by this voice, the freshmen, radicals or not, tagged along behind the rally. The procession was met at the door by the director of the lab – the "Doc," reputedly once a colleague of Bowra at Los Alamos, now an arch-enemy – flanked by an array of stout policemen. From there the demonstrators, chanting their slogans, went on to confront President Ronald McDonald and presented their demands for an end to military research on campus.

This concern for humanity and peace, Ramji thought as he stood at the back of the crowd watching demonstrators haranguing the Doc, can it be real, is it sincere? Back in Dar we thought only of our small community; sometimes we prayed for peace in the world, but not convincingly. What did we know of the world? We could not think of all of humanity as these Americans do, with such immediacy, such urgent concern. But then we did not have the power to destroy the world, did we? Nevertheless, how liberating, how exhilarating, to think that one belonged to a larger world, cared about it, could make a difference to it!

The Tech's President McDonald finally yielded to protests, announcing a temporary moratorium on defence-related research. And the faculty, with Peter Bowra as their spokesman, voted overwhelmingly in support of a moratorium on MIRV.

There *was* a different way to look at the world, and you didn't have to be a kook or some screaming wild-haired freak to be a part of this new thinking.

The year was drawing to a close, and to top it off on a high note before exams, Janis Joplin gave a scintillating concert in the armoury, ending with "Me and Bobby McGee" in that throaty voice that reverberated right up to Central Square. And as you emerged into the warm Saturday night stirred to the core you couldn't help thinking of yourself as a *student*, a passionate species apart that would not compromise its values as the adults had done.

Ginnie come lately . . ., the words of an old American song would come ridiculously to mind at odd moments. He was obsessed with her, dreaming of clandestine meetings in hotels, passionate encounters, steamy love scenes in back seats of cars; but nothing developed. As the weeks passed, she did not swoop in upon him, putting up at the Inn on Harvard Square or the Sonesta, as he imagined. At times he would be gripped by a wild fear – suppose she died suddenly, suppose the chemotherapy didn't work? But on the phone she was lively, it was difficult to imagine her being sick. And, as always, she was solicitous of him. John would be with her then. One day he told her quickly, "You know, sometimes I think that whole Christmas week – that New Year's – was imaginary." He thought he detected a brief pause, before she laughed and blithely replied, "My dear, count on it – it was all real!" And his heart sank. Because together with the passion and desire, there was, simultaneously, a small wish in him to be done with it, this cowardly sin of adultery and hypocrisy. But he was trapped, by memory, and by sweet anticipation.

Meanwhile, something had arisen, and he reported it in the form of a riddle to Sona: a naked fat ass has landed with a cat and taken over the room.

On the Sunday morning following the Joplin concert Ramji had been shaken awake by the bed heaving suddenly. Startled, he watched a pair of legs, thighs, and naked buttocks descend from the upper bunk and land with a thud on the floor. He gawked at the chubby girl who had jumped down – she wore a short dress and had a short crop of straggly black hair – unable to believe what he was seeing. Hi! she said cheerily to him, after which she proceeded in haste to put on her panties followed by jeans under the dress, and he was staring, thinking, Doesn't she wear knickers in bed? And suddenly there was Shawn's red head smiling triumphantly above him: Nice? he crowed.

Jeans on, the girl removed her dress by pulling it over her head, revealing naked breasts, and put on a T-shirt.

There came a blood-curdling animal shriek, frightening the already bewildered Ramji out of his skin, as a small creature bounded from the bed above down to his desk.

"Meet Husserl," the girl said and hurried out, presumably for the bathroom. Husserl was a dark grey cat.

"And the girl's Kate," added Shawn from above.

Ramji watched the door close behind her – chubby and unkempt, he observed to himself, and looks slept-in; he was ashamed at the thought. But how long am I going to last in this menagerie – aren't there any rules? – with a couple making open love, and a cat named shamelessly after a philosopher. He'd come late last night and plopped straight into bed in the darkness. They must have been in bed then.

Shawn had met Kate at the student takeover of the Harvard president's office earlier in April. Their hitching together was consecrated by a night spent in jail following that event, to which the cops had turned out in large numbers and a combative mood. Kate was a Radcliffe freshman and she became a regular visitor, coming Friday night and leaving Monday morning. Saturday was protest day for the two of them, and they would set off to demonstrate against the war, the draft board, or some injustice perpetrated against workers in Boston or Cambridge. On Sunday afternoons they went about distributing and posting leaflets around the campus, and for added effect they wrote graffiti on walls and notice boards. "Ali Akbar Khan, Emmanuel Kant," Shawn would write as his signature line, following which, "Bring the War Home," or "U.S. Out of Southeast Asia," and so on. They had a regular shadow in the Tech's corridors, a chunky YAP – Young American Patriot – with crewcut who would pull down the flyers and deface the graffiti, writing some of his own: "Love it or Leave it," "Communist Propaganda," "Bowra's an Ass." Kate's role was to trail the YAP, cross out or appropriately edit his words, and add some of her choicest.

Ramji came to dislike Kate. She was wilfully dirty, and she crowded the room, leaving her things all over, deliberately, he thought, to needle him. Nights, the two thrashed about shamelessly on the upper bunk. They offered to take the lower bunk, but Ramji declined, opting to keep the easy access to his bed. But he began to come in late and leave early.

"You want to try her?" Shawn asked him one day. "She's wild, man. She won't mind –"

"No!" emphatically, clenched mouth.

Why did he hate her so? She wanted to be friends, even though she called him Domino – apparently Shawn had told her about their first meeting, in which Ramji had confidently and innocently reported his theory about containing Vietnam. (No doubt they had had a good laugh at his expense.)

She frightens me, he thought, being candid with himself. She frightens me because I am so far behind them, in how far I can go. With sex, for example. The showdown came when he found her used underwear on his chair. This is it: What do they think of me? A Third World person they think they can walk over, and *they* talk of exploitation?

"You go," he told her. "I don't want you using this room." With his slide rule he picked up the panties and threw them towards her.

Shawn and Kate apologized, pleaded, and begged, but agreed finally: she wouldn't come to the room. But of course she did, only she kept out of his way.

The three of them were walking on a cold windy April night across Harvard Bridge, a thin drizzle raining cold needles on their faces. The river lay dark and miasmic below. April lets you down, he thought. Funny how you begin to think of weather, in this climate. You form expectations and then judge reality against them. Why would the universe know or care that come March 21 it should begin to smile upon you ceaselessly? . . .

"This meeting – I hope it's worth it. What a time to set a meeting –"

"Relax."

"Hm." He sniffed.

Kate was humming. She's from New York, she's used to this bone-chill. And he's from Boston, positively relishes the cold.

"It's Saturday night, no one else'll be around the house," Shawn explained.

"So the meeting's private. How do you know it's for me."

Kate stopped, he and Shawn stopped. "Look, buddy. If you don't want to come, fuck off."

They stood there, halfway across the bridge, faces wet, shoulders hunched against the wind, hands in their pockets.

"Take it easy," said Shawn to Kate. To Ramji: "You were invited and agreed to come. There's no point in going back now."

It was Shawn who had brought the invitation, saying, There's going to be a meeting of people who're interested in doing something for the Third World. I've spoken to the guys involved and they would like to meet you. A radical meeting? Ramji asked, intrigued. Sort of, Shawn had replied, Why don't you try it? Ramji nodded, all right. And so here he was, on his way with Kate and Shawn and wondering if he had not said yes too hastily.

"Do you know which way the wind blows?" a guy called out, as soon as Shawn finished introducing Ramji at the front door. There was a moderate buzz at this, and all eyes were on the guest.

"Uh. . . ." Ramji turned to look behind, towards the door, as though he should have noticed the wind direction, and there was laughter. "Oh – that's Bob Dylan," he said, recovering, and grinned at the one who had spoken. But who are these guys?

He was in the living room of the Student House, a low-budget coed co-operative he had once considered as a residence but rejected because it had looked too informal in the brochure. He had been right. The room was crowded with college types sprawled out on the hearth rug by the fireplace, crammed in on the stairs and the landings, and overflowing into the kitchen. There were no chairs around. Three people sat on an old sofa, which had been turned away from the fireplace to face the meeting: a strikingly pretty girl in miniskirt and boots, a rangy, bearded guy wearing a red beret, and between them Professor Linda Hodge, who taught a course called

Imperialism and History. She was in a red sweater and black skirt, beautiful as always, brown hair falling loosely to the shoulders. She was beaming, apparently waiting for the room to come to order once more before she continued her spiel.

"This country is at war, we all know that. We also know that wars have always been *fought* by young people, but *made* by politicians and the industries they serve. And so it is an appropriate irony that this struggle against the war machinery and American imperialism is being carried out mainly by young people on the home front. You are the true war heroes, you are the vanguard. No more will young people take up arms simply because their greedy elders tell them to – and use them against the people of the Third World, be they in Chile, in Vietnam, or in Cambodia, simply because these people refuse to acquiesce to the demands of Uncle Sam and his multinational henchmen. But imperialism is far from beaten. As Lenin said . . ."

Later food and drinks were served in the kitchen, and people milled about. Ramji learned that Linda would be on her way to Berkeley the next day. She had been denied tenure by the Tech because of her antiwar sympathies. There had already been two demonstrations to show support for her. He watched her from a distance. At one moment she looked up from her conversation and waved at him. He remembered uneasily that one day in class he had told her that it was fine to talk of large events, but he came from a small people and thought the study of history should take into account the lives of such people. She had smiled charmingly and told him that indeed some historians believed as he did. But Ramji had never been able to engage her for long. Her interest is in large systems; history à la Tolstoy and Lenin. Civilization and its discontents, imperialism and capitalism, declines and falls. And I tell her of the woes that befall shopkeepers . . . small people.

As he made his way through the room, he was surprised and flattered by the attention he got. He was quite exotic to the others present there. He was the man from Africa, an authentic Third Worlder, to whom they were sympathetic, yet it seemed to him that they could not quite understand him.

"Don't worry. There's revolution going on everywhere. Imperialism's on the retreat." The miniskirted girl, who had been sitting beside Linda Hodge before, had come to stand close to him. He stared, not comprehending, wondering what she thought he was worried about. She was bra-less, he noticed, and he blushed. "You don't have to be shy," she said. "You're in America."

Her name, she said, was Lucy-Anne Miller.

Her tall companion from the sofa came and stood beside her. "We should – you know . . ." he said.

"Excuse us, we're having a discussion," she told him sternly.

"Aw, all right, see you later then," he said awkwardly and sauntered off.

"Actually, I'm through with that jerk," she said to Ramji. "Say, let's move over there."

They went and sat against the wall under the stairs, their shoulders touching.

"I bet you know imperialism inside out – experienced it?"

"You mean colonialism?"

"Yeah, tell me about it. And don't spare the details, please. The racial stuff."

"Well, there was more of that in Kenya –"

"Must have been where you were, too. Whites-only stuff, segregation."

"Well, the public toilets . . ."

He was playing up to her, but what he was trying to say was true enough: public toilets designated "Europeans Only," "Asians Only," and "Africans Only" when he was growing up.

"Hey, listen to this stuff," she called out. "You want to know colonialism? Here it is, from the horse's mouth."

A small crowd gathered around him and he told them about the public toilets, and the "Europeans Only" clubs and restaurants.

"But after independence we didn't have segregation any more," he concluded.

He looked around him. They were listening to him. American guys and girls, holding plates of cheesecake or ice cream or lemon meringue pie, mugs of coffee, cans of Coke or Dr Pepper, slices of pizza, bagels. Long hair, beards, faded jeans, boots, sneakers, bare feet. But their heart is in the right place, at least they know about the Third World, have sympathy. . . . The girl sitting close to him, Lucy-Anne, was different from the rest: strikingly well-dressed, hair parted in the middle and combed down to frame her face, giving it a heart shape, the look of a saint. She drew him helplessly in like a magnet.

"You belong with us, man. You know what it's like out there, the battlegrounds —"

"You have to educate us, to authenticate us —"

"Yeah, all we know is hearsay —"

"Speak for yourself, man. I've been to 'Nam, I know what it's like there. Fucking cesspit —"

"Yes, but do you know the Vietnamese side?"

"And you think he does?"

"What's this group?" Ramji asked the girl.

"We are the Freedom Action Committee. We are bringing the war home. And we join in solidarity with the Black people's struggles in this country and Third World struggles in Angola, South Africa, and Mozambique."

Don't forget Ian Smith's Rhodesia, he thought. In National Service, less than a year ago, during the early-morning jog we would sing, "Kill! Kill! Kill! Kill Ian Smith, and kill Verwoerd; kill Salazar and down with the Americans!"

"You must know of the Vietnam War Crimes Tribunal?" she said.

He was now alone with the girl, more or less, the crowd having drifted away, though he felt they were keeping him in sight. He caught a whiff of marijuana in the air, sniffed a couple of times, nervously. If you got caught here. . . . She was staring at him.

"Wasn't Bertrand Russell one of the organizers?" he asked finally. There had been some hubbub back home because Russell had included the names of African presidents in his tribunal without asking their permission.

"Then you must know of the war crimes – the antipersonnel bombs, and napalm. It's a jelly that sticks to the body and burns, at two thousand degrees; burns babies and small children. And American bombers are doing to the environment what it will never recover from. The sheer arrogance of this country in the world. . . . The sheer arrogance of power –"

"I read that book," he told her.

She stared at him. "I'm sorry I didn't –"

"By Senator Fulbright. I got it from the United States Information Service. I'm afraid I didn't understand it."

He smiled ruefully at her. She smiled back. "You're an interesting person, you know, you're an interesting person. Not like those foreign-student nerds, who are trained here to go back and rule as American stooges and oppress their own people."

"Well. . . ." He didn't quite know what to say. The thought was somewhat disturbing.

"Do you think America should decide who rules Vietnam? Or your country?"

"No," he said. "Actually, America put pressure on us — my country — trying to dictate to us who our friends should be. West Germany stopped aid because we recognized East Germany. And one American ambassador recently wrote a book called *The Reds and the Blacks* because he thought we were becoming communists —"

That should please her. It did.

"There, you see. You are one of us."

"I just don't . . ."

"Yes?"

She was really close to him, their legs were touching. There was a faint smell from her, but not perfume. She is the type who uses Ivory soap, all natural. And she stares into my eyes all moony-moony, how could one possibly disagree? Only . . .

"I just can't belong to organizations. For one thing I may agree with you on one thing and disagree on another —"

"That's perfectly all right! None of us agrees entirely with the other. We're all ready to learn from each other. We sit down together and discuss our disagreements and what we don't like about each other, and our friends point out our faults to us. The revolution should always be kept fresh, as Mao said. There's no room for complacency. We're all against the American empire and the military-industrial complex."

"But still – I don't believe for one thing that all Americans – even Republicans – are bad, even if I happen to disagree with them."

That took some doing. And there was silence.

"Gandhi, eh. You believe in Gandhi," observed a bystander.

"Anyway," said the girl, "think about it. You are welcome to join our meetings, Saturdays, and criticize us, say whatever you feel. But remember, if you join us, you'll also have to face up to criticism. All this Republican stuff . . ."

She smiled at him – she's nice, you've got to hand it to her – and got up and went away. Soon everyone ignored him, the presumed Gandhian. This would be the time to push off, though he didn't relish walking back alone.

As he stood around listlessly, Shawn came by, a powdered doughnut in his hand, and told him, "You'd best be leaving now."

Ramji looked up in surprise, opened his mouth to say something, shut it without a word.

"The rest of the proceedings may not be to your, er, taste," Shawn said, with a smirk.

Kate came by and grinned. "Hey – you missed a great chance with that Lucy-Anne . . ."

Ramji thought he understood. He had heard what these meetings sometimes degenerated into.

As he walked out and turned onto the sidewalk, he heard laughter coming from the house, felt envious of those who found it so easy to have fun. Somewhat tentatively at first, then with determination, he walked towards one of the windows, stepping on a flowerbed to get closer. The window was a foot too high, so he moved a garbage can over and climbed on it to peep inside. A guy and two girls were groping each other in the middle of the room, and stripping. A door opened, and a girl with flowing golden hair came in clutching sleeping bags in her arms. One of the two groping girls, now naked to the waist, began French-kissing the guy, the other girl bent low to cup and suck at her breasts. The girl carrying the sleeping bags in saw all this, then dropped her load, and looked up suddenly to meet the peeper's eyes through the window. He jumped down, walked hurriedly away. Shame, shame, shame, Ramji; if you don't do it, at least don't lick your chops watching others do it.

He walked back alone across the river, eyes wet with painful tears. In the distance, the fraternity houses along the river; the Charles Street Station; the imposing, impersonal dome and columns of the Tech bathed in a cold light.

Summer arrived and the university became a quiet, almost idyllic place. Ramji found work at the physical plant, spending his mornings with a gang of workmen, going about with ladders and scaffolding and cleaning windows. There was time also to wander about and sit outside in the sun and read and to catch up on correspondence. He wrote more frequently to his grandmother, almost once a week now, though his letters were very brief and there was hardly anything new to say in them. Although their relationship had always been one of love, they had never shared their inner lives. But he did enjoy receiving her letters, which always began and ended with long prayers for him, and sandwiched between these would be some news from their neighbourhood. The Friday "musical mosque" was kept going, though it was relatively quiet. Some evenings Ramji and Sona would spend together, going out for pizza in Central Square or a movie in Harvard

Square. Sona was wrapped up in his studies, and even his summer job involved research in his field. The Ethiopians were away on tours arranged by their sponsors. Shawn had found a job in some factory outside Boston, where he hoped to radicalize the workers, and Kate went to New York, where her folks lived and where the antiwar protests proceeded nonstop.

Towards the end of July he spent a few days with the Morrises, going there on Friday and staying past the weekend. The boys were not home. On the Monday he'd accompanied Ginnie to the hospital for a checkup. On the way back they bought sandwiches and sat down on a bench at the local park to eat. As they watched the ducks paddling placidly on the small lake in front of them and a jogger intermittently come into sight through the thickets on the other side of the water, he had reached out his hand and she let him hold her.

"I'm a very sick woman," she said in a quiet voice.

"But the therapy . . . it's working?"

"We're not sure."

Then she said, "You should have a girlfriend – I'm sure you do," and he was hurt. She sensed this and leaned over to place her head on his chest. His heart was beating wildly, and he leaned back to make her more comfortable and very softly put a hand on her waist.

He realized, then or perhaps a little later, that he was a bit childish in his yearnings; he had refused to put his head to what he felt. Did he expect her to elope with him? She had a home and family, was twice his age – and dying of cancer. Still, he could not stem the love he felt for her, or forget the New Year's Eve they had spent together.

6

It was October in the new academic year. Chilly winds blew eddies of dust about on Mass Ave, and the student movements were back in full swing on the campus.

"Will you be coming for Christmas?" Ginnie asked him over the phone.

"No," he said. "Not this time." Just tell me, and I'll come running, he prayed, pleaded in his mind.

"It's going to be a quiet Christmas," she said, "but the doctor has ordered rest. Junior's spending it with his girlfriend, and Chris has got plans of his own, I'm not sure what."

"Won't you be lonely," he asked.

She changed the subject.

You couldn't forget that several hundred people died each day in that terrible war far away in a poor country; you could not but be confronted by that fact in the corridors and streets, over loudspeakers, in flyers and newspapers, on TV; you could not but form an opinion about it. And once you did?

Do you believe America should be in Southeast Asia? Do you

believe America should decide the future of Vietnam – and the rest of the world? No. Then why don't you join us?

America, this land of multiple choice, where ice cream came in thirty-one different flavours, and every city had a colourful baseball team, and there were a dozen television channels to flick through (and Johnny Carson or Dick Cavett for the late show), had yet another choice on offer: to join or not to join the protest. On one side Chomsky, Dr. Spock and Peter Bowra, Mailer and Lowell; on the other, Nixon and Agnew, John Wayne and the store owner on Central Square who said on TV, Send these kids to concentration camp.

Every day the picketers begged, beseeched, argued, and leafleted on the front steps of the Tech on Mass Ave, and, holding hands, they walked around in circles and in between the fluted columns – massive, intimidating, and as cold as the immoveable enemy – and they chanted.

If you're against the war, say it! If you oppose university investments in South Africa, say it! If you denounce CIA-sponsored assassinations, say it! Don't wait for McGovern – the next election is three years away – force the hand of that bum in the White House! Join the protest!

One morning he did not just walk by the picketers with a smile of sympathy but joined their line.

Sona was one of those who couldn't be sure, who couldn't take sides, to whom this war didn't matter so much. He was possessed by his twin manias: the running of the music mosque, which he did with devoted care and theatricality Friday evenings, and his pursuit

of the study of their sect of Indian Muslims, founded a long time
ago by an elusive Sufi saint called Shamas Pir. In his quest for their
origins, Sona had found an ally and sponsor, Marie Lundgren, for-
merly of the Sorbonne and currently at Harvard, Professor of All
Things Mystical, especially Islamic, who, in a rose, a stone, a brook,
saw the manifestation of God . . .

"It's not all like that, Ramji – not all mushy and mystical love
– though I admit Marie's a little like that."

"Oh, so now it's Marie, is it?"

"In America everyone calls profs by their first names."

"I'll be damned if I call any professor of mine merely Noam or
Victor –"

"And yet you demonstrate against the mighty American
government!"

Yes, Sona was immersed in the past, reconstructing, as he put
it, all the byways taken by a small community of Indians over four
or five centuries, who simply, and seeing no contradiction, had
extended their customs and beliefs and love for their gods to
embrace Islam. His excitement would get feverish, catchy, as he
explained his arcane discoveries – "Look, Ramji . . . this word . . .
there's no dictionary in *existence* that has the meaning even close to
what we had. . . . It's a fossil, it's *our very own*, a clue to our past!"
He was the scholar, the easy chair in his room surrounded by a wall
of books, half-read, unread, read-but-still-needed, books bought
cheaply from the religion-and-mysticism basement of the Harvard
Bookstore. And in his exciting world of Sufi and Hindu mendicants walking the busy highways from Punjab to Maharashtra in
the medieval India of small rajas and Mogul emperors . . . Vietnam?
It was a little remote.

The scholarly mind is like that of a shopkeeper's: Leave me

to my business, and you can go about your own. I will ask no questions, to each his own. What the scholarly mind needs is stable government, peace and order, and a certain sense of well-being, in which ambience it can peruse the faded manuscript, reflect upon historical confluences, scan the odd poem . . . enter some flight of fancy that is as absorbing as an average LSD trip but with yourself at the controls.

Sona of course resented being compared to the tribe of shop-keepers (which is what his family were). The two of them were returning from Friday mosque, having detached themselves from the others. The reason why their people were having trouble in East Africa, Ramji said, was precisely this attitude – ducking issues while going on with their trade. This was a time in America when you simply had to speak out, there was no neutral ground when lives were at stake, silence meant collusion . . .

"Look, you're proselytizing! You've picked up the Christian ethic, you want to save the world – you've become an American!"

The taunt was meant to suggest he was changing. It could, once, have hurt to the quick. But the instrument was blunted, if not entirely without effect.

Ramji had to concede that an opinion regarding the war was ultimately a personal call, a very private choice. Only, the temptation was too great to act the missionary, to share one's new conviction, to convert. War was a matter of life and death, of urgency. And what the heck, it had just been Moratorium Week, five full days of preaching peace – even the Tech's Ronnie McDonald had stood up to speak for it. Every college campus in the country had rung out with nothing but cries for peace.

The long tunnel that was the main corridor connecting the

outside world to the inside of the campus was deserted, except for
the few solitary souls like themselves caught in its dim transitory
emptiness, feet crunching its grimy floor, voices rendered hollow
and diffuse. On one side of the corridor lay the dark, cloistered
world of the mind, and on the other the bright and real world that
called and demanded meaning. The pamphlets announcing the
Vietnam Moratorium activities of the past week lay scattered
about, having served their purpose in mobilizing the Tech community into thinking about peace. All week long there had been
speeches and seminars, loud rallies on Mass Ave, emotional exhor-
tations in the corridors. Wednesday had been the Moratorium Day
itself, a day of your life you could never ever forget. At twelve-
thirty in the afternoon a solitary trumpet began playing "The Star-
spangled Banner," at which signal suddenly there was all around the
campus a moment's stillness, an awe-filled heeding of this call from
a distance. Ramji was in Fletcher Lounge, on a break from a
morning of leafleting. As soon as the trumpet finished, everyone –
or so it seemed – stopped what they were doing and converged in
one motion upon the green across Mass Ave, accepting blue armbands from volunteers, and gathered outside Henley Auditorium.
Over loudspeakers they heard the president, Ronald McDonald,
and members of the faculty make speeches endorsing peace.
Finally, after a minute's silence for the war dead, the Tech contingent set off eight abreast, behind the faculty, along Mass Ave,
packing the entire Harvard Bridge from end to end, onto Comm
Ave and Boston Common to join the tens of thousands gathered
there. Senator McGovern addressed the rally. It was the day the
Mets won their World Series game.

They had arrived on Mass Ave, Sona and Ramji, without

saying too much for a while, and several options presented themselves, one of which was to part ways, with this new sourness between them unhappily unresolved. A Dudley bus, carrying the Marlboro Man on its side, was gearing up speed and headed Boston way, having discharged the passenger now waiting for the walk sign to come on. Except for this brief spasm of life, the scene in front of them looked strangely depleted. But the night was crisp and clear; a return bus would approach soon.

"Listen," Sona said, offering the olive branch, "how about we go to the Square – sit at Pewter Pot and talk awhile."

And appear intellectual and do nothing. . . . But, "All right," Ramji said, grabbing at the chance to make up.

"Listen to this idea. Have you ever wondered if you could be deported for taking part in a demonstration? What exactly are your rights as a foreign student?"

"I don't think you can be deported for expressing an opinion . . ."

"But what *exactly* can you do freely? My Moratorium idea is to produce a pamphlet with that information, for the foreign students. I have already been to the Dean's Office and gotten all the information. It may be obvious, but a lot of the foreign students are too frightened to say what they think. They need to be informed."

By the time they'd caught the bus and arrived at Pewter Pot they'd discussed Sona's project. He would do the dogwork, prepare and mimeograph the flyers. And Ramji would assist in stuffing them in the foreign students' mailboxes the following evening.

And so they lingered in the crowded restaurant over tea and muffins, discussing home.

There's a game I sometimes play with myself, Ramji said. I try to imagine what it's like back at home, now. But which "now" – nine o'clock Friday night or, taking the time difference into account, Saturday morning at five? Depending on my mood, I imagine either . . . Friday night at nine, Uhuru Street is empty, people have come back from mosque, the shops are closed . . .

Upanga being suburban, Sona said, talking of the area his family had moved to recently, people linger outside the mosque, they go home in groups, chattering all the way, and the kids play in the lanes between the row houses . . .

They sat quietly for a while, drank more tea; all around them chatter and bustle, smoke, frantic waitresses trying to cope. Outside, Harvard Square, brilliant and busy as at midday.

"You know," Sona said, "you couldn't demonstrate like that back home."

"No. I'd be in detention somewhere and my family would be desperate over my whereabouts."

They recalled the friends they had left behind, whom they'd known, it seemed, since time began. What would *they* be up to? Having fun, now that they were in university, going out in large and loud groups with all those *sondis* from Girls School they had previously (and longingly) watched from afar. Ultimately, they would get paired off and married.

"Do you regret coming to America?"

"No. And you?"

"No."

There was no going back to one's previous state of being. The longer one stayed here, the more altered one became. The odd thing was that part of one's new consciousness was to become more devoted to the country one came from, and to appreciate more its problems. There was no doubt in their minds that they would return as soon as possible to their young nation and participate in its development.

Sona, feeling isolated during Moratorium Week, had gone and spoken to his friend and adviser Marie Lundgren. I think I should do something, he said, but I have no convictions in this matter – it simply confuses me.

Marie, an ancient, diminutive woman with silver hair, looked at him across her large desk in her book-filled and paper-strewn office, with twinkling, kindly eyes. Among her past students, it was said, were (besides illustrious scholars) one of Henry Kissinger's advisers, a Mossad agent, and a PLO official.

You could do something useful, Marie said to Sona. We scholars are not meant to demonstrate in the streets. What we are good at is sorting and presenting information. Sona thought that was an excellent idea – he would obtain information on foreign students' rights to demonstrate and distribute it. This was not quite what Marie had in mind, but she smiled and said, Go ahead, it can't hurt. And so Sona produced his pamphlet, entitled, "The Foreign Student and Free Speech: Your Rights." You are free to express your opinions, it said, after a rhetorical preamble; it warned against silly things like getting caught in the possession of drugs or attacking policemen, and it gave a list of phone numbers to call in case of arrest.

On Saturday night, at about nine o'clock, while he was stuffing the mailboxes at Rutherford House with his flyers, Sona overheard something that sent a chill up his spine: *someone was discussing him and Ramji.*

"They're using the foreign students . . . one of them is right here, putting flyers in mailboxes, another's on his way to the west side . . . I've got one here. . . . You're free to express your opinion it says . . ."

It was Steve Mittel, on duty at reception, talking on the phone. A solitary guy, Mittel — tall and athletic-looking, often seen manning the late shift here while absorbed in his course assignments. He was at his table now, round the corner from the wall of mailboxes so Sona couldn't see him. Who is he speaking to so intently, passing on information? What can they do — who *are* they? The FBI? Is this guy an informer? A quiet chap, but his close-cropped hair, his button-down shirt and trouser pants are a statement of sorts.

Shaken and disheartened, he continued the chore. The more he stuffed, the more worried he became. He had never shown his hand on the issues; this was the first time, and it was almost a neutral hand, yet here he was face to face with opposition. "They're using foreign students" — when there is a "they" there is also a "we." Would his name be filed on a record somewhere? A frightening thought, all he seriously desired was to be able to do his beloved research. When he had finished the job, from one of the phone booths in the lobby, so he couldn't be overheard, he called his own dorm in the west campus where Ramji had gone with his share of the flyers.

"Has a tall guy come there with flyers . . . a tall Indian . . . no? If he comes —" What, if he comes? "Tell him to wait there, his friend Sona is coming. . . . Yes, Sona, without the 'r' at the end. It's urgent. He shouldn't move." The joke about his name was getting pretty stale, he thought.

He hurried towards the west campus. The long walk through the Tech tunnel-corridor allowed him to compose himself. Perhaps he had overreacted, there was no real urgency; but it was no idle gossip he'd heard – not from Mittel's mouth. He'd sensed menace, and instinct told him to find Ramji right away.

As he crossed Mass Ave, the rhythms of music from a party came throbbing down from the direction of the Student Center. It's either the homosexual party or the Thai party, he thought. He'd seen posters around for both events. Tekle the Ethiopian passed him with a wave, on his way to spend the night at the Student Center library. Isaac the Cameroonian and Stavros the Greek had spent a fruitless time hunting American girls at a singles club, and were now also on their way to the Student Center. The sight of the building reminded Sona that he himself had a date there in fifteen minutes on which he had placed rather high hopes. Earlier in the day, while delivering an overdue homework assignment, he'd befriended Amy Burton, the professor's secretary, who actually also was an Eng Lit student. She had agreed to meet him for coffee that night. And what a lovely night, cool but not cold.

Where is Ramji?

When Sona reached the chapel, across the green from the Student Center, where the residences also were located, he ran into an odd-looking threesome emerging from the alley: Ramji supported by a guy on either side.

"Ramji!"

"He got mugged," one of the guys said. Ramji nodded wearily.

"It's all right," Sona said, "I'll take over from here."

"Thanks, guys," Ramji said gratefully, "I won't bother you anymore," and the two Americans disappeared. Ramji hobbled along beside Sona, using a shoulder for support.

"So what happened?" Sona asked, and Ramji told him. He had been not mugged but jumped on by YAPs, who had been waiting for him.

Ramji had first visited MacDonald House, the newest of the west campus dorms. Having finished stuffing mailboxes there he came out the back door, pulling up the collar of his coat against a wind gusting from the river, wondering if there was any point at all in doing the rich dorms with their carpeted corridors and panelled walls. He was walking in the dark alley between the chapel and Mac House when he heard simultaneously a brief shuffle of footsteps and a mutter behind him, some fifteen feet away, he sensed. He became instantly nervous, his hairs tingling, throat constricted; he reached out to feel his wallet in his pants pocket, as if that would make a difference if he was going to get mugged. He started to run, when from behind a dumpster ahead of him a big guy in an open overcoat stepped out. If Ramji had continued running, he would have been tripped, so he stopped, and said, "What do you want?"

"Got you."

Someone seized him in a tight neck hold from behind, pressing against him, another knocked the flyers from his helpless hands, and the third, the guy in front, punched him several times in the stomach. He was let go and crumpled to the ground.

"Fucking wog! If you don't like America, go climb up the tree you came from."

Ramji looked up, recognized a face. "I know who you are," he said, clutching his stomach in pain. It was the YAP he thought of as

Chunky Crewcut, the guy who went about writing over Shawn's graffiti. He was holding a camera.

"Hey!" There was a shout and approaching footsteps, and the three attackers disappeared.

"When I was down, they had the audacity to take a photo of me," Ramji said to Sona as they walked back to Rutherford. "I think they were right," he muttered, after a moment, "I should go climb up my tree —"

"Nonsense! This is America, everyone has a right to be here, even to protest."

"Tell that to the YAPs. What would they want with my photo anyhow — they can get a better one from the yearbook, or the registrar. You think they took it as a trophy?"

Then Sona told Ramji about Steve Mittel and the telephone conversation he'd overheard and how he'd suspected that Mittel might be a police informer. They mulled over that awhile, then concluded they'd done nothing wrong.

Sona walked Ramji to his room, then went to the Student Center coffee house to meet Amy Burton. At his desk at the Rutherford House reception, Steve Mittel was painstakingly writing up his homework.

7

*T*he great hall of Building 10, under the second classical-style dome of the Tech, overlooks Mem Drive and the Charles exactly halfway down the main corridor – where every moment of the working day scores of people are scurrying along in either direction, like neurons in a throbbing central nervous system going about their tasks acquiring fresh information, new knowledge. To take a break from this frantic activity is to feel wilted, redundant. And yet there are three tables set up here offering respite. Behind the middle table sits Ramji, eyeing intently the urgent traffic moving past. The white manila banner hanging from the table's edge proclaims in large red and black letters: "MARCH ON WASHINGTON: SIGN UP!" His pocket transistor is tuned to mellow WBZ-FM. Beside it on the table a ballpoint pen, coupons for bus reservations (seventeen dollars per round trip), an envelope full of money, a pile of pamphlets from the Mobe, the group that has organized the march. And he's also allowed a liberal space at one end for pamphlets left by assorted radical groups. You just can't refuse them, even the completely screwball ones ("The story of Dick the little Prick with BIG DREAMS") or the cockeyed ones demanding a STOP or END to almost everything. Before you know it you are part of the movement, you learn to live with the differences. The important thing is to end the war.

High on the white marble walls of this great hall, to either side of him, is a reminder of the two world wars: etched in gold, a roll-call of the Tech's contribution of lives. Only names on the walls now, all those young lives that once hustled through these very corridors twenty-five, fifty years ago. Where will *I* be a quarter century from now? . . . Bright sunlight pours in refreshingly through framed doors and windows behind him, beyond which lies a peaceful, lush green lawn.

Two Afghanis mind the stand to his left, their tape recorder playing lilting string melodies. And to his right is the SDS table crowded with its assortment of causes: support the dining workers' demands; support Maria Delgado, fired from the libraries for her political views; join the rally against Poseidon-MIRV-ABM; etc. Behind it sits an amiable guy with small goatee called Eddie Shapiro. The two Afghanis are fair green-eyed men, soft-spoken and polite. They have an open album of photographs on their table depicting the victims of torture carried out in their country, an article cut out from the *New York Times*, and for some reason pamphlets in Afghan. Eddie walks over to them every now and then to ask pointed questions. Finally they look at each other in exasperation as he arrives, and he walks back to his post guiltily, and stays put. But when the Afghanis have netted another interested party, he leans over and says to Ramji: "CIA – they work for the CIA, you can bet on it."

"Really?" Ramji replies. Just when he was thinking how nice they were, how as a fellow Asian he could identify with their reserve and politeness, even their music.

Two of the YAPs from the other night, Chunky Crewcut and companion, have passed by with the day's traffic, perhaps too many times, and he's met their looks squarely. He's filled with a new confidence, there's not going to be another instance of physical aggression from them, not without his making such a noise, they'll be sorry.

I'm going to D.C., he said to Ginnie when she phoned him last, three days before. And he told her what he'd been up to the past month. First the Moratorium, now the March. And she, bubbling over with her usual enthusiasm: Chris is home, he twisted his ankle playing lacrosse. . . . And Junior should get married to his girl by springtime. You can't hold back the hormones, Mormon or not.

What did she think of the war? What did *they* think of the war? They never mentioned the subject, expressed no opinion in front of him. He assumed that John, veteran and former intelligence gatherer – his job had been to cut clippings from newspapers, he once told Ramji – must support the military. And Ginnie would simply want the war to be over, regardless of the politics.

"Call me when you get to Washington," she said. "Call collect. You should come and see me before I go to the hospital."

"You're going to the hospital?"

"A minor operation, the doctor thinks I could do without some parts of my body and be no worse."

"I'll call." His heart sank.

Thursday, November 13, 1969.

Buses waited at Freedom Square on Mount Auburn early in the afternoon to take Boston-area protesters to D.C. All was orderly, even subdued. Mobe officials were at hand to assist, and policemen looked on, arms folded; the only evidence of the impending protest was the placards, at this stage simply extra luggage with the backpacks. Ramji arrived at the square with his fifth-floor buddies the Ethiopians, but having found their bus they were quickly dispersed in the mad scramble for seats and acquaintances. A girl from the Weathermen group had commandeered the quiet, studious Tekle and sat beside him, Ebrahim and Marek had found a seat together.

"Hi there," said a voice as Ramji stood perusing the available seats from the aisle. "Here's a place —" He felt a tug at his sleeve. "Seems you're looking for a window – here, I'll move over – you can have the window."

It was Lucy-Anne the radical, whom he'd met at the Student House some months before, looking rather different today – though no less enigmatic. He paused a moment before accepting with thanks. She had on an oversized faded army jacket over blue jeans, with a red beret and boots. Rather small feet, he observed as he sat down. As on the previous occasion beside her, his heart began doing a nervous double-time.

"I had a ride, you know, yesterday, could have saved a few bucks," she said, abruptly beginning conversation.

"Then why didn't you take it?"

"Oh." She was taken by surprise. "Very forthright aren't we. That's good. A fight, that's why. A lot of factionalism and politics. Informers. You're not an informer, are you? . . . No, you don't know half of what I'm talking about."

"No." This was going to be hell, he thought; and she's super-charged, she's not likely to fall asleep on the way.

He looked out the window for a while, as the bus found the interstate exit, settled on I-95. No forests on the way, he thought, recalling journeys taken back home; no wild animals crossing the road, no tea stops, the bus simply rolling along the concrete highway bypassing town after town; no mystery – and no inconvenience either, the bus won't break down or get stuck in the mud somewhere. The driver was a youngish guy, hair sticking out under his hat, already chatting up the people in the front seats, answering them: "I agreed to go, didn't I? Count that as my contribution to the protest."

Ramji turned, finally, to look at Lucy-Anne; she returned a blank look, seemingly a challenge.

"Tell me about yourself," he said.

"Oh? Like what?"

"Like – where did you go to school?" I've got you there, haven't I, now the shoe's on the other foot, and unless you quarrel, I'm going to find out who this Lucy-Anne Miller, this firebrand radical, is.

"I dropped out . . . from Glenmore." She paused, couldn't resist: "Know where that is?"

"Yes, in Pennsylvania. But why did you drop out – what year?"

"I got tired of the hypocrisy and racism. The college was nothing but an assembly line turning out faithful functionaries of the racist imperialistic state. There were only white faces around me, white and middle class and revolting; I got to hate them. If you saw a black person around, she was a domestic – a servant. And there is the whole black ghetto the other side of City Line. . . ."

"That's just like apartheid," he said, knowing full well this would get her approval.

"It *is* apartheid." She looked pleased, surprised.

"But why not get your degree first?"

This is the Third World speaking, we don't like waste, we can't afford it. All that money, effort – could be put to use?

"I went to work with poor black women – mothers; I babysat while they went to work in those large houses in the Main Line suburbs. And I organized."

Her family lived in Worcester, Mass. Her father was a doctor, her mother a housewife of Quaker origin from Philadelphia. They were important, her mother's antecedents, the way she said it. She had a brother, in law school, and a little sister of ten.

Ramji stared at her. The jeans, the army jacket; the small, delicate face with thin lips and large eyes, the straight beautiful brown hair falling at the sides. We gave her everything money could buy . . . he said to himself, recalling a popular song. Now she was a full-time raging activist, at the front line of demonstrations. Was that mark above her left eye made by a police baton? She brushed it lightly with the back of her hand, almost shyly, with a smile. "Protest's taken on a new meaning in America. Enough of the namby-pamby stuff. The keyword is *revolution.*" Bring the war home, smash the state. . . . And her parents, what did they think of her revolutionary activities?

"They're liberals. They support the antiwar movement."

But perhaps not the extreme form to which you would take it, he thought, but said nothing. She eyed him briefly, then took out a diary from her breastpocket and began writing in it. He looked away.

The bus had settled to a steady, almost lulling speed, and the mood inside was now more subdued, the initial excitement and brouhaha having abated finally. They had been joined by a hippie couple, who had clambered in at the toll booth. The two were now sitting in the aisle, cross-legged, facing each other, their meagre belongings between them. The guy had a light beard and long hair caught in a blue band round the forehead; the girl had two golden braids and wore a long patchwork skirt. Catching Ramji's stare, she smiled at him. Her companion edged closer to take a keen look at Ramji, then, apparently satisfied, joined his hands and said, "Namasté. I'm Shiva."

"And I'm Parva," said the girl in a soft voice, also joining her palms.

"Namasté," Ramji said hesitantly, intensely aware of the now-silent but very observant Lucy-Anne beside him. "I'm Ramji."

The guy nodded, the girl smiled again at Ramji, and the couple settled back. They looked marvellously contented and together, he thought, totally from another planet.

After a while the girl fished out from their things a packet of assorted seeds and a fig, which she and her boyfriend shared in silence.

Ramji tried to read but dozed intermittently instead. In his half-awake state, the late-afternoon sun pouring in through the window, his mind dreamily wandered off in all directions, bringing back memories of home, reviewing the new aspects his life had taken on in the past year.

There were cries of joy and relief as the bus exited from the highway and stopped at a restaurant, and all tumbled out, for bathrooms and food, some even for a few throws of a Frisbee to stretch the limbs. Ramji and Lucy-Anne shared a table with the Ethiopians and the Weathermen girl, whose name was Susan. The Ethiopians talked about the Eritrean war, charming the two American girls with anecdotes about the history of their ancient country.

"These friends of yours," Lucy-Anne said to him later in the bus, "they have quite a charisma among women. They're quite in demand, you know."

"They seem rather quiet. Especially Ebrahim. I know him well," Ramji said.

"You mean the Afro-head. He's made the most conquests —"

"Really?"

". . . and looks like Susan's the next one." She regarded him quizzically. "You're not exactly a love machine, are you."

"Well, if you're bent on insulting me . . . ," he began, not knowing what else to say.

"I mean, do you fuck?" Ramji cringed, blushing all over, and she pressed on: "Honestly, do you fuck?"

"But I do —" he spluttered out.

"Oh, I see. Is she an older woman? Knowing you, she's got to be an older woman."

So Shawn's been talking. Saying what?

"Let's change the subject. Where I come from, there are certain things we don't discuss." Give her a cultural guilt trip. It worked.

"Okay. Fine."

Do I fuck? The inhibitions I've grown up with . . . as soon as my arm brushes against someone like you, as it just did, my conscience takes over and begins an inquisition: Whose arm brushed against whose — who was in the way? Come on, it was no accident, admit you desire her. No I don't, I wouldn't know what to do with this macho type. Macho? Remember the miniskirt she wore? — weren't you just dying for a peep inside, the colour of her panties? And the soft features — the saintly look, as you once said, the martyr, surely you find that attractive. I simply don't desire her, she's not my type. Then why the nervousness, the racing heart? Because of you, you son of a bitch, goading me and nagging me.

It was grey and dusky outside. At the back there now began a singalong led by a regular of the Tech's Friday night Coffee House.

Lucy-Anne turned up her lips scornfully at the inevitable Tech anthem in the repertoire.

She opened her mouth, closed it, heard the song out.

Let the laser shine in, let the laser shine in,
It's the Tech I'm in . . .

Finally she blurted: "They're making a picnic of the revolution. It's no picnic —"

"They've only come to express their opinion on Vietnam. So have I," he said proudly. "I myself signed on fifteen of them."

After a short medley the singing died out, the mood in the bus went from cosy to dark and sombre. They were on an overpass, looking down upon a New Jersey slum: houses old and dilapidated: broken porches, shattered steps, rotten sidings, peeling paint; deserted streets, ancient cars, and not a soul in sight. A scene that takes the collective breath away in this bus, and for a moment at least you understand the anger of these activists, and of Malcolm X, and the Panthers . . . unless you are one of those who blame the poor for their own problems. Why not? Instinct, or simply faith, that there is collective responsibility.

Spirits picked up gradually, however, after they'd passed the slum, and hit the roof when they were queued up at a toll plaza and someone shrieked, "Look, they're also driving to the march!" and everybody peered out excitedly.

A Volkswagen Beetle in the left lane, weighted with passengers and decorated with stickers, exchanged with them delighted cries of solidarity and two-finger peace signs and clenched fists through the windows. Simultaneously, they were given the finger from the right-wing, two guys in a Mustang, and answered multifold and most appropriately in the same language: Fuck you too, buster. Two drivers in military uniforms received howls of derision but waved cheerfully back. Then quiet once more, as they gathered speed. How long before we get there? A few more hours. The sun had set, and headlights glared back from the dark. The hippie couple had left them at the toll plaza.

They passed Philadelphia, and after that came a sense of nervous expectancy. We're getting there, almost there. A pamphlet was passed around from the Mobe regarding discipline during the marches. The first activity, the March Against Death, would already have started, at six, but they could make the end of it.

"Where will you be staying?" Ramji asked Lucy-Anne.

"A friend's house. We're going to take it over – his parents are away for the whole week. You're welcome to crash, if you don't have a place."

"No – I'm going with Ebrahim and the lot; they have some Ethiopian friends at George Washington University . . ."

"I guess they do."

"What activities have you planned?" he asked. He imagined her in a motorcycle helmet jeering at the cops somewhere. And the line of cops in riot gear moving towards her, clubs raised. She didn't reply, so he asked: "Do you think you can bring about change only through –" what word to use? – "violence?" He was pleading, he knew, telling her, *Be careful.*

He said: "You don't have to hit your head against a brick wall to bring change."

"Sometimes you have to . . . to demonstrate, to shake the system up. A few people can make the difference."

They were quiet again. More flyers came their way, more reading lights came on. People were hungry, apples were passed around, as well as some very hard muffins. He told Lucy-Anne about the gaunt and rather grim bearded librarian who worked the graveyard shift at the Student Center library and looked like some angst-ridden character straight out of Dostoevsky. He gave out small brown bags of hard, stale corn muffins to foreign students, with a piece of paper slipped in, typewritten with a quotation from the New Testament and service hours at a local church.

The muffins induced Ebrahim to come by and chat, and Lucy-Anne was rather perked up by his visit. Ebrahim, that gentlest of guys, had one day pulled a real shocker on Ramji. They'd met in one of the aisles of the Coop bookstore, and after a chat, just as they were about to head for the cashiers together, the Ethiopian — who had happened to introduce Dostoevsky's novels to Ramji, specifically *Crime and Punishment* — took a box of Bic pens from a shelf and shoved it down his shirt. Ramji gaped, dumbfounded, then said quietly, "Why?"

They broke into a philosophical debate — like one of those they sometimes engaged in late at night over sweet black tea, except this was hurried and urgent and over a real issue — as they walked to the cashiers, the box of blue Bics still inside Ebrahim's shirt. Stealing is wrong, Ramji said. Period. Did you read how much profit they made last year, came the reply. What difference will this make, a small thing? But you can afford it with your handsome scholarship.

I donate to the Eritrean People's Liberation Front, came the answer. And, besides, they think we Africans are all thieves anyway.

But just before they reached the cash counters, Ebrahim removed the contentious item and with a gracious look of defeat placed it on a shelf.

A year ago I would have been satisfied at my good deed, he said to himself, my moral victory. Now nothing is clear anymore, it's all grey, even the simple crime of stealing – and there's only the individual conscience to nag. He felt suffused with a sense of his private guilt and helplessness.

Ebrahim went back down the aisle to his seat.

It became quiet once again, except for the lulling, reassuring hum of the engine and the sound of the tires belting away in the night. Then suddenly there was a quick succession of exits, a profusion of headlights, and destination looked imminent. Another bus, full of demonstrators, vibrant with song, was passed; the drivers waved to each other. And a crescendo of voices erupted; there were conversations all over the place.

– A helmet, if you can. Always advisable. A must if you're planning to take on the pigs.

– No, it just gives them ideas, see. It tells the cops you've come to riot. Let the crazies wear them.

– What crazies?

– You know, crazies.

– There are Crazies, Mad Dogs, Motherfuckers, Weathermen – which do you mean?

– Is Vaseline advisable? . . . I mean for tear gas . . . like, if were caught in a –

– Remember: this will be a peaceful demo. Any sign of

disruption and it could be Chicago all over again. And we lose public support.

— There shoulda been instructions —

— Don't worry, you'll be told.

— Vaseline can help, but it's not a good idea. If you don't wipe it off soon enough, you'll get burns.

— What do you do if there's tear gas?

— Run like hell.

"And regroup and attack the pigs again, asshole," Lucy-Anne muttered softly and with pleasure.

— Are they going to burn draft cards?

"How does the draft work?" Ramji asked Lucy-Anne.

"The rich get deferments and the poor go and get shot at. Do you have the draft in your country?"

"We have national service. It's military training plus farming. The military training is brutal. It's designed to make an animal out of you — a killer."

"I know." Pause; then softly, with a sideways glance: "Would you have killed?"

If taken to fight the Portuguese down south? . . . They had been told in the service that they could be taken to Mozambique, to assist the guerrillas. Would he have killed?

He didn't answer her.

"No," she said. "You're no Kenyatta."

"Certainly not. Why do your friends call me that?"

After his visit to the Freedom Action Committee meeting in the Student House last spring, the students there had debated calling him either Kenyatta or Gandhi, and had settled for the former, as Kate had sneeringly told him.

"To mock you, I think. But you're all right. I have an instinct for people. I can tell. And I think you're all right."

"Thanks," he said. He was rather touched, though he wasn't quite sure what she meant by "all right."

There are more people behind you than ahead of you, urged the marshalls in blue armbands; keep moving. And we kept moving.

So that Saturday afternoon I marched for peace; not for or against America, this mighty cauldron of a place, but simply for an end to the war, and this country's shameful, bullying role in it. And I was one among thousands, hundreds of thousands, an endless sea, a moving carpet of people; carrying placards and flags, and babies, supported by crutches and canes, in wheelchairs and strollers. . . . From the Capitol to the Washington Monument, moving to the beat of drums. Pennsylvania Avenue was cordoned off by buses and police, and Nixon was inside the White House watching football, they said, unperturbed by the marchers. But you bet he's concerned, his mouthpiece Spiro Agnew will come up with a statement soon enough. We can't all be wrong, thousands upon thousands, we feel it in our bones: Give peace a chance!

When Ramji refused a Viet Cong flag, blue and red with a yellow star, there was a scuffle; he was saved by a middle-aged woman carrying a placard that read MOMS WANT PEACE and walked with her awhile. My son's in high school, she said, and I don't want him drafted. If he's called up I'll take him to Canada, I think. . . . Oh why do these kids utter such obscenities? . . . With such marches Gandhi fought the British in India, and King the racists of

America; with such a march will there be peace in Vietnam? Cambodia? South Africa? Rhodesia, Mozambique, Angola? . . . PEACE NOW! PEACE NOW! Realistically speaking, this is not going to bring peace to the world; homo sapiens are not peaceful creatures. A girl carrying a portrait of Ho Chi Minh stumbled, a guy offered to hold it for her, she refused. Along the route a line of silent Weathermen in fatigues, standing to attention and shoulder to shoulder, holding up Viet Cong flags. . . . I HAVE A DREAM! Yes, we have a dream, too, of one day returning to our countries and working in a school or college; of paying back to our country. Ask not what your country can do for you, et cetera, et cetera. "Ho Ho Ho Chi Minh, Viet Cong is gonna win!" A stone flew into the demonstration, and two fellows from the march made a dash for the culprits among the spectators, but were restrained by marshalls. They don't throw tomatoes here; they shoot presidents, don't they. Bystanders joined the march. TRICKY DICK STOP THE KILLING!

Sona's pamphlet to Tech foreign students had worked a miracle. Fifteen of them raised their heads from Bessel functions and Landau and Lifshitz textbooks and signed up to go to Washington. Fifteen nerds, each one worth fifteen ordinary demonstrators, that's how difficult they are. You deserve a medal, someone told him. Remember, said a voice, Sona's, if there's a riot in Washington you could be hauled in for conspiracy. That's a new law. Conspiracy! — for God's sake, for manning a sign-up booth in public! America is the most powerful country on this planet, the most influential in the world, it has an interest in our countries, it sends agents there, and it sends Coca-Cola and movies, and sets up libraries and dominates the United Nations, the IMF, and the World Bank, surely we should say what we feel when we're here . . . but you've gotta watch it, said a guy at a rap session yesterday, the movement dies, the government kills it, with the aid of a tiny number of crazies who love to trash, because ordinary folks just get scared shitless to demonstrate about what they feel. STOP HARASSMENT OF THE CHICAGO SEVEN. SEND JUDGE HOFFMAN TO VIETNAM. And among the bystanders, a bunch of men and women screaming "Baby killers! Butchers!" at a Yippie contingent, referring to the Tate murders. How you can turn things around; you couldn't find more peace-oriented people than the Yippies. Pregnant Sharon Tate was murdered by the psychopath Charles Manson and his zombies. NO MORE MY LAIS. *And babies too?* – a reporter had asked one of the soldiers involved in the My Lai massacre. *And babies too*, answered the soldier. That was a shocker: Americans do that too? – we thought it was only the gooks and the huns and the nips who did that. Lieutenant Calley and his men lined up unarmed villagers and shot them; women and children, babies too. That was the My Lai massacre, that is war. THERE CAN BE NO REVOLUTION WITHOUT GENERAL COPULATION.

The speeches lasted five hours in front of the monument, but it was all like a concert, better, because you could simply lie down during a boring interval, tune off, close your eyes, and dream. Yeah, dream, about where you are right at this very moment on the grass, where joints are passed around, a neighbour chomps on a hotdog, and a girl and guy sit back to front, up close, the girl lifts up her long skirt and gives the bearded long-haired guy a real rub on the crotch, and it's all right, the sky is all colours and there are tears in your eyes from the light; or is it the cold November wind. Who are you? I am a guy, a simpleton, from the town of Dar es Salaam in the African country of Tanzania, belonging to a small Indian community called the Shamsis. It's so far far away, this city by the blue-green Indian Ocean, it could be in another galaxy; it could belong to another life, a past incarnation. . . . Once I didn't know what America was, where it was, this country of Elvis Presley, later I thought everything it did was good, the Kennedys, John and Bobby, were princes and God's answer to Communism, and now I lie stretched out here before the Washington Monument in the capital, the cordoned-off White House not far away, because I have come here with thousands of other young folks to demonstrate against a war we think is evil, fought, financed, sponsored in all possible manner by this country, and its hands are bloodied, so is its soul. . . . And finally the refrain over and over, led by Pete Seeger, with Peter, Paul & Mary and the others, All we are saying, is give peace a chance, over and over, oh over and over, hold hands and don't stop . . .

Afterwards, when the rally was dispersed, feeling at a loss Ramji followed a bunch of rowdies on their way to the Justice Department to demonstrate against the Chicago conspiracy trial. He kept his distance from them, and when they reached their destination he watched them first defy and then do battle with the police. His own voyeurism surprised – and repelled – him. Yet he could not restrain the desire to witness something daring and dangerous – and destructive; this manifestation of mad commitment.

As last night, too, he had watched.

He was sitting before the TV in the lounge of the dormitory where he'd been put up, and along came Lucy-Anne Miller with two guys, all three in boots and helmets, looking formidable, and immediately the focus of attention of every pair of eyes on the floor. These were the tough guys, they were taking on the government's troops, actually bringing the war home.

"We're going over to the rally outside the South Vietnamese

embassy, we thought you'd like to come by." She presented it as a casual affair, no hint of riot. But the way she was dressed gave her away, with her hair tied up, pants stuffed into her boots, pockets sewn up; tight jacket and that small bag for what – riot paraphernalia? Nevertheless Ramji agreed to go, and Ebrahim came along, if only, he suspected, to impress Lucy-Anne.

"Kenyatta – you hail a cab," Lucy-Anne said to Ramji, without a glint in the eye; perhaps she yet hoped to rouse the Mau Mau in him. In their battledress she and her friends were unlikely to stop a cab, and just as unlikely was the Afro-haired Ethiopian.

The driver nervously dropped them two blocks from the embassy, and they started walking. There were sounds of bullhorns, sirens, and as they walked, their eyes slowly began to water. Holding wet cloths to their faces, they hastened their pace, drawn on by the bullhorns. An obsessive curiosity had seized Ramji, such as a child feels towards something it's told is hot. You want to touch it, feel it's real, tangible. "You're assembled here illegally, please disperse." Lights blue and red and white from the police cars. "Come on – let's go!" Lucy-Anne said, and she and her two companions ran to join the demonstrators. ". . . please disperse." A canister of tear gas flew in the air, a crowd of young people raced back, then some of them took out stones from their bags and they started throwing, at the police, at cars, at windows . . . and Ramji and Ebrahim walked away.

"We did the same thing in Ethiopia . . ."

"Yeah, tell me about it."

And now at the Justice Department, the same scene, in daylight. A Viet Cong flag went up in place of an American one, which had been torn down. He watched for a while; a tear gas canister flew in his direction, and he turned to walk away; it fell far short. I can never have that madness, that commitment, he thought; that certainty. . . . It's better to be a sane coward.

On his way to the dorm he came upon a phone booth and decided to call Runymede as he'd promised Ginnie he would. He smiled at the thought of her – surely she would cheer him up. John Morris picked up the phone and they exchanged a few pleasantries. And then John told him, "You called at the right time, Ramji. Ginnie's in hospital."

Ramji asked, Can I come see her tomorrow, I can then take a bus back to Boston. John said that would cheer up Ginnie immensely.

※

John picked him up at the Runymede bus depot the next day, in the Grand Prix. He shook Ramji's hand warmly. He looked well, braced as if he'd just emerged from a shower, and smelling lightly of cologne. The red blazer and the checked permapress pants on him were utterly sporty and cheerful.

"Glad you could make it. The whole family's here. No problems finding a bus?"

"Amazingly, no."

"And how was the protest march in Washington?"

"Great. A few hundred thousand people . . ."

"You're not saying!"

"They say it was bigger than the Martin Luther King march a few years ago."

Their route took them through open countryside. It was a crisp sunny afternoon. Late autumn's leaves clung to the trees, blushed in the cool clear light streaming through them. It was Sunday quiet, hospital quiet, deathly quiet, as they arrived.

Three low white buildings lay parallel amidst large green park grounds, which a paved driveway entered between two white pillar posts. Two children played on the lawn, minded by an adult in a windbreaker; a man and a boy puttered about near one of the buildings with ladder and wheelbarrow.

"Quite a small place," John was saying, ". . . exclusive, and the doctor's an expert in his field . . . not cheap either . . ."

"And what happened?" Ramji asked. "I mean, why —"

"Well, they decided an operation would help. At this stage all we can do is take the doctor's advice."

"She'll get well, then?"

"You'll see."

The three buildings were edgewise to them as they approached and were connected by glass passageways. The hospital entrance was in the leftmost wing. As they reached it, they saw Junior and Chris at the garden benches, with a girl, playing charades. She was the boys' cousin, Mary, John told him. Ginnie's sister Pat's daughter. Yes, they were here, Ginnie's sisters, they had driven up from Baltimore.

"Will he ever return . . . ," Chris called out playfully, and the two boys grinned at Ramji and said "Hi there!" Ramji returned the greeting.

"Get on with it," Mary said to her cousins. "I said 'Cuckoo'."

Junior proceeded with the clues, miming a brood, negating it, with his hands.

"Sterile," Chris said.

"Sterile cuckoo," Mary shouted.

"Easy, huh?"

It was Chris's turn, and he took Junior's place. From the

entrance, Ramji watched him do an elaborate pretense of reading, and moments later, as John registered him inside at reception, they heard Mary's triumphant scream, "Story!"

"Oh, there he is," spoke Ginnie excitedly from her bed as they entered her room. "The rest of you, out, give me a few minutes with my lover boy. Pat, see you later, John, honey . . ."

Ramji looked helplessly at John as the relatives all filed out, with good-natured, indulgent looks on their faces.

"See you later," said John chirpily, and gently closed the door behind him.

"Oh, come here," she said, and he went and bent over her and gave her a long long hug.

She looked devastated. Oh yes, the face was still full from the medication, but now plain and puffy, all the glow was gone from it, and the suppleness too, the flesh was dying and pale and the eyes were sunken, the skin on the neck and arms was mottled. He smelt makeup and perfume on her.

"Come lie down beside me," she said, making room, and he stretched out uncomfortably next to her, on the edge of the bed, one arm around her.

"I'm all hollow, they've scooped out my insides, there's nothing left, only my connections –"

"But you're not connected now," he said, pointing to the IV, which was idle. "You're getting better."

"You're nice. Now tell me about what you've been up to, how was Washington?"

"Well, I was one among a quarter or half a million people, all peaceful, just walked, while the President watched football . . ."

"I envy you. I've always envied you, you know. You're just starting out – at the beginning of a great discovery . . . like . . . like
Columbus!"

Gone, gone the life and the loveliness; the voice, the bubbly
cheerfulness now coming at him all seemed disembodied. He
wanted to sit down and weep. She felt weak, too, on his arm,
perhaps they really had scooped out her insides – what else can you
do with a cancer? She had been a big woman, beautiful and
sensual . . . all that a long time ago, she was now a helpless, hopeless patient in this cruelly heartless room with white paint and a
stainless steel trolley and uneaten hospital food you discreetly
turned away from.

He sat up on the bed, holding one fragile hand in his. He asked,
"You don't think, for instance . . . that I've been ungrateful –"

"Ungrateful? How?"

"Demonstrating against American policies –"

"Don't be silly. We are not policies. The government is not the
people –"

"Come again?" he teased, catching her eye.

"Well, not always – Ramji, you were always too clever for me.
In fact, John and I have taken great satisfaction in watching you
grow, find your space – don't get spaced out though, isn't that what
you kids say?"

"Yes." I have to make my confession, he thought. I have to say
it, if it's true, which I think it is, I'm going to say it, or I'll forget it
and not believe it. . . . "You know, I've loved you since . . . since that
day . . ." Night, actually, but that sounds inappropriate.

"Yes, I know – though love is a complex thing, isn't it? And I've
loved you too, in my own way."

What way is that? A mystery for me always.

The family was let in, and Ramji stayed a little while longer, then said to John, "I have to make classes tomorrow, I think I should go."

John drove him all the way to the Port Authority Terminal in Manhattan, and Chris came along and was quite chatty. He was still a Buddhist and had finally left the military academy for the public school in Runymede, so he could be close to his mother.

8

Carnal desire, pure and simple, thighs touching in a Greyhound bus — accident or deliberate, does it matter, can one tell? — brown corduroy against blue denim.

The girl he sat with was reading *Siddhartha*, the bible of the mooney-eyed liberation-seeker following the Eastern way, and she caught him trying to take surreptitious peeks at it.

"Great book . . . read it?"

"Yes . . ."

She smiled at him, waited for his endorsement, and he hesitated.

"And? . . ."

"I found it too thin. It was all right, I suppose . . ."

"It's allegorical, you see."

"I *know*. . . . I prefer Dostoevsky, there's more stuff in it, it's heavier —"

"You would."

He stared at her. "Tell me, why do you say that?"

What do you know about me, why this smugness? Have you found Nirvana already?

"Never mind."

He leaned away, closed his eyes. The first time he read the Grand Inquisitor's indictment of the Saviour in Dostoevsky's *Karamazov*, he'd called up Sona in the middle of the night to tell him, Hey, you won't believe what I've just read, it goes straight to my heart, it reads my mind, and it's scary. And Sona said, It sure is powerful, but d'you know what time it is, for Chrissakes! And Ramji put down the phone, sensing Sona was not alone, probably was with that Amy girl he was seen with nowadays . . . what a development . . .

Her name was Lyris Unger, his bus companion said; their thighs were touching intermittently, they were smiling at each other, talking college-student lingo – You know? . . .

A slim girl, not very tall, with a long face, brown wavy hair combed back, wearing high, dark brown leather boots into which she'd tucked the legs of her corduroy jeans. She had a button pinned on her sweater, showing a white lotus inside a sky-blue circle, with the inscription "ONNE . . ." printed in orange inside the flower.

He pointed at the button. "Are you . . .?" He had seen posters of the Divine Anand Mission around campus, offering "One-ness" with the entire universe.

"Yes, I am a disciple."

"What's he like, this guru? I mean –"

"He's called Satguru. He's far out, really good." She sounded almost wistful. "He's not like those Indian gurus, who're only after your money –"

"He's not Indian?"

"He is . . . and he isn't. He has divine birth," she said mysteriously.

"Yes? How?" Curiouser and curiouser . . . but I'm after one thing only and –

I don't believe myself. What about Ginnie, whom you held a few hours ago, scooped out as she put it . . . and dying? Yes. But she'd hardly deny me this irresistible heat flowing through denim and corduroy, in fact she'd encouraged it, perhaps it's all I need, to be normal, and free at last . . . not that I'll ever not love her . . . or forget that golden face full of laughter. Go on, she'd say, go on. . . . But is it real, this up-close invitation, these intermittent, almost casual nudgings? Dammit I should take a risk and find out, girls don't feel your thighs just to frisk you. All that warmth touching and boiling me up . . .

"Why don't you come to the ashram for a darshana and see for yourself? You should really try his teachings. Some people just come for his Rama-naam-bhakti – that's what the chanting is called – it releases all their pent-up tension from the rat race of the world. Satguru likens it to a bath in the Ganges."

"Naah," he said, too flippantly. "I don't need that bhakti and meditation. You see, my people have always believed in meditation, to escape from the illusion of the world, which we call maya. And we have a mantra, and also a guru who comes from a long line of gurus, but they are called pir – sometimes also called guru, and would you believe it, also satguru and swami and so on –"

Fool, you Ramji; you blew it there, you egotistical navel-gazing nerd; do you think she cares about your spiritual life and your traditions? No wonder she sized you up the first instance; Dostoevsky indeed, all words and no action. You should have said, "Fine"; better still, "All right – I'll come, but you'll have to be my guide there and show me the ropes. . . ." Instead, she's turned away, disgusted, to look out the window – better the concrete of the I-95 than you – and her leg has moved away. Free at last – to do what? Jerk off in your room? Tough.

The bus entered Arlington Street Station. Welcome to Boston, check your belongings, watch your step, check for connections, et cetera. He recovered his carry-on from the overhead rack, allowed himself to be nudged up the aisle to the door, got off the bus; and waited for her. She came down, went to pick up her bag, and as she began to leave the unloading bay, she ran straight into him.

"Sorry," he said. "Let me get that –"

"It's all right, I'll manage."

But the bag was heavy and she let him take it through the station and outside to the curb. She smiled her thanks as he put it down.

"I'm taking a cab . . ." she said and began looking for one.

It's no use, he thought hopelessly. Failure stared him in the face. "I might drop by," he said to her back in desperation. "Listen. This Satguru – is he really what you say he is? . . ." She turned around to face him. ". . . He sounded like a far-out guy."

"You should really try him out," she said firmly. "You should come to the ashram and see for yourself."

"I guess I should." He watched her expectantly. Then he took the dive. "Is now a good time . . . I mean, I guess it's late?"

"It is, a little. Lights are out at ten. Let's go and see anyway. There is an early morning darshana, too. You could spend the night there and be in time for that."

Right on.

The Satguru Divine Anand Mission was housed in a large grey stone mansion in nearby Newton, that arcadian hideout and bastion of the gentry. In one of the upper wings of the house were Satguru's apartments. His close staff occupied adjacent quarters. The remaining part of the upstairs, accessible through separate stairs and looking out upon the garden, the driveway, and Beacon Street, were the devotees' rooms, fifteen in all, partitioned from the original large bedrooms. Downstairs were three more guest rooms, the kitchen and dining hall at the back, and a library, a devotion room and a meditation room.

The foyer and the main hall that they entered were hushed, suffused with yellow light from antique wall lamps. The walls had a textured brown wainscotting below a wood trim, the rest covered by wallpaper of intricate curvilinear designs in shades of purple and blue. On the floor was a red oriental carpet. Three other doors led out from the hall, and a majestic gleaming wood staircase went up, curving around itself once, before terminating at a balcony that led off on one side to Satguru's quarters.

"It's a palace," Ramji said, gazing up at the ceiling, at the chandelier, not quite managing to adjust his voice to the silence, and so it echoed loudly.

"Shh," Lyris whispered, putting a finger to her lips, and they both giggled.

"It was a gift to Satguru's father, who was also a great spiritual teacher," she said.

There was a whiff of incense in the air, and soft music was playing that he thought was strangely familiar. She watched him as he paused in his tracks to listen.

"I know it," he said excitedly, not quite managing the whisper, and again she put a finger to her lips, and they smiled.

It was a song to Krishna the sweet lord, currently on the charts. He said the name out loud and she pulled him along by the arm and said, "It happens to be one of his favourites."

She showed him a guest room with three beds, in one of which someone slept huddled inside a blanket.

Ramji hesitated as she made a move to depart. "I might wake him up, perhaps tonight I could spend in your room – I'll sleep on the floor . . ."

"Yeah, sure you will," she said sarcastically. Then: "All right, come along."

She was as hot as he, as he'd known all along.

"Aren't you supposed to be celibate," he said, "or is this" – he was ensconced snugly between her legs – "supposed to symbolize mystical union?" Careful, Ramji, with that cynicism.

But she was relaxed, and warm and wet. "Among the inner circle, yes, perhaps."

She was of the outer circle, consisting of newer, or less committed, members, those who had careers, or families, and who were not ready to abandon all.

"But this is forbidden, I'm sure," she said. "Screwing in these rooms."

And so a relationship formed, based purely on fucking, a convenience, and the convention that if you fucked, then you formed somehow a unit; and based of course also on growing acquaintance and friendship. But a chasm existed between them, bridged only in those couplings.

A chasm of what? Of foreignness: We're foreign to each other and don't really matter to each other, we need not even bother trying to come close. After all, her mother and father were doctors in New York City, her grandfather and an uncle lived in Brookline, she went to Brandeis, and she had a brother in private school in Vermont.

Early the next morning they went downstairs to the devotion room for the daily darshana, a session in which the devotees met their guru, having spent the previous half hour meditating in their rooms. By six o'clock the devotees were all gathered, seated in rows on the floor, awaiting him in silence. There were roughly equal numbers of men and women, about twenty in all. A couple of logs had been set going in the fireplace, beside which stood a small dais, about six inches high, on which all eyes were transfixed, as if expecting the Master to materialize at any moment, right there. A constant drone of tanpura filled the room, creating by its few plangent notes an aura that embraced the gathering in a purpose and a frame of mind, enhancing the feelings of devotion and longing. The Master arrived through the door at the back of the room, escorted by a female devotee walking behind him with eyes lowered. He went to the dais and sat upon it, his legs crossed under him, and he placed his hands on his knees as he gazed down at the rapt audience beaming at him with bliss. His ruddy, clean-shaven face shone serenely at them. He seemed to be in his late twenties and was of medium height, and unlike other gurus, he was not chubby but actually slim and good-looking. His lips were full, his forehead was large and pronounced, and his dark hair was combed back.

After a minute or so of gazing at his disciples, the Master began to speak; Lyris gave a nod of assurance to a fidgeting, uncomfortable Ramji. His voice was pitched high, with little modulation, carrying a tension that drew the audience powerfully along; in the background the tanpura droned.

"In New Haven the other day a young woman shoved a Black Panther flyer under my nose – actually shoved it." A few devotees shook their heads in a show of disapproval. "'What do you have to say about this?' she asked. 'You can't hide the boys and girls from what's around.' Referring of course to the poverty and injustice against which the Panthers purportedly have taken up cause. A valid point, but, 'Sister,' I told her, 'the path of action is noble – if you pursue it righteously. Are you sure that in your protests your actions are always righteous?' The path of love, of devotion to the Lord, reaches the same goal – only it is easier. The Lord is your engine, your locomotive. The Gita says,

The unwise work in pursuit of selfish ends
the wise one works without attachment for the good of all;

that is the path of action and it is noble; but says Krishna to Arjuna,

Give me your mind and your heart, give me your
worship and your love;
then truly you shall abide in me;

such is the path of devotion, the path of ecstasy."

After a brief pause, Satguru said, "Say 'Rama-Naam' with me," and closed his eyes and sat up even more erectly. The disciples did likewise and the devotion began, "Rama naam, Rama naam, Rama naam . . ."

The chant went on for quite a while, during which Ramji opened his eyes momentarily a couple of times for a quick look around, as he felt sure others did. The climax finally came – "Raa . . . aaa . . . m . . ." – in one long sonorous syllable, ecstatically pronounced, diminishing, abating into an echo, a nothingness, into which the Master re-emerged, and went on, "Now concentrate on your temples, see the multicolours of your humours, and go down down down, concentrate on your solar plexus, touch that button, release that fount of energy . . . and let it overflow, bathe you in its cool glow, release you from those worldly cares . . . and now connect, connect . . . connect with your neighbours, open those ego-dykes of personality, let it all overflow and become one ocean of wisdom, one, onne . . . ONNE . . . AUM . . ."

The disciples held out their hands to their neighbours, eyes still closed, "connecting" in rapturous silence.

This devotion, called Rama-naam-bhakti, was meant to bring a sense of "Onne . . ."-ness with the universe, which Ramji understood to be the hallmark of the Divine Anand Mission. It did nothing to him.

The devotees opened their eyes, slowly let go of each other's hands, and looked at the Master expectantly. Satguru said, "Well?" The mood relaxed. This was the beginning of the question and comment period. A young man said the cross-legged posture distracted him due to the pain. It was recommended that he attend the afternoon yoga classes. Nothing comes easily, practice makes perfect, practice both in mind and body. A girl asked: The orange light that one sees during meditation, is that a good sign? No, she was told, it reflects the passions. Curtail thinking, become unconscious – but don't fall asleep. (Modest laughter.) Is the objective inner peace, or is it enlightenment? a woman in her thirties queried, enlightenment is surely wisdom and knowledge, and therefore with respect to the world. . . . When you find it, you will know what it is, the Master said. The two are the same. Enlightenment removes turbulence of the mind and heart as light removes darkness. But the path is treacherous, it looks easy but is not, the ego has to be smashed . . .

There was a minute of silence as Satguru and his disciples beamed at each other; then Satguru joined his hands in a pranam, and the disciples began getting up. Each went up to the Master, knelt, kissed his left or right foot, took three steps back, then turned and left the room. Only Lyris and Ramji remained now, her hand on his arm as if to stay him. Satguru's gaze fell upon them, and Lyris got up, gestured to Ramji discreetly with a hand, and he followed. They went and knelt before Satguru, and Lyris kissed the foot closest to her, at the heel.

"Satguru-ji, Swami-ji," her voice was tremulous, "I've brought a friend – Ramji. He is in need of spiritual guidance but has . . . has a . . . a sceptical mind . . ."

Ramji sensed the guru's gaze upon him. Years of religious upbringing had taught him to keep his own eyes lowered at such moments and instinctively he had done so. Now he felt uncomfortably compromised.

"Better a sceptic than an indolent mind; a sceptical mind is already engaged . . . it knows what it wants but stubbornly denies itself. But it needs to be saved before it destroys itself. With the right insight and love it can be made to see –

"It is natural at some point in life to want to rebel," Satguru said, in a changed, more casual voice than before.

"Ramji is a Gujarati name," observed Satguru more pointedly, after a moment's pause. "A holy name."

"Yes," said Ramji.

"You are welcome here," the guru said, and Ramji felt pressure on the back of his head and his forehead was touching the guru's other foot. Not a bad-smelling one, at that. Oh God, what's going to happen to me, this utter humiliation; how low can you get, kissing the foot of a dime-a-dozen-in-America guru. Smash the ego.

The Mission's brochure, of which Ramji found a carton of copies in the library, explained clearly what Satguru was about. He was the son of the great guru Anandaswamy, who had in 1932 come to the West with a message of hope and enlightenment from his own guru, who lived in a retreat outside the famous city of Rishikesh on the Ganges. After establishing a centre in London, he had come to the New World, specifically (and symbolically) to Boston. America possessed the fresh mind of a child – or youth – but was deluded as the young always are in the exuberance of their possibilities and their energies, without the wisdom of experience, unaware of their limitations. It was ready to receive the ancient wisdom of the East. The Divine Anand Mission, its headquarters now in Boston, soon gained renown in America and Europe; its founder's melodious voice spoke at many prestigious venues, including Madison Square Garden in New York. The likes of Albert Einstein, T.S. Eliot, and Aldous Huxley had benefited from his vision. A faded photo of Anandaswamy (in trousers, Indian kurta, and turban) with Thomas Stearns Eliot (in three-piece suit)

was shown at the bottom of page two of the accordion-folded brochure. And then suddenly an *apparent* scandal broke out in 1939. One of Anandaswamy's disciples, an English girl called Carol Brown, announced that she was carrying the child of the guru. Shortly thereafter the mission was closed in Boston, and the couple went to live first in California, where the child was born, and later in Switzerland.

The scandal was only an illusion, the brochure explained, it was the "lila" – play – of the Merciful Master, who had outwardly suffered ridicule and humiliation but actually taken a leap into the future. Having foreseen the Second World War, he had postponed his mission and planted a seed to blossom in the years of peace ahead. The divinely conceived son, named Edward Anandaswamy, had been trained to continue the mission. In a ceremony in Lausanne in 1964, he had been anointed by his father, and Satguru Edward Anandaswamy declared himself ready to guide mankind on the path of perfect happiness of the soul.

Anandaswamy the Elder had not been inactive in Europe. He had written six books on spiritual philosophy and an autobiography in 1960 called *To Break a Destiny*. He regained some of his earlier reputation and was awarded honorary degrees in Germany and America. Finally he left his mortal body and obtained union with the Universal Soul in 1965.

He was profoundly influenced by his two meetings with Einstein, who, he wrote in his autobiography, "was one of the great souls whom the Universal Soul sends forth at critical times to enlighten the world. In his catholicity in all matters and indeed in his pursuit of unity in the physical world, he demonstrated (as did Spinoza before him) his awareness of the essential unity of

everything in the Universal Soul Itself." In a footnote to this statement, written in 1966, his son traced the influence of Einstein's
pursuit of unified theories on his own concept of Onne . . .-ness.

The ashram had a manager and was run like a dormitory. Residents
paid rent and gave gifts to the guru. Televisions and stereos were
not allowed, and close friendships among devotees were discour-
aged; you were there for yourself, on your solitary quest, and your
relationship was with your inner self and your master, Satguru. At
the management's discretion you could be asked to leave. One
meal every day was communal, an early dinner of vegetarian fare
in gleaming stainless steel utensils, in the Indian fashion. Forks and
knives were allowed, but grudgingly; you had to ask for them.
Occasionally Satguru turned up and ate by himself on a side table,
with his hands; there would then be utter silence in the room, all
cutlery laid aside.

Ramji was allowed a free bed in one of the guest rooms in
exchange for hours he agreed to put in every week in the publishing department, which produced brochures and flyers for the
Mission's activities. He kept his room at the Tech though rarely used
it, going to the campus only to attend lectures. His relationship with
Lyris was maintained discreetly. He was often in her room, even
when she was not there, and sometimes they went out together. But
there were other secret liaisons among devotees as well.

He attended with diligence his remaining classes in November
and December, having sneaked into his dorm room early a few
mornings to bring out his books. He avoided friends, grew a beard,
let his hair grow further, and in the manner of the Master wore a

white cotton kurta instead of a shirt. He stopped going to the Friday music mosque, and his mailbox in that period received a dozen messages from Sona which he ignored; in the last one Sona said he was moving in with Amy Burton, the girl he'd been seeing for a while; there was an off-campus phone number.

He had called Ginnie once early in December, at the hospital. She was preparing to return home.

"You'll come to see me, won't you?" she said.

"You bet," he replied, "maybe right after Christmas."

"I'd love to see you again."

Christmas came, and went; Lyris had gone home and returned in mid-January.

But Ramji didn't go see Ginnie, he didn't call her. There was a new coldness in him, an indifference. It was as if he had detached himself from his former self, as far as possible. And yet – God knows I love you Ginnie, have loved you – in many different ways as you yourself said, and I know you of all people would under-stand the life I'm leading. In your laughing, carefree way you'd say, It's all right, Ramji. But I don't know how to face you anymore, I don't seem to be the same person, the Ramji you knew. I am car-rying on a relationship with a girl I don't really care that much for, I am at this ashram under false pretenses and merely to escape from myself . . . I am not a nice person at all. I have become cynical, insensitive, brittle . . . a shell of myself.

He thought he would write all this, and more, in a letter to her, composed and recomposed it in his mind, began to transcribe it on paper; never sent it.

In December also, Ramji and Lyris had gone to protest the police shooting of Black Panther Fred Hampton while he was in bed. The Freedom Action Committee gang were there, drumming up a riot, as were Shawn and Kate. He avoided them all, but very briefly once met Kate's eye and turned away. She must have recognized him, despite his beard. She herself looked different that day; her hair had grown and she wore black cords, and the hiking-style boots looked new. Kate and Shawn, he had already learned, had moved off campus.

Gradually, the question of Satguru's genuineness or fakeness lost importance for him; the ashram had an atmosphere that could only be called spiritual; it had a calmness and a purposiveness that was not overbearing. No one brought up his strange behaviour at the morning darshana: he would not chant but sit quietly in a back row; at the end he would stand up, do a pranam but without going up to kiss the Master's feet, and leave. At that moment of departure their eyes would meet. It seemed that Satguru, with his liberalness and compassion towards him, was winning him over. Ramji took yoga classes, attended lectures. There was barely any theology to contend with, and the philosophy, from the Upanishads, was attractive and liberating.

His work at the printing press, located in the coach house at the back, gave a regularity to his life that he enjoyed. A group of devotees drove around college campuses in a van, distributing the Mission literature and explaining the message of "ONNE. . . ." When a place had been deemed suitable to receive him, Satguru would go there and hold a few devotional sessions. There were branches of the Mission in over twenty campuses.

In the new semester he arranged to take only self-study courses at the Tech. The ashram became an almost total retreat, a quiet hideout in whose spirituality he allowed himself to be suspended, wafting in an atmosphere pervaded by gentle sitar ragas and bhajans and Sanskrit recitals, without commitment to anything or anybody.

There were days of forgetful bliss, yes, when he could have kissed the Master's feet at morning darshana in gratitude for allowing him into this refuge, of place, of mind. There were times when he even thought he could feel a glowing sense of euphoria, when the Guru said to hold hands and "connect." But could he lose himself entirely? Could this place completely claim him, cut him off and subsume him? No, he knew he would eventually emerge from it.

In the first week of March, a packet of correspondence arrived at the ashram, collected from his mailbox at Rutherford and forwarded. This is how your life catches up with you. There was a letter from John, dated approximately six weeks before, January 15.

"Dear Ramji, this is to inform you that Ginnie passed away peacefully on December 23 at Runymede General Hospital. According to her wishes she was cremated. I am sorry to be the bearer of such tidings and we all miss her very much as I am sure you do. We tried calling you a few times but there was no response. Ginnie was of a cheerful disposition and would have wished us to remember her at her best. I continue to look forward to your visits to us in Runymede . . ."

He read and reread the letter, I wish I had called her, at least once, heard that voice for one last time, that beautiful laughing voice . . . I could have gone to be with her in her last hours, I could have held her hand. Instead, where were you, Ramji? I knew she was dying and I hid myself away.

He took one Aspirin, then another. Do I have a headache yet? . . . But I want to cry, so much to cry. . . . Then cry, you nuthead, let the tears come out, you rockface, but they flow internally as in Indian film songs, you drink them in and they are no good. Damn you, Ramji, let go and simply grieve . . . grieve for all you've lost, Ginnie and your hopeless innocence and your simple faith and . . . and . . . There was a bottle of pills on Lyris's desk, he poured them out, all gleaming in potency, little bombs or M&M's depending on your point of view, all colours, red white blue, yellow, shit brown, orange, even black for God's sake, you can play a marvellous game of Go with them, in Technicolor, or is it Eastman or Kodachrome . . . He took out a pad of square-ruled paper and arranged the pills on the intersections, you here, you go there, but it was much nicer to form a multicoloured design the way the Chinese did using schoolchildren holding coloured flags or boards and singing "The East Is Red." . . . He swallowed a red pill, and another, and another and another and he went out as he'd so much wanted to.

"OD'd himself right outta this world. Holy nirvana, man." It was Johnson, the black cook at the ashram, who had become Ramji's friend recently and been plying him with a lot of questions about Africa.

"How long's he been out?"

"Twenty-four hours, at least." Lyris. "Moaning and groaning, Jesus, and in *my* bed. He took all the reds, who asked him to take the reds, they're from Mexico and dangerous –"

"Holy karmic nirvana, musta' been all those letters he received . . ."

He was cold, sweaty, smelling of piss. "Lemme go." Ramji staggered away to the bathroom. His head was cracking open, his body shivering in great uncontrollable spasms. He slipped onto the floor, clutching the side of the bathtub.

Voices outside.

"I'm not touching him. You sort him out." Lyris. So much for exotica, we are all vegetable underneath, and when we rot, we rot.

Johnson and Robin, the latter a full-time cop and part-time devotee, helped him clean, plied him with bread and sweet milk, and tucked him into a freshly made bed in his own room where he stayed two days.

Later that week in the middle of the night he was pushed over and she came in beside him; familiar smell, familiar flesh, she always wore a flannel nightie; Lyris. In the morning on his notepad, just "Goodbye!" with a flourish.

"She's moved on to the fourteen-year-old wonder from India," Johnson said. "That's the second of Satguru's devotees who's discovered Guru Maharaj-ji and his mother. They like it easy, these kids, instant nirvana: close your eyes, swallow the phlegm, see the red light back of your eyes, that's it."

9

An anguished, horrified look on a girl's face, her right hand reaching out and upwards – for what? – beside her a fallen comrade; behind, in the distance, a column of guardsmen. It became an emblem of raging dissent, that shooting at Kent State University, Ohio; and that look of horror screamed out to a troubled nation: What have you done? Don't shoot us, we are your children!

It seemed to Ramji he was beginning to wake from a long sleep. Nixon had announced the invasion of Cambodia and campus after campus erupted in riots during the early part of May. And it seemed as if the ashram itself was seeing an invasion from the world outside. A portable nine-inch TV had materialized from somewhere and at night some of the devotees gathered around it in secret to stare at a world apparently in flames . . .

Venerated, paternal news anchorman Walter Cronkite told it the way it was, with a colour map of the United States pinpointing riot spots throughout the country. Harvard Square saw mass demonstrations once more, tear gas and bloody encounters with police clubs; Central Square was trashed; a camera caught a rock-thrower in the act and the newsman asked: Why the destruction, if you say you're for peace? For Kent State, the thrower panted, his missile lurking in his palm, and for My Lai, and six hundred thousand Laotian refugees, for South Africa and . . . and . . .

But in less than three weeks the strikes were over; the news of the day at the Tech, before it broke up for summer vacation, was a science colloquium.

And that was what finally brought Ramji back to reality. Somewhat paradoxically, perhaps, it was an event that also heralded his scientist-hero Peter Bowra's departure into the cloudy world of mysticism.

"I was right," Lyris said, sidling up to him as far as the auditorium seats would allow. "Satguru is all right, but too intellectual — all ego." She prodded the side of her head with a forefinger. "But Guru Maharaj-ji is *it*, direct, the source."

It was two months now since she'd left him and the ashram for the other guru.

Today Satguru was speaking at a Tech colloquium, the same weekly forum that had seen some of the world's great scientists in the past. By all indications at the ashram, Satguru Edward Anandaswamy was *excited*.

The event had been billed as a Bowra-Satguru joint colloquium on the Tao, titled "The Cosmic Dance," and the auditorium was packed, having drawn a diversity of people from near and far. Even the saffron-clad tambourine-clanging Hare Krishna mendicants were on the scene, on the green outside the Student Center.

About six weeks ago one morning the legendary Peter Bowra showed up at the Divine Anand ashram. He had been expected by the Master, though the devotees were taken by surprise. They had not failed to note that the air was clear of incense that morning and a rather enchanting recital of the Gita was playing over the loud-speaker. As soon as the scientist was wheeled into the great hall, the awaiting Satguru fell on one knee, saying with a flourish, "Ah, the great master, welcome!"

"Wait a minute," Bowra said, coming to a stop, "I thought *you* were the great master."

"Ah, but you have held death in your hands, the weapon of Shiva —" The reference was to Bowra's work during the war on the atomic bomb project.

"Isn't it Krishna — in the Bhagavad Gita, as Oppie said — who proclaimed, 'I have become death'?"

"But Shiva is the destroyer. . . ." Satguru smiled.

"But these are symbols anyway, aren't they?"

"Exactly. Unfortunately, people quibble over symbols and lose sight of the great —"

"The great equation," Bowra put in, "if that's what you meant to say."

The two were soon locked in a private discussion in the library, after which the scientist left, much as he'd arrived, with a great flourish. A few days later the colloquium was announced, and it promised to become a much-anticipated event in the Boston area.

"In every scientist's life," Peter Bowra began his introduction at the colloquium, from his wheelchair behind a small table on the stage, "there comes a time when individual phenomena — such and such an equation, such and such an effect, the brick and mortar of the scientific endeavour — cease to hold the mind." Perhaps this restlessness was due simply to an awareness of one's own mortality.

But what began to hold the fascination for the mature scientist was the greater picture – the Holy Grail of all the great minds of the past. One could call this Holy Grail the equation of state of the universe, one could call it a unified field . . .

Bowra's own research for a single overarching pattern in the behaviour of the universe had brought him, after useless detours in the arid world of Western philosophy, to Eastern mysticism. He had begun to entertain what only a few weeks before had been unthinkable for him: the notion of a supermind, or soul. He was struck by those mystical systems of contemplation that from the beginnings of civilization insisted on a unified view of everything. And so he found himself in the halls of the marvellous colonial-style mansion in Newton – what a happy coincidence, that name! – the ashram of the Divine Anand Mission, whose teachings were partly inspired by Einstein's search for the Holy Grail.

Satguru went to the podium, which was beside the professor's table, and greeted the audience with a namasté – a joining of the palms, and a brief bow. Then he recited a verse in Sanskrit, after which, in a British accent somewhat loosened by his stay in America, he gave a brief introduction to Indian mysticism and mythology. When he finished, he nodded to Peter Bowra, and for the rest of the session the two men conducted the proceedings together.

"And so where does the connection come in, between science and mysticism?" the scientist asked. "In the past few weeks we have exchanged notes on our respective disciplines. While our approaches to the secrets of the universe are diametrically opposite, we were struck by some remarkable coincidences. We would like to share them with you."

Lights were dimmed, a slide image came on the screen: a bubble-chamber photo of particle trajectories; beside it a projection of the god Shiva dancing. The lines and curves of the bubble-chamber image could be interpreted, without too much assistance, as forming an outline profile of the dancer. Many such parallels were shown; between icons and diagrams, equations and musical scores, ideas and ideas.

"We are not saying these different-looking phenomena, the subjective and objective if you will, are precisely the same," said Bowra. "That would be too simple. What we have shown are just a few data – some patterns, symbols, and images – worth contemplating. This is just the beginning."

The colloquium was a resounding success. The mere fact of such a bold presumption as that of combining modern science with Eastern mysticism in order to understand human existence was itself remarkable and exciting, a sign of the free spirit of the times.

Ramji and Lyris parted with a brief hug. She left through a side entrance, and he headed for the lobby at the back. There he ran straight into Sona, who held a Styrofoam cup of coffee in each hand, one of which he proffered to Ramji, and an Oreo cookie in his mouth.

Sona said: "Or don't you take coffee anymore. What's happened to you, Ramji? You could be mistaken for a guru yourself," he added, looking Ramji up and down – Ramji with a kurta over his pants, long hair curling at the back of the neck, and a beard.

Sona was in a blue Tech windbreaker and beige Levi's bell-bottoms. There was a certain acquired confidence, a composure in his bearing which made him seem very much a part of his milieu now, and no longer the wide-eyed genial foreigner. He too sported a beard, but his was trimmed, a neat goatee ending in a point. Could the American girlfriend Amy have done so much for him?

And now here he was, come to bring the apostate back into the fold . . .

"Actually, I do have what you might call a disciple of sorts," Ramji said, "so you could call me a guru I suppose. . . ." Let him stew for a bit. (He was referring to a young man who had recently gravitated towards him to learn the ropes at the ashram.)

"Playing the Indian card now, are we?" Sona asked.

"Why not? What did you think of the lecture?"

"Why you or anybody else can't see through this charade — the guy's a divinity school dropout, for God's sake! Then proclaims himself a guru —"

"He must have been some good to get in. And divinity school is just theory. Who needs that? People seek the real thing. He's the son of the famous Anandaswamy —"

"Yeah, conceived while the great teacher himself was demonstrating a yogic position to a beautiful, gullible young woman, I'll bet. What do *you* learn there — Kama Sutra?"

They crossed Mass Ave to go to the Student Center. The Hare Krishna mendicants were still vigorously at it, twirling about and singing, jangling their tambourines, watched by a small crowd as the late afternoon sunlight streaked in brightly from the west. Ramji felt an old familiarity, a closeness returning between himself and Sona beside him. We've known each other forever, he reminded himself, and we pick up where we left off almost without a thought. His concern for me is touching.

"I wanted to get away," Ramji found himself explaining, "and the ashram has a peaceful atmosphere, conducive to meditation and reflection . . . even spirituality. . . ." (If we don't mention Lyris for now.)

"Escape," Sona said scornfully.

"Perhaps."

"Who was the girl with you, back there?"

"I met her on the bus from New York once."

"She with you at the ashram?" That searching look, it was more than academic now, there was gossip behind the curiosity.

"She introduced me to it."

"Stinks. Look —"

Sona, the designated mukhi of their little student community of Boston, picked by popular acclaim. He would have made the perfect village headman in some distant past: learned, protective, keeping the fold together — or at least trying to.

"Look," Sona said, "all this mysticism and devotion this guru teaches, you know we have it in our tradition, we grew up with it — what's wrong with what we have? You don't have to run off to find it anew —"

"I just want some space . . . to be. To be left alone from the past, not worry about what I'm called, and what I'm *supposed* to be. . . . I am what I am."

"So said Popeye. It's not so simple, is it. You can't run away altogether."

"Perhaps not."

Sona brooded for a while. They had arrived at the Student Center coffee house and ordered coffee. The place showed evidence of a recent modernist onslaught by an architecture student project; the tables and most of the chairs had been removed and replaced instead by a tall and coarse-looking multilevel screwed-on structure of wood, red pipes and translucent plastic, provided with seats inside nooks and corners for people to sit in. For those unwilling to undertake the climb to search for a suitable place, there was a large cartwheel that served as a table, surrounded by a few chairs, which is where Ramji and Sona sat. The place was quite deserted.

"Look. We are a community, with a history, language, identity. Would you that it all evaporate into nothingness?"

Surely not into nothingness, but into something else perhaps. But Ramji didn't quibble. He felt curiously unmoved by Sona's plea for communal integrity.

"What about your courses – how long do you plan to stay at the ashram?"

It would be nice to tell him: Forever. Or, better: I have renounced life, I've become a seeker of truth, a mystic, and I'll wander from place to place and have a few disciples of my own . . .

But what he said was, "I'm leaving it. Actually, that lecture confirmed something I've known all along. For me, it's the mind, not the soul; mine is the world of science and mathematics, reason. *I* don't want beatitude, infinite wisdom, permanent enlightenment. Donnez-moi la confusion et un peu de lumière."

"Who said *that*?"

"I did. And further – listen, for you are the mukhi – if there is a traditional God out there, I don't think He has the time or the inclination to hunt me down because I don't bow and praise him and humiliate myself. If He is there, I give him a nod of respect – which I would give even to Nixon – and go my own way. Vive le Ramji libre!"

"What's with this French stuff – a new phase?"

"I'm reading Camus."

"Welcome to the world, anyway," said Sona with feeling.

Little could he know then what a surprise the world was preparing for him. The politics of dissent he had become engaged in, before he abandoned them for the quietude of the ashram, were soon to catch him in their trajectory, in a manner that he neither could have foretold nor would have chosen for himself. Indeed, over the long term they would never let him go.

10

In early September amidst the excitement of Rush Week, a bomb exploded near Kendall Street Station, destroying a good portion of the ancient building that housed the Institute for Strategic Studies, or ISS.

It was a Friday night, a little past sunset, and Kendall as usual at this hour was deserted and forbidding. There was no witness to the explosion when it occurred, save one homeless soul. Out at the front end of campus, though, Mass Ave was festive, a rock band had just wound up its performance on the green outside the Student Center. It was here on Mass Ave that, in typical overkill, five fire engines and six police cars appeared in a jangle of sirens, drawn by a garbled warning phone call and the presence of student crowds. The mistake was realized and the fire engines began a hasty departure, when one of them backed into a police car. Flashing blue and red lights and the heavy breathing of automobile engines as from overgrown beasts added to the bizarreness of the scene. Overjoyed students surrounded the crashed car, and for a moment there looked to be the makings of a riot, with shouts of "Pigs! Off the Pigs!" and the possibility that the car might be overturned, whether in jest or as an act calculated to inspire a cop into a bullish deed and the crowds into a frenzied retaliation.

Sanity prevailed, however, and someone said, "ISS's been bombed!"

"A couple more bomb threats too," said one of the two cops, who were emerging unscathed from their badly dented vehicle. "Now if you folks'll kindly make room . . ."

The students made room for the two to walk through to one of the other squad cars, then they went quietly, en masse, to Kendall Street to see what had happened. A police cordon was already in place when they arrived, and they stopped obediently behind it, positioning themselves into an intent crowd of watchers on the farther side of the intersection, in partial darkness. Flyers soon appeared among them.

Ramji, who had come with the crowd of watchers all the way from Mass Ave, snatched at a flyer:

STRIKE TERROR INTO THE PIG STATE! ONE MORE BLOW FOR THE OPPRESSED PEOPLE OF THE THIRD WORLD! The Institute for Strategic Studies is one of the lynchpins of the Warfare Terrorist State that goes by the name of the United States! . . . The ISS has formulated the policies of the Warfare State in Vietnam! . . . signed: Third World Liberation Front

There was a shout and the sound of a scuffle behind him some-where as, apparently, a couple of people distributing the flyers were hauled off by police. At that moment, Ramji found himself reminded of someone he had not seen, had hardly thought about, in months — Lucy-Anne Miller. He glanced at the flyer in his hand, again looked at those words. Surely not her. . . . But she liked to talk of the Third World. . . . Smash the state, bring home the war, enough of the namby-pamby stuff. . . . According to rumours circulating in the crowd, it seemed one person had been killed by the blast, the panhandler who always used to sit at the side of the building.

Ramji peered before him, towards the bombed building, an old one-storey yellow-brick structure partly hidden from view by police and fire vehicles.

Late Wednesday night a commune in Brookline was raided by the police. Seven people were arrested in connection with the bombing, four of them while they were in the final stages of preparing to leave town.

News of the arrests made the next morning's headlines. When Ramji picked up the early edition of *Tech Speak*, his worst fears about the bombing were realized. None of those arrested were familiar to him, but: the police were seeking two other suspects, a couple named Lucy-Anne Miller and Jason Perly. The news preoccupied him all that morning. She couldn't have done it, he would tell himself — not this. But then again, why not? He simply had a soft spot for her, and he hoped that she wasn't involved. At lunchtime, as he came down the fifth-floor corridor of Rutherford to go to his room for a quick bite to eat and pick up some books, he was mulling over the news once again. Of all the stupid things, to be involved in a bombing and hoping to get away with it. What a waste of a life.

He flung his room door open, and there she was, the object of his current anxiety, seated on his green armchair, one leg over its armrest, looking up from a book: Lucy-Anne. She was wearing brown cords and a green army jacket; the book was *No Exit*. He opened his mouth, checked himself, closed the door.

"I'm no James Bond," he spluttered angrily at her. Somewhat ludicrously, in his mind flashed an image from a movie seen in boyhood, the British secret agent entering his room to find a squeezably soft, gorgeous Russian blonde in his bed – while two Russian agents film the resulting love scene through a spyhole in the wall.

"My, my. Testy, aren't we," she said.

"What do you expect? . . ."

She didn't respond.

"You guys bomb a building, kill a man in the process, and you come here . . . for *what*?"

"They're framing us."

"What? . . . Don't you live at – here – '641 Macedonia Ave –'" he said, reading from the paper, "and what have we here – 'gallon containers, fertilizer, pipes –'"

"Don't you see –"

". . . 'the oven had obviously been used to dry fertilizer, an FBI spokesman said,'" he finished. "You live there."

"I didn't do it."

"Do you have an alibi?"

"For when, Sherlock? We were all in and out."

"What do you want me to do? You'd like to see me in jail? Or perhaps back in Africa up my tree, taking the revolution with me?" Then he remembered, he screamed at her: "And *who* gave you my bloody key?"

"Shawn," she said calmly. "He thought his place would be watched. Look, we were on our way to Canada, via Maine, someone — the pigs — blasted the car with a shotgun Monday night. We're waiting for another car. I'll leave Saturday. How about that?"

He didn't say a word.

"Look — I didn't bomb that building. But it deserved what it got," she muttered angrily. "Except for that bum, of course. . . . Don't you *see* what they're doing in places like that? They're divvying up the world — *your* world — into spheres of influence, friendly countries and the not-so-friendly, which can be destabilized —"

"But I don't believe in bombs," he pleaded with her.

"They're as American as apple pie," she retorted sullenly.

From the corner of his eye he noted the black phone on his desk. He'd come back to have lunch, but now he had lost his appetite. He picked up a couple of books from the desk.

"I'm going," he said brusquely. "Classes." But then at the door he hesitated and turned to look at her, adding more gently: "Help yourself to anything in the fridge."

She returned his look with what he could only think of as a kindly smile.

The overwhelming feeling he had as he left his room was of being suckered; of knowing that and not being able to help it; of being so predictable. She had *known* he wouldn't turn her in. Suppose right now he went ahead and proved her wrong? . . . Of course, she could be innocent and telling the truth; that was the saving grace.

He returned at ten in the evening, noticed the downstairs lobby packed with YAP guys — four of them leaning against the counter, on the other side of which at the table sat Steve Mittel, apparently their man at Rutherford. Clean-shaven and sporting crewcuts, all of them.

"Hi," said Chunky Crewcut. The Intimidator. The sight of his jeering Neanderthal-looking face filled Ramji simultaneously with rage and fear.

"Hi," Ramji replied with false cheer, walking past rapidly to get to the stairs.

"He's got a white chick in his room, likes them white, he does," one of them said behind him.

Ramji looked down from the first turn of the stairs. The distance was safe, so he could make a run for it to the first-floor rooms. Taking a breath, he said angrily, "What's that to you . . . KLANSMAN! What are you going to do about it, KU-KLUX-KLANSMAN! Are you going to burn a cross outside my door?" All his anger from that previous night when they attacked him came pouring out now, in uncontrollable surges. And almost everyone from the rooms had come rushing out to the staircase, staring down at the scene from their landings. There was little sympathy at Rutherford for the right wing, and they all began shouting abuses at the foursome.

"Assholes!"

"Creeps — lay off!"

"Go back to Baker House!"

But the four were not leaving. They were big and hungering for bony contact.

Ramji climbed the stairs to his room. Lucy-Anne was there, looking rather like a tart on the job: with a blonde wig and gaudy makeup, in miniskirt and boots.

"Hullo. Where are we off to? Isn't that . . . a bit too obvious?" Besides, what does it say of *my* taste.

"Yes, and no. It's distracting – no one would expect to see me like this. I've already got a few whistles and a proposition. I went out for a while."

"Oh yeah? Anyway, those YAPs are on your scent. They're waiting downstairs. We may not last the night."

We: he was already in on the conspiracy, was he. Pray God morning comes quickly. It's Friday tomorrow. She seemed a bit shaken by what he'd said, and he told her to sit down and made some tea and tried to calm himself. Later he heard voices down the corridor outside, went to the door and peeked. Who should be sitting outside the resident genius Billy Blair's room some five doors away but Chunky the goon with a girl. Keeping vigil for guess who. Trust Billy to keep such friends. But a YAP? Ramji shrugged nonchalantly, closed the door. They could be planted there all night.

Obviously they were not sure of themselves, whatever their suspicions were, or the cops would have been here a long time ago. Maybe one of them *was* police – but then, who had heard of undercover cops disguising themselves as right-wingers? They went around as radicals. Someone must have recognized her this morning, outside Rutherford perhaps. So that outfit's not such a bad disguise after all.

He voiced his approval out loud, and she said – well, tartly, he thought – "It's worked before."

The trick on this tightrope was to appear as normal as possible, let everyone think this foreign student's picked up a white girl off the street. He wanted to ask her, Are you *sure* you were not involved in that bombing? That sounded terribly inane, and besides, what would she answer?

He said, "So what shall we do?"

"Let's play cards." She brought out a deck from her rucksack and they played gin rummy for a while.

Suddenly, there was a knock on the door. Ramji and Lucy-Anne looked at each other, then he got up and opened the door slightly. It was Steve from the desk.

"Your mail, I brought it up. . . ." He gave a quick look inside, adding: "Sorry about those guys downstairs. Uncalled for." And he left.

"Is this some kind of harassment? Who asked him to bring my mail up?"

"Maybe he's just a nice guy."

"And he thought he'd come and check up on us. Here, let me teach you a game called Zanzibari." They began playing, and she seemed to enjoy the game.

"Is it really an African game?" she asked.

"Yes," he said, proudly, nostalgically.

Later she wanted to go to sleep. "But I have to go pee first," she said.

Outside was the men's room, which could be converted with a sign hung outside, but that was too involved and risky.

They both threw a glance at the basin. Fat chance, he thought.

"All right, turn off the lights. I'll use the window."

"What?"

"It's all right – I've checked the ledge. It's quite wide. I've noticed you store your doughnuts there, don't you . . ."

"And a squirrel keeps stealing them. Spare my doughnuts, though. Are you sure – you won't topple off . . . or be seen?"

"Turn off the lights."

He did so. She went to the window, climbed up and out onto the ledge. He couldn't help himself from trying to discern the sounds. He heard only the rustling of clothes. She was facing him. "Don't gawk."

She slept on the bed while he worked, using the desk lamp, or tried to; he filled some mugs with water and poured them out the window where she'd crouched.

He couldn't sleep, sat on the armchair staring vacantly ahead. The dark was soft, a dim glow poured in through the window, from the yellow night lamps in the courtyard down below. He tried not to think about this circumstance he found himself in, but that was not entirely possible. It was like after a sudden accident, a fall perhaps, and one could not quite believe what had just happened.

I could go out, lock her in, and call the police. Would I? No, but I don't quite know why.

She says she didn't do it. Do I believe her? And if I knew for certain that she actually did do it, and was therefore one of the people responsible for that bum's death, would I *then* call the police?

There is a look of such innocence about her.

She had washed the makeup off her face, borrowed his pyjamas, which she rolled up at the bottom, brushed her teeth, and, with a shy "Well, goodnight," had got between the covers and gone to sleep, facing the wall. As if the yellow brick wall oppressed her even while she slept, she turned away from it later to lie on her back, her head partly turned to face him.

A perfect upbringing, storybook style. A house something like the Morrises', he guessed. With a mother and maid, Thanksgiving turkey and a Christmas tree. She gave all that up for the Third World, she says, for me and the world I come from . . .

The general politics are correct, I think. But she has no inkling of the world I come from. In our house when I woke up and went to brush my teeth, there would be inch-long cockroaches scurrying about. Nothing romantic in that. And in my country Indians like me are sometimes called foreigners even though we've been there more than a century. There are people who want to leave, go away to Britain or America, does she realize that. . . . I am Indian and African and all screwed up with Western education, and all she sees is "Third World." Yet she has the sympathy, from somewhere; and notwithstanding that innocent face of a child fast asleep she may have – has she? – killed someone . . . for that sympathy, for that Third World cause? – as she says – or simply due to some inner confusion, unhappiness, rage? . . . or a combination?

But she says she hasn't done it.

To distract himself, he picked up from his desk the day's mail (which Steve Mittel had brought up), went through it one by one but without much heart.

Grandma wrote: "Beta – dear – May God grant you good health, wealth, happiness, etc. I am well and happy here, thanks be to God, don't worry about me. I am overjoyed that you have started writing regularly again. . . . The rumours are true that a few people have been taken away at night; but only those doing illegal things . . ."

Preventive detentions without trial had recently gone up, back home, for all sorts of reasons. You could be kept in a secret prison or exiled to a remote highland region.

With Grandma's letter came one from a couple of African tailors who were their neighbours back home. A few weeks ago Ramji thought suddenly of writing to them. This was their reply. They were thrilled at his letter, "danced with joy" at his success in America, from where they were certain he would return "a big man."

And one from Lyris: A group photo taken at the Divine Anand Mission in January, and a Guru Maharaj-ji flyer – "Who is Guru Maharaj-ji? Come and find out" – with her phone number scrawled on it.

He got up, opened the door quietly, looked outside. The corridor was clear; the only sound came from the radios in the open rooms of the night-beavers toiling away, separately lost in their world of tangled hairy formulae. At such a time he might have strolled up to Ebrahim's room for a small chat and a glass of sweet black tea; but not tonight, there would be too many questions.

He lay down on the floor next to the bed and tried to sleep.

The next day, Friday, he spent between his classes, the libraries, and the coffee house, avoiding his room as if it were infected. He had brought up the *Times* and the *Globe* for Lucy-Anne, but perhaps earned a curious look or two in the process: who had heard of Ramji going down specifically to buy a paper, let alone two papers, first thing in the morning? He shouldn't have done it. Pray Saturday came without a hitch and she went off to the woods of Canada and he could forget about her.

Friday at six, Ramji returned, prepared to go to the mosque. It had become more a social occasion now, this little private prayer meeting they had begun two years ago. Its location had changed from the music library to two attached seminar rooms above it on the next floor. The Friday mosque was where you went to be with people who seemed familiar, even if you'd never met them before, whom you could trust more or less unconditionally. Hopefully some family people would bring home-cooked samosas or kebabs, if not more. And later some of them would go to a movie if there was anything worthwhile. And hopefully too that new girl from Smith College would return – a homestyle East African beauty in a miniskirt, a rare thing. She had come for the first time last week and sent the guys' blood racing.

He glanced at Lucy-Anne. She was sitting on the bed, back against the wall, flipping through a book. They had not talked much since he came. He sensed she was keeping out of his way – or simply acting hurt because he had avoided her again all day. She was not in her tart's disguise, and she'd confirmed that she had stayed inside all day. The YAPs were not around, which was a relief; perhaps they were convinced she was only a pickup after all.

"Would you like to go to Friday night mosque with me?" he asked. She raised an eyebrow, and he explained, "It's not far – in the Humanities building. It's more a social event, though non-members wait in the outer room during prayers. Very informal."

She should be unrecognizable in the wig, he thought. His concern for her at the same time aroused a sense of dread in him, a quaking in the pit of his stomach. Am I getting in deeper . . . abetting a bombing suspect . . . and perhaps not only a suspect – if she is innocent, why run away to Canada and not stay to defend herself?

"I'd love to," she said brightly and began to get ready.

"Go easy on the makeup, though," he said, and they exchanged a smile.

They left by the side entrance and, hurrying past the main doorway, saw Shawn and Kate absorbed in a discussion outside while apparently waiting for someone. Kate was gesticulating. They called out brief hi's, not to draw undue attention, and walked on towards the Humanities building.

Today, the second Friday of the new term, there was a large attendance at the mosque. It was actually noisy when they arrived, and Lucy-Anne turned somewhat pale at the sight of so large a group. Amy was talking good-naturedly with a few guys and, apparently in a bid to tease them, had drawn the attractive Smith girl Samira into the discussion. Samira, however, had come with a guy of her own, an American. This semester there were two other newcomers, students at Harvard, who had already begun to undermine Sona's prestige by insisting that proceedings at the mosque were not being done in the proper Islamic way. Today, for example, having arrived early, they had evidently moved Sona's little platform, behind which he always sat as presider, so that it faced west now, and the congregation would have to face east, towards Mecca. Sona moved it back to where it had always been. It was clear now to everybody that the music mosque would no longer be the calm and harmonious communal gathering it had been; it was now a theatre for opposing ideologies.

Towards the end of the ceremonies, Sona sang a beautiful hymn with a lilting melody containing traditional Indian references. It told the story of how a famous king restricted his queen from practising her faith and how by a series of miracles she made him yield. It was all about the call to duty, and when it was sung in the main Dar es Salaam mosque every New Year's Eve, people claimed they got goosebumps, so powerful was its message. The hymn also marked the annual change of regime in the mosque back home, the implication of which Sona hadn't quite thought of.

As Sona concluded the hymn, with the king putting down his sword and saying, Queen, tell me about this faith of yours, one of Sona's detractors spoke up: "But Sona, where is Islam in this song you sang?"

Before Sona, getting red in the face, could find a response, there came quick, urgent voices from the outer room, where the non-members were, then the sound of angry swearing, and a loud squeal. After a moment's hesitation, a few guys from the congregation got up and made a dash for the lobby, the others followed not far behind. Two very official-looking men – short-cropped hair, light suits, compact builds – stood at the doorway ready to leave with a handcuffed Lucy-Anne between them, her face contorted in a grimace. The Feds turned around and took her away.

As she left, Lucy-Anne looked behind at Ramji and shrieked: "Asshole! You traitor – betrayer of your world –" There was venom in her eyes.

Ramji gaped, watched her as she disappeared into the corridor, unable to grasp what he'd just witnessed. Did she really think that *he* had turned her in?

How had it happened, what had just transpired? How did those men know where to find them – was he being followed all the time? Who else – besides Shawn and Kate – knew where to find him at this hour? Steve Mittel could conceivably know, and therefore all the YAP guys. Who else had seen him leave with the bewigged Lucy-Anne? Enough people surely, and someone must have seen through the disguise, after all. And he thought he was being smart, avoiding his room all day – that was another sure giveaway. You can't fool the pros.

But Lucy-Anne – how could she have uttered those words – did she really think he had betrayed her, set her up *in the mosque*? After all he'd been through on her account – the anxiety, the risk? If he had wanted to, he could so easily have turned her in simply by sending the cops to his room in his absence. How typical of these radical types, with all their ideals but no trust in common decency. And here he was left standing, burning with embarrassment, all eyes upon him wondering what exactly he had been up to.

He agreed to spend the rest of the evening with a solicitous Amy and Sona, so he could recover from the shock. The thought of spending the evening by himself in his room was appalling. The three of them went to see a film, and later at a café they chatted late into the night. Apparently Amy liked to sit for a discussion somewhere after every movie, and with, "So – what do you think?" at Sona, take the movie apart.

This they proceeded to do for some time, with Ramji putting in his half-hearted bits now and then. Earlier on he had explained to them what the evening's drama at the mosque had meant.

When he reached his room late in the night, he ignored the telltale signs of Lucy-Anne's presence and got straight into bed. But it felt like a strange bed, her tormenting presence very much with him.

The next morning, Saturday, the phone rang at nine, waking Ramji up, and Dean Johnson of Undergraduate Affairs asked a nervous Ramji to be present in one hour in the President's office in Building 10.

"Mr. – er – Ramji," the President began, after the preliminaries, having waited for Ramji to sit down across from him. He picked up a paper from his desk. "I surmise from this pamphlet you helped distribute last fall that you are not destructive; you have kept up with your course requirements and Mr. Neville the Foreign Student Adviser very much corroborates my estimation." He paused. "But if you are not careful you can be drawn into violating the law . . . even in participating in a violent act."

Ronnie McDonald was a tall studious-looking man, with circular-rimmed glasses. He was sitting rather erectly, in front of an arched window that overlooked the Charles River. Ramji had never been this close to him before. Dean Johnson was younger and more athletic; he was always seen dashing about in the corridors, and as front man for the administration, much disliked by the activists. He had pulled a chair to the President's side, like a secretary. The two federal agents of the previous evening sat on either side of Ramji, their chairs turned to face both him and the President and Dean. They were introduced to him as Mr. Harrington and Mr. Butler and had the hungry look of those who had come bearing a complaint. Of the four, only the Dean was not in a suit; he had on a navy blue sweater.

Ramji kept quiet for a while, trying to understand the President's gambit. What does he know, what doesn't he? He knows everything of course, he's got the full dossier. He sat with his hands clasped between his knees, wondered if there really was a tremble in one of them, or if it was simply the posture in which he had been caught, causing twitches of protest in the leg muscles.

Make a clean breast, he thought. If necessary, beg forgiveness. Crave it. Crawl on knees.

"About Lucy-Anne. I had no choice really, she simply walked into my room —"

"You could have picked up the phone," one of the agents said. "According to our information you went out of your way to assist her in hiding —"

"But she was not a fugitive from justice," Ramji said, thinking: I've had it.

"It is not as simple as that, is it," President McDonald suggested. "She lives in the, uh, Dagger-and-Poison Commune, which as you know was raided by the FBI and where bomb-making materials were found." The President paused awhile, then added: "A man has been killed; thousands of dollars worth of property has been damaged — thank heavens the computer and files were saved. Surely it's the duty of law-abiding citizens to assist in official inquiries of . . . such terrorist acts."

"For your information, on Friday morning a warrant was issued for the arrest of Miss Miller," said the second agent.

There was a long, painful silence. I'm not going to be kicked out of the Tech; but the U.S. — that could be a different matter. Hi, Ma, I'm back — kicked out by imperialist America.

"Who do you think phoned you with the tip?" Ramji asked.

Ronnie McDonald drew a breath and sat back. The four interlocutors exchanged quick looks.

"That settles it, then," Dean Johnson said, softly.

"I think that it does." The President.

The first FBI agent picked up the slim briefcase at his feet. The other stared intently at Ramji for a few more moments, then took the cue from his partner and relented. Both stood up.

"You did the right thing in following your instinct," the first agent said to Ramji.

The two agents left, shaking hands with the President and the Dean, with deference and thank you sirs, and a nod towards Ramji, who stood gaping at the open door behind them, wondering what to say. As he turned round to face the President, Dean Johnson came to him and escorted him to the door.

"You know better than to do something stupid," he muttered.

"I didn't make that phone call," Ramji began to protest, but the Dean didn't seem to understand.

*T*hat all recollections, unless forcibly extracted, contain at their core at least a germ of vanity I would hardly quibble over. But, much more than anything else, for me these memoirs are a balm; I take to them like a plunge into cool water in a heat wave, and emerge only at my own peril. Is this dwelling in the past an act of surrender then – of having lived, and then nothing more? I pray it is not. For I know she will return.

I am told I should consider myself lucky I am not in a country where even the least suspicion of wrongdoing is enough to put one into the clutches of so-called "research bureaus" and their truth-extracting torturers. To which I answer, Of course I appreciate that; but am I supposed to feel grateful for not being tortured? I receive a smile, and a "No, of course not." My interrogator is a far cry from the agents whom I met once in a university president's office, all of a quarter-century ago. He tries hard to be chummy . . . but I must return to him later. "In all the time that's passed, how did you look back on your first years here," he once asked.

It's twenty-seven years since I first set foot on the soil of this country; the earth has gone round the sun so many times. The Vietnam war is over (but who won?); Mandela was freed and became president (and the world sings Nkosi sikelele, God bless, all is forgiven); the Berlin wall came down and the Soviet empire imploded; we lost Elvis and John Lennon; the Shah of Iran was deposed as was Haile Selassie (dictators replaced by more dictators, and where is my friend Ebrahim now); thousands of species of life, biologists tell us, became extinct, as did, in my own (former) country, the Aasax language. And what became, what's become of me?

Whenever – and it has been often – I think of my first years here, in this land, it seems I had walked through a portal – a passageway – to emerge into a state of enchantment. There was no walking back of course, no undoing of that spell. There was now a certain looseness in the step, an exhilaration, a sense of freedom. I had an awareness of a larger universe than the one I had known and of all manner of possibilities, of *choice*: in one's beliefs and actions. I wouldn't say there was any less anxiety in this freeing myself of the faith and the moral order of my ancestors, of the sense of guilt and sin which keeps one bound to their universe. There *was* terrible fear – of hell and damnation – awesome anxiety and loneliness, which only appear diminished now from this distance of years and seen through the intervening medium of nonbelief.

Okay, so you finally got rid of that monkey on your back, God, that Old Codger in the sky, and you walked away a free man, an individual at last with destiny in his own hands. But what else, Ramji, what more did you come away with?

Perhaps – and I need to say this – There was a sense of smug self-satisfaction and arrogance, at having been if not anointed then at least touched by the magical "sixties" with its mark of righteousness and belonging on the right side always, its belief in the underdog, in the "oppressed" against the "oppressor." For we of that generation were convinced we had been given the revelation of political discernment and a belief in *engagement*.

And all that followed seemed to fall short of those inspiring years, seemed a betrayal. That too.

Betrayal — how subjective a term, depending where you stand. For example, who betrayed Lucy-Anne, that night she was arrested? Or was she betrayed at all? I have asked myself these questions often enough in the intervening years. Now that I am in the hands of someone who might know the answer, I realize these questions have lost their urgency. Did Lucy-Anne believe it was I who betrayed her to the cops? It seems impossible to me that she could have believed that for very long. After all, had I wanted to, I could have given her away sooner, and without embarrassment to myself.

From the newspapers I had learned that Lucy-Anne had been released on bail a few days after her arrest. A photograph showed her walking away from the court with her parents and a promi-nent New York lawyer. I never tried to contact her. One day, almost a year and a half later, I ran into Shawn and Kate in Central Square. They told me that Lucy-Anne had been acquit-ted on a technicality. The news had been in the papers a couple of months before and I seemed to have missed it. I never ran into either Shawn or Kate again.

But more than questions about Lucy-Anne and betrayal, what has nagged at me all these years is whether or not she had lied to me about her innocence. And, further, if I *had* known she was involved in that bombing, would I have acted any differently? That almost three decades later, I would be confronted by a horrifyingly similar dilemma is something I could not have dreamed up in my wildest fantasy.

The Friday night of Lucy-Anne's arrest marks the end of that period of enchantment for me. I recall the months and years that immediately followed as a period of diminished intensity, of relative calm, both in my personal life and in the scene around me. It was a time in which to observe and to reflect, and to carry on. I recall vividly sitting up half of one hot August night to watch George McGovern secure the Democratic convention to tumultuous cries for peace; then sitting up another night a few months later only to see him lose the presidential election by the greatest margin ever. There was the Watergate Show with Chairman Sam Ervin, and the end of the war; the pathetic I-am-not-a-crook Nixon resigning, and gleeful media pictures of the new president Gerry Ford stumbling. The gullible and gentle Moonies and the gullible and abrasive ESTers offering truths for which the hunger was gone.

For me, there came the years of hard work, when I began to study the philosophy of science, while making annual guilt-ridden resolutions to go back to Africa, to do my bit for nation-building. But instead of going back I took a job at a Cambridge electronics corporation editing brochures. This was a far cry from the career in science I had once dreamed of, but I realized I no longer had a head for the hard-core nitty-gritty of the discipline (as Peter Bowra might have put it), though I remained a believer in its perspective of the world. Gradually I also developed an interest in Swahili philology (perhaps to assuage my guilt), which I studied in the evenings at Boston University. This period of study and employment coincided with a disastrous love affair, and I have often been tempted to put my failed patriotism at least partially at its doorstep.

Sona too remained in Cambridge, and we continued to see each other. He and Amy lived together for a couple of years before getting married, and I rather envied him his settled life. His scholarly work now preoccupied him completely. He had already resigned from the "musical mosque," which moved out of the Tech and became a more formal, established affair.

About a year after Ginnie's death, five months after the ISS bombing, I received a letter from John Morris, announcing that he had married a woman in Montclair and had moved in with her. She had three young children, two cats, and a dog, he said, and he was very happy. It had been Ginnie's wish that he remarry as soon as possible. There was a phone number, but I could never find the will to call him up.

Back home – how haunting is that term *home* – back home times were hard. A mad dictator called Idi Amin had taken over the neighbouring country of Uganda and expelled all Asians, having received instructions from God in a dream. Asians from my own country were being driven out by the rigours of socialism, the whims of arbitrary bureaucrats, nightmares of a local Amin. Now that I had a place of my own, I thought of inviting my grandmother to come and visit. Instead she asked me to come back, *and get married.* Along with her letter and newspaper clippings, she sent me a photograph of a distant cousin in Zanzibar. According to the clippings, five members of the revolutionary council in Zanzibar, led by a sheikh I had always believed to be ruthless and extreme, had each chosen for themselves an Asian girl as a bride. This despotic measure, as announced by the sheikh, was an effort to help along the integration of the races. There were fears of more such forced unions, and many Asians were in extreme anxiety and on the lookout for suitable husbands for their daughters. Now I was being asked to be one such son-in-law. Our girls are in danger, said Grandma in her letter; you must help your cousin. She is a good, decent girl. . . . I sent Grandma a long and (I now think) callous lecture to accompany my refusal: If we Asians had integrated with the Africans before this, such problems would not have arisen; I could not marry a girl I had myself not chosen, the world had changed from the day of arranged marriages; and so on. It was half a year before she replied. By this time, the protests were so strong, that it became unlikely that more forced marriages would take place. But I could never escape the guilty feeling that I had disappointed my grandmother, and hurt her. The newspaper reports of the abductions of young girls by African dictators helped me to convince a judge to grant me the status of a permanent resident in the United States.

And so I followed the route of so many visitors to this country. I allowed convenience, the temptation of the good life, and the assurance of safety and freedom to detain me, even as I held on to the image of the errant patriot, needed, missed in his native land.

And then my grandmother died, and home had never seemed so far away.

Lucy-Anne: *You betrayer of your world!*

No, I would not come to blame her for subsequent feelings of guilt and betrayal, but she certainly took a hard poke where one day it would hurt.

One Christmas I visited Toronto, where a large number of my people had arrived from East Africa and formed a thriving community. It was 1979, the Shah of Iran had been deposed; Americans had been held for weeks now as hostages in the former embassy in Tehran. On my way back from Canada, I faced a dour immigration officer who seemed far from well-disposed towards dark-skinned foreigners – a sentiment not uncommon at border checkpoints in the best of times, and this was hardly one of those. He seized the moment (as we used to say), found something wrong with my passport – the photo seemed to be peeling – and questioned me for a long time. My bus left without me, having deposited my luggage in the blustery cold outside the immigration building. I waited in an inner office dreading all sorts of outcomes; now and then someone would peer in through the glass walls to see I was not up to any mischief. And then suddenly, after an hour of detention, my nemesis walked in, handed me my passport, and told me I could go. There was a New York bus early in the morning, for which I could wait. Bristling with embarrassment and humiliation, I resolved to wait outside, lest these watchdogs of the home of the brave change their minds, or sniff out something else.

"I guess you need a ride," a voice said as I stepped out and faced the chilly air anew.

I turned to my right, from where the voice had come, and eyed the man suspiciously as he stepped forward.

"I vouched for you," he said. He was taller than I by a couple of inches, in a black duffle coat and holding a woollen cap in one hand as if to show more of himself – balding up front, sunken-eyed, long angular face, and a fluffy pointed beard. A vaguely familiar face, I thought. We stared at each other for a few moments.

"How did you vouch for me?"

He smiled enigmatically.

"I'm going to Boston," I said.

"So am I."

"Oh. We must have passed each other – Park Street Station, wherever . . ." I grinned.

"Ten years ago, and a month maybe – to be more exact. Washington, D.C."

"You were there?"

"Who wasn't? But I saw you there."

His name was Stan Allen, he'd been to Northeastern, and he was two years older than I. We spoke at length and excitedly about those times and how important it was to keep their revolutionary spirit alive. It was time to entrench, we agreed, hang on to the victories won, resist the backlash and the lazy thinking, educate the public, break new ground. By the time we arrived in the gloomy shadows of the Berkshires he had offered me a partnership in a small company dedicated to the distribution of publications put out by alternative and radical presses, those crucibles for new and far-out ideas and truths the mainstream dared not touch.

In the spring I moved to a suburb of Chicago, where our company was based. It was time to move away from the city that had been my cradle in this new land, so to speak, and from a region which carried so many reminders for me of an era now ended, of people disappeared, of a tormenting romance recently ended. I sought a new life in a new place. I began to frequent Toronto, where I met many of my old classmates and acquaintances. But while I could not completely feel part of the community after my long absence from it, I could not help returning to it to try to re-experience what I had lost. One day, I met a vivacious, pretty Dar girl who seemed the perfect complement to me; we were strongly attracted to each other, and after a courtship that lasted a few months, we married. At last, I thought, I was coming home. If only Grandma had been alive to bless my future!

Today it was cool and clear. I went to sit at the Rose Café, a place a few blocks away. Darcy arrived, driven by my intrepid young patrons Hanif, Leila, and Lata (the first two are his grandchildren). The teenagers were treated to sandwiches, after which they hurried off to the beach, which, it being Sunday, promised much (a session of tea-leaf reading, for one), and Darcy and I walked back here, to my place. A brief, unimposing visit, spent mostly in quiet chit-chat. When I see us together now, and juxtapose that image with my memory of when and how I first saw him, I cannot but be struck by a poignant awareness of time. "Don't think of time that way," he says, "You're still young." His support touches me, for even though I pretend to a certain cold detachment at this juncture of my life, I do need my hand held occasionally. I am utterly alone. I have not recovered from my loss, and I harbour a fanatical hope. I see her around corners or across the street on a bicycle; I hear her humming a taarab and laughing at a joke. Any moment Rumina will come and pause briefly at the doorway with a smile, and walk in.

II

A GRAND REUNION

1993, a week in midsummer

"What revels are in hand?"

– SHAKESPEARE
A Midsummer Night's Dream

1

*W*ell, folks, here we come, Ramji mused to himself as he entered the Schuylkill expressway, sat back, and began heading across Philadelphia towards Glenmore. The Ramji contingent arrives in full force, in modest midsize conveyance, no doubt, but ready to play the reunion game. And who knows what lies in store . . .

He had had forebodings about this visit. On one hand, he had wanted to go, to be with old friends and stay up to party, and reminisce, and banter. But reunions were always a two-edged sword, weren't they . . . you came back from the close encounters revitalized but also somehow wounded.

"We're here," he said with a smile to Zuli, who had sat up, having nodded off the last half hour or so.

She smiled briefly back, began to get out her makeup kit from her handbag.

He threw a look behind him towards the back seat, at their sleeping ten-year-old twins, and called out gaily, "Hey kids! We're here, the city of brotherly love and —"

"Where – where is it?" Sara said as they both jumped up, looked out their windows.

"We're only passing through – but do you see the rowers on the river . . . nice, huh?"

The late afternoon sun shone bright still, the riverside was busy with joggers, vendors, dogs, the usual summer weekend crowd.

"I hope we're not too early?" Zuli said. She had turned a bit tense at the prospect of meeting company, which was a normal reaction from her, though Ramji thought she always made a favourable impression wherever she arrived, raised eyebrows by her tall, pretty looks, by her forthright opinions.

"Oh no, we're on time," he told her, looking forward to the prospect of winding down after the long drive from Chicago, which had not been entirely free of disagreement and tension.

Four weeks ago the invitation card had arrived, saying

You are invited
to the "mustardseed" midsummer's party
at the home of
Jamila and Nabil Henawi
July 4, 2:00 p.m.

Quite simple, illustrated with an airy cherubic figure floating above the text, and a champagne bottle and bowl of fruit below, just the motifs for the occasion. And a little Stars and Stripes under the date to give the Fourth its due. How's that for design, Jamila said to him when she'd called to discuss the get-together, I did it myself on the computer. The bowl of fruit has been ruined though, what a pity. Never mind, Ramji had reassured her, it looks just great.

Ramji felt happy for Jamila. That card was a notice to her friends: I'm coming back! And a rallying cry also. After a long immersion in motherhood – this she'd said to Zuli over the phone – we've *got* to take back our lives!

During her years in New York in the seventies, during which she and Ramji had known each other quite well, the "mustardseed midsummer's" at Jamila's had been an annual event much celebrated among all those who knew her – a motley crowd of young professionals recently arrived in America from all corners of the globe. No one who was invited missed it for anything, and if she happened to be away that part of the summer, early July, she had to come up with a substitute, usually a bash on the day of the U.S. Open tennis finals in early September. It was at one of these annual parties that she had met her husband Nabil.

Oh, I hope this works, she'd told Ramji, it does seem like such a good idea.

Of course it's a good idea, he'd said. Especially, as he now reminded himself, after the tragedy of her nephew Abbas's murder in a West Philadelphia street. Not that Abbas was close to her, but, still, he was family, and she had felt guilty for neglecting him. There had been family complications too – concerning the burial, for one thing, and Abbas's wife for another – to worry about. Ramji always felt a bit vulnerable when Jamila called and assumed her confiding manner with him – a leftover from their past relationship, over for more than a decade now.

Jamila had organized her midsummer party to be the finale to a week's grand reunion (her words) starting today in Glenmore among her closest friends. There would be (he began mentally ticking off the names) Salma and Aziz, also from Glenmore; and Iqbal and Susan from D.C.; Sona would also arrive from D.C. (though he lived in Boston, had done so ever since their Tech days), and word was that he would bring along a student; with Jamila and Nabil, and Ramji and Zuli, that would add up to ten people altogether; and then the kids, a bunch of them, all now beginning to grow up. This would be the first reunion in four years. The last one had been in Toronto, and before that there had been one in Boston, both of them small ones; nothing so extensive as now, with everybody present.

And nothing in such lush surroundings either, he said to himself, taking the Glenmore exit. Zuli drew a deep breath beside him, murmured, "This certainly *is* the right side of the tracks," and he grunted his agreement, saying to himself, Nothing but the best for Jamila, she always made sure of that. A suburban shopping plaza met the kids' approval by its displays of all the fashionable designer names, a park and tennis courts they passed were met with similar approbation, before they wound through a shady and narrow road with majestic homes looming from the high ground to their left. They turned finally into a cul-de-sac with slightly more modest and modern offerings. The driveway they entered was long and already had several cars parked in it.

As soon as they had stopped, Zuli took the lead, getting out and walking up ahead with a tired "Hullo! *Hodi?* We're finally here!" towards the back door that opened into the driveway.

Jamila materialized at the threshold, exclaiming, "Oh welcome, you're finally here – you must be exhausted . . . so nice to see you, Zuli . . . you look wonderful as usual . . . ," at the same time throwing a concerned eye towards Ramji. He grinned at her and waved, and the two women kissed, Zuli saying, "And you're the same as ever, Jamila, time doesn't wear you out!" Jamila looked a bit taken aback but smiled graciously and went on to welcome the twins.

"Is everybody else here?" Ramji asked as they all went in, and Jamila said, "No, only Salma for now . . . ," then called out, "Salma, they are here, the Ramjis. Come meet them." Jamila paused, apparently realizing that she may have caused offence by referring to Zuli as *a* Ramji, then went on, placing a reassuring hand on Zuli's arm, "Salma is inspecting the food – by the way, the theme today is South Indian crossed with East African – let's hope she gives me the Good Housekeeping seal of approval!"

Salma stepped down from the kitchen and there were more greetings all around. Salma was petite and darker than the other two women. A fellow Glenmorean, she was Jamila's critic-over-the-shoulder. The two could not have been more different in their ways. They did not like each other very much, yet here they were, from the same background in East Africa, thrown together in this small town. In her distinctively husky voice Salma pronounced, "It's all perfect, Jamila – but if you want my honest opinion, really . . . the potato-chops would have been better fried, not baked."

Jamila shrugged, said rather good-sportedly, "We can't all be perfect." But then as Salma and Zuli huddled together, discussing their kids, Jamila turned to Ramji and made a face to mimic her local nemesis, muttering savagely, "Miss Constant Comment, always the last word . . ."

She almost got caught with a contorted face, both Zuli and Salma turning towards her at the same time, but Jamila saved herself in time with, "You know Sona's bringing a girl with him?"

"A girl!" exclaimed Zuli.

"Yes, a girl," said Salma solemnly with a nod.

And Ramji thought, My, my, how interesting, this must be a new development. He never let on about it the last time we spoke.

By the time Sona and his companion arrived, the others were gathered in the living room, a happy backslapping bunch exchanging news and greetings, some of them with drinks in their hands. There was a sudden silence at the sight of the couple as they entered: beside Sona stood an apparition, alien and forbidding – a woman wearing a blue scarf over her head and shoulders, in the traditional Iranian way; she wore a long wide cotton dress, she had clasped her fingers together in front of her as she took a few measured steps forward, and she was staring back at the gaping crowd. Sona introduced her. Her name was Rumina, and from up close she seemed quite young, in her twenties. There were a few awkward moments (during which people looked at each other as if wondering how to greet her and whether to hide their wineglasses) before it became apparent that she was quite normal, and the mood lightened once more. Susan and Rumina began a lively conversation about something of common interest, the city they both lived in.

"So who's she?" Ramji teased, when he and Sona had drifted towards each other and found a chance to talk.

"Tell you about her later," Sona said.

"I hope you've warned her about Aziz's offensives."

"I can handle him."

Aziz Pirani waved at them from a distance, eyes gleaming mischief through his dark-framed glasses, but he didn't come over. Probably charging his batteries, Ramji thought. Aziz was the loose canon at these events, a master of verbal indiscretions, but he could be a lot of fun . . . we certainly are a tolerant bunch, aren't we . . .

Over the years these reunions had become more an occasion for the men, for the "old boys" of Dar – Ramji, Sona, Iqbal, and Aziz. They all spoke the same lingo, they had all gone to "Boy-school" in Dar es Salaam at around the same time, they had known each other forever, it seemed. Among each other it was as if they shed the veneer they had acquired in adulthood and as family men, and they became the schoolboys they had once been; they would get silly and nostalgic, they would bait and tease each other without mercy. The wives, it appeared, had once again indulged their husbands. Out of kindness, perhaps, or for bargains already struck – or prices to be extracted in due course. They themselves were not given to such long-lasting and close relationships or losing themselves in youthful hijinks and runaway nostalgia.

Tea was announced and they all trooped out to the dining room, where a gargantuan display awaited them. There were dhosas, idlies and sambol, samosas, potato-chops, chicken tikka, kebabs and salads, gulab jamun, and cakes and a flan from (as Salma proudly announced her contribution) Dessert Storm no less. But before they began, the children – all between the ages of seven and twelve – were brought in and all regaled with a boisterous rendition of "Happy Birthday to You" and given presents for their birthdays, whenever they occurred during the year; and they were compared and admired and, not for the first time, became the objects of flagrant and wishful matchmaking on the parts of their parents. A lament went up for the shortage of boys (the score was three to five), and the kids – amused, flattered, embarrassed, and annoyed all at once – disappeared.

And the adults were left to their devices.

Ceremoniously, the main dishes were passed around, half a dozen condiments hard on their heels, and conversation ranged from recipes and restaurants to how the community was doing in the various cities of North America, from the global economy to the novels by Indian authors that were on their summer reading lists. Salma proceeded to dish out desserts and Jamila and Zuli brought tea and coffee. The stranger in their midst, Rumina with the headscarf, joined in the conversation when she could, though she looked hopelessly out of place. Ramji felt sorry for her. At a sudden lull in the conversation, Sona said, "Now . . ." and all looked at him rubbing his hands gleefully.

"I mean – what have *we* been up to recently? . . ." Sona asked.

"We're not going to start one of those, are we," Susan said, sitting back with a groan.

"Why not?" Aziz said, then unctuously, and obviously having fun, went on, "It's quite all right, you know, we don't take these things seriously . . ."

And so followed what Ramji, whenever he thought of these events, could only describe as a ritual bloodletting, a hurting and wounding of each other, using words like knives and goads, teasing and taunting to the accompaniment of collective mirth and laughter.

Aziz began to leer predatorially at head-covered Rumina, who murmured uncomfortably, "Someone please change the music, please."

"Why, it's Kurt Weill," Jamila explained. "I put him on for

Salma, she's into opera, aren't you Salu?" Salma had only recently discovered opera – Jamila's forte – and must not have graduated far beyond the more gentle sounds of the popular repertoire; she reddened, and Jamila, having had her dig, eased off with, "Oh, okay, I'll change it, it's playing a second time anyway – what shall I put on, do you think?"

"Just turn it off," Iqbal suggested.

Which was when Aziz, waiting for his chance, lunged into attack mode. "Yes, Sona, talking of who's been up to what – *you're* a fast worker, aren't you? A little bit of *faculty* involvement, is it?" He threw a sly glance towards Rumina, who was sitting diagonally across from him. "Some *fatherly* concern? . . ." he said coaxingly. "Surely not a little . . . of that . . . er, harassment business everyone is talking about these days? . . . oops!" He grinned happily, drew back.

"Conflict of interest, at least," said Salma quite pointlessly. "What would Amy say?" she asked, referring to Sona's ex-wife, which seemed even more pointless.

Sona turned red. He looked at Rumina, they all looked at Rumina, hurt and embarrassment clear across her face. She got up and left the room. Susan followed.

"Now see what you've done," Sona said, rebounding. "I've nothing to defend myself against, as you'll find out soon enough to your eternal disgrace."

"Hey . . . ," said Aziz, backing off. "I didn't mean to –"

"Sure you did. Rumina's from Zanzibar, and I only brought her here to meet other East Africans." Then Sona grinned at Aziz. "But tell us, what news from the land of the dead?" When that line didn't seem to go anywhere, he went on, "I hear the funeral business is quite lucrative these days . . ."

That brought Aziz, an actuary by profession, plummeting down. "Hey . . . now that's really below the belt – who's been talking? The funeral parlour's only a business interest, a minority partnership . . . and *community* work, damn you! Wait till you guys start croaking and your spouses come running for discounts."

That wasn't enough to get him off the hook – laughing, curious eyes upon him from all sides – and Sona pursued: "Are you sure you don't have a go at the dearly departed with pliers, to remove the gold teeth, for instance – after an auto accident, perhaps? . . ."

"Tell them," said Salma, but then went on herself. "He's worried about his kids. It's okay to be bohemians in rags when you're still young. But when your kids are growing up, that's another matter. Who can afford college fees nowadays?"

Everyone looked at her and, not wanting to sound too hard up, she quickly covered herself: "But the parlour wasn't my idea – it's not our type of thing –"

"And it's a hassle, believe me," Aziz said.

"What, to put on a black suit and so on?" Iqbal asked in mock innocence, that manner a specialty of his.

"The gold, I'd like to know more about this gold bit," Zuli said, at the same time her eyes – and by consequence everybody else's – falling on the gold bracelets adorning Salma's arm.

Salma reddened, said, "That's not true, he's not into gold extraction . . ."

"The great Aziz Pirani," Ramji murmured, recalling their days of boyhood dreams. "The local Elvis and Einstein all rolled into one – now an undertaker?"

"Better than an underwear maker," the great Pirani murmured, pleased at the mention of past glory, now gloating at Iqbal.

"It's *manufacturing* and selling underwear, you oafs," shouted Susan from the other room. "And what's wrong with that?"

They laughed, and Iqbal, blushing at the secret of his new venture already out, said with a smile, "Anyway, they are called foundation wear in the business. And this one's also an investment – I'm a restaurateur first and foremost."

"Isn't it funny." Jamila said, "Whatever professions we studied for and practised, we can't seem to stay away from business. It's in our blood, isn't that how we say it? Even Ramji – now who would have thought."

"Who indeed," Ramji said lamely and waited for the onslaught, thinking, Uh-oh, here it comes, an assault on my money-making disabilities. A few years ago he had invited his friends to invest in his business, a book-distribution company. Was he glad they'd simply laughed off his suggestion: the company was now foundering.

But Sona came to his timely rescue, changing the subject. "About the, uh . . . foundation wear . . . how do you actually go about designing it –"

That was when the remaining three women left the room.

Eventually the four men came into the kitchen, bleary-eyed and tipsy, a little subdued also, evidently having had their fill of each other. They flashed rather sheepish grins at Salma, Jamila, and Zuli, who had gathered there to chat and who now looked up at them in amusement.

"I am surprised," said Salma, with a wink at Zuli, "that our men don't kill each other – the things they say to each other – even in jest . . ."

Jamila gave an exaggerated shiver. "Reminds me of the Muharram festivities I used to go to with my cousins – the self-flagellation and drawing of blood, and then the celebration –"

"And what are we mourning?" asked Salma.

"Our loss of home and dispersal to the four winds, for which we gather periodically to perform this bloody ritual," Zuli pronounced with a lofty gesture of one hand, adding, "I'm quoting my husband, of course." She threw a swift look at him and he acknowledged with a grin.

"Aren't you glad you're the sane ones," Aziz retorted.

"Takes a woman to keep her head about her."

They stopped the banter to watch Susan and Rumina, who were standing together beside the swings outside in the backyard.

Susan, as always, looked prim, a little too well maintained (in surprising contrast to the quite dissolute-looking Iqbal), what with the makeup and neat pageboy hairdo. And Rumina – she was laughing now, rocking back and forth on a swing as though prepared to take off, and apparently without a care in the world. Her headcover had fallen back on her shoulder.

"Pretty, nuh?" Salma said. "I wonder who she is? Are you going to tell us, Sona?"

"Talk to her and find out for yourselves," replied Sona.

"She's not one of us, obviously," Zuli murmured. "We gave up covering our heads decades ago. And when our grandmothers did cover, they didn't do it this way, did they Sona?"

"Right," said Sona, the community historian.

"Well, we *have* to find out who she is," said Jamila.

Later that night, the day's noise and commotion having finally departed, there remained only the hush of sudden quiet in the house, now at one with the deep suburban stillness outside. Susan and Iqbal had taken Rumina to stay with them at the home of some other people they knew in the area; and Sona had agreed to put up at Aziz and Salma's. Zuli had retired, and Ramji, sleepless with all sorts of echoes of the afternoon in his head, decided to sit out in the kitchen to recover, and was tempted to a cup of tea by Jamila, who hovered in the kitchen, puttering. He wondered if Jamila was detaining him with the tea, and the dessert that followed, and concluded yes. Zuli will have something to say about this, but it doesn't matter.

There loomed over the impending tête-à-tête the shadow of a past intimacy. Ramji and Jamila had known each other for a long time. They had been nodding acquaintances in Dar; boys and girls there pretty much stayed apart. Then he had met her accidentally in Cambridge and they began spending time together in a hectic, uncertain, unresolved, and, to Ramji, tormenting relationship. He thought: if he wanted he could easily leave the kitchen now, pleading sleepiness or the bathroom, even as she was putting away a stray item in the dishwasher.

But he didn't and soon she came and joined him at the table. They exchanged niceties, he declining more dessert, and they worked up to a neutral friendliness that they realized with relief would be the nature of their relationship in the coming week.

"Would your wife approve, your sitting with me like this?"

"Perhaps not," he said. "She's jealous — which is good, I suppose."

"Wives are jealous, no matter what. But, tell me, how's it working out?"

There had been other meetings in the past, over the sixteen years since they'd ended their involvement, but nothing this close, alone. Never these questions, which had been often in the mind.

"All right, I suppose. I have nothing to compare with." Liar, he thought to himself . . . but why should I tell her? "How about you and Nabil – the great love of your life, as you called it . . ."

"Is that what I said?" She blushed.

He's just right, Ramji, she'd told him, he is what I've been waiting for all my life. When you find someone like that you'll understand.

"Well?" he asked. "Everything hunky-dory – with two kids and an expensive suburb and a brand-new car. . . ." He had seen the Acura in the driveway.

She smiled, dimly. There was bitterness yet in his sarcasm.

"I know, I know –" he told her, "things change with time; kids and middle age and a mortgage and life insurance and college costs round the corner; and it's hellishly difficult to live close to another human being –"

"Perhaps it's best then that we decided not to come so close." She eyed him, having spoken this half-truth about the past. It was she, after all, who had insistently maintained a distance between them.

"So, how is Nabil doing? I hear he's dabbling in mysticism – news travels, you know. I suppose it's middle age and premonitions of mortality – that would do it to most people."

"Would it do it to you?"

"I am anachronistic. And I pay for my obstinacies."

She didn't ask him how. There would be time for that. But:

"Ramji – talk to him, please. Talk to Nabil. When you get a chance, I mean. I don't even know what it is with him – mysticism or whatever . . . every other Sunday he goes away on secret meetings. It could be some fundamentalist group, for all I know – can't you reassure him –"

"With what? But I'll have a talk with him . . . perhaps he'll wind up converting me."

"Thank you. You've not changed," she said.

"Yeah?" He looked at her over his poised teacup.

"I mean in your friendships."

"Maybe. Meanwhile, be nice to Zuli. Convince her you're not interested in me. Never were. That shouldn't be hard to do. Huh?"

He stood up and ambled away.

2

Ramji did not go straight to bed. Instead of turning into the guest room where Zuli, he hoped, was already asleep, he went on to the living room and sat down in an armchair. There in the darkness by himself he began to recall those days so many years ago, days that for him were dominated by the presence of one person, Jamila.

Nineteen seventy-four, the dog days of summer.

Grandma had died the past winter and it seemed to him that now he was quite alone in the world. A telegram had arrived from an uncle he barely knew: "Ma expired 14th instant; funeral services took place 15th." It was the 15th, February, when he read it. What bureaucratic language to announce death. And "expired," what a word. "Died" was just right, simply died; mort, tot, kaput, khalas; finished. Finished? Not really, she would always haunt him, the old healer and singer and dancer, as he thought of her sometimes. In his absence many changes had taken place back home – in that country in Africa that would gradually over the years assume the shape of a thorn to prick his conscience. There had been the business about the introduction of forced marriages on the island of

Zanzibar, news of which had come from Grandma and left him bitter and angry.

It was 1974, yes.

On television, the wethead was dead, as hairspray commercials announced with emphasis and joyfully, Archie Bunker still made his bigoted observations, yet we laughed, and Alka-Seltzer always tamed the spicy Italian meatball . . . and the Watergate hearings . . . and. . . . He smiled wistfully. Who remembers them now, once vibrant images long since consigned to the junkbox of private memory?

Foolishly, he admitted now, he had accepted her invitation to this reunion, and Jamila was always larger than life. He hadn't thought a lot about those days – their days – in a long time.

Early June, streets awash in sun. He would sit for coffee or lunch outdoors, on Tech Square or on the green next to the Student Center, watching human traffic, so different in the summer. Convocation time, dreamy-looking alumni looking lost and found, happy families with minor anxieties. . . . And he, working and studying, with no one in the world, free yet envious, thinking, How I wish I had a home to go back to. But you do have a home, it's just that there's nobody there . . .

In the evenings he would stroll on Harvard Square, visit the coffee shops, and the bookstore on Mass Ave, which, obedient to the demands of a new era, was now filling its former Eastern Religions shelves in the basement with books on management; and later, after coffee, he would sit on the pavement and watch a music group or a juggling act or whatever perform next to the newsstand, the summer sky only now beginning to darken and lights coming on everywhere. And one such listless evening, having sat down with a crowd in front of a classical music group, his ears perked up at a voice, an accent. He thought, It's home, dammit, I'm sure, those *inflections* . . .

". . . and I said, 'That's ridiculous, you don't serve drinks on Rockefeller Plaza,' and she said, 'It may be ridiculous ma'am, but. . . .' The cheek, I tell you . . ."

His eyes, having searched and found the speaker, met her eyes: Of course, the look, the style, I even know the girl –

"Hey, aren't you –" she exclaimed, excitedly.

"Yes –" Yes what? He remembered – "You're Jamila Lakhani?"

"And you're Ramji. Hey, come and join us."

He got up and joined her. There was another girl, an Indian from Kenya, introduced as Palu, and an American, Sibyl.

"This is Ramji," she introduced him. "Hey, I'm sorry I don't even know your full name."

"It's okay," he laughed, didn't volunteer it.

The girls were former classmates from college in Minnesota; now Jamila had landed a job at the foreign section of a large bank in New York, Palu had just become engaged to a Pakistani jeweller in San Francisco, and Sibyl was at the *National Geographic*, also in New York.

Jamila: How to describe her? . . . *Life!* Unabashed, silly, and quite naive at times, but that zest – pure, simple, authentic – simply won you, and everyone, over. That evening after the concert on the Square she actually went over – tugged him along – to compliment the members of the quartet on the last piece they'd played, though she got the name of the composer wrong. But so what. And, it turned out, the players quite appreciated her zeal.

Jamila wore a long white skirt and red T-shirt; the long hair he remembered from Dar – a single ponytail halfway down her back – had only recently been cut she told him. How d'you like it, my new hair? He didn't quite care for it, but he said, That's the fashion, is it? And she said, All you Indian men like us to look traditional . . .

The girls had been promised the use of an apartment whose occupant was away for the weekend, and they were somewhat stranded, waiting for the person who had the keys. So Ramji said, Why don't you come stay with me – my roommates won't mind, one of them is away anyway. They accepted gratefully. Jamila was excited about Cambridge, the intellectual hub, I'd like to meet some real intellectuals while I'm here – sorry for asking, but are you an intellectual? We'll invite some real intellectuals for brunch tomorrow, Ramji said, how about that? And so next morning there came Sona and Amy, and an Iranian philosopher named Mahmood and a whole bunch of other people, and that evening they had dinner at the Algiers, a popular basement restaurant, which had been described by *Time* magazine in an article on Cambridge. Mahmood pointed out a clamorous group seated two deep in a corner, said, There's the PLO table, and no one was quite sure if he was pulling their leg, Jamila's in particular.

Two weeks after the girls left, late one night, Jamila phoned. "Hey, thanks for your hospitality, that was very nice, we wrote you a letter, I hope you got it." He said he had. "Listen, there's a Ravi Shankar concert in Princeton on Saturday. Would you like to go?"

Ramji demurred: All the way to Princeton for a concert? Then staying the night? Too complicated.

"And you could spend the night in New York . . ."

Soon he would never be found without his wallet-size train schedule. And he frequently made the trips, long train rides you wished would last forever, carry you in their gently jolting rhythm to the eternity of eternities . . . and then at the sudden end of it a girl like Jamila, a whirlwind who swept you off your feet, to concerts, films, record shops, tennis matches, brunches, parties . . . whatnot. Even wine-tasting.

With her he came to meet a lot of other people, who had also come as students and were beginning to stay on. Among them were Salma, Aziz, and Iqbal.

But if he were to write an account of their life together, he would call it "Not a Love Story." How about that for recalling old times.

What do you say about a girl who loves Beethoven . . . whom the Beatles do not quite excite as much, except the odd song that reminds her of Dar . . . who plays tennis in full gear and with boundless enthusiasm but whose game leaves much to be desired . . . for whom life is the joy of process — *being* — though that is not how she would put it . . . and who is guaranteed to sweep you up in her enthusiasms and for that is the envy of all those who know her . . .

Perhaps he would call his account "Swept Away," after a film they saw together once . . .

There was not, between them, a burning fire. There was instead the tepid warmth of smouldering possibility, though, even then, he knew in his heart of hearts that the affection and sympathy they had for each other would never fully ignite into passion and love. But he hoped, yes; and they *were* together so much, after all, every other weekend almost, and all their acquaintances knew about them: Ramji and Jamila, odd couple, yes, but couple nonetheless, and she was drawing him out — and he giving her a certain intellectual respectability?

And sex. *And sex?* He gave an exaggerated shudder. Grotesque, that's what sex was, could it have been otherwise, coming from where we did?

The first night he spent in her room, she made a sofa up for him, then said, "If you want to sleep in the bed, you can – there's room." She was tired, feeling irate that day. But what did she mean? That was hardly an invitation to share an intimacy. He said, "I'm not Mahatma Gandhi." The Mahatma, after all, could control lust lying down beside a woman, but not he, Ramji. That made her laugh and that was that.

Or was he mistaken. Had she expected him to say yes, was this her way of saying it's okay, we can do it? With Lyris, a few years before, it had been so easy, spontaneous, a single urge driving them on from day one. With this Cutchi girl, this Shamsi . . . how impossible. He wanted to do the right thing, not to act like a Westerner with a hit-and-miss attitude to sex. It was also a question of maintaining her respect: if he'd goofed in his decision that night, she might have thought sex was what he was interested in. *Had* he acted wisely? She never let him know. They went on as before, and he spent many nights in her room. Chaste.

One night in Philadelphia, returning from a play, they went to an Indian restaurant in West Philly and, coming out of it, after a few paces in the dark and rather scary streets – not far from where her nephew would be murdered almost twenty years later – they were accosted by two guys. This is it, Ramji thought; not another soul on the street, a pretty Indian girl with me. He was sure, though, that the restaurant owner was watching from inside; perhaps had called the police, perhaps was too scared to do so. In any case, they were robbed of money and her credit cards. Fortunately, the muggers didn't molest her – no rape, thank God – but then one of the guys returned, gave a violent push to Ramji, who staggered to the ground against a parked car, and then gave Jamila a long kiss on the lips.

Utter humiliation for the man. And the woman? They went back in silence (to Aziz's place, where they'd put up and borrowed the car); and all the way he smarted from the barbs of blame in her looks, blushed from the guilt and the shame in himself.

The question of sex hung between them, unresolved. But it also gave her an escape hatch out of the relationship; she remained uncommitted. More and more he desired commitment, but could not get it.

Finally, he decided he would sweep *her* away. He would take the initiative, and the risk that came with it. It was on a weekend when both his roommates were out of town, so she agreed to come visit him, by herself, which she had never done before. He felt confident; there was already a close relationship between them, wasn't there?

Perhaps she guessed the intent. They'd had a wonderful Italian dinner that evening. No running around this time, he had requested, no movie, no concert afterwards. Just strolling about, talking about this and that, themselves, their families, arms brushing against each other's, both fully conscious of the moment. Once or twice she threw a look at him and smiled. Oh yes, she knew the intent. That night, with a violin concerto playing in the background, they made the beds, hers a sleeping bag on the floor, as she wanted it. They turned off the lights and got into their beds. And then immediately he got into action, fully aroused, one hand lowered down, playing tenderly with her hair, her hands, which did not fight his but stroked it, such nice shapely hands she had (still had, he'd watched them as she gave him the tea) – and then her neck and chest, and then her breasts, how soft and small they felt, he squeezed and rubbed harder and harder against the aroused nipples until she protested. Come down, she finally said, in a tremulous voice. That was it, he thought, he'd crossed the Rubicon. He lay on her, full of passion, foreplay, kisses. But she said no to lifting that nightie, go on just like that, up and down and – Oh, fool, Ramji, as he told himself many times later – he had done just that, pleasured her with their clothes fully on. At the end she fell asleep and he felt used.

Was it her Indianness, the tribal sameness of her, that kept him from going all the way somehow, that created a fear that he should not violate her? If she were not so familiar, from the same background, would he have gone further, just taken her? One did not talk of date rape in those days. What did she *think* she was doing, an Indian girl in that situation? . . . Or did she feel she knew him well enough? Or had he got it wrong all over again!

The next morning she was irritable, as if the previous night had all been his doing, somehow he had taken advantage of her. They had coffee in silence.

"Let's talk about it," he said.

"What?"

"About us – last night. Did I do wrong? What –"

"I don't want to talk about it."

"Why?"

"I don't want to discuss everything in my life with you."

She refused to eat, pored over the Sunday paper, telephoned friends in several cities, telling him she would pay for the calls; acted as if it was all over between them. Good, he thought, I'll bear the pain for a few days and finally be free.

They parted on an uncertain note about their relationship. But the following week she called as before, as if nothing had happened: Rostropovich is conducting *Scheherazade*, I've bought tickets. And he said bravely, Aw — I wish you'd called earlier — I've agreed to go to Toronto then. . . . Oh, I'll ask someone at the office, she replied. And to himself, he said, Well done, Ramji, hold your head high, stand steadfast. But he felt lousy.

A couple of days later she called again: I hope you're still coming to my midsummer party. Of course, he said, feeling elated, his resolve to keep his distance from her already wilting. It was to be the Fourth of July weekend, two weeks away. It was at that party that he met Nabil, who impressed him as rather a smooth-talking guy with all the right European affectations to impress the women. But the following week Jamila called and told him, "He is the one for me, Ramji, what I've been waiting for. . . ." Ramji could never recall her words exactly. He had hurt so.

3

*T*he next morning at the Henawis' house, the kitchen was swarming with children itching to burst loose and go outside as soon as they'd had their breakfasts. As Ramji sauntered in, he saw that Jamila and Zuli, apparently having just attended to the kids, had paused at the counter for a breather. Jamila was explaining something to an overly attentive Zuli – Is a friendship in the making, after all? The subject of the lecture seemed to be the kitchen itself, the new jewel in Jamila's crown – it had been recently, and expensively, renovated. The eating parlour, where the kids had gathered at the table under a skylight, was a new extension and overlooked the backyard lawn through glass sliding doors. The two large and robust plants, a feature of the area, had been somewhat crowded out today, shoved against the walls, and the upright piano, moved here recently when the kids lost interest in it, cried out against its location and current mistreatment. A well-used baseball glove rested casually upon it.

"Dad," Rahim said to his father, "guess how many kinds of cereals they have – twelve!"

"Ama*zing!*" said Ramji approvingly. "And I bet they have the juice of every known fruit?" He looked at Jamila ruefully: "We'll have our hands full keeping up with the Henawis when we return home . . ."

"None of your smart comments now," she warned with a friendly grin. "You don't have to live with a Salma in town setting all the standards."

Her eye rested fleetingly on Zuli watching them.

"Okay kids," she announced with a clap of her hands, "I see you're finished, you may leave now . . . take it easy. And Aisha," she caught the eye of her eldest, "you are in charge — and remember who the guests are."

Aisha, long-faced and sloe-eyed, acknowledged her mission with a significant nod at her mother and followed the rest of the kids out to the backyard, and the adults then sat down to a breakfast of scones and croissants, with butter and preserves, and home-roasted coffee, which later they went out to finish on the backyard patio.

Nabil was at work today and so there were only the three of them. He would be in and out all week, Jamila told her guests; they should feel free to do what they wanted, outings with the kids and so on; the evenings, of course, the adults should plan to do things together. Salma was available if they needed her during the day. She would bring the other four kids over in the afternoon.

The morning was bright and clear, though the ground was wet in patches, in the shade, it having rained the previous night. A neighbour, a stout middle-aged woman, waved vigorously, walked to her car, drove away. "She's a lawyer," Jamila said. "And further up the road we have an Indian couple, both doctors — you'll get a chance to meet them." She and Nabil had moved into their ranch-style house five years ago. It had been owned before, for thirty years, by a German doctor and was well maintained but small. The attic had now been converted to her two girls' bedrooms and the back of the house had been extended.

"I do so envy you this house – you must have time, too, for the garden, it looks so well tended," said Zuli.

"Oh, we've contracted out the lawn and plant care," Jamila said casually.

"Better still," Zuli said. "We've just lost our young maple, the azaleas froze from lack of winter care and the climbing rose died . . ."

They watched the four kids playing outside, and discussed schools, activities, and expenses, and the individual quirks of their children, always careful not to get too carried away talking about their own. Their kids, they agreed, were still the main focus of their lives, but would not be so for long. What seemed remarkable, watching them, was how much their kids *belonged*, in a way in which none of them ever could, here or anywhere else, despite their ardent protestations when the occasion demanded that they were fully American.

"How lucky they are," Zuli said, at length. "They have the world ready-made for them. We came with nothing, more or less . . . had to make it on our own."

"Yes, but we had a greater sense of adventure," Jamila said spiritedly, "which they won't have. They won't have to fight, they won't have a lot of choice. In a sense I feel sorry for them, poor kids!"

"Well, in some ways the sky's the limit for them, I suppose," Ramji said. "But we did arrive *somewhere* – and we haven't done badly at all." The last comment was aimed at his wife. He was a little piqued, first at her narration of their garden's recent woes, and then at that tone of regret that could reveal so much to an alert Jamila.

Ramji got up to go, to meet Sona, who had called earlier, and Zuli had said she would look after the kids. Jamila had offered to take her for lunch and fabulous shopping later, reminding her that there was no sales tax in Pennsylvania.

"They do go back a long way, don't they," Jamila murmured at his back, "him and Sona . . ."

"Yes. That's one past relationship that doesn't bother me at all −" They exchanged a look, and Zuli backed away a bit. "I mean, the first thing they want to do when they're both in town is to sit down together and have a long chat, bring each other up to date, I suppose. It's enviable, really."

"It is."

They sat quietly for a while. Both took time to exchange words with the kids. And then Jamila asked, softly, with a twinkle in her eyes: "And his other past relationships? How do they bother you?"

"You tell me," Zuli said. When Jamila didn't respond, Zuli went further: "What *exactly* was there between you two? May I ask? Or isn't anyone ever going to tell me?" She had spoken with feeling, but the expression in her eyes was hidden by a sudden glare of the sun that made her first squint, then look away.

"Nothing," Jamila lied. "There was exactly nothing between us. There was just this group of friends, most of whom are here this week, and we were part of that. There were a few rumours, but that was that. Hasn't he told you that?"

"Yes. But maybe *he* felt something for you – some sort of look would come over his face whenever your name came up. Anyway, it was all a long time ago."

"And, as I told you, there was nothing. Listen, when I met my Prince Charming from Egypt, that was it. I had no doubts."

Zuli seemed to brood on that and Jamila thought, Perhaps I've said the wrong thing. . . . I'm sounding happier and chirpier than I actually feel, and she's wondering where *she* went wrong. So she told Zuli about her recent problems with Nabil, to say, Look, my dear, life ain't exactly a bowl of cherries for me either, but I'm still in there.

"Anyway," Jamila said at length, "don't you think this reunion is going to be special, that our lives may not be the same afterwards? I felt it even as I sent the e-mail to Ramji telling you all to please come – you knew I did that?" It was before she had called and spoken to both Zuli and Ramji.

"No," Zuli said, "but never mind, that doesn't matter. What did you mean, our lives may not be the same afterwards?"

"I'm not sure . . . but the last time we were all together the kids were still young and we were so preoccupied with them, so this time around feels like a watershed of sorts, don't you think?"

Zuli got up thoughtfully. "I don't know – maybe . . . perhaps. But shouldn't we be going? I do want to check out the stores."

They packed their four kids into the back of Jamila's car.

Ramji walked to the shopping plaza along a narrow road called The Winding Way, and it was just that, with tall trees on either side and small residential streets all leading away from it on the right. The corner houses he met were large, stone-built. He passed a parkland to his left, with a little wooden bridge in the middle, presumably to cross a stream, and further up on the same side there was a school, closed for the summer, then a seminary, also deserted. A solid, well-established neighbourhood, he thought. There was no one else out walking, though once a kid on a bicycle meandered past him. Cars drove by speedily, familiarly. Imported cars are all the rage here, he thought; Japanese and German. He became conscious of himself and wondered if he looked respectable; a strange face was likely to be stopped anytime. Who had told him about such a place, this very location, a long time ago? Where a black face was likely to be that of a house maid? . . . It had been Lucy-Anne Miller.

Where was she – Lucy-Anne? He wondered whatever became of her.

One day about five years ago, in the course of his work, inspecting publications submitted to the company for distribution, he came across the title *Dissent to Nowhere*; the author: Shawn M. Hennessy, from a college in Iowa. With a strange feeling of excitement, and an eerie sense of déjà vu, he flipped through the pages, avidly poring over the words written by his former roommate. All sorts of memories, recollections of arguments they'd had, demonstrations they'd attended, flooded into his head. But this book was a confession, repudiating the sixties' student movements as the excesses of crazed, misguided, and spoilt middle-class youth. Shawn the fiery radical who would march for the rights of cleaning ladies and tenement dwellers, and all the poor of the world, now saying this! There he was, the new Shawn, full-length on the back cover:

a stern long face, with close-cropped hair and a higher forehead than Ramji remembered, in jeans and jacket, feet spread apart, arms crossed in front: a new certainty, a commanding presence.

How easy for these rich American kids to renege and say it was all misguided, a mistake. We're home, repentant, and all's forgiven. He had come to view the sixties as his period of rebirth, from ignorance and narrow-mindedness into enlightenment and an awareness of the world; what a bitter pill to see it repudiated thus. It was as if the priests themselves, who had been the most fanatical, had turned against the faith – giving it a bad name, so you couldn't talk of Third World exploitation or the growing difference between rich and poor without looking utterly ridiculous.

In 1979 he had joined Stan Allen in a partnership pledged to distribute publications aimed at keeping alive the radical spirit by which they had both been touched; and here they were now, promoting and selling academic books written to trash that spirit. Which was marginally better than their even more recent sales initiative, placing do-it-yourself, occult, and get-rich-quick titles in the bookstores, along with CD-ROMs and war videos. Welcome to the nineties.

He couldn't help but send a letter to Shawn, saying how he'd come across the book and asking what he'd been up to since they last saw each other. Back came a prompt but rather controlled cheery response: What a surprise, a letter from his former roommate! How time had flown! They were all older and wiser now! Shawn was divorced with two children, a boy and a girl aged twelve and fourteen. Kate Webber lived in Chicago and wrote for *Harper's*; would Ramji mind if Shawn gave her his address, she was at work on a book about the sixties. They should stay in touch!

And that was that. No phone call from Shawn, though Ramji had sent him his own phone number and an invitation to call.

Sona was seated at a corner table of Le Coffee Break, a fashionable (by Jamila's report) local hangout, with his *New York Times* in front of him, very much in the manner one would find him Sunday mornings at the Pewter Pot or the Blue Parrot in Cambridge. There was vanity in that egghead, some pretense, too, but he was a good, reputable scholar.

Sona was shorter and better built than the gawking Ramji. He had never been chubby, but his face had grown fuller in recent years. He had started to bald, and there were white strands in his goatee, which went well with his reading glasses and crimson cardigan. He looks rather like a devil, Ramji thought, sitting down. Then another, fleeting thought went through his mind – *Is he going crazy, with that single-mindedness of his?*

"You're wondering if I'm crazy," Sona said with a twinkle in his eyes.

"The thought does cross the mind periodically," Ramji said, trying to sound flippant, and pulled up a chair.

They had been to high school together, had arrived on the same plane twenty-five years ago one rainy August evening in Boston. Besides Amy, his wife until recently, and perhaps more than her, Ramji was his one confidant in the matter that seemed to dominate his life above everything else. Every time they met or spoke over the telephone, Ramji would be brought up to date on discoveries, controversies, frustrations.

Sona's cause had to do with the history and beliefs of their people, who over the last few centuries had maintained intact a syncretistic belief, combining Islam and Hinduism. Recently, though, the community had chosen as a matter of policy to purify itself of so-called Hindu idolatry and move closer to a cleaner, mainstream Islam. Sona, as an influential professor, had – somewhat rhetorically – called the new trend a submission to Arabism and Arabic Islamic imperialism. He had gone one step further: For their faith to take root in this new country, the Shamsis must adopt the values and icons of America, and he suggested Emerson, Lincoln, and Martin Luther King as examples. Now, he said, e-mails were arriving full of hatred for him and he had even received threats.

"Nonsense," said Ramji. "Our people are benign – they don't carry out such threats. For one thing, they are cowards."

"My grandfather was killed in a community feud," Sona said, referring to a celebrated case of a hundred years before. His ancestor, an immigrant from India, had been stabbed to death by several assassins while returning from mosque early one morning, in a small coastal town in Tanzania.

"That was a different time and place."

Though what do I mean by that, Ramji thought. There was a time, in their student days, when Ramji felt not only annoyance but also . . . a little contempt . . . at his friend's lack of commitment to the political issues of the day. And yet all the while Sona had been as political as anybody could be; only his politics were of a different sort.

"They are rewriting history – *my* history, *our* history. They are hiding books and manuscripts, burying them away, either out of ignorance or fear of the orthodox, mainstream reaction. Someone has got to speak out –"

There *was* a madness in his single-mindedness; but was it something noble or simply pigheaded? In the matters of the world, what

did this religious argument among a small people signify? But to
Sona, it was everything, it was his life. Amy had presumably tired
of this obsession, to which she obviously came second place . . . and
now this girl he'd brought along?

"And your companion – Rumina. . . ." Ramji pictured the mysterious girl in the hijab-headcover, surely a symbol of Middle
Eastern orthodoxy if anything, and a far cry from Amy, with whom
Sona had lived in sin for a year before they got married. "What
does *she* think of your mad obsession?"

Sona laughed. "She's a former student of mine, from back
home, Tanzania. There's nothing between us. Actually, I've brought
her here for *you*."

A sly look, gleaming eyes.

"Well, thank you, the wife will appreciate this –"

"No, seriously. She's interested in your work in Swahili philology. I always wished you had carried on with it – instead of dropping out and getting into that useless business of yours."

Hardly useless, Ramji wanted to say; very useful, someone had
to do it, and we have achieved a lot . . .

"After the press I've given you," Sona was saying, "she's determined to talk to you. In all of America there must be not more
than three people she can talk to about her work, and one of them
happens to be you! And don't let her innocent looks fool you. She's
very bright – and charming. You'll have to be careful!"

4

"**M**itumba," Rumina said, to Iqbal, and turned to Ramji and caught his gaze on her.

It sounded like a musical note, the way she said it – "Mi-tumm-ba" – a string plucked, then released, her voice rich and very lovely.

The hijab-headscarf gives such beauty and shape to a female face, Ramji had been thinking. And a certain delicacy, softness, an innocence – or does that simply come from an imagination tantalized by a partial view? The scarf is not a veil, yet it's also a veil, for with the face framed like that, by the white cloth, you never know what it's really like. She's a mystery.

"Yes?" she said to at him with wide eyes and dimpled cheeks.

Is it the hijab that makes the eyes look so big?

"What is "mitumba"?" he asked her. "I don't believe I know the word."

"I'm surprised, knowing your specialty in Swahili and all that. Mitumba," she explained quite sweetly, "are the used clothes – shirts, jeans, skirts – that are bought cheaply, in bulk, by weight, from America and Canada, by the wholesalers of Dar es Salaam.

They then sell them to dealers, who sell them to ordinary people throughout the country."

"Wait a minute – you mean people are wearing foreign hand-me-downs in Dar?"

"Many of them, yes. Of course, there are some who believe mitumba are dead people's clothes and don't touch them!"

"There must not be many tailors left in Dar now . . ."

"I suppose not."

Rumina and Iqbal had been talking about Jamila's nephew, Abbas, whose line of work was mitumba.

They were sitting on the deck at the back of Aziz and Salma's house, on their third evening: Ramji and Nabil, Iqbal and his wife Susan, and Rumina, on deck chairs strewn around a table, while their hosts were in the kitchen, on the other side of the glass-door partition, busy with preparations for a late barbecue dinner. Lights from neighbouring houses filtered faintly through the shrubbery, but Aziz and Salma's deck was still clothed in the hue of twilight. Iqbal the restaurateur had brought some wines to taste; Rumina and Nabil were having coffee. Sona was meeting other friends tonight. Jamila and Zuli and the children had dashed off to the Philadelphia mosque for services and would join them soon.

The ghost of Jamila's nephew seemed to hover over the proceedings of this evening. Now it appeared that he had been Rumina's classmate in Dar. Then who exactly was she? He asked her, "What's your family background – I mean –" and she answered abruptly but nicely, "Is that important?" He felt rather slighted and turned away to catch a wry look from Nabil.

Abbas had been murdered in West Philadelphia. He had been mugged and then quite pointlessly shot in the head. The whole thing had been witnessed by two undercover cops. The killers had escaped, and the cops' identities had not yet been revealed.

"Where exactly did he live?" Ramji asked Nabil.

"Close to where he was killed, they had an apartment there."

"They? Did he live with someone?"

"He was married. You should ask Jamila about it," Nabil said, excusing himself as he ambled away inside.

Where was Abbas's wife, then? That obviously was what Nabil didn't want to talk about.

Ramji looked at Nabil. He was – had been – everything that Ramji wasn't but, as he had sometimes thought, would have liked to be. Suave, handsome; intelligent without sounding academic; liberal, but not anxious, committed, or guilty. He was a gentleman in the European fashion, as Jamila delighted in pointing out – kissing hands, yet in a self-mocking way that achieved two impressions at once, knowing when and how to hold doors open for ladies, how to help them with their coats; he knew about good food and wine, was conversant with art and music. Ramji had been jealous, yes, he admitted this to himself. *He's the one, Ramji. . . .* To add salt to his wounds, Jamila had said – yes, he remembered this also – "Do you like him, Ramji, you have to give me your approval: what do you think?" And Ramji had replied, "Of course I approve, he's a great guy!"

And now here was Nabil in middle age, with a pained expression on his face, looking shrunken, a little bald, less confident. Fatherly, avuncular, definitely not threatening. Metamorphosed from a butterfly into a pupa. (Now *that* was being cruel.) Had all that former sophistication been simply a mask that refused to grow with him into middle age, and crumbled and fell away to reveal the original boy from a Cairo tenement, some Midaq Alley, only much older?

Is there any hope for us? Ramji thought gloomily. No there isn't, we are all doomed. . . . His thoughts took flight, alighting momentarily on that other butterfly, who had stung like a bee, the boxer Muhammad Ali; grounded and wobbly, shaking from Parkinson's and drawing out all our gut-wrenched pity. Even our childhood heroes mock us. . . . What irks me is my own middle age and feeling of uselessness . . . and this mysterious girl in hijab telling this old-timer, Is that important?

Aziz and Nabil came out, heading for the barbecue with trays of meat and vegetables, and Aziz was saying, "Let's face it, if I want my wife and children to have the standard of living they're used to after I'm gone, the minimum coverage I need is for a million."

Nabil said, "I agree – what is a million in this day and age?"

And what's a million to me? Ramji wondered, smiling inanely at the two. When you're crossing your forties and the fifties loom over the horizon, you inevitably ask yourself, What have I accomplished? And with everyone he knew, it was the bottom line that counted, acquisitions, net worth. And yet I refuse to believe I took a wrong turn somewhere . . .

Iqbal, who had stood up to refill glasses, was holding forth on how he developed his menu at his Georgetown restaurant, the Kilimanjaro.

"Ndizi Tamu, for instance, Sweet Banana – but that doesn't sound authentic enough. The way we are used to it is with coconut cream – fresh – and grated coconut, and sugar. Now do you think these Americans will go for it? And where would you find fresh coconut in Washington, D.C.? So you substitute a little rum, and you call it the dessert of Swahili kings – the Sultan's Banana –"

He roared with laughter, delighted with himself, and Susan cried sharply, "Iqbal!" though the others were also quite amused.

"So you change and invent as you go along. Is that authentic?" asked Rumina.

"Of course it is, my dear; recipes develop, they don't remain constant. Have you had my Chicken Zabibu for instance?"

"Yes."

"Did you notice any zabibu in it – grapes?"

"No . . . don't remember."

"Then take my word for it, there was no zabibu. Now, didn't that taste to you like authentic Swahili food? Nouvelle, if you like . . ."

"Sounds nouvelle all right, but I have to come visit your restaurant again."

Salma had brought out candles in colourful tinted holders and placed them on small tables, and the night seemed quite romantic.

Soon the others returned and the deck was crowded to capacity and fermenting with predinner excitement. The children were reporting to all who would listen a blooper made earlier during the evening prayers. Aziz called out, "I've just put the meat on – won't be too long now!"

Salma said, "Jamila was supposed to call before leaving the mosque, so he could start."

Jamila replied, "You know, I clean forgot!" With a sigh she plonked herself down on a chair beside the trolley of wine bottles, saying, "Oh good, you saved the wine for me," creating a ripple of amusement which surprised her. "Did I say something wrong?" She looked around unperturbed and picked a bottle of the new Napa Valley chardonnay, only to meet her husband's disapproving eye.

"Surely – immediately after prayers . . . this indulgence is a little inappropriate," Nabil said, looking peeved.

"Dear, why be hypocritical about it? Those who drink wine, do so. As Omar Khayyam says –"

"I'm sure he didn't say that after prayers, and –"

"Oh, all right," she relented, muttering, "you're turning into an ayatollah," and again everyone laughed, including Nabil.

"At least wait a little while," he said, to appease her.

Amid smells of smoky meat and cooking spices and the voices of her hungry guests, amplified duly by too much wine on empty stomachs, Salma's voice rang out: "Listen – listen . . . *Jamila* –" She had climbed on a chair at the centre of the deck, and there was finally a hush around her.

"Listen, before dinner gets served there's going to be a strip . . . tease." She paused just long enough between the last two words. "The tease is, someone's going to remove a piece of clothing – just one. Can you guess who the person is? And it's not me, let me tell you!"

"Really, Salma," Zuli said, "surely we're not into this sort of thing."

"Aren't we?" Aziz wisecracked from the grill.

Jamila giggled, looking around, saying, "And it's definitely not me."

The children, who had been served their dinner inside, had all now come to watch the scene through the wide-open doorway. Nabil went over to induce them to go in, his elder daughter stamped her foot and mouthed a silent "no." Ramji tried to glare down one of his twins, Sara, also to no avail. He shrugged and looked at Susan, who had taken a step in the direction of her children, as if ready to act. But to do what? Suddenly shield them from indecent exposure, lascivious adult mischief? Rumina was smiling rather broadly, and he thought that rather perverse. But what *was* the matter with Salma? She and Aziz indulging in perversions of their own?

Salma, on the chair, called out: "Rumina, come here."

There was a collective intake of breath; Ramji looked first at Zuli, then at Jamila, then at Rumina, who had gone to stand close to Salma.

"Earlier this evening, Rumina gave me permission," Salma said, "to do this —"

In one clean motion, she drew away Rumina's head scarf. There was an audible gasp, at the face, the new look, the person revealed: the face appeared fuller, the neck long, and the curly hair was knotted into pigtails that fell to the back and sides.

There were shouts of approval and laughter: Bravo, now that's more like it. . . . You're a beautiful girl, why were you hiding under that scarf? . . . And Rumina, face blushing, lowered her eyes. She had on a halter-top dress and a lot more of her was revealed than she had perhaps anticipated.

"So, now having had the tease and the strip — how about meat!" called out Aziz, and everyone groaned.

After dinner, Napoleon brandy was offered, and Iqbal and Susan, glasses in hand, danced dreamily together, outside on the deck, to a romantic jazz number put on by Aziz. They were joined, much to everyone's surprise, by a neighbouring couple out for a stroll. Nabil stood up, and Jamila pulled him along past the open doorway, and they too began to dance. Salma and Aziz were quickly clearing up inside. For a while, Ramji watched the three couples dancing outside, then turned and caught Zuli's eye; in the moment he took to hesitate, she looked away and went to help their hosts in the kitchen. In the living room behind them, partly visible, the six children also danced. But their dance was not like the adults', body to body, close and yearning; instead, they danced every which way and individually.

Later, back at the Henawis', with Nabil gone to bed, Zuli, Jamila, and Ramji sat in the living room over cups of mint tea. The husband and wife had taken the sofa, and Jamila had pulled a chair across the low seering table from them. Jamila was elated with the evening's development and needed to wind down. Zuli had a serene look on her face.

"These reunions are always a revelation, aren't they," Zuli mused.

"As for tonight's revelation," Jamila said, obviously speaking of Rumina, "if she was such a believer, why did she let the hijab come off so easily?"

"She's still young," Ramji said, earning a stare from the women.

"Anyway," Jamila said. "Let's talk about me. I'm so glad all you guys came. It's made a difference. To *him*." She looked towards her bedroom. "He actually stayed up late – something he's not done in *months*! And he *danced*! Oh, thank you for coming, I do hope this is going to work – I so much want him back!"

She was leaning forward and there was a plea in her voice, so that Ramji and Zuli were both touched.

"But what *happened* to him?" Zuli asked. "Why did he become so religious, all of a sudden?"

"Ever since the Gulf War . . . ," Jamila began. "And it's not just religion, it's some Sufi sect in New Jersey. Oh why can't he take it with a grain of salt the way the rest of us do?"

"It'll be all right," Zuli assured her, "see if it's not. He cares about you – he's got to make it work."

Jamila went to bed, and Ramji apologized to his wife about the debacle earlier on.

"I meant to ask you to dance . . ."

"Sure you did."

"As it is, you know I'm a lousy dancer –"

"Then why do you say you meant to ask?"

She leaned over and put her head lightly on his shoulder. He put a gentle hand on her head, caressed her hair.

He would have liked to squeeze her, draw her closer, kiss her on the eyes and mouth, but he was afraid; he wasn't sure how she would respond to a rush of tender passion from him. This fear in him, and her withholding from him, had come up over the past few years to stand as a barrier between them.

They had thought, as on previous occasions, that this family trip away from the bustle and tensions of daily life would bring them together, rekindle love and care; if not that, at least help each of them accept the inevitability of compromise for the sake of continuity, familiarity, companionship, at the onset of middle age. But a few hours out of Chicago and they were at each other again. This time the quarrel was about the presents they had bought or failed to buy. It was not a pleasant trip, but they had kept up a pretense for the twins' sake, with the McDonald's stops, the pop and potato chips for the road, songs even, and an amusement park on the way.

Her eyes were closed, her hands rested on her lap; he watched the long lines of her body, inhaled her sweet perfume. She's a beautiful woman, Ramji, that lovely face with the high cheeks and the pointy chin . . . laughed easily once; strands of grey showing up, but just a handful. They worry her, speak to her of a wasted life. That is the crux of the problem, you didn't amount to anything for her.

It was twelve years ago that he had gone from Chicago to Toronto to visit some of his friends who had arrived recently from Dar. There was an Eid festival on that weekend, a few thousand people had gathered at an immense hall near the airport for a fun fair. There he saw, in charge of a blood-donation booth, a tall and beautiful girl. She had short hair, wore high heels, and had just finished speaking rather crisply to a passerby. Ramji was feeling exhausted and obviously looked it, having walked a few times through the noisy proceedings, and when she caught his appreciative stare she shouted: You look like you could use a blood transfusion yourself! He had laughed and they introduced themselves. That evening he called her up and asked her out for lunch the next day. She was an executive secretary at a law firm downtown. They met as arranged and soon realized that they got along fabulously. The lunch lasted a couple of hours, and they agreed to meet again.

He liked Zuli's forthrightness, and her back-home interests – she was not embarrassed by her passion for Indian films and songs and by the food they went to eat the next couple of days in India Town. She had had a disappointing romance; he didn't ask her for details, and he didn't give her any about his own past relationships. She seemed to like it that he was not just another "Paki" – Toronto's deprecation for Indians; he was different, with a past in the U.S., he had dropped out of graduate school to join a business that was not a doughnut store or a hardware store or a motel. Her parents were also in Toronto, though they lived with her sister, and he got to meet them all that first time.

When he left for Chicago, it was with the understanding that they would call each other. They wound up speaking every day on the phone, yearning to see each other again. Ramji was convinced he was in love; so, it seemed to him, was Zuli. Within a month he was back to visit her. In Toronto's Kensington Market she accepted his proposal of marriage. And there, walking together on the sun-drenched, littered streets, they stopped to watch a garishly dressed toy monkey drummer that had been stood upon a display table outside a Chinese variety shop and was beating relentlessly on its drum for the benefit of the steady human traffic. Delighted by each other, by the monkey, impulsively they had gone and bought it as a good-luck charm, a memento. Zuli's easy laughing manner came like a refreshing breeze to blow away the residue of the complicated, painful relationship he'd had with Jamila.

And now . . . could any two people be lonelier, sitting so close together, even touching.

The differences between them, which they initially idealized, had gradually become occasions for bitter and hurtful quarrels. He could not muster enough enthusiasm for the middle-class aspirations she soon began to reveal in their suburb of Chicago, and he could no longer pretend to share some of her passions, for example for the Bombay musicals about (as he would describe them) rich fantasy-teenagers in heat. She found him – at his worst – a smug killjoy, an inadequate provider with a burnt-out idealism who had learned nothing about real life. And then after every such quarrel they would try and reach out to each other, but there always remained an unbridgeable divide with the potential for so much pain.

And if Adam had lived? He would often think that if the child had lived, their life and love would have been different; all the joy and expectation had been simply quashed by the still-birth. Tradition demanded full burial rites, including naming of the baby, thus compelling them to think in terms of a death in the family. And the rituals only enhanced the grief, sanctified it – at least for Zuli. The sight of the dead baby – its thick black hair, the delicate fully formed features and the pale blue cheeks – which had been pulled out roughly by the nurse and taken away in a basin, would haunt her always. And in case she flagged in her grief, forgot the stillbirth, there was a perpetual reminder, because with full burial rites came the requisite annual services for the soul of the dead.

They had named the child Adam. A stillborn Adam – their friends had been startled. Trust Ramji to come up with such a name. An oxymoron, as Aziz quipped, at a previous reunion in Toronto, which happened to coincide with the annual services, when they expected sympathy and commiseration; trust Aziz to come up with something so out of place. And Zuli had never for-given her husband for heartlessly picking the name, for somehow fooling her into accepting it, all for the sake of his cynical, agnos-tic world view and his wordplay. That of course was not quite his own version of how they had come to name their dead child. He too had been grieved, but more for her sake. He could not pretend to a mother's grief, or to a belief in the religious mumbo-jumbo. "Adam" for him meant the first one, for there would be others. She had not been convinced by his arguments.

The widened gulf between them was bridged only, and nar-rowly, by the joint devotions of parenthood; thankfully, they had a healthy pair of twins, Sara and Rahim, to quell the grief and fill up the emptiness.

Ramji squeezed Zuli's arm and she sat up, giving a smile; he leaned towards her and kissed her on the cheek. They discussed the kids, how they were doing so far.

5

The next morning, Jamila was busy touching up, altering, and agonizing over the redecoration that the downstairs of her house had seen in the past weeks. She was convinced, as no one else present could be, that the dining room wallpaper had not quite the warm tones of the matching drapes; moreover, the painting she'd acquired for that area, of a period tennis match in progress in patrician surroundings (viewed through an impressionistic haze), hung one – perhaps two – inches too high. Salma's decorator acquaintance responsible for these lapses having departed for the beach, Salma was on her way with husband to verify for herself and bring her kids along as well to play with the others.

"Do you think Rumina is part African?" Jamila asked Ramji from a perch upon a chair, adjusting the hinges on a kitchen cabinet door with a screwdriver. "From the hair, you know, and generally . . ."

Rumina had just called to speak to Ramji, saying could she come over to consult with him about some work she had done as a student. Ramji, having spoken to her on the kitchen phone, now hung listlessly about watching the cabinet doors being tested for shutting speeds.

"Generally what?" Ramji asked Jamila. "Why don't you ask her?"

"I'll ask Sona," she said. "She wouldn't wear a hijab just to hide her hair now, would she?"

"That's not the usual practice. And she did remove it, didn't she?" Ramji said.

"Yes, but I still wonder. There's a story there. Who were her parents, and so on."

"You certainly do pry, don't you."

"I do like to find out," Jamila admitted, still up on the chair.

Salma was preceded by her voice. "You could at least have let *me* eat," she was complaining to Aziz.

"I didn't know you were *that* desperate," he said, defending himself.

To which she, entering through the kitchen door, retorted, "Not desperate. Just hungry. . . . Hi everybody. I was just complaining he wouldn't wait to let me eat a muffin before leaving —"

Salma in these reunions was the odd one out, somewhat of an outsider. She was Kenya-born, the others Tanzanian, and that made for much of the difference between them. The Kenya Asians, having lived under the superior gaze of haughty British settlers in the heyday of colonial rule, tended to formality in their appearance. As if conscious of her dark skin, Salma always wore rouge; and she liked to dress, in Jamila's description, maximally. Today she had on a black vest over a white shirt and khaki culottes, with high-heeled red leather sandals. Large brown African beads graced her neck. The clasp purse was cheetah skin.

Ramji and Jamila had first met her in New York. She was from a wealthy family, had recently arrived from Kenya and become one of the Silver girls: typists and clerical help awaiting their green cards while working at minimum-wage jobs, which immigration lawyer Alan Silver and his secretary Moira had found for them. Jamila was awaiting her Silver assignment before she luckily found her job in the rather exclusive international section of a bank. Whatever their education, joining Silver's legion was a sure way for the girls to acquire a green card. (The story was different for the guys.) Their employers were all Jews and there was enough of the racist name-calling by the girls against them, before the reality of what was what in the new country had sunk in. There was a shortage of eligible men on the East Coast, giving rise to some desperation in the girls, and Salma's hooking up with the rather handsome Aziz Pirani was generally considered a coup by all who knew her.

Rumina arrived, without a headcover, and wearing a white cotton dress; and all looked up at the apparition from the previous night.

"That's more like it," Zuli said with approval, and there was agreement all around. Rumina murmured thanks.

"May I borrow your husband for a couple of hours?" she asked sweetly, of Zuli. "He is one of the few experts in my field of study."

And Zuli said, "By all means, yes, check him out."

To which Jamila quipped: "But there's a fee for overnight!"

And so, everybody laughing, Ramji and Rumina left the house. The plan was to go to a quiet place where she could tell him about the manuscript she had brought. It was her master's thesis, she told him. Recalling his college days, he thought how most kids were so charged up about their first piece of work, they brandished it about to the slightest acquaintance, confident of its intellectual break-throughs and far-reaching consequences; and most of them in ten years' time wished it were buried somewhere unreachable. So how do you handle her? Sona had cleverly passed her on to him.

They started at a casual pace along The Winding Way towards the mall. There was a Borders bookstore further up from it on the main Glenmore road, which they quickly settled on as their destination. Alone with her he felt awkward and foolish, having so easily succumbed to the flattery of a young woman's attention. What would the three women they'd left at the house be saying to themselves by now, what malicious gossip would Aziz be cooking up? But the girl beside him, as though herself finally alert to this situation, was deferential, as befitted the fact that he was her teacher's friend after all. Twice she pulled him in by the arm, away from the narrow, winding road when approaching traffic seemed perilously close, then let go, a little embarrassed. She must think me quite ancient, he thought.

Once they reached the main road beyond the mall, they could walk more relaxedly on the sidewalk.

"Tell me about what you do," she said with a hop alongside him.

"Oh, am I walking too fast?" he asked apologetically.

"Rather," she said, panting. "So – what sort of business is yours?"

He told her: We look at the lists of books our publishers have scheduled for publication in the coming season and we select all those we would like to distribute. Twice a year we have sales conferences when the publishers come and present their new titles. Some of our publishers actually have rather odd names – Black Tulip, Caligula, even Cat's Pajamas!

She was delighted.

"Why did you decide to drop . . . leave your studies, I mean?"

He brooded for a while, looking down at the ground as he walked. "An overactive – but fruitless – love life."

"Oh."

"A subject not to be discussed in the presence of the others."

"I understand."

What did she understand? He glanced at her sceptically, caught her eye, and she gave a short chuckle: "Oh, all right! I don't understand!"

"How about you?" he asked. "You haven't told me what you do in D.C."

"I have a temporary job with a Senate foreign relations subcommittee on Africa, as a translator. It's not going to last long, though. I'm not sure whether to go back to school or not."

They arrived at the bookstore, and before entering it, he paused at the door and pointed in the direction of the grey brick ivy-covered walls visible further ahead up the road: "Someone I knew long ago went to Glenmore College."

"Who?" she asked.

He shook his head, lied: "Too long ago – I barely remember her."

For a good hour they browsed among the aisles of the large and well-stocked bookstore and selected some books to give as presents.

Finally over coffees at the upper storey of the store, he said to Rumina: "I must confess I may not be able to help you much with this —" he indicated the buff envelope she'd brought along. "It's been such a long time since I looked at Swahili poetry." Better come clean, he said to himself.

"That's all right. You can try," she replied.

"So I may have brought you here under false pretenses."

"Oh, did you now? I thought it was I who brought you here." Her eyes flashed at him mischievously.

"I guess you did," he conceded.

Is she hinting at something — or is she merely a tease, likes to see them make fools of themselves. She seems delightfully — breathtakingly — fresh and young, smooth-skinned (now, now, hold that old lecher's eye . . .); unburdened and sprightly; still in her twenties, I guess. All those years she's got ahead of her, like money in the bank.

"I'll keep this copy then," he told her. "I'll read it, and maybe write to you —"

"I would like that, thank you."

The material she had brought for him was a long Swahili poem written in the sixteenth century, during a time of distress, when the town of Mombasa was under foreign attack. It had seen numerous assaults from the sea by Portuguese and Arabs, and had earned the appellation Mvita, or "wars." She had edited and commented on the poem. He could still be able to say a few things on the subject, he thought. He had, after all, at one time studied several varieties of the Swahili language, going to Boston University in the evenings, and had been versed in the academic literature.

"You know, Milton mentions both Mombasa and Kilwa in his *Paradise Lost*. I wonder where, in what texts, that knowledge existed . . . Portuguese accounts, I suppose. I picture the angel Michael and Adam kneeling on top of a mountain, at the edge of Paradise, and Michael pointing out Kilwa and Mombasa along the Indian Ocean coast, dhows bobbing in the harbour . . . and Adam looking at the whole panorama of East Africa. . . . Maybe that's where the angel then sent him, and Louis Leakey found his remains in the Zinjanthropus!"

She had been staring at him, and he felt embarrassed, exposed, by his excitement.

"Have you ever been back?" she asked, indulgently.

"Regretfully, no. Never. I could have gone while I was still a student, I suppose. I never managed it."

"Why? . . . An overactive and — what was it? — fruitless love life?"

"That, too," he said to her beaming face, "but. . . ." And he explained to her patiently the difficult political climate of that period; and even how, when the Asians were afraid that their daughters would be taken away by African politicians as brides, his grandmother had sent him a photograph of a cousin and asked him to marry her. "Of course, as you can see, I didn't." He told her of the death of his grandmother, and that he had nobody left there.

It was, he thought, a wonderful thing talking to a young person outside business, outside family, outside the *sansara* of daily life, the *janjaara*, the hustle-bustle. So was she an angel, come to remind him, Harken! Wake up to life! He smiled at himself.

"A penny for your thoughts," she said.

He smiled even more broadly. "I used to read that phrase in Enid Blyton. Did you read her?"

Yes, she had. And no, Elvis and the Beatles were not big in her time, it was Michael Jackson.

"*Rumina mimina . . . ,*" he murmured. "You wouldn't know that."

"Repeat that, please."

"It is a ditty some African girls used to sing at the back of our house while skipping rope – *Rumina mimina/maziwa na sukari,*" he recited with the proper stresses. It meant "Rumina pour out/the milk and the sugar."

His grandmother's house had been the old-fashioned kind, low, with a corrugated metal roof, mud walls, and cement plaster. Behind the backyard fence was an African settlement where his grandmother would send him to buy vitumbua or maandazi, sweet breads fried by the women, for breakfast. There would always be a group of young girls staring warily at him, having stopped their game of skipping rope to do so.

"Well, I'm half African," she said, "as you've guessed."

"Not really."

"But I *am* half African," she said, leaning forward to press her point. "In school they called me *nusu,* for 'half' – I'm half-caste."

He stared at her. "Does anybody ever use that word anymore – 'half-caste'?"

"Oh, it's common. All us half-castes were lumped together. My father was the African."

"And your mother?"

"I don't remember her."

He wanted to ask why, but he didn't. That would be prying.

As they walked back, a feeling of contentment infused him. He hadn't felt so with himself in a very long time.

6

Ramji and Zuli had planned to spend the next two days with their kids in New York before returning to Glenmore on the eve of Jamila's "mustardseed" party. A few months ago a former school chum had called up Zuli from Long Island, where she'd moved from England, and an old, almost forgotten friendship had been re-established. This would be their first meeting in twenty-three years, with families, and there was some apprehension about that. The twins for their part were dying to see Gotham, the Big Apple, the city of everything big and notorious, "cool" and "nasty." And so Zuli with Sara and Rahim left by the Thursday morning Amtrak train, with Ramji staying back to attend to chores (a business call from his partner Stan, for one thing) and to follow in the family car later in the day.

Having dropped off Zuli and the twins at the train station, Ramji drove to Glenmore's popular Le Coffee Break to meet Rumina. He had read her material late the previous night and had jotted down some observations. In this he was perhaps (why "perhaps"?) cheating a little; he didn't have to do this, he had already promised to send her his comments by mail. But Rumina was leaving this afternoon, and he'd felt a sudden craving to see her one more time. (He didn't want to admit that this was perhaps his real reason for wanting to stay on.) Family life seemed such a closed world, a relentlessly single track cluttered with routines, and predictable even in its upheavals and recoveries, that the prospect of a mere flutter, an ephemeral, fleeting moment of verbal seduction and daydreaming, was irresistible.

Rumina had already arrived and found a table, and she looked up with a large smile as Ramji approached.

"You certainly know how to keep a girl waiting, don't you," she said impishly.

She had been delighted, he would even have said flattered, when he'd called her earlier this morning and told her he could meet her later to discuss her thesis. Iqbal and Susan were gone, to Providence, and she had been alone in their friends' house, packed up and biding her time before she left for the train station. She had no desire to wait for Jamila's party on Sunday. "I think I've had enough of this company." "Oh?" "I don't mean you, of course," she laughed.

"It's quite a rendezvous, isn't it – this place." He gave a quick look around as he sat down. The café seemed full but not crowded, and there was an air of suburban gentility to it, reinforced by Vivaldi playing in the background.

"Yes. I was just thinking there must be a lot of affairs being arranged here!"

She giggled when he gave another look around as if to check out her surmise, then stopped abruptly and blushed a little, her hands clasped in front of her on the table.

"I see you're in a naughty mood today, on the day you're leaving. I think we look quite respectable, though."

"I think so too," she said.

She beamed. Her hair was now gathered back from her face and held with a barrette, a red and white beaded disk. She wore jeans and a long white and green cotton shirt, the front of which was decorated with a solid black map of Africa facing a silhouette of Nefertiti in profile.

The waitress came, they gave their orders, he a large espresso, she a "frostino."

"Look, I brought your stuff. I've read it and made some comments, for what they're worth. But read them only after you've left. I don't know what you expected of me."

"Let me be the judge of that. You are too modest. Sona warned me . . ."

"Yes? What?"

"Never mind," she replied, and he flinched at these words, which his kids sometimes used, to cut him off, to his great annoyance.

"Well," she gave in, watching him, "that you were diffident and modest, that's all."

What's she really like? She's just a girl and I've brought her here under false pretenses; a Muslim girl . . . a lovely girl, really, with a string of admirers I bet ready to jump to attention with a blink of those big round eyes of hers.

The poem she had edited was called "Enerico na Fatima"; it told the story, set in medieval times, of the love of a Portuguese commandant for a young Arab widow in Mombasa. Every afternoon for a few days Enerico would go to sit across the street from the widow's house, and gaze up at the latticed windows of the women's quarter; with him would sit an old Swahili poet he had hired to recite verses relating his love for Fatima. One afternoon the poet arrived alone, but this time, his love verses also told the tale of what had befallen Enerico. The *mreno* had been arrested by his superiors and put in prison. When the poet had finished his recital, a servant appeared from the house and paid him a silver coin, which he accepted as a token of Fatima returning Enerico's love. In the story, Enerico died shortly afterwards in the prison, from fever.

In her introduction to the manuscript, Rumina had narrated the story with quite a bit of pathos, assuming rather naively – in Ramji's opinion – that it had a factual basis.

She was eyeing him.

"Why did you take the hijab off – did you wear it always?"

That caught her by surprise, she coloured, paused, then she answered him softly: "Since I was a teenager . . ."; and then, speaking up but just a little more: "I guess I was ready to take it off."

"I guess you were." He shouldn't have asked, not now, but perhaps that was simply in self-defence – to maintain a safe distance?

"You're leaving today," he announced jovially, to make up, and sat back like a proud uncle, watching her.

"Yes," she answered brightly. Then, leaning forward, she said earnestly, to his unbelieving ears: "Listen, why don't you come along? How long will you stay in Glenmore; aren't you tired already of this suburbia?"

He felt a tremor in his hand; he put his cup down. This was an actual invitation he'd just heard. There was nothing better he would have liked, then. Nevertheless, . . .

"The suburb's nice, actually," he said, sounding confident and strong, "but anyway, I'm going to New York later in the day. Just pounding the pavement there again will be worth this whole trip. Zuli and the kids are already there – I'll join them, and then, after we return, Jamila's party. Then home."

That seemed to deflate her for a while. He watched her sit back and sip her iced concoction through a straw, having stirred in three sugars – gathering strength, as it were. Then once more, intensely, she implored him: "Look – *come* to Washington. Seriously, why don't you come? There's a taarab concert, at a private house; you do like taarab?"

The restaurant across from their house in Dar es Salaam used to play taarab on the radio – lively coastal music, with harmonium, tambourine, drums, and Swahili lyrics sung to Indian film songs, about the wiles of women for one thing . . .

"Yes I do, though I've never exactly been to a concert."

His heart was leaping. He had not expected this . . . hoped, maybe, for something . . . and here it was. This invitation to do something crazy, something that would liberate and rejuvenate – *revivify* – him. He wanted it, and he didn't. But he had lost control over himself, it was all up to her.

"You can take a train to New York tomorrow, early in the morning. It's called –"

"The Early Bird, or something like that." He laughed.

". . . and meet your family," she continued, on a lower note, watching him expectantly. Victoriously.

They stared, eye to eye, gauging each other. And he thought: Well, why not? "Perhaps we can ask Sona to come along, surely he loves taarab," he said, unconvincingly.

"Yes, we'll ask him," she replied with a smile as they got up to go. "And thank you for looking at this," she said, picking up her manuscript. "That means a lot to me."

He dropped her off at the suburban train station, promising to meet her at the main railway station in Philadelphia in the afternoon, where they would catch the Amtrak to D.C.

Is this how flimsy a man's resolve is, like a tattered rag, that at the slightest come-on from a pretty young woman it shreds to pieces risking all? And how far would I go? Would I give up everything, if the moment were right? . . .

"From what I've seen around me in this neighbourhood," Jamila said, "children don't always mind break-ups. Sometimes they even come to expect it from their parents."

She and Ramji were sitting together in her kitchen having lunch, and, somewhat disconcertingly, the subject of marriage fatalities had loomed up. It was curious that, from among their generation of Shamsis, they knew of only a few divorce cases, way below the touted national average. All their friends were still with their original spouses, except for Sona, and he only half-counted, having married an American.

Ramji said, "I think it's because we Indians would rather go through a painful marriage than see our children suffer the grief of a broken home."

"But that's nonsense," Jamila replied. "And anyway, why are we talking divorces? Do you know anyone who's getting one?"

"Not really . . . and I thought *you* had brought up the subject. Listen – I've decided to go to Washington this afternoon. Rumina has invited me to a taarab concert, and Sona might come along too.

I'll call Zuli when I get there, but if she calls in the meantime, please tell her . . . and that I'll meet them in New York tomorrow."

Jamila caught herself gaping, then said slowly, "Certainly . . . ," finally recovering with an upbeat "Don't worry, I'll tell her. You go ahead and live dangerously for a day – haven't we all done it?"

"Oh?" Ramji said.

She gave him the briefest but most telling look and he wondered what mischief *she* had been guilty of.

On the train, they chatted animatedly about themselves. Absorbed in the moment, Ramji would find himself forgetting why he was there. A train ride was the ideal escape, into a provisional state of existence beholden only to a constant mind-numbing rhythm, a clacking and rumbling beat that was out of ordinary time altogether.

An escape – is this what he was up to? Escape . . . into what? This girl had simply invited him to a concert, admittedly to embark on a little escapade, something out of the way, a detour, but what else had she offered? What did he expect?

And what did he know about her?

Tomorrow he would go to New York, having flirted a bit, having been a little unfaithful, and he would join his family and embrace them tightly, the more so for having courted danger and survived.

There was something indestructible about the family experience. It was bonded in blood – the blood spilt together, in all those pains and sorrows. There was joy, too, of course. But joy was relief. Pain was endured, wept over, overcome, and it made you stronger. Together.

For Ramji there had been one long bloody moment of such bonding, one night in particular.

A normally strong-willed and accomplished woman, exposed in that most open and vulnerable of postures, wet and wide-eyed and clutching at anything with her long fingers, whimpering – with pain, with fear, with grief – and pushing, pushing out dear death from inside her.

Ramji grasping her hand: Oh God . . . let this end now.

Never mind – if you feel it's coming, give it a push, give it a push. Otherwise it's all right, the doctor will soon be here. Don't fret, it'll soon be over.

She gets up, with help, goes to the toilet. Call me if you need me, yes, and she waddles in, door half open. And then, Oh God, she shouts, I think it's come, the head, the hair, it's *coming!*

Ramji runs and presses the emergency button, the Barbadian nurse comes instantly, Good, she says, good, it's over, my dear, and goes in and pulls out the dead body, the tiny little corpse, and the placenta, carries it out in a basin, Ramji helps Zuli to bed –

Then she weeps, Oh God, I saw the hair first, thick black hair, and head, it was so *real*, it was my baby –

The next day Ramji, her father, who had come with her mother from Toronto, and the mukhi from their Chicago mosque took baby Adam for his burial.

Beside him Rumina had fallen asleep, was leaning sideways against his shoulder. He recoiled, inwardly. If he moved she would wake up. Surely I felt the pressure of her head all along, why feign surprise?

Can she be as sweet and innocent as she looks?

There was still a chance. As soon as the train reached the destination, he would simply take the next one back. And nothing would be lost. He had succumbed to temptation – almost; all right, his hormones were still raging, and that was good. But it takes courage to admit to foolhardiness, think of others, one's responsibility . . .

He simply didn't have the will to turn back now.

She unlocked the door, went in, held it open for him. "*Karibu, karibu sana*," she said, a little shyly, the traditional Swahili greeting.

"*Ahsante*," he replied, and entered, and heard the door close behind him. There was a slight smell of perfume in the air, something Eastern, he thought, perhaps Zanzibari, but only a trace. How so like her, he thought, and realized he was presuming to know her.

Rumina's apartment was in downtown Washington. It consisted of a large room which had been partitioned by a shelf into a bed and a living area, together with a small kitchen and a bathroom. It reminded him quaintly of places he'd known in his younger days, though it was a lot neater than anywhere he had lived on his own. There were hangings from Africa and a poster on the walls.

"Small, but it's sufficient for my needs," Rumina said, and he nodded.

She put on a cassette of taarab music for him, as she'd promised on the train, and its lilting, joyful sounds, which he had not heard in years, seemed to relieve the restrained mood that had suddenly come over them inside the apartment.

Your voice is heavenly, like a santuri, I beg of you let me hear you, over and over . . .

"I'm going to lie down for a while," she said, watching his face light up at the nostalgic melody, the lyrics. "You can do the same, if you want to – this is your bed –" she pointed to the sofa on which he was sitting.

"I'll be all right – you go ahead and rest. I might even take a shower."

"Sure. Make coffee or tea or whatever." She slipped off her shoes and went to her bed.

Ramji sat and flipped through some magazines, then put them aside. He glanced towards Rumina and saw that she had fallen asleep as she had lain, in her travel clothes, on her back. Her full lips were open, her breathing was light. He turned away and lay down on the sofa for a while, but felt uneasy; he wasn't used to naps for one thing. The music stopped. He picked up the towel to go for a shower.

Walking to the bathroom, he glanced in her direction again. He stopped and stared. The face was flushed, the curly hair dishev-elled. If I go to her bed and kiss her, she can't possibly stop me, he thought. But why am I thinking this? . . . Just let it be, Ramji.

"What are you thinking?" she asked.

"Oh, you're awake."

"Yes. What were you thinking all that while you stood there in silence?"

He paused. "Nothing . . . I forget what it was, actually . . ."

"How convenient!"

"Yes, isn't it." He slowly went to her bed and sat down beside her. She sat up. "You want to know what I was thinking," he told her.

"Yes, tell me," she said, eyes flashing a challenge.

"I was feeling a little bit like Enerico sitting outside Fatima's house, in that poem in your thesis."

"But you're *inside*!"

"Well, it felt like *out*side . . . the distance – you wouldn't understand."

"But I do." Just like that – flat, no inflection, and with all the confidence in the world.

"Oh. Do you?" he said quietly. He took both her hands in his, held them, played with them. They felt warm, and small, and quite limp. "What do you understand?"

"Enough . . ."

Her eyes had a tender expression; they would always caress him in that manner, and embrace him; the memory of them would continue to haunt him when she was no longer with him.

He said, "I was thinking, as I stood there, that if I came and kissed you on the lips you couldn't . . ."

He put a hand on her forehead, swept back a few locks of hair. He caressed her on one cheek, saw her mouth tremble, then he leaned forward and he kissed her.

"Ramji," she said after a moment, pushing him gently away.

"Did I take advantage?" he asked, not quite sure he'd done that.

She paused for a moment, then said, "You have to be sure it's what you want –"

"I am sure!"

Am I? Sure of what, what exactly do I want? But these and other questions remained as yet unarticulated, existing only as a painful, anxious feeling in the pit of his stomach, a mixture of guilt, excitement, desperate yearning.

"Are you sure you're sure?" she asked.

"Yes." He couldn't help himself. In a barely controlled voice, he went on, "Sona told me that he brought you for me — humorously, of course — but little did I know . . ."

She took his hand. "I feel so happy . . . but what does it mean, for Enerico and Fatima?"

"Let's hope he doesn't die of fever."

The little room could not contain the excitement they felt. They went out for a walk, and they talked, they sat down for coffee, and they talked and talked. They did not quite know what they meant, working out impossible logistics for other meetings, choosing unlikely places for future trysts, as if it was the most innocent and casual deal in the world, not something that would cause pain and disruption in the lives of those who depended on him.

That night, though they'd lost interest, they went to the concert. It had, after all, been his excuse for being here. And by going there he felt he could still legitimize his escapade.

The concert was in a narrow old house in Georgetown, an old two-storey red-brick structure. The front door was wide open, a harmonium was being tuned somewhere inside the building, and the corridors were jammed with loud, cheerful people in a variety of national costumes. There was a distinct exoticism to the place, a happy alien-ness.

Welcome Rumina, he heard called out several times, in the Swahili manner, and she answered, *Ahsante*, thank you. He himself received a few quizzical looks. Some of the women took Rumina aside to chat, some of the men flirted with her. She was clearly quite well known here. She spoke in Swahili or English, and her fluency and manner with the former brought home to him with a pang how long he had been away from it, how distant from him had become the typical humour and grace of the language, which had once been so familiar to his ears.

The concert began in the front portion of the house, a living room and adjoining dining room. The area was packed to overflowing, the air stifling with heat and the mingled odours of sweat, perfume, and beer. There were five musicians, including two singers, a man and a woman. Ramji and Rumina found a place to sit on the floor, not far from a fan. The music, though a little too loud, was accomplished, and in other circumstances they might have been thrilled with the performance. But their hearts were elsewhere, and so during the intermission they agreed between them to leave.

Outside it had rained and the night was warm. He felt as if he had stepped out from the world as he knew it – as if he had jumped off a moving train onto a station platform. And did he expect that the train would be sufficiently long that he could jump back on it when he was ready? It didn't matter, tonight.

Back in the apartment, on the sofa, they continued to talk, his head on her lap, inhaling her presence, aware of her flesh, his fingers intertwining with hers. He revealed everything about himself to her – his childhood; his dreams, fears, and disappointments over the years. Her mother and father were dead, he learned, but she seemed reticent about her past, encouraging him instead to unburden himself. There was pain buried inside her somewhere, he sensed, and he hoped she would let him in eventually, let him comfort her.

He could have gone on all night in that mode, dreamily, meanderingly revealing details of his life to her, but she was tired and it was time finally to sleep. She helped him make his bed on the sofa, and as they kissed goodnight, he said, "Let me be with you . . . let's. . . ." And she told him, "Not this time, Ramji, but next time – promise." It seemed, in spite of his intense desire, that this was right.

But as he lay in the makeshift bed, he was besieged by all manner of thoughts, memories from the past, fears about the future, doubts about the present. He thought of his relationship long ago with Jamila, in whose room he had also slept on a sofa. How different Rumina was, how free of affectation. And Zuli? – they couldn't have made a greater mistake than to have married each other. . . . He heard Rumina get out of her bed, anxiously waited while she walked around the partition behind which he lay. She came and knelt beside him. "Come," she said.

"Are you sure?"

"Yes, come."

And so he spent the night in Rumina's bed.

He could have taken the first train out next morning to reach New York in the early afternoon; he didn't. Later in the morning, still unrecovered from the night's lovemaking, he couldn't reach Zuli on the phone at the hotel. When, instead, he reached Jamila, she told him to prepare for the worst – and that woke him up. It was best, she said, that he return straight to Glenmore.

She explained that Zuli had called her the previous afternoon to ask what time Ramji was setting off for New York. When she heard the news, that he would be delayed because he had gone off to D.C. with Rumina, she was totally freaked out. And despite Jamila's covering for Ramji ("I believe Sona went too – practically convinced Ramji to go," which was an outright lie), Zuli had not been appeased. "You'll have to make big amends, Ramji," Jamila told him. "But don't do anything now. Act innocent – as I hope you are." If she was waiting for confirmation, Ramji did not provide it.

Ramji finally took an afternoon train out. At the station, as he waited with Rumina for his train, the chattiness of the previous night was no longer there between them; he felt pulled down by anxiety, and neither of them spoke a word for a long while. He had no idea at this point how the future would unfold. They had agreed he would call her frequently, they would try to set up meetings. And they would go on from there. "Ramji, are you sure," she'd asked this morning. "If you have doubts, tell me right now." Of course I'm sure, he'd replied. We belong to each other now. But what did he really mean by that, he wondered to himself. It was time to say goodbye, and he took her hand, pressed it in his, then kissed it. She was cold. "I'll keep in touch," he said.

He started to walk down the platform, then turned and looked behind him. Rumina had not moved, was staring at him; further along, when he turned again, her eyes were still fixed upon him.

7

*I*f he deceived anyone, it was himself. He should have known he could not cheat successfully; he should have known he could not belong to two worlds at the same time, that he was liable to fall off into the space between.

Finally it was the day of Jamila's once-famous and now revived midsummer party. She had been in a state of high excitement since the morning, fussing over food and drinks, rearranging furniture, perfecting the decor of the house. Everything had to be right for her official return to the world. The children stayed out of her way, as did everyone else, except when pressed into service. Ramji found all the bustle and tension a welcome diversion from his anxieties.

He had picked up Zuli and the twins that morning from the train station, with apologies and explanations ready. They were not needed. Zuli had arrived with a kind of ominous determination, with the distant manner and curt rejoinders Ramji knew so well at the ready. He found himself at once relegated to the role of outsider to a new clique of three. "We are going back on Monday," she informed him on the way to Jamila's; the implication being, he could go with them, or not, as he wished.

"What do you mean, 'we'? Don't I count?"

"Since you prefer to make plans independently from us –"

"For God's sake – why don't you tell me what's on your mind?"

"Why don't you tell us what's on yours."

Touché. Still, the quarrel had a feel of familiarity, and Sara and Rahim by their manner – bored annoyance – suggested they'd seen it all before: Get off it, guys, patch it up. And soon he found himself asking them about their time in New York, telling them to stop arguing, putting on the parental cap as it were. So perhaps reconciliation was possible. But then, could he lead a double life? He wasn't sure anymore. How could he give up Rumina – what of the passion and love which had entered, finally, into his life?

Was a guiltless, painless freedom ever possible? What a question.

Enerico and Fatima, he said to himself, Rumina and Ramji. Forget about it. Just catch yourself: you stumbled. Count your blessings and keep walking.

Which is what Jamila told him when he returned the night before. It's not worth it, Ramji. The risk is too great. Think of the collateral damage – are you ready for it? And then in a lower voice, I've been there, Ramji, and I caught myself in time. She and Nabil seemed to be on better terms in the short time their house guests had been away. Things had happened between them. He wondered what kind of secrets she kept.

Ramji and Nabil were assigned to take all the kids out to the mall for lunch. And later, while the kids scoured the shops, the two men had had a long chat. Ramji found himself warming to Nabil for the first time since they had known each other. Nabil told him more about Jamila's nephew Abbas, who had married a Puerto Rican woman called Alicia. They'd had a baby boy. Over the last few days he and Jamila had arrived at a bargain. On her part, she had promised to take an interest in Alicia and the boy, which she had thus far failed to do. And Nabil's part of the bargain? He had agreed to tone down his religious fervour. He smiled with embarrassment, and Ramji's eyes widened, as Nabil revealed that for a few months he had joined a group of dervishes in New Jersey — the whirling kind. He would give that up for now, for Jamila's sake. A family is a wonderful thing, isn't it Ramji? — we should treasure ours. Did that look in his eye signify anything? Yes, it did. Who would have thought Nabil would turn out this way — indulgent husband of the indefatigable Jamila, now busy preparing her party of the decade.

The guests started arriving at three; they came from as far as New York and Washington. Ramji had known some of them a long time ago, Jamila's posh friends at the UN or the World Bank, with E.F. Hutton or J.P. Morgan, graduates of elite business schools and schools of economics, with manners to match. Nabil had been one of them.

Ramji waved at Iqbal and Susan in the distance; they had stopped over briefly on their way back from Providence to D.C. If Rumina had stayed on, she would have returned with them . . . but Rumina had wanted nothing more of this middle-aging crowd. . . . *Aren't you tired of all this suburbia?* . . . *Suburbia's quite nice actually.* . . . *I feel like Enerico.* . . . *But you're inside!* . . . Today was not only the "mustardseed" party but also the Fourth of July and the day of the Wimbledon tennis final. Champagne flowed to begin with, strawberries were relished. A small crowd had set themselves up in a corner of the living room to watch the all-American matchup between Sampras and Courier. And true to the spirit of American abundance and overkill, there was laid out in the dining room a lavish spread of cheeses and salads, sandwiches, cakes and trifle, spring rolls, pakodas, and samosas.

Drink in hand, Ramji meandered through the bacchanalia, among people who all seemed very much the same to him, with most of whom he could not muster any fellowship or sustain a conversation.

In a section of the living room, Sona was holding forth in a loud voice. He was reunited with Amy (who had come with their daughter Emna), at least for today. This was Jamila's doing. Her sense of propriety, of order in the universe, had been wounded by the fact that Sona and Amy, both friends of hers, had managed to avoid each other since their divorce. This time Sona was already here in Glenmore, and Amy, who had always been present at Jamila's midsummer parties, had very much wanted to come to relaunch the tradition. Well, why shouldn't she? But Jamila didn't tell either of them the other would be there.

This hadn't spoilt anything, for now the exes were sitting next to each other, on the rug in front of the fireplace, and Sona was telling all and sundry who had gathered around how he had met Amy the day he was doing his bit for peace during the Vietnam War.

You'd never have guessed, listening to Sona and Amy, that the two were now divorced. Ramji wandered off into the kitchen, behind Jamila.

"Happy couple there," he said to her. "Are you planning to bring them together again?"

"The way some of us are going, certain people had better come together." She saw the look on his face, softened. "I'm worried, Ramji," she said, in a low voice, "about you. Please — work something out; apologize to her — for not going to New York and taking off on your own. She'll forgive you. At this age we all need each other . . ."

"I don't know what I want," he said painfully. "I don't know what to do."

"Don't be an idiot, Ramji," she muttered. "Wake up. You're not young any longer! You don't know what you'd be getting into! . . ."

"I'll try," he said, with a helpless look at her, and came out from the kitchen into the dining room, though he did not quite know what he was going to do.

Sona and Amy had now drifted away from each other, and Ramji went over to where she was sitting on the couch with Zuli. There had always been a middle-aged look about Amy, he thought, with her soft features, conservative clothes, and her lush brown hair in a French roll or (as now) in a bun at the nape of her neck.

"How nice you came all the way from New Haven for Jamila's party," he said to Amy and pulled up a chair to sit with the two women. He met Zuli's eyes, noticed with relief the ice in them had melted.

"Listen," Amy replied, "I wouldn't miss the relaunch of Jamila's midsummer bash for anything, even if old bozo there," she looked towards Sona with affection, "were here — which I didn't know he would be. And hey — besides, with you guys in town —"

They were all distracted by one of Jamila's banker friends talking nearby in a very German accent.

"I'm glad we haven't lost touch simply because you and Sona broke up," Zuli said.

"Hey, I'm glad too. Initially I wondered, is he going to take away all the friends he's introduced me to?"

"No chance of getting back together, eh?" Zuli asked. "You two looked quite terrific together."

The remark pleased Amy, and she gave a grateful look, putting her hand on Zuli's arm. "Listen, when it's over, it's over," she said. "But you can remain friends."

Neither Ramji nor Zuli replied, but there was the briefest exchange of looks between them. The three of them took a moment to watch Sona, who stood captivated in the middle of the room listening to Aziz. The subject was insurance, and Sona was very much on the defensive by now, sheer arithmetic having convinced him his insurance policy was inadequate. Sona was saying, by way of consolation, "But when she's finished college. . . ." To which Aziz countered graduate school and unforeseen illness.

There was a shout from the TV area; the tennis final was apparently over. Sampras had beaten Courier and was grinning and panting at the television camera, trying to come up with the requisite words to explain his triumph.

Amy got up to go and talk to Jamila and Salma, who were standing together, leaving Ramji and Zuli facing each other. Ramji asked how New York had been.

"Okay," she said quietly. "We did the things we wanted to do."

"I'm sorry," Ramji replied, "it was thoughtless of me . . . abandoning you all. . . ." He would never be able to tell afterwards how fully sincere he had been at that moment, but she seemed to relent a bit, in the loosening of her features.

"You'll have to tell me about Washington later," she said.

"Of course," he answered.

Jamila announced one last round of champagne, this one to toast the Fourth of July. Her daughter Aisha played the national anthem on the kitchen piano and some of the guests sang along.

※

The party was over by six. Salma and Aziz, Jamila and Nabil, Ramji and Zuli, and Sona sat around in the living room, adjusting to the sudden lull after the storm of the past few hours.

"All in all, it was a success, don't you think?" Jamila said, looking very pleased.

They all agreed with her. This was the final day of their reunion, the final scene as it were. Iqbal and Susan were gone, Sona would leave that night, Ramji and Zuli the next morning. What happened next was perhaps inevitable, but no one could have foretold how far things would go. But for someone at the edge it takes only a small push to fall into the awaiting abyss.

"I always like to meet your classy friends, Jamila," Aziz began to tease. "Once they've left, I can't help but feel good about myself."

"You bet. They'll probably all be calling up their insurance agents by now," said Sona in rueful humour. "I'm going to call mine tonight, you've convinced me."

"Couldn't you talk of anything else besides insurance policies for once," scolded Salma.

"Oh, come on, I also talked about other things," Aziz protested, red-faced.

"Such as?" Sona asked.

"Cheap cemetery plots!" Ramji couldn't resist. He had heard Aziz going on about that too, much to the discomfort of a few of Jamila's out-of-town friends.

"Well, what do you expect? Swahili?" Aziz retorted, triumphant, grinning broadly; having stung, he was out of the corner and dancing. Ramji felt a chill in the atmosphere. Perhaps the scent of a kill was just irresistible. For Aziz goaded on, relentlessly: "And I see Rumina didn't come, Jamila. Zuli, you've got to watch this husband of yours and his Swahili interest."

"Actually," Sona said, matter-of-factly, attempting to steer away the conversation, "Rumina is a fascinating person. Would you guess that she was an expert on Zanzibari doors?"

To which Aziz said: "Really? And what else besides?"

And Ramji, in all seriousness: "Sona, what exactly is her family background?"

A moment of silence fell.

Disaster, disaster, disaster. A shot in the foot. He only wanted to appear casual, unflustered, innocent. But he gave himself away. Guilt was written on his darkening face, in his pounding heart, if anyone cared to listen to it, and now in this clumsy ruse. Sona looked at him in surprise, and Zuli cried out: "Why, doesn't everyone know? The girl is the daughter of Zanzibar's Sheikh Abdala."

"Wha-at?" his voice almost a shriek, uncontrollable. For a moment he couldn't see anything, until he pushed through the darkness, met Zuli's eyes, and he knew she knew. She looked pained, enraged – and in the next instant the silent communication between them was also public.

He looked helplessly, searchingly at Sona, who said, simply, "Yes, that's right."

Sheikh Abdala, a populist leader of the 1963 Zanzibar revolution, whose specialty had been his verbal attacks and veiled threats against Arabs and Asians. And as a minister in the Revolutionary Council, he had announced the sinister edict –

"Wow! The guy who announced the forced marriages in Zanzibar," Aziz said.

"Yes," Ramji said. "Yes, the same one." And the teenage girl he picked for himself chose to end her own life rather than stick with him. Her brother had finally knifed the Sheikh to death. Ramji, in his room in Boston, upon hearing of the assassination, had drunk to it in celebration.

"And Rumina? –" Ramji asked no one in particular but with a pleading look towards Sona, his voice small, dry. I'm getting into it even further, but there's nowhere else to go.

"But how did *you* know, Zuli?" Salma asked. "None of *us* did."

"Amy told me, this afternoon," Zuli said. "Sona must have known."

Sona nodded. "It didn't matter to me whose daughter she was – and it was up to her to tell people if she wanted to."

"Her mother? –" Ramji asked. But no one answered.

I'm a half-caste, Rumina had said. Now it was all so painfully clear, and also why she was so well known to the African crowd in Washington. She was Sheikh Abdala's daughter! That is why she was so reticent about her past. She knew it would be hard for him to swallow. He had even gone so far as to explain to her all about the forced-marriage episode and what difficult times those were.

I've made an utter fool of myself in front of everybody. He looked pathetically at his wife. Her face was stone. Whatever understanding they had reached over the past few days and the overtures they had made only an hour ago were now shattered.

And Sona – why hadn't *he* told him about Rumina? His idea of surprise?

"You knew it. . . ." He was looking at Jamila, saying it to whomever it applied.

"I didn't, I swear —" Jamila said.

"You see, you should have been insured," Aziz crowed.

"I would have made a bundle, wouldn't I."

Salma and Aziz got up to go. Sona edged towards Ramji, as if by imparting closeness he could give comfort. Aziz, as always, having done more damage than he realized, apologized in a good-natured way.

A dreadful quiet oppressed the household that Sunday evening. Jamila convinced Zuli they should go with the kids to the local park to watch the fireworks. They called up Salma first and agreed to meet her there with her kids. After they had gone, Nabil and Ramji contemplated various options open to them. Jamila had got it right; one needed to escape from the house and its remindful echoes of destruction and unbearable hurt. Nabil proposed they go see Alicia, Abbas's widow, and Ramji agreed.

On their way to West Philadelphia, they stopped at a supermarket and bought some tea and cheese and a six-pack of cola. Nabil had also brought along food left over from the party.

"She had to move to a smaller apartment," he explained, parking the car outside an old red-brick duplex, which had a small patch of grass in front enclosed by a short wrought-iron fence. Inside, they went up long narrow stairs — unswept, dark, and creaky, and permeated with the strong odour of recent cooking.

Alicia's apartment was on the second floor. "Hi," she said to Nabil shyly at the door. "Come in." She was a woman in her twenties, short and heavy, and was wearing a loose dress and bedroom slippers. Nabil introduced Ramji, who as he went in almost stumbled over a baby on the floor; the child was six months old, he guessed.

"What's his name?" he asked. "It's a boy?"

"Basheer," she said, accepting from them the two packages they'd brought. She offered them Seven-Up or tea.

They opted for tea and she went to the kitchen to make it. Nabil went and sat on the stuffed armchair in front of the TV, Ramji sat on the bed. The child crawled up in front of them and they started playing with him. Nabil picked him up, put him on Ramji's lap.

The room was narrow and crowded. The two windows were both completely curtained. On the table, across from Ramji and against a wall, was a framed picture of Alicia and Abbas, and another one of baby Basheer. Ramji put the baby down and went up to take a closer look. In the first one, Alicia wore the blue uniform of a security guard and was sitting on a chair; beside her stood Abbas in shirt sleeves and jeans. The baby photo was close up and charming, taken professionally soon after birth. There was a third photograph, evidently of Alicia's family, taken a few years ago, judging by how much younger she seemed to be in it.

"My folks," Alicia said to Ramji, as she brought in the cups of tea. "They're in New York."

"They're close, then. That's good."

"Yes. My mother was here last week – but it's not easy for her to get away, you know, she works."

Ramji and Nabil stayed a little over half an hour, during which time they watched part of a news broadcast, the baby's sagging diaper got changed, and, twice, police sirens went howling past on the street below. According to Alicia, her husband's murderers had still not been captured.

"I know them," she said, "I see them on Chestnut – by the taco place and –"

"And the police?" Ramji asked.

"It seems the two cops who saw them are on undercover assignment on a much larger operation," Nabil explained to him. "Don't worry, they'll be captured eventually," he told Alicia. "But we want you to come and visit us. We'd like to see more of the two of you."

Alicia gave him a sullen look.

"Jamila will call you," Nabil said, the accusation in her look not lost on him. "Then you can come and visit. You should even think of moving closer to where we are – I am serious."

It was such a depressing and lonely scene they walked out of that afterwards on the way back they did not have much to say to each other. Even the walk to the parked car in the dark had seemed like a hazardous venture in that area. How easy it had been, Ramji thought, to lose sight of this brutalized world from the heights of sheltered suburbia.

But Alicia and her son were real and they now had a patron in Nabil. He felt envious of Nabil, with his family and his newfound faith, and now this cause. And here he was with his own life a shambles.

When they returned, their families were back. Zuli had excused herself for the night. And once more, as on the first night, Ramji found himself at the kitchen table with Jamila. This time she offered him brandy, saying, "You look terrible."

"So . . . what did she – what did Zuli say?" he asked.

"I'll be honest: she's raging – mad as hell and insulted. But give it time," she said. And after a while: "And this Rumina business – I gather it's over?"

"It's over," he said wearily.

"Good." She put out her hand and he took it.

"And you – all right?" he asked.

"Me? I think I'll be all right," she said and squeezed his hand.

It was much later that night, when everybody had gone to bed, that Ramji called Rumina.

For more than an hour beforehand he had sat by himself, trying to think. Most likely his marriage was broken. Zuli would never forgive today's humiliation, even if he crawled back to her on his hands and knees. He did not see himself doing that, though he was sorry he had hurt her. The fact was, he hadn't been able to help himself, he had seen a vision of happiness for himself and made a grab for it, come what may. And what a fall he had taken.

"I thought you'd forgotten about me," she said, sounding very pleased. "Are you alone there? I mean, can you talk freely?"

"I learned today your father was Sheikh Abdala," he said, his voice quivering with emotion.

"Oh. I meant to tell you. . . . I was only waiting –"

"That's not enough. You should have told me first. I feel horribly cheated. It's not something you keep secret – it matters."

"But why? I am still me."

He was silent.

"Ramji?" Low voice; pleading.

"Yes? . . . Look – I can't handle this . . . this history . . . any of this . . . not now, anyway, it's too much for me. . . ." Pleading, also.

"Tell me when you're ready then," she said.

After a moment's pained silence, they hung up.

*H*ow to continue with this narration, when on one side myriad reminders constantly tug at me, to take me away to relive every moment of the bliss, dwell upon every tender word and sigh and gesture of the love that became my prize; and on the other side, at the end of it all, bereft of that love, I am confronted with a visual reminder of a tragic killing and exhorted to understand it. And understand it I must, that is my responsibility.

Still life, post-destruction: a snapshot of a dwelling above a bombed-out bookstore in the Midwest, in ruins, portions collapsed, contents flung about, a gash in the far wall, shafts of daylight from outside; the vantage point is probably from a corner still supported. In the midst of the debris, the upper portion of a woman's body, the dress olive green, the hair golden, a hyphen of red lipstick on a smudged pink doll's face; the rest of her body could be under the broken masonry but isn't, I know; it's been blown off by a bomb. Also dead, her husband and child, nowhere in this picture.

The question arises again and again: How did a person like me get involved — however obliquely — with a horror such as *this*?

That's what he has to find out, says my interlocutor, Federal Agent Will Jones. He eyes me intently as if to gauge my thoughts, then quietly takes the photograph from my hand and slips it back into his collection.

He is the investigator who arrived one morning a few weeks ago, not long after the bombing depicted in the photograph and the events that followed, in the aftermath of which I found myself amidst the shambles of my own life. He is a psychologist, but his job is not to cure me. Rather, he comes with the belief that by digging deep into my background and my mind, he will find some answers to what makes a community of normally law-abiding citizens produce acts of reckless violence. Our interview, he says, by shedding light on the background to that bombing, will be our little contribution to greater peace and harmony in the world; and I have little doubt that I and what he thinks I represent are destined for the government's data bank of global malcontents and malfunctionaries. Open a window into your mind, says Will, show us your loves and hates, your fears and despairs, your beliefs and history; only then can we understand you. He lumps me with a people, among other small rootless people of the world with grievances. Is he wrong? Can I talk about myself without reference to a group?

He is not unresourceful. In the initial days of our interview, he brought with him a tome or two in his briefcase, reference books on foreign peoples, but he's given up, having realized perhaps that these groups can cause as much trouble inside books as outside them.

"Why does each people think they are so special?" he once asked. A question more appropriately addressed to my friend Sona, whose life's mission it has been to study the distinctiveness of just one community.

"To themselves, they *are* special, aren't they?" I said. And when they fear annihilation . . . I almost added, but didn't. When they fear annihilation, they are apt to take measures into their own hands? . . . Isn't that why we are here, you asking and me answering?

Over the weeks, I've come to be fond of Will – we seem to understand each other, and talk like contemporaries, which we are. He is a boyish-looking man, with sandy hair and a red face, a tight build. A Yale man, in fact, a year younger than I. "Like you, I was on scholarship," he says. His father was a baker. Not good enough a background for the CIA boys? – I smirk knowingly. He bites into an apple: Our success rate is greater, and you can see why: we have patience and time – and resources. We deal with people, not ideology, unlike those other, much-maligned guys.

Let's see, he once said, when he was trying to find out if I was of revolutionary pedigree: Were your people – family, if you insist – involved in the Indian Mutiny of 1857? The Indian independence movement? Any relation to the Assassins of Persia? Not involved in the African independence struggles either? . . .

Quite off the mark, of course. I said, We are a peaceful people; all we've ever wanted is to be left alone; ninety-nine per cent of us have never seen an actual gun, let alone held or fired one –

Will pulled out the picture he'd just showed me from the stack, pushed it towards me, saying, "A lot of people who do this sort of thing say the same thing, that they are a peaceful people, all they want is to be left alone."

I look at the picture: *Still life, post-destruction: broken torso of a woman in olive green.* . . . Why me, how did *I* come to be connected to this?

Regular as a pendulum, twice every week he's arrived at my door, and prodded and probed my memory, asked me questions about my background and ancestry, taken away my impressions about people I have known and whom he finds interesting. And I have indulged him, partly because I don't think I have much choice. Partly because I am lonely and his company is congenial. He is a good listener and does not jump to easy judgements. But also, I must admit, talking to him has helped me draw out from my mind details I had quite forgotten, and his questions have suggested departures which I might not have taken on my own.

He has in his possession statements from people from my past . . . he let that drop one day, quite inadvertently, it seemed then, but perhaps it was deliberate needling on his part.

"What do you think your friends at the Tech thought of you," he asked, "your former roommate Shawn Hennessy, for instance?"

"Well, as someone who was naive at first, but who learned fast; idealistic but unwilling to resort to just any means . . . a little nerdish perhaps –"

"And a jerk-off, in bed? Sorry –" he said, but he looked, if anything, amused.

If I could, if my complexion had allowed it, I would have turned beet red. "There's nothing wrong with self-gratification, as nowadays we're admitting," I blustered, "it's not a sin –"

"Who's talking of sin?" Will said.

It began dawning on me that Will Jones – or someone else in his organization – had spoken to Shawn; and others, too? Our interview would surely be only a part of a larger file; this friendly but persistent fellow from the agency, my companion for a couple of days every week, Tuesday mornings and Friday afternoons, must know things about myself even I don't. And so I said to him once: "You must know – who called the cops on Lucy-Anne. Was it anyone we knew?" We were sitting at my dining table, with its yellow and green and brown khanga tablecloth and desk lamp, which also doubles as my writing table. Will smiled slyly at me, reflected a while, then replied: "I'm surprised you have to ask. You must not have read his book."

"Whose book?"

"You mean you really don't know," Will said. "Your room-mate. Shawn Hennessy."

I felt, that instant, like one might after a sudden checkmate, being one-upped mentally and abruptly, with a tightness in the pit of the stomach it takes minutes to get over. I got up to pour more coffee for us, which I did with some effort to keep a steady hand, and I said, simply, "That f— traitor." I recalled to mind Shawn's subsequent academic career, our one exchange of letters, and thought, *But not surprising, after all, is it . . .*

Will had raised an eyebrow, watching me as I returned to the table. "Traitor to what, though?"

"His friends."

I could have guessed: the most likely suspect, if you gave the matter some cool thought, someone who knew precisely Lucy-Anne's and my whereabouts that Friday evening. But that's in retro-spect. To have guessed *then* about such a casual betrayal would have been to admit to the flimsiness of the radical movements and their causes – a cynicism that is more modern and sinister.

"Why would he turn informer?" I asked. "Did he believe in the war after all?"

Who else had he informed on? Was there ever a file on me, for instance, to which he had contributed?

"The fact that his brother Pat went missing in action in Vietnam. That might have been sufficient to turn him into a patriot. Perhaps he stopped believing in the extremist element of the peace movement."

"What ever happened to Pat? Did he return safely?"

"No. He was sent up in space by the Russians, that's what a psychic told his mother." Will smiled.

If he was expecting a smart comment, I didn't give him one. I asked:

"And Lucy-Anne? You must know where she is?"

"Yes, but I don't know if I'm allowed to tell you." He paused, then added: "Perhaps it's best not to think of her – at least not yet."

I walked with him to the end of the block, then he left, saying, "Till Tuesday, then."

And what of this man Darcy, who had once come to my grand-mother's house for a pain in his back and helped me decide my future? A hero of sorts to me then, he would again play a part in changing the course of my life.

One evening we sit on a bench across from his apartment, the black ocean in front of us, the sky clear and starry, listening to the waves coming in, and he says, "If I hadn't invited you here, you would not now be in this situation."

Nor would I have met my Rumina again. And to think that it was she who had reconnected us in the first place, after all these long years. The Rumina present now in every rush of the waves upon the beach, every break, every swish and gurgle of water on sand . . .

Darcy smiles thinly, and continues. "In any case, it was not a good idea to involve a young person in an old man's causes."

"I'm hardly a young person."

"You were still in your teens when I was the age you are now."

Old? Yes, he's old and defeated now; he was defeated even before he landed on these shores two decades after I did; only I hadn't realized it. To me, when I met him again all those years later, though he appeared somewhat marked by age and frailer, he was still the awesome, fearless Darcy. The original, genuine dissident.

Will says, another day: "This young woman – this Rumina, did she lure you into coming here to California or was she used to lure you? . . ."

It had been quite straightforward, really.

One day a phone call came to my office in Chicago.

"My name is Darcy, I am calling from Santa Monica. I don't know if you remember me from Dar es Salaam . . ."

Mister Darcy! My heart was racing. How could I not remember. "Of course," I said, "you used to visit my grandmother –"

And after asking questions about me, my well-being, he said, "Yes, it's been a long long time."

He'd been given my name, he said, as someone who could assist him. He had recently taken over a political magazine with an interest in the Third World called *Inqalab*, and he was looking for marketing ideas. And so we talked.

At the end of the call I realized he hadn't told me who had given him my name, and I asked.

"I believe she's a friend of yours," he said, "Rumina Abdala. She's in Los Angeles, I came to know her in Dar."

What was Rumina doing in California? When did she go? . . . But I didn't ask.

A week later the phone rang, a sweltering July midnight. Rumina.

"Oops – what time's it there, I clean forgot the time difference –"

And so we had an innocent chat, on the surface. She had a pretext, a question, could I suggest publishers who might be interested in publishing her thesis? I gave her two names in Amsterdam; what was she doing on the West Coast? She'd been invited to a conference there and had decided to stay. She liked the climate, and had found a part-time job teaching Swahili at a university. She had been there eight months already and would probably stay for the time being. We made no reference to our past intimacy — it had been almost exactly a year since Jamila's reunion — though it hung heavily behind each calculated response we uttered. In that intervening year I had come to think of that brief and happy time we spent together as the prelude to an impossible dream and, therefore, best forgotten. Now there was fear at broaching the subject, and uncertainty, and of course the dark shadow of her past, which I did not believe I could ever feel neutral about. She called one more time, and again there was that sense of uneasiness, of fear stalking our conversation, despite the outward cordiality. Nothing might have come of these tentative gestures — except that Darcy rang again, two weeks to the day after that first time.

"Look, I've been thinking," he said. "Why don't you come and join us here at *Inqalab*, help us reach out to more people. You have knowledge of the market —"

"I'm flattered." And I was thrilled, too. To be invited by the old warrior to join him!

He explained his plans for expansion, concluding with: "I've made inquiries about you . . . and you're what we used to call a *ndugu*. We need you, the cause needs you."

Rumina called a couple of days later: "Do you think you will take up Mr. Darcy's offer?" Unable to hide the excitement in her voice, the tremor of happiness, and reminding me with a pang of the girl I knew in Glenmore – her freshness and youth and surprising boldness.

So who used whom? Did Darcy use Rumina to entice me to come over, or was it the other way round? In either case, it doesn't matter now.

※

The Swahili term *ndugu* that Darcy used for me – it seems to disturb Will. In the seventies, this word became the equivalent of the "comrade" of communist countries. But, I tell Will, its first meaning is "little brother," which always takes precedence. So *ndugu* from Darcy was no small tribute. Will smiles quizzically, indulgently, as if to say, Whatever pleases you. But we are back to the photo of the bomb scene: the debris and the victim.

He says: "The line between Darcy's company – Inqalab – and this . . ." (He pronounces the word "Ink-alab," the last part to rhyme with his "A-rab.")

"But there is no straight line between the two," I reply.

"No. But there is a point of contact – hence we are here, and so on."

Touché. That's the point, isn't it. If you make it a habit to stand under trees and get caught by lightning, whom to blame. Dissent is all right, he says. But it can become a habit; like tobacco or coke; or promiscuity (I beg off from that one, it's his example); one day you just might get hit, *kapow*! Then where are you? Involved in something like this. Or this:

He brings out another photo. This one is smaller, in black and white. It is from a much earlier explosion: September 1971, Kendall

Square, Cambridge; Tech's ISS. A man had been killed then, but there's no body in this picture. I hand it back to Will and we let it go at that.

Though nothing explicit had been revealed, or discussed afterwards with my wife, I had exposed my feelings for Rumina that afternoon in Glenmore. It was the last straw in a marriage that Zuli and I both knew had been crippled for years. There was no forgiveness – for me to crave, for Zuli to give. Shortly after our separate arrivals back in Chicago, Zuli and I decided to live apart, and I moved out. Within a year we were divorced.

I was living then in a suburban apartment complex to be near the kids and their school. I had not felt so alone in a long time. I had no friends in town, family and work having been my sole pre-occupations for more than a decade. Now the kids were a matter of weekend visits under sanction from a possessive mother, and at work the company in which I had minority partnership had moved so far from its original mandate (into New Age and do-it-yourself titles) that I was already open to other possibilities. And so, having accepted Darcy's offer, and having told the kids beforehand of my impending departure, one morning I went to their school and said an emotional goodbye to them outside the principal's office, promising them I would call frequently, and we would meet regularly. I then picked up maps from the AAA; I left a note for Zuli at the house I now suddenly felt a mawkish attachment for; and I headed west and south on the highways.

So you absconded? Will says. Just like that. Yes, I reply. My one struggle was moving even farther away from Sara and Rahim. I could only hope they would one day understand. I felt at the time

I had nothing to lose and everything to gain: first, to assuage a conscience which had never fully recovered from a belief I had betrayed my world, as Lucy-Anne had put it so dramatically once. And then, to try and find a relationship with Rumina. I couldn't get her out of my mind now.

III

PHANTOM OBSESSIONS

(Fall/Winter, 1994–95)

"The fire is in the minds of men
and not in the roofs of houses."

– FYODOR DOSTOEVSKY
The Possessed

1

California. Had it always been in the mind? Go West, young man, they used to say, didn't they – whoever they were – the movies most likely; or, as Grandma would say, citing ancient lore with wide-eyed confidence or, later, a knowing smile at my teenager's newfangled scientific scepticism: The sun will rise from the West, that's where the Lord will come from, salvation. Later still, hippies beckoned with flowers and pot and freedom from the norm, and West Coast girls were . . . and Berkeley was radical Mecca, that's where the revolution came from, and I thought Grandmother had been right after all. Ultimately, I learned to settle down, adopting East Coast values and ways, succumbing to a fast-paced world of subways and trams, and grey gritty streets in biting cold, and narrow spaces and tight living – in spite of which, supposedly, there was more history and culture and irony. And California, too good to be true, always far out and a little too much; the last escape on this continent, where the sun god ruled; and the sea, the sea.

With his exhaust pipe clunkingly defying its recent life-time warranty – he would have had to return to Reno to make a claim – Ramji had driven into Santa Monica and westwards still to where the road must end, where the ocean was bound to be, and here he was, and the shimmery mystifying vastness lay before him.

When he was in his teens in Dar es Salaam he would go to the seashore to study for examinations, sit on the same stone bench every afternoon, hardly a soul in sight. There would be absolute quiet, except for the rhythmic burble and burst of waves, the occasional rustle from a branch overhead, in which to cram all those theorems and trigonometric formulas, and lists of exports from the shires of England; and lines from *Julius Caesar* – appropriate political drama for Africa during the decade of the popular dictators.

In those green adolescent days in a small African town, looking out to the sea and what lay beyond, he dreamed of . . . what? Doing something incredibly wonderful or great. A major scientific discovery, for example. A new theorem. Or even, in the moral or heroic domain, risking his life to rescue a drowning child or a girl from the treacherous hold of a receding tide – as a boy from his school had done a few years before. The boy had lost his life but attained the status of an angel. (So it was believed.)

And now, looking out across another ocean, what did he seek? What did he have to give?

Between Darcy and Rumina the pull was enough to bring him over. Desire for a young woman, and desire to do something useful, make amends, in whatever small way, for the past. It was towards the past he was now looking, in a manner of speaking, across the Pacific Ocean, towards Africa and India; though he was uneasy at this unexpected symbolism, what it might portend about his quest.

How would Darcy seem to him now, from up close? Would the old charisma still be there? Darcy's voice had carried an easy, unaffected authority, when they'd spoken to each other over the phone in recent months, but Ramji also detected in the tone a paternal familiarity. They had rather warmed to each other. Did Darcy wish to see in him some sort of lost son? And had he, Ramji, come here chasing lost dreams? He cast aside the thought; nothing ventured, nothing gained. At the very least there was a common cause between them.

And Rumina? Could they simply carry on from where they'd left off, without regard to what had once come between them?

He must have stood there an hour, lost in thought, before coming to with a start. He checked his watch, turned, and walked back to his car and drove off to look for the offices of his new employer, where he had arranged to arrive at about this time.

Inqalab International – the Company, as he would learn to call it, would come to think of it – had found mainstream occupancy and quiet anonymity in Santa Monica, at the rear of a commercial development on Pico Avenue named the Aerospace Business Park. Between the forbiddingly modern glass-encased main building and a fair-sized yellow-brick warehouse at the back ran an elongated one-storey block of modest offices with glass doors and front panels, one of which was Inqalab. The Company name was painted in gold on the door, beside a logo consisting of a golden globe circled by what could have been either the red petals of a flower or the raging flames of a fire. *Inqalab* was the Urdu-Hindi word for "revolution."

There was no one at reception, or in the adjoining front office, but the sound of lively chatter and the telltale aroma of Indian savouries seemed to emanate from the back through a passageway.

He headed that way, past two more offices and a conference room, and came into a large, square, and brightly lit workroom where everybody was gathered around a table laden with food.

"He comes! The messenger from the east!" said a loud voice. "He's crossed the continent to come and join us! Welcome! Ramji, may we presume? And you have duly found parking for your camel?"

"And you must be the revolutionaries!" Ramji grinned.

Half a dozen people had looked up or turned to face him as he entered. The guy with the robust though not quite sincere-sounding welcome had a handsome boyish look, he was short and clean-shaven, with close-cropped hair. He introduced himself as Zayd Afzal, one of two associate editors, the other being Indra Basu, equally short but dark and pudgy, who raised a hand in greeting. Between these two stood someone thin and frail and not much taller, who was staring at him – it was Darcy. He came forward and put a hand on Ramji's shoulder and said warmly, in a familiar drawl now crackled with age, "Welcome. We've been waiting for you."

One day, long ago – this must have been the late fifties – two young men came to their house in Dar and said to Grandma in grave earnest voices: Ma, have you heard, the Governor has put Mr. Darcy in prison. We are collecting donations for his defence. But isn't this Darcy a *sheytaan*, Ma asked, he speaks out against the Community, he doesn't pray, and he married that woman. But he's one of us, Ma. Grandmother put her hand in her bosom, pulled out her tiny black coin purse and gave the young men a crumpled five shillings from her small monthly allowance. Over the next few years of the boy's life, this "Darcy" would become an awesome and rarefied presence, one invoked by exciting news and rumour. He was the man who'd defied the Governor, who spoke better English than the British, who did sinful things like smoke and drink and arrogantly get up from mosque, on the few occasions that he came, during a sermon. But then one day, the man himself arrived at their house, in a beige suit and red tie and polished brown shoes. He came supported by two young men, and sat down on a straight-backed wooden chair. Kulsa Bai, he said to Grandma, relieve me of my pain. He said this with familiarity, though they had not spoken before; but each had a reputation townwide. Grandma was caught by surprise, took some moments to regain her composure, then offered the visitors tea and biscuits. First the pain, said the sufferer, barely able to lift an arm to detain her. Grandma eyed Darcy from the doorway and said, It won't go away with one visit. Start now anyway, he said. But you'll have to believe in the treatment. I will believe, he grumbled, what makes you think I won't? At her bidding, painfully and laboriously he went down on his knees then flat on his stomach, on her spotless and gleaming linoleum floor, and extended his arms over his head. Grandma began to prod and feel his back with her right foot, all over, and he would say, No, not here, a little to the left, that's too far, and so on, until she found the spot, and he groaned, Yes here, quash the *sala*. She closed her eyes, whispered some prayers; then spoke, Shall I break the knot? She had to repeat it so he understood, and he said, Go ahead, go ahead, yes; at which, stepping on the pain, she crossed over to the other side of him; and then she crossed back.

The *sala*, the pain, was quashed it seemed after a few visits. Grandma's treatments were always free of charge, but after Darcy's cure, he left the boy a present, a genuine Parker fountain pen.

Though Darcy remained a subject of rumour and news, there was now also a certain tangibility to him. He greeted Grandma in mosque during his rare visits, and he occasionally even dropped by to see her at home, during the day, when Ramji was in school. One time he brought a slide rule for the boy – a teenager by now – and what a valued, exotic, beautiful gift that was!

And then just before Ramji was to leave for America, Robert Kennedy was shot dead, the Kennedy who'd come to Dar and won their hearts, and Ramji suddenly said, I'm not going there, shocking everyone – his teachers, his friend Sona, and Grandma. But Grandma prevailed. She told him, Go and speak with Mr. Darcy. And so, one afternoon, he rather timidly stepped into Darcy's office, which was behind a common storefront, on a dirty street across from Hindu Lodge, the vegetarian restaurant. It was dusty, and the boy had to walk a path between stacks of old newspapers and magazines to an old wooden desk at which Darcy sat. The man looked up over his reading glasses, screwed his pen shut. Yes, young man, what can I do for you? And Ramji, first introducing himself, in case Mr. Darcy did not know him by face, explained his dilemma. He was afraid to go to America, he said, where a great man could get killed so easily. They had amazing things there, but what values did they have? He realized as he went on that he didn't have just one reason but a mass of fears. There were many temptations in America . . . he didn't want to lose himself there. He didn't want to leave Grandma alone. He would be homesick. And the man said with an understanding smile, For you, my boy, there's nothing more important than your education. Go and get it wherever you find it. See the world and learn from it – and come back to us. That is your duty to your country, to your people. I myself have a son in America. And don't worry – we will look after your grandmother, she'll be safe and sound when you get back!

And now, two decades and a half later: the same man, old and shrunken, the clothes identical to those he always wore. What had he actually thought then? Had he smiled to himself at the boy's naive view of the world, of the Kennedys?

There were four other people in the room: two young men, Sajjad and John, who did the printing and setup; a slightly older impish-looking man in a safari suit standing between them, called Mohan, a travel agent from next door; and a woman in a pink and blue sweatsuit who said, "Hi! I'm Naseem. I made all the food here, I run a catering agency," and later, when he'd accepted a plate from her, "I was among the first to come to L.A. – when I came, there were fewer than twenty-five of our people here."

"And now?"

"At least five thousand," she said proudly.

There was no sign of Rumina. They had agreed that she would meet him here at reception.

Ramji was given a quick tour of the premises, after which he found himself behind closed doors with Darcy, Zayd, and Basu in the conference room and library. They had all brought their drinks inside with them. He was now one of them and they wanted to make him feel at ease. When they quizzed him about recent political events though, somewhat startled, Ramji found himself sounding equivocal and without strong opinions, obviously not up-to-date, perhaps disappointing to the other three men. They seemed to have a somewhat exaggerated idea of his "radical days" – that he had been some kind of firebrand organizer. Where had they got *that* idea from? – from mention he himself might have made to Darcy, about his student days? Zayd even referred to the free-and-easy ways at Woodstock. Had he but been there to participate, Ramji thought! He had questions, yes, and ideas; but those could wait.

The Company was in the process of establishing the capability of publishing and printing bilingual multicultural texts, Darcy said.

"The idea is to make inroads into mainstream culture," Basu explained, "subvert the homogenizing melting-pot, even as it goes out and chews up world culture in its maw."

"In the ass," Zayd said with a grin and Basu smiled.

Darcy looked at Ramji with a pained expression. "Don't mind these extremists – I am here to tame them."

There seemed a striking complementarity to Zayd and Basu, sitting across from each other at the long table: one light-skinned and ebullient in his manners, the other dark and reserved. From what Ramji had learned, they went back a long way together, were in fact the original founders of the Company.

The main inspiration behind everything here, Darcy said, the driving force, was the monthly journal *Inqalab*, "the Global Newspaper of Radical Analysis."

"Of course, the journal is political, polemical, its position is deliberately antagonistic. It's the devil's advocate – although I shouldn't use that term, it puts us on the side of the devil! – and that is precisely because we work with certain presumptions about power politics in the world – and how information is controlled –"

There was a voice, a distinctly familiar and thrilling voice, in the passageway outside. It drew all his attention; he listened to it, watched the closed door facing him, from behind which it emanated. It seemed to him that the other three people in the room had paused to do the same.

"It's Rumina," Darcy said.

At the same time there was a knock on the door, which then opened, as Rumina first showed her face and then stepped inside.

"Hullo," she said. "Sorry, am I intruding?"

"Not at all, not at all," Darcy waved away the apology. "Come in, we were just getting to know our man better."

"And we still have a long way to go, by the way," threw in Zayd with a chuckle.

Ramji had got up from the table. "Hi," he said; in diffidence, partly, yes, but also shock. He moved two slow steps towards her. It took him a few moments to connect, regain his sense of reality, and respond appropriately. He managed a smile, as they stood facing each other. She doesn't look different, it's the same Rumina. Then why did that first sight of her send a jolt through me, as if I'd forgotten what she looked like? . . . Am I disappointed? How can that be, there she is – that same round face, curly hair gathered at the sides in two delightfully abbreviated braids; and the twinkling, laughing eyes. A little plumper and darker than I remembered, but lovely, life itself.

She laughed. "Do I look so different?"

"No . . . no," he stammered.

"You must be tired – you've only just arrived and they've put you to work?"

"Well, I spent the night at a motel before coming into town; not tired at all. Besides, they had a reception all ready for me, samosas and all that. . . . It's nice to see you again."

Naseem had followed Rumina into the room.

"Ramji," Naseem asked, "what are your plans? Do you know where you are staying?"

He hadn't given that any consideration, had thought he would somehow go along with whatever possibilities turned up. And now here was Rumina before him, and he badly wanted just to get away to be with her in private.

"We should go out to dinner first," Darcy said. "And as for living arrangements, you can stay with Naseem as a paying guest — until you find something suitable of your own."

"That is," Naseem put in, talking to Ramji, "if you like my humble abode. There is a separate entrance and you will be left undisturbed. I live with my son."

There was an awkward silence, and then Naseem added, ". . . unless you have made plans, of course."

"I have prepared a guest room for him," Rumina began slowly, then hurried out with, "and there's an apartment going near where I live, that he can look at tomorrow morning . . ."

Her voice trailed off, and Ramji hesitated. Around him they were all waiting for his response: Jump, Ramji, jump: jump left, jump right, which way will you fall? There was Zayd, watchful as a hawk; and Basu, bemused; Darcy, indulgent as a parent; and Naseem, holding her breath as though watching an intimate scene unfold on TV. They must all have known something was going on between them, and they had probably all wondered, exactly what manner of relationship?

Ramji said, "Yes, I think that's what I'll do, thanks. Besides, we have some catching up to do."

"Yes, you go along," Darcy said. "You need a rest too." And to Rumina: "He's all yours!"

All right then, the rest of them said, cancel the dinner plans for tonight, some other night perhaps, and then they said their good-byes. Ramji looked at Naseem and said he would let her know tomorrow – regarding where he had finally decided to stay – and she said, Anytime, you're welcome.

As he left with Rumina she pointed out the yellow warehouse building outside in the complex. "That's the Shamsi mosque," she said with a smile, "in case you need to go and pray."

He hesitated, then said, "I stopped praying a long time ago. I thought you knew that."

A thin drizzle fell as they drove to her place, taking her car, leaving his Company parking area. The evening traffic was thick and the going slow through the kaleidoscope of reflected city lights. They were on Sepulveda Boulevard, she went on chattily; along this stretch it coincided with the Pacific Coast Highway, which went all the way to San Diego. She lived in Hermosa Beach, in the South Bay area. Of course Santa Monica was more fashionable, but she liked where she was. It was full of young people, very informal, good for cycling and volleyball. The beach was close. The library was excellent. There was a Borders, and another bookshop she really liked, called Maktaba's, which had books on Africa.

He was unresponsive and broody, and soon she stopped talking. Then after a while she said, "I'm sorry for hijacking you, I suppose you would have liked to have dinner and relax and chat with the rest."

He looked up, surprised. "Not at all," he told her. Quite the contrary, he might have said, I wanted nothing more than to get away with you. . . . But am I sure this is right for me, even as I desire her so terribly, too much perhaps? Is she my inevitable end, my conclusion?

"About this apartment – what's it like? How far from you?"

"We can think of an apartment tomorrow . . . if you like."

Eyes agleam – but I'm only imagining that. There was always a great deal of mischief in her. She could be a djinni, a temptress, he mused. Zanzibar had always been full of them.

Neither of them spoke after that. Left to his thoughts, he recalled their time together in Glenmore, then Washington. She probably had the same thoughts flitting through her mind. Same? Wouldn't it be interesting if two people could share the same memories, experience exactly the same images? That would need a hard-wiring of the brains, wouldn't it . . .

She turned right, off the main road, into one of parallel streets sloping to the beach, then took another left into a residential street called Salal Avenue. Her apartment was the upper level of a blue duplex with white window trimmings. It was reached by an external staircase at the side of the building, leading up from the front to the back door.

He followed her in, and let the door click gently shut behind him.

She turned to face him, her cheeks flushed. And as she had done once before, months ago in D.C. – but now her eyes were aglow, hands clasped in front of her at the chest, a questioning look on her face – she said, in Swahili: Welcome. And he replied, exactly as he had done that time, *Ahsante*, thank you. They stared at each other for a moment. Then, overcome by a rush of emotion, they fell into a desperately tight, silent embrace.

Later, in the bedroom, amidst tender caresses, bodies gratified but hearts still craving, there were answers, assurances, excuses.

"The last time you said you were sure – doubly sure . . ."

He said softly: "Yes."

She lay on her back, arms behind her head, he facing her, raised on one elbow beside her, drawing patterns with his finger on her midriff.

"And after that? Cold, stony silence. Mister Heartless. Did it matter so much to you that I was Sheikh Abdala's daughter?"

"It did, then. But I can handle it, I think."

"I don't think you were really angry that I didn't tell you. You just got cold feet, admit it."

"That too," he said, after a pause.

She turned on her side, asked: "How are the twins – they must hate being called that – Sara and Rahim?"

"They're doing fine."

Two faces loom in his mind, a girl with a ponytail, a boy with tousled hair . . . what would they be up to now . . . returned from school and snacking, and perhaps bickering as they eat . . .

"Yes. I tell myself they'd have distanced themselves in a couple of years, and would have left after three more years." And Zuli – would they have moved closer as he'd hoped so often, if Rumina had not happened?

They had a late dinner at a Vietnamese restaurant down the street, which even at this hour, 10:30 p.m., was moderately full, then strolled along the beach. A three-quarter moon was out, a free spirit slicing through clouds, and the tide was high and the waves lashed gently at the shore. A few other people were out for a walk, and in front of a house there was a gathering of young people chatting in low voices. As if in celebration of openness and the elements, most of the houses they passed had full-length windows and glass doors, through which they could see tidy living rooms and kitchens, in darkness or flickering with the shadow-play of a television still on.

"When was the last time you walked by the sea?" she said.

"Twenty-five years ago," he said. "I thought I had got it out of me, the sea. . . . Reminds me of home, a bit, but home's on the other side of the ocean, straight ahead of us."

"Only it's not home any longer."

"And we're not who we were."

They walked on in silence, she clutching his arm, he saying silently to himself, It will be all right. It will be all right.

2

Afterwards, when he would recall this brief span of a few months, and when it seemed to him there was nowhere to turn but to the writing paper or the computer screen in front of him, it was his time together with Rumina that became the most vivid, the most painfully real: tender moments of love, a romance opening like a fairy tale; her touch, her smell of fresh soap or, in the evening, of a faint perfume or (to tease him) a seductive Zanzibari attar – the eyes twinkling, a sarong hugging the contours of her body –, her various hairstyles, the dimples on her cheeks . . . all the pleasurable details of her presence and being. What else was she to him besides her sensual presence, which so thrilled him? After a long time, and perhaps for the first time, he felt actually loved, by a woman. He adored her for that, and he was grateful. And also, with Rumina he was finally living an existence which he did not feel was alien to him, and so, in a manner of speaking, she had brought him home.

In their spare time he and Rumina would sometimes drive around and explore the vast metropolis that is Los Angeles in all its diversity. So many of the places had a mythic feel to them, simply from their names, long familiar to him through movies and television and the detective fiction of his youth. And yet here they were – Sunset Boulevard, the soaring office towers of Century City (in one of which he went to visit an old classmate of his, a lawyer), the palatial properties of Beverley Hills.

They loved to cook together, elaborately: something traditionally Zanzibari – a rice bread and coconut-based curry with cilantro, green chillies, and ginger, or a vegetarian Gujarati thali with an assortment of greens and daals elaborately served with pickles on gleaming aluminum trays, or a lush saffroned biryani or pilau, or goat trotters, or brain fried in the richest spices.

Their landlord was a Swede with the large proportions and bearing of the stereotypical Nordic woodsman: Svend Nilsson – also gruff and good-natured – had an occupation not far off the mark either, that of a designer of furniture. He occupied the floor below them, with his French girlfriend Josie, using the backyard and its shed for his practical work space. The apartment was small, opening at the back where the kitchen was; it had two bedrooms on one side of the main corridor, which opened into the living room in front, with a four-foot bay window that gave an unhampered view of the western sky and portions of the beach. Between the kitchen and the living room was a partition of half-height shelves. Rumina had been induced by discounts into furnishing this room with Svend's designs, some still in their provisional stages, using Scandinavian pine and glass, and black and white veneers – a starkness she had cleverly subverted by using appropriately placed African hangings with warm greens, yellows, and reds. Svend would visit, to check out the wear on his hinges and joints, he said, but also to chat, and he would never turn down an invitation to a meal.

Twice a week Rumina went to UCLA to teach Swahili, which she loved with a passion. Three days a week she did the morning shift at an espresso bar run by a women's co-operative in a quiet part of Santa Monica where the only steady clientele came from the nearby daycare centre and supermarket. A partnership in the enterprise was hers for the asking. In her spare time Rumina pursued another passion, a study of traditional Zanzibari door designs. Meticulously, while Ramji read or watched television, she would reproduce, with pencil on paper, from photographs and from memory, and from drawings she received by mail, doors covered with intricate floral and abstract motifs.

On Fridays she would come to the Company offices in Santa Monica after work, and if it was late they would sit outside on a bench and watch people emerge from the Shamsi mosque next door. A couple of times, if it was early enough, she urged him to go in – saying, They are your people – and he did. At times she brought food for the mosque, this being the Shamsi tradition, though quite alien to hers. The prayer hall had been converted from a warehouse, using wood panelling, broadloom, and drapes, and minimalist furniture consisting of low tables for ceremonies, and a podium; at the entrance were display cabinets, a notice board, and a book table. Sometimes, as Ramji and Rumina sat watching, older folks in their walking shoes would emerge from the mosque and gather outside, then walk around the parking lot a few times, to practise for a walkathon that was scheduled for some weeks away. This was a far cry from the little mosque they used to run in the music library at the Tech in Cambridge, Massachusetts, when a presence of twelve was considered a crowd, and Sona was mukhi, the presider. Nowadays a presence of a hundred was considered paltry and lamentable. People of the Community all over America were questioning their identities, reading up on their history, and even — as Sona claimed — rewriting it.

Is one entitled to this happiness? I was taught of second chances but only when the outcome was spiritual. The world is a prison, we were taught, existence is bondage to the body. Those who are wise opt out of involvement in it, and so they escape the endless cycle of birth and rebirth. *That* was your second chance — to opt out. But a happy rebirth, a second chance to a life of *this* world, to sensual, homely happiness? It goes against everything we believed in.

But one cannot completely detach oneself from one's previous existence, he knew that. He had had a wife, and a home, for thirteen years, they had a set of twins who would soon reach their teenage years. He could recall vividly the first news of their conception, the first sight of them on ultrasound, their first day in school. He could not pass by a sporting or a children's clothing store without, instinctively, thinking of their needs. They were a part of him. He now called them on Sundays; Zuli would pick up the phone and, answering his query with a curt, "I'm fine, thank you, and you?" hand over the phone to Sara or Rahim. He hoped he would be able to spend some time with them before they grew up, that Zuli would not come in his way. What influence he'd had she had not much cared for.

Gradually over the weeks Ramji and Rumina began to reconcile themselves to that past, which had once caused a painful rift between them – a past involving the violent revolution in Zanzibar and her father Sheikh Abdala, who had been one of its leaders; together they began to undo the potency of their memories of that terrible episode of the forced marriages, which had installed the Sheikh as an embodiment of evil in Ramji's mind.

When Ramji was growing up, the island of Zanzibar, although it had exotic associations elsewhere, did not capture the imaginations of those who lived on the mainland across from it, in Dar es Salaam. Its importance had been in the past, in the days of its slave market, when it was an urban commercial centre, while the mainland was still tribes and villages. When he was a boy, Zanzibar, *Jungbar*, was a laid-back kind of place, an island in the sun some fifty miles away, where the ships stopped on their way to Mombasa, Aden, and Bombay. It had the distinction that its Indians spoke a curious blend of Swahili and the Indian language Cutchi. There was the vague knowledge around that it had an American tracking station, and it was a free port. But it was basically a backwater, which routinely got trounced in soccer by the other East African countries. Then one morning in January 1964, Zanzibar – tiny, friendly *Jungbar* – was on everybody's lips: it had become the site of a bloody revolution, every radio station had carried that news. And the amiable voice on Zanzibar Radio itself had been replaced by the harsh tones of someone calling himself the Field Marshall, giving notice: All you imperialists, your days are numbered.

Worried faces appeared everywhere on the street where Ramji lived – a lot of people had relatives on the island. Many of the older folk, including his grandmother, had in fact immigrated to Zanzibar from India, before going on to Dar and other places on the mainland. What Ramji recalled clearly of that January morning of the revolution was that the Arab restaurant down the road where he went to buy bread or maandazi for breakfast did not open.

The days that followed were filled with news and rumours about the revolution. The new government was African; the ousted one had been backed by Arabs, who had ruled the island for more than a century, so there seemed to be some justice to the change that had taken place. But the refugees who came pouring in to their relations' homes brought stories of rapes and killings and plunder. According to the newspapers, Cubans, East Germans, and Russians had been sighted on the island. Not long afterwards, Tanganyika, the neighbouring mainland country, formed a federation with Zanzibar, perhaps to neutralize a communist threat, but the new country so formed, Tanzania, rapidly turned socialist. The Chinese soon arrived and were best friends. And the American ambassador in Nairobi, William Atwood, wrote a book called *The Reds and the Blacks* to explain the situation back to his people; it was banned in East Africa.

One of the leaders of the Zanzibari revolution was Sheikh Omari Abdala. Ramji remembered reading the issue of *Time* that had given the Sheikh's biography and called him one of Africa's most brilliant politicians. Apparently Sheikh Abdala had gone to university in Moscow, and a few days prior to the revolution he had returned home with a Russian wife.

And then, some years later – after so many people had fled the island in fear (and when so many still continued to flee it), after the seizure of so many properties and businesses by a dictatorship, and when so many languished in jails – *that* happened: the forced marriages. It was 1972 and Ramji was in Boston when he read about them in the newspaper clippings his grandmother sent him. Five members of the Revolutionary Council had each claimed for themselves, by decree, a young teenage girl from the Indian community as a bride. The youngest of the men was Sheikh Abdala, in his thirties; it was he who had announced this first bold step in a bid to integrate the races. The oldest of the men was in his sixties. All were married, some had more than one wife. In the weeks that followed, two of the girls, including Abdala's coerced bride, killed themselves. Finally, some months later, Sheikh Abdala was assassinated by a brother of the girl he had married by force; the killer was shot dead by bodyguards.

Sheikh Abdala left behind a daughter. Her mother, Elena, had gone back to Russia in 1967, when Rumina was two.

Late one night, they were sitting on the sofa, side by side; she with her back against the cushion, her legs crossed under her, and he having turned to face her, caressing her knee.

The past swirls in dark eddies around us, he thought, but we have to take the menace out if it . . .

I don't believe in murder or assassination for any cause, but when I heard of your father's killing, I quietly celebrated: a warm feeling in the heart, like a glass of eggnog on a chilly December night. Can you believe that, Rumina? I could have stood a round of drinks were I so inclined, I felt like running out into the street and shouting for joy, O my wish has been fulfilled, someone finally went and got one of those lecherous bastards. And it is his daughter I'm making love to . . .

"He loved me," she said of her father. "He played games with me and told me stories. And I loved him. I remember him clearly – I was six when he was killed. It happened at the airport, he had just returned from Dar es Salaam. They rushed me to the hospital, from home. I had never seen him in pain before, and there he was, helpless on a hospital bed, doctors and nurses around him, and tubes coming out of him. He held my hand and I climbed on a stool so we could see each other."

"And . . . ?" Gently – we're talking of Sheikh Abdala, but he was also her father.

"I looked into his eyes. They were wet, gleaming . . . I knew my father was crying. I still wish I could know what he was trying to tell me."

Two tears rolled down her cheeks. She wiped her eyes and he took her hand. She looked at him gratefully.

He asked, after a while, "And the girl he married . . . do you remember her?"

"Yes, I remember her. At meals, and sometimes playing with her. She was a lovely girl, Zainab, thin, with long hair down to her waist which always took a long time to wash. I wanted her so much to be my sister. My father loved her, I know that."

Did *she* love him? – Ramji wanted to ask. That man whose memory I've hated for more than half my life. Instead he said quietly: "But can you justify taking a girl by force – at gunpoint?"

Rumina's eyes widened and she drew a quick breath – Is this the end of our relationship, Ramji thought in a moment of alarm – but she recovered.

"No. But in a year or two she would have been married off by her father, against her will, most likely. I'm just giving you another side to the event. You don't know her family, I did. And my father had known the family a long time, they used to be neighbours, he had seen Zainab and liked her . . ."

She was crying now, and Ramji took her in his arms and held her. "It's all right, Rumina — we have to be able to talk about it . . ."

She is humanizing him for me, he thought; and it feels strange to see Sheikh Abdala as a loved and loving father.

Rape was a heinous crime then, not so routinized into our language and consciousness as it is now. Of course we believed in virginity then, the purity and sanctity of women; rape was worse-than-death. But was it the idea of black, communist too, impregnating white, Indian, virgin, that made the crime seem even more terrible; made our — my — horror and anger so obsessive? Perhaps there was a twinge of racism in my reaction? But still, what justifies such an abduction of a girl from her home, her family, her hopes and dreams?

"And your mother — she never tried to contact you at all? Did you think of visiting the Soviet embassy?"

She shook her head. "She didn't contact me — and she must have heard about my father's death. I have no memory of her. Until I was ten I believed that my mother had died, and whenever I formed a picture of her, I would imagine someone who looked like Zainab."

After her father's death she was brought up by Zainab's people, the Gulamhusseins. They treated her well, she said. Her father had had two brothers and a sister; every Eid her uncles came by to give her gifts of money. Only when she was much older did she realize that Zainab's family had taken out insurance in adopting her — after all, one of them had killed a member of the first Revolutionary Council.

When she was ten the family moved to Dar es Salaam.

"We lived opposite Odeon Cinema," she said, her face lighting up, "but we were not allowed to see movies. My guardians — the

Gulamhusseins — were very conservative. Once, though, a few of us girls from the family stole into the women's show, wearing veils to disguise ourselves, and we saw *Pakeezah*!"

She was sent to the International School, with a team of other girls in hijab-headscarves. It was here, as a teenager, that she recovered her African identity — she learned about the history of Zanzibar, its slave trade and its domination by Arabs from Oman; she learned about who her father was — a son of a dockworker. She gave up her adopted last name, Gulamhussein, for her father's name, Abdala.

"And Darcy? How did you meet him?" he asked.

"The International School organized a trip to Europe for the twelfth graders, and those who couldn't afford the ticket were told to seek sponsors. My family wouldn't pay for my ticket. So I went to Mr. Darcy's newspaper office and asked him for a job. 'Can you type?' he asked. 'No,' I said. 'Even if you could, I don't have a job,' he told me. I broke into a giggle. But he did find me a sponsor. Only later I found out it was his son Amir, in America."

There were questions he had, but didn't want to ask, and there were thoughts he had best put aside for another day.

And then one day they put the past finally behind them, after he confessed to her his own terrible thoughts about her father. They had come to visit the Yoga Shrine on Sunset Boulevard one Sunday, and as they sat on a stone bench in a cool shaded spot, tucked away among palms, pines, and banana trees, watching the peaceful water of an artificial lake, suddenly he could no longer hold his secret inside him. He told her how he had rejoiced at the news of Sheikh Omari Abdala's murder.

"I had to tell you — be absolutely honest with you. This is where *I* come from, what I am. Please don't hate me for it," he said in a low voice.

She sat motionless for a moment, then leaned her head on his shoulder, tears running down her cheeks.

"How can I hate you?" she said. "But it's over now, isn't it?"

And he met her look and said, "Yes, my dear, it's behind us."

3

Ramji had come from his previous job with a detailed knowledge of the niche markets for political books and magazines that the Company could tap: the left and radical; the academic and multicultural; the ethnic. Within weeks of his arrival he had worked out promotional strategies for both the magazine and the books. He succeeded in having *Inqalab*'s look changed from that of a tabloid to a standard newsmagazine. The emphasis, Darcy said, should be not on shrillness but credibility.

The magazine's contents were no more radical or extreme than those of half a dozen or so periodicals, or some of Chomsky's books, which you could pick up a few blocks away at Santa Monica's Promenade on Third Street. But the distinction was that *Inqalab*'s perspective was not entirely American, and it was not delivered from the distance of high objectivity. The magazine's concerns were more rooted in issues pertaining to the so-called Third World, issues to which Darcy with his first-hand knowledge of Africa brought a sense of immediate reality; the (occasionally unbridled) passion with which *Inqalab* expressed itself was due to the memories of racism and colonial domination that all four of its principals could attest to.

Of course, the new man on the Company masthead had to live with certain compromises, tolerate some ideas that made him squirm, allow his name to endorse some opinions with which he did not quite agree. Basu's ardent and earnest Marxism, for one, seemed as out of place in the world around them as the *Daily Worker* would be on the trading floor of a stock exchange. (Though Ramji liked plump Basu, a gentle man, in his white shirt and black pants and threadbare grey woollen Indian waistcoat that was a symbol of his devotion to his homeland. He was from Calcutta, and like many compatriots of his whom Ramji had met, he operated with the happy presumption that a nice guy like you obviously thought the same as he, how could it be otherwise, it wasn't even worth considering: didn't you share ethnicity, a history under the colonial yoke, Third Worldness? There.) Zayd bristled on matters concerning Islam. And terrorism was a subject too lightly taken up by all three editors: not, they would insist (oh, no), to condone, but to understand the causes. For Ramji there was something disconcerting in this attitude; how far was understanding from actual sympathy, and then, down the slippery slope, condoning? And what was one to make of the gentle Basu's humorously stated though nonetheless cynical aphorism, "Today's terrorist, tomorrow's statesman"? But Ramji was convinced that the concerns of his co-principals for the wretched of the earth were genuine. To him they were far truer than the reckless, spoilt, and ultimately fickle radicals of the sixties – his former roommate Shawn Hennessy came to mind – who had (having awakened from the acid trip of commitment, as it were) scurried behind cover of nostalgia and academic analyses while rejoining the ranks of the world's affluent.

And so, in spite of a few misgivings, Ramji held firm to the belief that in coming to Inqalab International he had rightly followed a destiny, heeded a call of conscience. In his desperate desire to believe thus, he could not see those doubts for what they were: gaping holes in his idealistic universe.

One Saturday afternoon Darcy was a speaker at the Tomonaga College of Applied Arts in a seminar on American policy in Africa. A small thin figure in his trademark beige suit, with red tie on white shirt, he stood at the side of the table of speakers, half-turned towards the white board behind him as if at any time he would go and write something on it for emphasis. The bony right hand would move as he spoke, but not enough to distract, two long fingers stretched as if holding a cigarette (which he must have done in his younger days). In that rich voice of his, with its distinctive crackling edge, he seemed to have the large audience, who almost filled the hall, mesmerized, giving instances and reminiscences of imperial practice gleaned from over four decades. "And I asked the ambassador – whom I met again in Virginia not long ago – I asked him, 'Did even our most cherished freedom-fighters have a price in American dollars?' And he said to me, 'But they were among our cheaper investments.'" Someone from the audience finally asked him why he was here, in this America he considered evil. Which question he dismissed easily with "But Sir, America is everywhere. What better place to speak about its sins abroad than right here at its heart." A helicopter passed low overhead and he, making reference to the famous murder trial going on a few blocks away, said,

"There's another Simpson juror being sent home," drawing a laugh. That was vintage Mr. Darcy, in new surroundings, adapted quite well, thank you. He was a pleasure to watch.

Afterwards, he came and stood with Ramji at the tea table outside the auditorium and asked, "Well, how did I do?"

"Splendidly," Ramji replied.

Naseem the caterer came breezing in from outside to join them. "Don't stuff yourselves with these cookies, leave room for my famous biryani tonight," she said, speaking to Darcy and referring to a get-together at the home of Darcy's son that night. It was Ramji who was actually guilty, with a couple of cookies stashed in his napkin. She took one from him. A few people came by to chat briefly with Darcy, some others whom he must have offended pointedly avoided him; a Bengali Indian woman in sari stepped up and gave him a large hug. Then Darcy and Naseem drove off in her hatchback marked SANTA MONICA CATERERS, of which she was the owner, manager, and chef. Ramji stared after them, speculating on the relationship, and reflecting on this Darcy he found a little hard to reconcile with the image of the outcast radical he had carried with him since childhood and the provocateur he had seen performing so electrically earlier at the seminar.

From Tomonaga College Ramji walked over to the Promenade, where he bought all the radical magazines he could find and sat down for coffee. In the years following his marriage he had found himself embarrassed to be seen with such material; and what he had dismissed as mere rich people's toys in his younger days evoked in him responses that rather shamed him when he caught himself, as when lustfully eyeing other people's Land Rovers and BMWs.

His acquiescing to middle-class desires counted among Zuli's partial victories over him. She had wanted no trace of his political views to disrupt their relationships with their neighbours or, as she put it, pollute their children's minds. Once, he remembered, a few years into their marriage, she had locked him inside the house on the day of the protest march he had planned to attend after the American invasion of Grenada. And so now these magazines, a little more of getting back his own life. He read for a while before getting up to go. From one of the shops in the mall he was moved to buy a couple of baseball caps for his kids.

Ramji walked to the Company offices and tried calling Zuli in Chicago to discuss further his proposition that since now he was more or less settled, Sara and Rahim should visit him. Zuli had sounded reluctant the last time he presented this suggestion to her. Rumina had had no objection, had shown not an iota of jealousy; it was a wonderful idea she said. But no one was home in Chicago that afternoon.

He worked in the office till a little past five, when Rumina picked him up to go to Amir Darcy's house.

And yes, she said in answer to his question, they do seem to have a thing going between them, Darcy and Naseem. "I don't think the family's so thrilled about it, though outwardly they are all amity itself. How old would you say Naseem is?" Fifty, fifty-two, he guessed; and Darcy twenty years older.

Darcy's marriage had been controversial, Ramji recalled. There had been talk about "the woman," an enchantress who, through magical spells, had won over the brilliant young man that Darcy had been and induced him into marrying her. She had been a

Sunni Muslim and perhaps a little older than he. Since then, Darcy had lived at odds with his community. His wife had died a few years afterwards and had left behind a son, Amir, who had grown up and gone to America and become a dentist. Darcy became a solitary man, of radical and fearless politics. And now, Naseem? — how unlikely a companion.

Amir and his wife lived on the outskirts of Brentwood, an area currently under siege by journalists and tourists, for it was where the football star O. J. Simpson, on trial for a double murder, had his residence. Amir's Moorish-style white house had a massive studded front door that opened onto a long corridor, divided by an arch and decorated with Middle Eastern-type art objects on its white walls: a dagger; a painting of three women peeping out through their black veils; framed samples of Arabic calligraphy — all reflective of the Community's current fascination with its supposed origins. Amir's wife Naaz had come to greet them. She was a breathtakingly beautiful woman, with a husky, seductive voice; her black hair had just a touch of brown to lighten (or perhaps heighten) it, and she seemed to glide before them in an elegant cream silk top with matching pants. As they followed her to the kitchen and den area, where the others had gathered, their eyes fell on a slim young woman in a long yellow dress, her head covered in a printed silk scarf, very hijab-like. She was standing with Darcy.

"Meet my granddaughter Leila in the veil," Darcy said with a friendly grin as they approached.

The girl said firmly but with affection, "Bapa, it's not a veil, as you well know."

"Come and have a scotch — or something," Darcy said to them, adding for Rumina's benefit, "there is tropical punch too, and it's safe."

Darcy, out of his suit for once, was wearing a printed shirt over cotton slacks, and sandals. He helped them with their drinks, then came and stood between them, beaming, paternal. And fragile, vulnerable right here in the bosom of his family, Ramji thought, or is that simply how I want to see him? . . . But I've never seen him like this, a party man straight out of Hollywood, out of *Gatsby*!

Leila joined them and put a friendly arm around her grand-father, who stiffened instantly before yielding. She was a good few inches taller than he, and her angular face seemed to owe more to him than to her mother.

"Tell him why you cover your head," Darcy said to her, lifting her hand from him but holding on to it. "Maybe he'll drum some sense into you."

"Will you, Ramji?" she asked, in a voice spoilt and childlike. "Is that your real name?"

"Of course. And don't pay any attention to what your grand-father says, wear anything you like," he told her in a friendly, elder-brother way.

"But what *do* you think of women covering their heads in modesty?" she asked.

"Ramji thinks the hijab adds to a woman's beauty," Rumina said, teasing him.

"Is that how she snared you?" the girl asked him vampishly.

"Yes, I would say so," he said, and stopped there, unwilling to be drawn into further discussion on the desirability of the headdress. But he had his opinions, which she divined; and so she gave him a piece of her mind, which she'd obviously been itching to do.

"Nobody tells me to wear hijab – it's my wish. It's my Islamic identity. I follow the injunctions of the Quran for modesty – they are quite clear – and I make a political statement as well."

And she walked away towards her mother.

"Don't worry, it's just the current phase," her brother Hanif said, having come over, making a circular motion with a finger to his head to indicate his take on the status of her mind. He was a big strapping youth, darker-skinned than his sister, with jet-black gelled hair. Easygoing too, but with a certain vacuousness, a rootlessness of spirit perhaps: he was intensely inquisitive, not about what people did, but what they thought, no matter what the subject. It was a relief when he drifted off to corner someone else.

Basu and Zayd had arrived, Basu having come with his wife and daughter; Zayd's wife, who was American-born, apparently kept away from places where there were men and drinks. They did not have any children of their own but had adopted two kids from Pakistan. Zayd and Ramji had over the months settled into a mutual tolerance, a forced friendliness laced with the occasional sarcastic bite of a casual remark. To Ramji, Zayd was religious in the worst – that is to say, political – way; despite his loud professions of faith, there was not a trace of piety in him. Zayd dismissed Ramji as a romantic and not fully committed to the cause. The fact that he was not far off the mark in the first part of his assessment fuelled Ramji's ire.

Zayd was currently covering for *Inqalab* the trial of a blind Muslim cleric who was being held on suspicion of instigating the bombing of the World Trade Center building in New York City. He had just returned from Manhattan, excited by news of the cleric's previous association with the CIA. But Zayd's passion these days, which he shared with Naaz, was attempting to follow the trail of the Phantom Author, a status report on whom seemed to be the main attraction of the evening.

News about a phenomenon termed the Phantom Author had broken into the print media several months earlier. Also called the Holy Pimpernel, the Blasphemer, and much more by some of the more sensationalistic commentators, the Phantom had been mailing out anonymous public letters pertaining to the Muslim faith and, it seemed, offensive to many Muslims. Copies of each provocative letter were sent from a different city to selected and well-placed people, and to news and other organizations. Ramji had read quoted excerpts from some of these letters, but he had dismissed their author as an academic crank whose day in the sun would inevitably pass. But the Phantom continued to receive attention and to persist in his campaign. For Zayd he had become a cause. "You want a terrorist, here's a terrorist – bombing people's hearts and children's minds. What's the U.S. government doing?" Apparently nothing. Therefore, Zayd said, the Muslims should take it upon themselves to do something about that perfidious character.

The lights were dimmed for the evening's pièce de résistance. A slide projector was set up across from a bare wall. A slide was put on. A political map of the United States came up, on which several cities were circled prominently in black, with red lines of diverse lengths radiating from each. Zayd, who was an engineer by training, received from other Phantom watchers in the country regular reports of "sightings" – details about places where a letter had reached – and of simulation studies that were under way to calculate the home base of the mysterious writer. The map, he explained, standing beside it, was the telltale track left by the Phantom.

"With every new missive he tightens the noose around his neck," Zayd said dramatically, looping his own neck with his fore-fingers and thumbs.

"Is the man condemned then," Ramji murmured, thinking what a clever fool the poor mischief-maker had been and wondering what would happen to him if his identity were uncovered. Had he broken any law?

"Yes, he is condemned," Zayd said, and without further elaboration continued his discourse on the mathematics of Phantom detection.

"The question is, what are the correlations among the mailing points – the cities from where he mails those letters? What airlines service them, for example, and how conveniently? Do the points receiving the letters lead back to an epicentre, which is most likely his base? Remember, that point is real and he is working around it. The Phantom has been clever – he's mailed his letters only from the major cities; presumably, he's close to a major city himself. So you see . . . the noose tightens."

"You . . . you seem to have followed him pretty closely," Amir said admiringly, from the chair where he was sitting beside the projector.

There was the barest trace of a flinch on his wife's face at this brief stutter, which melted quickly into a look of affection. Amir, tall, fleshy, and bald halfway back, was well liked, a people person; a generous, uncontroversial man, the big breadwinner of his family.

"Yes, I have my own file on him," Zayd told him, "and there are definite patterns to his activities . . . like fingerprints."

"What will you do if you find him?" Ramji asked the question he had been toying with.

"Why, he should be exposed . . . to the people," Basu said. He turned to Ramji and added, "Let him face the consequences."

"Such as? . . ."

Naaz said, "When I was young, when a thief was caught in our neighbourhood the crowd beat him up. That was people's justice. That's consequences for you."

"But surely," Ramji said, this time to needle Zayd-the-hunter, "if we believe in political dissent, then there is room also for religious and cultural and all sorts of dissent. The point is, the Phantom should also be allowed to speak. No?"

Howls of protest and ridicule exploded around him: But he's gone too far! This is not dissent, it's violence, it's personal attack! He *should* be stopped! Punished! If that other satanic author had received his due —

Darcy was standing at the back of the group, near the doorway, a sardonic gleam in his eye, unwilling to come to Ramji's rescue; Rumina was beside Darcy and looking anxious. There was an embarrassed silence, then an eruption of good humour and fellow-feeling as dessert was announced.

"It's always nice to withdraw from a crowd and be alone, isn't it?" Ramji said to Rumina, echoing a thought he'd often had after a raucous party such as the one they'd returned from.

"Yes . . . ," she said, beside him, and he turned towards her, wondering what she was thinking.

They had gone to sit on the beach. It was a cool night and for a while they sat together in silence, wrapped in a shawl, watching the black form of the sea straight ahead; the tide was low, the murmuring waves far away. At moments like these, he thought, you can't help but become aware of your ultimate loneliness. . . . He gave her hand a squeeze. She had told him recently that she sometimes missed all the girls she had been brought up with; but then she added that that was a long time ago, they all had lives of their own, with families, and she had him. He had suggested once that they try and search for her mother, start by writing letters, but she had shaken her head. She did receive letters from Tanzania, but there was no one there really close to her now.

"Do you believe that life exists in the stars?" she asked at length.

"Yes, in some of them."

Following her eye he looked up at Orion overhead in the sky; a constellation, he told her, known to Indians as Trisanku, the remains of a mortal abandoned both by man and the gods.

There came the sound of voices; low, but fairly close to their right, from a man and a woman, and they both turned to look. The couple was some twenty yards away. Perhaps they had been there all the time. The man was stark naked and crouched on his knees, visibly hard and primed for the woman who lay under him on the sand.

"It won't do to disturb them now, will it," Ramji murmured, turning away.

Rumina looked at him and nodded. He held her close, and they kept their eyes averted from their neighbours.

4

Darcy was telling his life's story; but in the manner of the preacher he had once been, he began with an anecdote that at first seemed to have nothing to do with the subject.

A long time ago, in the 1920s, there was an old white house on a beach in Zanzibar that was for many years known to be haunted; the ghost was that of a German diplomat. This ghost of a white man would appear in European-style white attire, complete with a sun helmet, called the topee, and shoes. He was tall, and seemed nimble and athletic. At nights he liked to stroll about in the compound, sometimes pausing for a drink from the well there; during the day he could be seen through the windows walking inside the house. Finally, a local exorcist claimed to have got rid of the ghost in the house, and a wealthy family rented it for the use of a young couple who were getting married. The wedding festivities were held in the house, and it seemed even then that something was not quite right. A cauldron of wedding biryani was first found to be missing, and then after much hullabaloo, during which the servants swore their innocence, the food was discovered in a room on the second floor. More surprisingly, the door had to be broken open — it had been locked from inside. How did the food get in there? It would have taken six strong men to carry the steaming cauldron up the flight of stairs; but without being noticed? and the locked door from inside? But the festive spirit had peaked, there was no inclination at this jolly hour to probe further into the strange occurrence. Food was served and the celebrations proceeded well past midnight. Not long after they were over, and the guests and families had departed, leaving the couple to their house, at four in the morning, just when the muezzin was beginning his call to prayer, a long and chilling cry tore into the quiet hour. People came running from all directions towards the source of the sound, the house on the beach. The sight that met them was horrific. The bride had been thrown clear through the couple's window and landed close to the well, the length of her trajectory suggesting superhuman strength on the part of the assailant. The groom was a nervous wreck, muttering incomprehensibly. He never recovered, and he never told exactly what had happened. But the fact came out that the German had been a homosexual; and after that terrible night the groom was rumoured to have become a homosexual too. In fact, years later, as a tramp in Dar es Salaam, he attained notoriety by trying to waylay boys outside a local school, and the boys in their turn teased him mercilessly. Aside from this proclivity he was supposed to be simply crazy.

"The exorcist was my father and the groom was my uncle," Darcy said, speaking in the apartment of Rumina and Ramji, where he'd come to spend his Sunday afternoon.

Darcy had called up Rumina during the week and suggested the invitation. "We can talk about the past, and listen to music from Zanzibar, and I can get to know you and your man better. Just make sure you have a bottle of scotch handy, I'll pay for it of course." And she, devoted to him, sensing his lonely call, said that, of course, he was most welcome to visit them.

Naaz and Naseem brought him over. The two women were on their way to the Golden Club's practice for the Friendship Walk, which had been organized in aid of international relief and also to give a positive image of the Community to the media. A man from the *L.A. Times* had promised to show up today and Naaz as the Community spokesperson was excited and all dressed up for the interview, in designer sweats, a thick girlish hairband over the head and a gold bangle on one wrist for good measure. The Golden Club members were fifty-five and over, and Naseem was their volunteer chaperone and trainer though, as she reiterated, "I still have a ways to get there." Naaz, in her early forties, had an even longer way to reach the Club age.

As soon as the two women left, Darcy nodded to Ramji, who brought out the scotch. And the old man, clearing his throat after a sip of the lubricant, began his prologue. Ramji and Rumina sat in rapt attention in front of him, thrilled at the privilege of hearing his confidences.

"I know the story – or rather, I've heard it told – though not the part about the man being homosexual," Ramji said.

Darcy nodded, saying, "Spoils our good image of ourselves to talk about homosexuality. We considered it evil or laughable – still do, sometimes." He threw a meaningful look towards the outside door in case Naaz and Naseem had stopped there on their way out, to eavesdrop.

Darcy was born in Bombay, he said, and brought to Zanzibar as an infant. His family were missionary traders, servicing the Indian Ocean from Calicut to Zanzibar throughout the nineteenth century, perhaps even earlier. His father Sherali, however, decided to settle in Zanzibar. He was a clove and cashew merchant and a renowned exorcist.

As a young man, Darcy moved to Dar es Salaam, on the mainland, just prior to the Second World War. There he acted as his father's agent and became a respected preacher.

Did he also exorcise ghosts, they asked. He looked distant, didn't give an answer. Perhaps it should have been obvious; it wasn't, quite.

He said instead, "Our people were backward. Religion and superstition were the same for them. There was no recourse to philosophy. Only magic and miracles. And blind worship. And the sins of poverty – envy and backbiting and inbreeding and intolerance. Any criticism of the Community and there would be a full-scale riot. I'm afraid I was no different – at first."

There was a group of educated Indians in town who used to meet and discuss independence for India. What he heard about their arguments attracted him, and he joined the group. It was low-key; this was after all wartime, and there was concern about government spies; Gandhi and Nehru were in jail in India and Jinnah had formed the Muslim League. Immediately after the war, Darcy went to London to study law. But he returned a few years later, before he could get admitted to the bar.

Why? He didn't say. Those must have been exciting times, Ramji imagined, picturing a young Darcy railing against British imperialism at Hyde Park Corner every Sunday. What colour suit did he wear then? And whence the name "Darcy"? Was there such a name in the tradition? Darcy was not one to tell all, to share the intimate secrets. It was impossible to imagine him insecure, afraid, though he must have faced his share of snubs by the whites in Africa. Perhaps in England he thought he could get away with his fair skin if he changed his name. Who would admit to such a weakness?

Ramji discreetly picked up the bottle of scotch and went to the kitchen to make tea. Naseem, flushed from the walk and in high spirits herself, soon came to fetch Darcy. Naaz had gone home disappointed. The *Times* reporter had stood her up.

"So the spin doctor was disappointed," said Darcy. He chuckled. "Has she tried *Time* or *Newsweek*?"

"I wouldn't say that in front of her if I were you."

"I won't. So how was your day?"

They left after the tea.

The man had been independent and forbidding once, had defied the highest authorities in his former country; in California, his former arrogance now seemed oddly to wilt under the various onslaughts from three women: Leila, his darling granddaughter, taller than him by almost a head, her hand placed patronizingly on his stiffened back (a gesture no one else could get away with); the small and compact Naseem, his over-diligent minder in sweatsuit and sneakers; the roundly sensual and scented Naaz, bullying, cajoling, confronting, making no bones of the fact that his cause was bunk and he was past it, even as his stature drew her respect and attention. Seeing him thus, taken over or besieged, you couldn't help feeling sorry for him: there is no getting past growing old, and dependent.

Rumina would graciously withdraw (or be nudged aside, as Ramji observed), whenever the three women approached Darcy in her presence, and watch sometimes with that dimpled smile she carried when she was with him. To them she simply didn't belong, wasn't community, family, or even race.

Darcy adored her and grew attached to her and Ramji's company, spending many pleasant hours in their living room or sitting with them for coffee somewhere. Among them there were things to talk about, to remember. Darcy was their past, a rich source of history, and there was a wholesomeness to sitting before him and listening to his stories. He could recall Ramji's parents: father a civil servant, mother a secretary who wore short hair and dresses, a typical Westernizing couple of their period. But he had not known them well, had never spoken to them, his preoccupations had been elsewhere. Darcy admitted once that Kulsa Bai's — that is, Ramji's grandmother's — spells seemed to have worked on his back problem, despite his scepticism. He also remembered a press conference given by Rumina's father Sheikh Abdala, remembered shaking hands with her mother Elena at a reception at the Soviet embassy in Dar.

Sometimes Darcy would fall silent, as when Ramji (sounding rather like a schoolboy) told him how he had held him in awe ever since he heard of the British governor putting him in prison.

Rumina jumped in: "Look — you've embarrassed Mr. Darcy."

And Darcy said, musingly, "We're all too human."

How human? Too human, Ramji would tell himself much later, only I was unwilling to concede him his humanity; I, who had never completely grown up, needed a hero.

One Friday evening the three of them sat on a bench outside the Company offices and watched Naseem's Golden Club come out from evening prayers and do one of their practice walks. Naseem marched in front holding a luminous baton in one hand, the gang of seniors straggling behind valiantly in a group, each wielding a baton of his own. Naaz, in an attractive green sari, traipsed after the seniors clicking away with her camera. Then she came over, in a cloud of exotic perfume, and spying an opening between Ramji and Rumina, squeezed into it, all warm flesh and silk. A very deliberate move, calculated to annoy, if not hurt, Rumina.

"So, you are finding out everything about the Darcy history — which is more than I am privileged to hear, let me tell you," she said to Ramji, pouting.

"Well —" Ramji said, but the old man cut in.

"Not that you've ever shown any interest, my dear."

"But I *am* interested, Bapa. I am married into the Darcy family, your history is *my* history, and the children are *entitled* to know of their background. Just tone down the politics —"

"I *am* my politics."

"And see where that's got you? This is no longer your silly sixties — it's the nineties. Your politics could have cost us our citizenship; and it gives the Community a bad name — do you know how much effort we are putting into creating a good solid image in this country?"

Naseem came over, having led her cohorts five times round the parking lot, and Naaz said, All right, let's go, and they all drove to Darcy's place. Once a month, on Fridays, the Darcy family met to spend an evening together, and today was that Friday. Leila was to come by later to show a video clip she had produced for a project on Muslim women; her brother Hanif would come with her; and Amir was away at a convention. Darcy sat on the broadloomed floor of his living room, leaning back on a bolster, as he railed against the free market and the IMF, the root source of the corruption in the country he had left behind. Naaz meanwhile went out and returned with an open bottle of red wine. "Isn't it a good thing you're out of it all now," she said to her father-in-law and flashed a conspiratorial look at the others.

Naaz had trained as a pediatrician in Vancouver, but had given up her career to run a lavish household and devote herself to the Community and her children. She would have liked nothing better than to knock the old man off his pedestal. And at times, when she had him in her presence, it almost seemed that she had succeeded.

Amir and Naaz believed that due to his politics, Darcy not only endangered his life (he had been beaten up twice in his career, the second time not long ago after he wrote an exposé on the business practices of a local consortium), but also risked not being allowed to come to the United States (he published a story that offended the U.S. embassy). The story that offended the American embassy concerned the so-called Pork Riots.

In a suburb of Dar es Salaam a Christian butcher gave a piece of pork, apparently out of mischief, to a Muslim boy who had been sent by his mother to buy some beef. Within the hour, in the ensuing riots, the butcher's shop was burnt down. A demonstration was organized the next day in the city against the sale of pork, during which some very suspicious-looking young men were sighted. They looked foreign. You could tell foreigners by their clothes, and their walk. There is a typical Dar es Salaam walk, a lazy amble, and these men didn't have it. Their clothes had designer labels. They were fair-skinned and dark-haired, some of them had beards. Middle Eastern money had been pouring into mosques in recent years; religious animosities, Muslim and Christian funda-mentalism, Canadian and American quacks with miraculous healing powers, had all been on the increase on the local scene. The young men in the demonstration were reported by some media to be Iranians. But Darcy produced a report claiming that two of the young men had been interviewed in his presence, enticed upstairs to his office by his two female assistants, and had boasted of having come from the United States. He concluded that they had to be American-hired agitators.

The American embassy protested; and a local man gave an interview in which he said that all the *gasia*, the palaver, was about nothing, his nephew who lived in America had simply brought over the Iranian boys as his guests to the country. The story sounded fishy, the man was not available for further interviews, and so Darcy's paper, the *Clarion*, did not retract its version. Its editor and proprietor, however, was a little apprehensive. His visa application to go and visit his grandchildren was pending at the American embassy.

But the Americans did not make life difficult for him. The visa arrived without delay, perhaps was even hastened. He had applied for a resident permit, a green card – so he could begin to spend long periods with his family. On the day he went to pick it up (he said he felt like an outlaw in the castle of the Sheriff of Nottingham), he was invited to meet the cultural attaché, Darlene Blake, a heavily madeup elderly woman. In the course of this interview, Mrs. Blake, treating him with a deference that accorded with his age and status, gave him a short list of addresses of foundations and people who might help him put his media experience and activism to use in the service of the immigrant community in the States. He was not unappreciated, her manner told him; and there were more sides to America than he might have realized. It occurred to him, though, that the addresses had possibly been given to him to keep him out of trouble, perhaps even for his own good.

In Los Angeles, of all places, in his son's home, he found himself in the midst of the Community, which he had shunned in the past because of its narrow-mindedness and backwardness. His daughter-in-law's false piety repulsed him, her interest in the Third World was a public-relations gimmick. In his new home in affluent Brentwood he was irritable and unhappy, at a loss for what to do.

This was when he discovered the newsmagazine *Inqalab* and became friendly with its editors, Zayd and Basu. It was, despite its limitations, tailor-made for him. With his experience and abilities, what could he not do with it! What he needed was a sponsor, to help him get the paper out of its financial hole and put him in charge.

He wrote without much enthusiasm to the addresses he had been given, and was surprised when he received two replies to his queries, both of which required him to travel for interviews. The first of these was from an elderly woman, a former volunteer nurse in East Africa. Darcy spent a week at her farm in Virginia and nothing much came of the visit besides goodwill.

His second interview was in Houston, with an outfit called the Overland Foundation. He was sent an airline ticket, given a room for a night in a high-class downtown hotel. When he went for his interview he was met, much to his surprise, by a man who turned out to be an educated and cultured Pakistani, and with whom he shared a love for Persian and Urdu poetry. By the end of the interview, Darcy had obtained a commitment for assistance if he took over Inqalab International and expanded it to include cultural publishing to benefit ethnic communities.

Darcy was a professional newsman and brought to the journal a vital credibility. It was a measure of its success that it reached far enough and was believed. But as subsequent events went on to prove, that success was ultimately its tragic failure.

5

On the night of January 20, 1995, a Friday, in the main street of the town of Ashfield, Michigan, a bookstore was bombed. The blast demolished the front end of the store and a portion of the residence above it, killing all the occupants, a family of three. In a picture that shocked the nation and provoked a presidential remark, the upper portion of a woman's body was shown among the wreckage, the rest of her body presumably blown away by the explosion.

This was the climax of the letter-writing campaign that had become known as the Phantom Affair; or rather, in retrospect, this was the first of its two climaxes.

In the weeks following, Ramji would stare at that picture, close up, many times over; the shambles it depicted would seem to him a visitation from the past come to make a mockery of his new life, the second chance he had given himself. But he'd first caught that grisly scene on TV on Saturday night, the day following the bombing, after the president's comment. The news depressed him. The tragedy of the dead family was real, and poignant enough, though in the scheme of things not an unusual news event for the small screen. But he was bothered by the possible consequences of the incident. By its connection to the Phantom Author, it was bound to touch the lives of all Muslims on the continent, good and bad and apostate alike, from the mainstream to the heretical fringe. What possible end could the bombing achieve? Who could be responsible for the madness? Who *was* the Phantom?

Ramji had initially paid little attention to the Phantom phenomenon, but after he came to Los Angeles it seemed impossible to avoid keeping at least partly abreast of the Phantom's activities through Zayd's obsessive interest in them. No one else at the Company took the Phantom seriously, though Basu gave Zayd a sympathetic ear, and Darcy was mildly concerned that the magazine had not merited a Phantom letter.

Apparently inspired by the tactics of the notorious Unabomber, the writer – who signed himself simply "K. Ali" – had been targeting well-placed academics, newspaper editors, columnists, imams of mosques and church leaders, even chapters of B'nai B'rith, sending them his notorious communiqués, which always began with the words THE PEN IS MIGHTIER THAN THE SWORD. Each time, exactly fourteen copies of a single letter would arrive at different addresses in the United States and Canada. They were mailed from different cities. In one well-known letter, published in the *New York Times* and reprinted throughout the country, K. Ali had openly stated his mission, which was to disseminate arguments and protests against what he termed "the current Arabic-dominated practice, study, and interpretation of the Islamic faith."

"My aim in these letters is to ring the knell of freedom, call upon thinking Muslims of diverse cultures to declare a Boston Tea Party and throw overboard the tea of imposed colonial practices which are narrow-minded, backward, and opposed to new interpretations."

What was offensive to many Muslims (and what got Zayd's goat in particular) was the manner in which the author, in a bold expression of his freethinking, cited and pronounced extremely critical opinions on certain controversial incidents from the early history of their faith. These citations and opinions only reinforced the negative views of Islam currently in vogue in the Western world. The Phantom's extreme pronouncements inevitably were quoted and requoted, only to increase their offence in the eyes of concerned Muslims and their sympathizers. Undoubtedly there was a malicious pleasure to be had in the knowledge of hot-headed clerics and orthodox priests being subjected to such a provocation. The Phantom by his elusiveness had acquired an aura of mystery, and the media came to call him, variously, and sometimes gleefully, the "Holy Pimpernel," the "Unawriter," and the "Blasphemer." It was pointed out that the paranoid tone of the letters, the us-against-them mentality, was characteristic of terrorist thinking. But commentators also saw in the letters a "*cri de coeur* of a man or woman caught behind the prison bars of tradition and custom, too frightened to disagree in public." This image was popularized in a caricature of the author that appeared in many newspapers.

In academic circles, it became a matter of prestige to belong to the select few who had received the Phantom's attention. (The first letter, according to rumour, was sent to an eminent, but controversial, Islamic scholar at the Institute of Advanced Studies in Princeton.) Inevitably, meetings were organized by university and college groups to discuss the contents of the letters. One such meeting, at nearby Tomonaga College, was addressed by both Basu and Zayd. Ramji had not attended it, and consequently the gulf between him and Zayd was that much the wider. To Ramji it seemed wrong and dangerous to blow the issue out of proportion; and it was incomprehensible to him why Basu should involve himself, except out of typical left-wing sympathy. Ramji did think of asking his professor friend Sona to write a sober assessment of the Phantom phenomenon for *Inqalab*, but he recalled, with a startle, that some of Sona's views were not dissimilar to the Phantom's and thought better of it. Zayd would surely not take kindly to a serious consideration of the "cri de asshole," as he put it, in a magazine of which he was one of the editors.

There had been a public event to which the Phantom Author apparently made a visitation and turned the proceedings into a farce. The event was the annual meeting of the American Religion Society in New Orleans, at which, Ramji thought, Sona might well also have been present, because of his specialty. Late at night, copies of the Phantom's Letter Number 19 were slipped under the hotel-room doors of many of the conference participants (thus deviating for the first time from the usual method of dissemination). One of the recipients claimed to have seen an intruder in the hotel corridor at 2 a.m., whom he scuffled with and briefly apprehended, later describing the person as "a dark-skinned, though not entirely black, female." This description cast suspicion on the sole Indian and Bangladeshi participants, who in an emotional press conference vehemently denied association with the Phantom and condemned him. It dawned on the learned academics that in their excitement they had turned into hunters; they also realized that anyone could have walked into the hotel from the still-swinging Bourbon Street and delivered the letter.

As time went on, it seemed to Ramji that the mysterious messenger had became more important than the substance of the messages. After the learned commentaries and the liberal pronouncements of sympathy had been superseded by other matters in the press, there remained the contest between the Phantom and those determined to hunt him down. The hounds were out and panting, nostrils flared.

Although the federal authorities refused to consider the case as one of disseminating hate literature and to act accordingly, a profile culled from various sources, including crime experts, was in circulation for the benefit of the amateur sleuth. There were studies of the typefaces, the paper, the postmarks, even the fingerprints, not to mention the quirks of language and punctuation. Simulation studies from several universities were reported, all of them inconclusive though promising, with the arrival of more missives, more definite locations of "focal points" where the Phantom might be found. The Phantom was believed to be a man. His signature, "K. Ali," was a pseudonym. He was thought to be a mischievous, frustrated, and frightened academic versed in Islamic study. Evidently he had been to an American university. His knowledge of the sceptical, secular, and Western interpretations of Islam seemed thorough, greater even than his knowledge of the traditional ones. The contents of many of the letters — for example, a short piece on the compilation of the holy book after the prophet's death — were academically sound though less known even to the Muslim public. His knowledge of Islamic Studies departments and their staff seemed detailed and up-to-date. It seemed obvious from the way he berated the predominance of the Arabic language and tradition that the Phantom did not come from the Middle East. There had been suggestions that a divorced man without children or close family ties was behind the letters.

Perhaps the author had at last become wary of the hounds hotly on his scent. In his now famous manifesto, first published in the *Times*, he had promised a total of ninety-nine letters. But soon after the delivery of his Letter 33 there appeared a book, *A Personal Handbook of Dissent: 101 Letters*, reproducing the already published letters and adding new ones. This seemed to be the conclusion of K. Ali's campaign.

A publisher in Canada addressing an annual writers' gathering had protested passionately against book censorship. A few months later, she received at her office in Toronto three thousand books and a letter from K. Ali expressing admiration for her fine speech and requesting assistance in distributing the books. The proceeds from their sale were to be used in aid of children who had been orphaned as a result of the ongoing conflict in Bosnia. Simultaneously, letters were mailed from Seattle, Washington, to bookstores, with instructions on how the book could be ordered. The publisher, in a press release, said she did not believe that books should be suppressed for their contents, or out of fear of intimidation, and so she had distributed *101 letters* as quickly as possible. She wished she had not been selected for the purpose, and she had expressed no opinions on the book's message. It sold out in North America within a few weeks.

Within days after the book first appeared on its shelves, a store called Book and Video Haven in Ashfield, Michigan, was bombed. There seemed no doubt that the explosion was related to a provocative window display of K. Ali's work. There had been protests and a large demonstration in the town regarding the display, and the store owner had received threats. A media expert concluded that, judging from the size of the explosion, it was another example of an ongoing terror campaign by "Mideast nationals" in the United States. The FBI promised speedy arrests.

And so the self-styled liberator of Muslims from orthodoxy and Middle Eastern domination had set off something he had obviously not intended. But the cycle of events had to go on, reach its conclusion, and, in the process, would strike like a bolt of lightning a conspicuous and sympathetic target in its path.

6

*I*t was the following Monday.

Noon break began quietly at the Company offices, as always in an atmosphere of serene calmness, with a lull in the daily exertions, close attention paid to the simple needs of a packed lunch, and restrained chat in the large, bright common work room at the back. Ramji was on a high stool before a PC, contemplating the pages of a forthcoming catalogue of Company publications, Sajjad and John sat together munching sandwiches over sections of the *L.A. Week*, careful to curb the rustle of paper. Halfway through the hour Mohan arrived from the travel agency next door to tell the young men, whose mentor and hero he was, about his latest sexual exploit. The quiet was broken, but not shattered entirely, for he had a matter-of-fact, low-key manner of narrating even the most risqué of his adventures. This time he had met the perfect-looking chick, he said, a beauty with real class, a Catherine Deneuve look-alike (which did not mean much to his two young admirers, but they trusted his taste) in the Torrance public library, checking out tomes of Hegel and Kant. He had walked her to her bike outside.

He described for his rapt audience the natural unvarnished beauty of this woman, her quiet charm and grace, her long limbs and lovely blonde hair. After much difficulty (she would not return his phone calls at first) he managed to date her, and then he accompanied her to her apartment.

"And you made out." The two boys smirked, anticipating details of the feat.

"Hold on, guys, it's not so simple as that."

A teasing smile as Mohan waited for his cue.

"What happened? Give, man!"

"We made out, a little, not all the way, and it was nice, and we drank wine, and we made out some more, and it was going smoothly, you know, and then she stops. Just stops. 'What's the matter?' I ask her. 'Is it that time of the month?' And she said, 'You know I charge for my services.'"

"What!" "Wow" they exclaimed, and Ramji thought, At last a deviation from the script.

"A high-class hooker – probably earning her fees for a Ph.D. at UCLA. 'How much do you charge,' I asked her. She was gorgeous and having gone so far . . . oh man –"

"How much?"

"Five hundred bucks."

"*Five hundred bucks!*"

"And worth every penny, I bet – only I was broke . . . I've got to get my hands on those pesos, now."

Meanwhile a thirtyish, good-looking man had arrived. He stood just inside the room, watching the scene with amused interest. Mohan, becoming somewhat conscious of himself, took off, saying to Sajjad and John, "She promised a discount. Talk to you later."

Ramji looked at the visitor, feeling ridiculous at his own engrossment in the tale, and said, "It's nice to have simple obsessions —"

The man, who had been watching Mohan, turned to Ramji and said, "I would like to see the editor of *Inqalab* – Mr. Darcy —"

"I don't believe Mr. Darcy is in, is he?" said John, and Ramji shook his head. "Come, let's see — I believe the other two are around," and John took the visitor down the corridor. A minute later he returned, motioned behind him with his thumb. "He's with Zayd."

The matter should have ended there. John and Ramji began discussing the layout of the catalogue, Sajjad began tinkering with the imagesetter. Zayd's voice could be heard intermittently. Darcy was away at Stanford on assignment with the Africa Club. Basu was somewhere, buried in his room perhaps; the Bengali newspapers had arrived yesterday.

Some fifteen minutes after the man was taken to see him, Zayd came over to the backroom and beckoned from the doorway: "Ramji, come and listen to this."

As Ramji walked into Zayd's office, the visitor stood up respectfully, hesitated a moment, then stretched out a hand.

"Hi, I'm Ramji," Ramji said, shaking hands.

"Michel," came the reply, somewhat softly.

Ramji wondered, Have I heard right? and looked towards Zayd, who had gone on to sit behind his large desk. There was a computer monitor to one side of it, and in front of him the *New York Times* for his daily fix of international news. Behind him on the wall was a black and white photo of himself shaking hands with an Iranian ayatollah, pictorial evidence of a full interview which he'd obtained during a visit to Pakistan. That interview had been widely quoted.

The visitor had an angular face with pronounced cheekbones, a straight nose, high forehead, and thinning hair; and he was expensively dressed, in a sports jacket and jeans, and a collarless black and white checkered shirt; his platform shoes suggested vanity – he was not exactly short.

"Michel is from your home town – Dar es Salaam," Zayd said from his chair.

"Michel?"

"Former name Mehboob."

"I know you," said Michel, suddenly sounding animated as he met Ramji's look. "I used to see you around. My elder brother – Alnoor Somji – was your classmate, wasn't he?"

"Why yes," Ramji said, pleasantly surprised. "Isn't he in Calgary now? How *is* he?"

Ramji had run into Alnoor, his classmate of many years, once in Toronto, at a Community event, after a period of almost twenty years, and had barely recognized him.

"He's doing great," Michel replied, sounding more subdued.

"And you must have been the kid who used to follow him around when we were teenagers," Ramji said, with a gleam in his eye. "Well, what brings you to L.A., Michel-Mehboob? And do you get *Inqalab* where you are? Where is that – Calgary?"

"Michel comes from Michigan," Zayd put in.

There was an uncomfortable silence in the room, and Ramji felt the beginnings of uneasiness. He glanced towards Zayd, who for no apparent reason nodded at him. Michel was sitting with his hands between his knees, fingers intertwined, as if poised to speak his mind but holding back. A bro from Dar, thought Ramji, observing him, brother of good old Alnoor Somji, chartered accountant, about whom I could tell a few stories (just as he could about me). . . . Was Michel in some sort of trouble? What kind of trouble? . . . Perhaps the guy is simply broke and wants some money. No, he's too well-dressed for that. Not an immigration problem either, he looks savvy enough. Then what? Zayd, sitting back in his stuffed chair, contemplated them both thoughtfully. Ramji realized he had an elder-brother status with respect to their young visitor, which Zayd was in the process of exploiting.

"What's this about?" Ramji asked finally.

"You see . . . ," Michel began, "you see . . . ," looking guilty as hell, Ramji thought, and asked him: "What have you done?" And then, more gently: "Have you done something?"

"Nothing criminal, I assure you." He paused, eyed Ramji a moment, looking rather like a schoolboy, then he blurted out: "But they'll try to get everyone who made speeches at the gathering in Ashfield, Michigan —"

A long moment's silence. Zayd played with a pencil on the op-ed page in front of him.

Ramji said, slowly, "The bookstore bombing . . . ," thinking angrily, therefore protectively, How did this idiot get involved with that? and turned towards Michel for an answer.

"Yes," Michel said, leaning forward. "But I was in no way involved in that bombing — I swear."

I swear. That's what we would say as kids to give our word. I swear upon God. I swear upon my father, my mother, by my faith. But what does Michel's oath amount to, a man on the run . . .

Zayd was saying, "Michel has some information that he thinks should come to light. That's why he has sought us out – especially Mr. Darcy. It is about the Pork Riots in Dar es Salaam."

"But what do the Pork Riots have to do with the bookstore bombing?" Ramji asked.

"That's what I want to explain," Michel said.

Zayd continued: "He says his information deals with U.S. involvement with fundamentalists abroad. He also has his own ideas about the bombing. He wants to tell us about that and what exactly happened in Ashfield – before they start making the arrests."

"I'll wait outside," Michel said, pausing to eye them both before walking out.

Zayd went on in a lower voice, "He insists he'll tell the full story only when Mr. Darcy is here. I don't think it's a bad idea to wait – Mr. Darcy will be back tomorrow. And then we may well have a whale of a story on our hands. . . . But meanwhile" – and there came a significant look on Zayd's face – "meanwhile, Michel must have a place to stay."

"I can't keep him," Ramji put in quickly. "I hope you're not suggesting that. Get that clean out of your head. Let him stay in some hotel, if you want my advice."

"Impossible," Zayd said. "He would have to give his address and a credit card and whatnot for that. I can't keep him. I'm travelling on Wednesday – besides which, Michel is your countryman, one of your Community –"

"That doesn't make him my *responsibility!*" Ramji's voice rose sharply, desperately.

Zayd was staring at him. "If you want, I can tell him to go," he said quietly. "Just say so."

Ramji looked away. To his right, facing Zayd and occupying a good portion of the wall, was the U.S. – a slide of which Zayd had shown with much enthusiasm at the Darcys' party several weeks before, to illustrate his lecture on the Phantom Author's movements. Ramji felt a chill in the heart. He couldn't believe what was happening.

"He is one of you," Zayd went on. "And he's probably innocent. He insists he is."

An appeal from a compatriot, a Community member; we were brought up to believe we are all brothers and sisters, we stand by each other. We come from the same neighbourhood, went to the same school and the same mosque . . . rows of fidgety boys sitting together on the floor, and a monitor minding you – how can you forget. You could end up losing your faith, but you would never really abandon a brother. Give him a place to stay in an hour of need? Surely this was the right thing to do. And so Ramji drove home with Michel beside him, prey to all manner of thoughts. He was dreadfully afraid. It was as if the blue skies of California had been shadowed by a sinister sepia tone and the world was not the same. Soon he was on Lincoln, caught in the afternoon traffic, heading south. There was no going back.

"You asked for Mr. Darcy when you came," Ramji said to Michel as they left the office. "You must have been surprised to find me there."

"I had no idea," Michel said, "until Zayd told me there was someone else at Inqalab whom I might know . . . real coincidence, meeting you here like this."

"It sure is," Ramji said dryly. After a pause, he added: "There must be something you were up to in Ashfield that made you want to leave town and come all the way to California. Can you tell me, what *was* it?"

This was perhaps more bluntly put than he intended, but he got a quick response:

"I made a passionate speech at a rally, and then I attended a meeting. That's all I did. I came here because of the story I have to tell. My version of the events will prove that I am innocent."

They had said nothing much after that, except for some perfunctory comments on local geography. Then Ramji told Michel that he lived with a Zanzibari woman who would also be Michel's host. Rumina had not been home when Ramji called from the office to explain about the guest who would be arriving with him.

Reaching Hermosa Beach, Ramji turned into Pier Avenue. He parked the car as close to the beach as he could and they walked out, Michel the embodiment of calm — even when they passed the two parked police cars which were a regular feature of the area at this time of the day (and which had quite slipped from Ramji's mind).

They arrived at the boardwalk and began strolling casually along it.

"Do you do this every day?" Michel asked. "Come here for a stroll?"

"Yes," Ramji replied. "I like the feel of the air here, and the sea. . . . Sometimes Rumina and I come here at night and watch the stars."

A couple of surfboarders were out riding the waves, a volleyball game was under way. A flock of squawking seagulls flew past.

"Tell me," Ramji asked quietly, "what exactly happened in Ashfield?"

Michel took his time before answering.

"The bookstore had on an offensive display of that book by K. Ali in its window."

"And?"

"Well, naturally the Muslims of Ashfield protested. The bookstore made the display even bigger and showy with more books about Islam that were offensive. The manager's a real right-wing jerk. There was a big rally with speeches. I called the book an act of terrorism and said we should defend ourselves from such acts . . . that the bookstore was aiding an act of terror." He looked up and said, "That's what your magazine *Inqalab* said, didn't it?"

"Well, *I* didn't say it."

Zayd and Basu had written that opinion, jointly, in an article, arguing that the book attacked what many people held dearest, which was their faith.

"Then what happened – how did you propose to 'defend' yourselves?"

"There was a secret meeting, to discuss strategy, what should be done to stop the display and sale of books, which I attended. Nothing came of it, just talk, the usual thing, everyone wanting to be heard. And then a few days later – the bomb. It took the whole town by surprise."

They stepped off the boardwalk and out onto the sand to avoid the joggers and the more intent walkers.

"Do you believe those books should have been destroyed?" Ramji asked, impulsively, not quite sure what he intended to make of the answer yet feeling a desperate need to know more about this visitor.

"I said so, yes, at the rally. I was angry. I'm not sure I meant it.

A lot of people were saying it. Strong feelings were expressed. But I was not involved in that bombing. You must believe me."

They had stopped, and Michel looked Ramji straight in the eye. "Not in any way," he said quietly but emphatically.

"You know who *is* responsible, though . . ."

"I think so. But I must tell that story from the beginning – it involves Mr. Darcy."

"In exactly what way does it involve him?"

"It's a long story."

"And your family – do they know you are here?"

Michel shook his head.

"Let's go home," Ramji said, and they started back to where the car was parked. They passed a florist, and Michel said he wanted to stop.

Rumina was home when they entered the apartment and Michel presented her with a bunch of carnations, saying "Enchanted." And Rumina was enchanted too. She took the flowers and gave a broad smile, saying to Ramji, "You didn't tell me we were having a visitor . . ." and to Michel, "Welcome, I'm afraid we are not prepared –"

"That's quite all right," Michel said, "but I must apologize for this unannounced visit –"

"Not at all," she replied.

Ramji said to Rumina, "I called before we left but you hadn't arrived yet." He explained that Michel was the younger brother of an old friend of his and had brought an important story for *Inqalab*. He needed a place to stay for a couple of days.

"You are our first ever house guest, please make yourself at home," Rumina said to Michel.

Ramji showed Michel to the spare bedroom. The two of them cleared it of the boxes and the various odd items which had come to be stored there over the past months, and they put fresh sheets on the bed.

That night, after a surprisingly relaxed dinner, they all watched the evening news, Michel wide-eyed and leaning forward with concern, Ramji worried to death and fidgety, ready to switch channels for Rumina's benefit, and Rumina grumbling: "You guys are always complaining about the media but you can't stay away from it." The bookstore bombing came up as a brief item towards the end of the newscast. The FBI officer in charge of the investigation reiterated the commitment of his agency to bring the perpetrators to justice, even if they had to be brought into the country from elsewhere. "Let me put it this way," said agent John Esposito, "our primary leads so far are to local extremist elements, but foreign agents or even governments have not been ruled out."

"Fanatics," Rumina said forcefully as she left the room, and then called out from the kitchen: "They give us all a bad name. I say, boil them all in hot oil . . ."

Ramji caught Michel's eye. "Don't give her even a hint, under any circumstances," he said, and got the brief answer, "Don't worry, I won't."

Michel seemed to settle in easily, unobtrusively. It was tempting to think of him as a boy. There was a naïveté about him, a certain delicacy. He had the relaxed manner of someone who'd never worked hard, but depended on parents or on girlfriends who didn't mind giving to such a sensitive soul. How did such a person become a suspect in the bombing of a bookstore? And, Ramji wondered, how did I become the one to protect him, and in my own household?

Here I am again, harbouring someone on the run from the police. The coincidence was laughable, were it not so dangerous. Twenty-five years ago, Lucy-Anne Miller had walked into his room and expected shelter because of the sympathy he had shown for her cause, if not for her methods; and now here was Michel. But Ramji didn't want to draw any quick lesson from this close analogy between two events so far apart in time; he had all his anxiety to preoccupy him.

And yet, when the three of them talked about the past, the lives they had left behind in East Africa, how the Community had established itself all across North America, and where various acquaintances had ended up, theirs seemed like a natural reunion of compatriots, with enough in common to last till eternity.

"I have a morning shift tomorrow," Rumina said, standing up. "I can show you around L.A. after that, Michel, if you like."

"No – that's not possible." This from Ramji, too sharply.

"Why not?" she asked.

"I . . . we have work to do, there isn't much time. We go to print Thursday and his story has to be in."

"That's right," Michel said. "But thanks."

There was a short silence while she pondered this. Her eyes found Ramji's.

"After the work then – you won't keep him all day – how about that?"

Ramji couldn't insist.

Later, in bed, she said, "He's such a gentle person, isn't he? So well-mannered. I can't believe he'd get involved in politics. What kind of story does he have, anyway?"

"Read about it in *Inqalab*," he murmured, trying to be flippant, then added, "I don't know the details yet . . ."

"He's quite young – I mean, not very old – isn't he."

"Yes."

And closer to you in age, he thought. Isn't he the type women can't help falling for? The sensitive helpless kind. Except you don't know what he's running from. If I told you now you'd need no convincing that the poor boy was entirely innocent.

From behind the door came the jingle of a TV commercial. A special offer, only on TV, not available in stores . . . with a free gift . . . shipping and handling . . . phone number repeated three, four, infinite times . . . after all, who can read a number this late at night?

I'm *afraid*, thought Ramji. I wish I could tell you that, but my dear I don't want to scare *you*, cast a dark cloud over your world. Why couldn't I have said, *No, no, no, I don't want to be involved? If you're even remotely connected with it I'm not interested, don't come near me, go elsewhere.* But he'd say, *I didn't do it, I swear, and I'm not a fugitive. At least listen to my story.* I have been trapped, but there must be a way out of this, it has to be handled calmly like a chess game, all variations considered.

The television's still on. The weather channel goes on forever . . . there's always the weather, it doesn't go away, merely changes. Strange, how TV sounds never become a murmur even when they are at their lowest. They needle and irk and drill into your bones, through the door, the skull, and simply drive you nuts . . .

Suddenly, uncontrollably, he gave a shudder. His throat constricted, he could not breathe. It took a moment to compose himself, and he let out a deep sigh. Rumina, beside him, sensed his anguish.

"What is it?" she murmured.

"Nothing," he said after a moment, his voice betraying all.

She took him in her arms, murmuring, "Tell me, *mpenzi*, tell me."

"It's just that I love you so much," he said.

"*Naijua*, I know."

"And . . . I don't want to lose you."

She snuggled closer.

7

The next morning Rumina had to leave early to go to work in Santa Monica. This was not her normal shift at the coffee shop, she had been called in an emergency to fill in for someone who had quit working there – a pattern that Ramji had found increasingly familiar in recent months. He was up with her, at seven, while their guest was still in his room. Do you want to meet for lunch? she asked Ramji as he saw her to the door, since we'll all be in the area? He made a face: Aw – I don't know if we'll be able to get away . . . sorry? That's okay, she nodded. They embraced, and she left.

By an arrangement he and Zayd had made at the office, Zayd had undertaken to call Darcy at his San Francisco hotel the previous night and let him know of Michel's arrival. So there was nothing else for Ramji to do but wait for Darcy to call as soon as he arrived in town.

There was no news on radio or TV regarding the bookstore bombing.

Ramji tried calling Basu, just so he could talk to someone and be reassured about his delicate situation, but Basu was in the shower. Ramji then got Zayd on the phone, and Zayd, who persisted in talking in code about "the package that's recently arrived from the east," assured Ramji that Mr. Darcy had been "apprised of the development," and not to worry. They had something precious in their hands, he told Ramji, it would make "glorious copy."

Soon after, Michel came out of his room. "Sorry I slept late —"

"Don't worry, it's not that late," Ramji told him.

Michel gave a brief nod. "Rumina's already gone, I see," he said, sounding a little disappointed. He volunteered to make fresh coffee and went to the kitchen.

Darcy finally called, at a little after ten. It would be prudent, he said, to meet with Ramji and their visitor at the Promenade in Santa Monica. Only he would come.

Ramji and Michel drove to Santa Monica, parked the car at the office, and then walked up to the Promenade. The meeting had been set for one. As arranged, Darcy was waiting for them at the corner patio table of a self-serve sidewalk café. He stood up, and, with a surprised look at Michel, as though he had expected someone different, said, "Well, well," and shook him warmly by the hand.

"And how are you?" Darcy asked. "You've come on urgent business, it seems."

"I've come for your advice and help, Mr. Darcy," Michel said with deference.

"Inqalab will do its best," Darcy replied, immediately putting a formal distance between himself and the visitor, as Ramji observed.

They picked up their coffees and returned to their table, and after a while Darcy turned to Michel and said, "So, tell us now what you have come to tell us."

Michel began straight off with a plain but loaded statement. For several years, he said, he had been involved in the activities of the Restore Iran Movement. By this revelation, he succeeded in quite stunning his audience of two, who had not the remotest idea of any such connection. Having made his impact, Michel had paused.

"And this pertains to the bombing in Ashfield?" Darcy inquired quietly.

Michel nodded.

"And, from what I've been told, also to the Pork Riots in Dar es Salaam. You were not there at that time, were you?"

"I was. I'll come to that."

"Hm." Darcy seemed lost in thought, but after a moment he nodded and said, "Go on, then."

The politics of Iran's Islamic revolution, and the Pork Riots in Dar es Salaam – Darcy had had a story to tell, linking the two, as Ramji recalled with excitement. That story had been Darcy's last journalistic coup in Dar before he left for the States. Darcy had boasted about it. And here was Michel making the same connection. It was now obvious why Michel had wanted to talk to Darcy in particular: Michel had been in Dar during the riots and he had known about Darcy's revelation in the newspapers there. A bit of Darcy's past, it seemed, had come stalking him. Incredibly, though, Darcy, sitting back in his chair, legs crossed, showed not a twinge of excitement as he let Michel proceed.

Michel's story began in 1969, when he was sent to school in Lausanne, Switzerland. There he met several Iranian boys and girls and immediately took a strong liking to them and their ways. He was intrigued by their country, and one summer he even paid a visit there. He spoke as if he felt that his roots lay there, which was highly unlikely given his surname, but neither Ramji nor Darcy challenged him. Michel returned to Iran a few years later to attend university in Shiraz. He loved the country, and during the five years he spent there, he learned the Farsi language. He also became close to a local girl, the daughter of a politician.

Later he went to study pharmacy in the States. Two years into his course the tragic (as he described it) revolution happened in Iran. He spoke of his grief at the loss of that beautiful country to religious fundamentalists. In Michigan, where he was at that time, Michel was introduced to the Movement.

And the girl? – Ramji asked. Michel said he had not kept regular contact with her, but after the revolution he lost touch altogether. Recently he had learned that she was married and living in the San Francisco area.

His manner was composed as he told his story, his voice remained flat and neutral despite interruptions from his two listeners. He wore denim jeans and a rugby shirt, shades in his shirt pocket, Gucci sandals. He could be in Geneva, Ramji thought. He doesn't look the least bit worried that at this very moment the FBI could be out looking for him.

Darcy, beginning to look more relaxed, would set off on the odd tangent, to discuss at length some aspect of the history of Iran (for one thing), before returning to Michel's story. There would be the trace of a smile on him, and the look of an indulgent father. He wore his trademark beige suit and red tie.

It was beautiful outside, sunny; not many people were about. Pigeons loitered between the tables looking for crumbs. Once, the sound of laughter a few tables away startled them, as if they'd been caught in a foolish, or guilty, moment. This had come, coincidentally, just after Darcy, inspired by mention of Iran and the ancient romantic city of Shiraz, all of a sudden broke wistfully into a few lines of poetry by a Persian poet.

"Why don't you tell us about the recent events in Ashfield," Ramji said to Michel, impatiently. "You can fill in the background later." He turned to Darcy. "We may not have much time – *those* events may soon catch up with us."

"There will be time," Darcy said. "Let him tell it the way he wants to. This way, too, he won't forget the details. And pardon my poetic digression – that seems to have irked you."

"Not at all," Ramji said, and lied.

Michel continued. He had obtained his nickname in school, in Switzerland; and he adopted it as his *nom de guerre*. They all had one, in the Movement – Michel, Pierre; Irma, Françoise, Debbie. It gave them a sense of professionalism, though most of them were hardly professionals. They were divided into cells. At the top – according to rumour – were some members of the Iranian royal family; but the man whose name was whispered as the real guy in charge was someone called Robin. He was believed to have been a general in the former Iranian air force.

Michel's involvement with the Movement was casual, during weekends only. But his Iranian friends devoted most of their time to it, and he joined them when he could.

In those first months in the Movement, he simply attended demonstrations in several cities. The Tehran hostage crisis was on, and there was an expectation that the Americans would attack the new regime. It was a godsend, this crisis, a strong ray of hope — and a weakness that the revolutionary government, out of sheer obstinacy, had exposed itself to. Those in the Movement wished fervently that at least one of the hostages in the American embassy in Tehran would die or be killed, to provoke a response from the U.S.; there was talk of sending someone, a suicide killer, to shoot a hostage and put the blame on one of the Ayatollah's followers, even of sending poisoned food parcels. Then the Carter fiasco happened, with the botched attempt to rescue the hostages, and a mullah was shown in the news exhibiting a dead U.S. marine — and even then there was no landing of troops.

They worked for Ronald Reagan, demonstrated against Carter; collected signatures at subways, exhibited photos of Iranian torture victims in shopping malls. After Reagan was elected president, the hostages were released, and those in the Movement knew that the long haul had now begun and counter-revolution would not come easily. That was when the cells tightened; the situation was grim, with a lot of waiting and no instructions. There would be small meetings — five to six people exchanging information. And then instructions began coming again, directed and regular.

He attended one military training camp, in Arizona, after which, under intense pressure from his family, he withdrew from the Movement.

The training was in weapons, yes. Handguns, grenades, machine guns. Workshops on explosives, which only a few were allowed to attend.

"Were you one of the select few?" Darcy asked, eyeing Michel intently.

"No." Straight, without a change in tone.

"Good. At least that simplifies matters."

At that, Michel coloured a bit and looked away, met Ramji's eyes. But by this time Ramji himself was feeling distinctly uneasy about Darcy. The man had been disruptive, and even flippant, with his lengthy digressions; he had taken time to recite poetry. He seemed utterly detached from the purpose of the meeting, at least as Ramji had envisioned it.

"Let's pause here," Darcy said, looking at the other two, "and discuss procedure for a moment."

It was agreed that Ramji would produce a written account of Michel's story, with the latter supplying the details as required.

"Details about that training camp in Arizona might be of interest," Darcy told Michel. "For example, were any Americans ever present there?"

"We saw them once."

"Where?"

In the log cabin that was the headquarters. A jeep and a sedan had come to the camp late one evening, and there followed a lengthy meeting in that cabin. This was just after the Carter debacle, and it was believed that volunteers would be dropped into Iran. So at night he and some fellow trainees walked towards the cabin in the dark, stopped some yards before a clearing, and watched. That was a U.S. army jeep. For sure.

Darcy nodded abstractedly, then he looked impatiently around, and outside at the street – they had been sitting at the same spot for a couple of hours – and announced, "And I'm all for a change of scenery now. Let's go to the restaurant across the street and have a bite to eat."

Ramji had come expecting to hear Michel's entire story that day, including his version of what had transpired in Ashfield. And Ramji had anticipated that soon, perhaps the next day, they would arrive at some sort of resolution concerning Michel and his story. And so he stared in utter disbelief as Darcy ordered a scotch with his sandwich; and when the man took his first relished sip, Ramji had no doubt that the day's proceedings were effectively over. What was wrong? Had he so completely misread the significance of Michel's arrival, the urgency of his circumstance – that he could be named a suspect any time in the bookstore bombing, and that he had come here to give a version of that event? Meanwhile here was Darcy holding forth on the Iranian situation before and after the revolution; asking questions, interested in everything about Michel's family background; taking delight in an account of Michel's experience at the Movement's training camp. (A bala-clava-clad Robin had addressed the recruits, in the company of a miniskirted woman in boots, who reputedly took one recruit to bed every night she spent at the camp.) One thing Darcy did not seem intent on pursuing was the last part of Michel's story.

Finally, Michel took a bathroom break, and Ramji had his chance. He turned to Darcy, saying, "We have to hear the full story as soon as possible. I think we have to decide upon a course of action."

"Don't worry," Darcy said. "There's time for it tomorrow. We can guess roughly what it's going to be, can't we? I'm sorry for the way I've been acting – but I'm tired now. I need time to think. We don't want to rush into anything. We have to know what this young man is about. I'm going to be making some inquiries." He looked pointedly at Ramji and asked, "But why did you take him home instead of asking him to stay at a hotel?"

Ramji explained why.

"No need to take unnecessary risks," Darcy said.

Ramji, to his own surprise, replied, "But he's not charged with anything."

"The question is, how did he end up in such a lunatic situation, involved with a book-burning rally."

Michel, having observed them in conversation, had strolled off outside. When he returned, they all agreed that the meeting would continue in Ramji's apartment the next morning.

Ramji drove home with Michel, as anxious as when he had first got up that morning. Perhaps, he thought, Darcy was right in taking things easy. Nevertheless, this was not the Darcy he had come such a long way to work with, someone who would have been delighted to see his story about the Pork Riots vindicated, someone who would normally have been alert as a hound to the prospect of an unofficial and perhaps darkly secret version of the events in Ashfield.

"What did you think of Mr. Darcy?" Ramji asked Michel. "Was he quite what you had expected him to be?"

"He's quite a cool customer," Michel said. "It's hard to say what he's thinking."

"You're right."

Did the magazine *Inqalab* have much impact on the Community in Ashfield, Ramji asked.

Only some people seemed aware of it, Michel said, he and his friends, and they used to discuss its contents.

He wanted to know more about Zayd and Basu, and Ramji told

him that they had founded the magazine as a cultural newspaper, with a very different name, when they were both in Queens, New York, in the eighties. Michel had been quite taken by their views on the Phantom, which he and his friends in the community had seen in *Inqalab*.

"Have you actually read the Phantom's book?" Ramji asked.

"No, but I've heard portions. They were read out to us at the rally."

"They can't have been too offensive if they were read aloud."

"They were," Michel said forcefully. "Have you read the book?"

Ramji took a long moment to reply. At length, he said, "Yes."

"And?"

"I can see how it could offend, but I didn't find anything that offended me." Some of the opinions expressed even seemed familiar to me, he might have added, but he didn't.

That night after dinner Michel helped Rumina with the dishes, and the two of them struck up a lively, intense conversation. He liked her, Ramji observed with a pang of jealousy, very much. Even when she told him to go inside and sit with Ramji, he insisted on staying to help her.

A ladies' man, as I suspected: What does she tell him about me?

She was beaming as she came in; he followed right behind her.

"Yes, I'd love to," she told Michel as she sat down on the love seat, across from Ramji, and Michel disappeared. "His girlfriend," she said archly.

Michel returned holding a small framed picture.

The two of them were standing side by side; Ramji was startled to see that she was a white American. She was slim and of medium height, with a scarf round her head and wearing a large red T-shirt, and she was leaning slightly towards Michel, her brown skirt reaching a little below the knees. Wisps of blonde hair showed from under the scarf, her blue eyes gazed intently at the camera, lips curled in a smile.

"What's her name?" Ramji asked.

"Shirin," he said, then added, "We met last year."

"She's very beautiful," Rumina said. "How did you meet – or are you not telling?" she asked playfully.

"You won't believe it – how I met her. It was through a personal ad."

That stopped Rumina in her tracks, her mouth gaped open in amazement. She turned to Ramji.

"Not the *Inqalab*," said Ramji; though the idea of having personal ads had been tossed about.

"No, a Muslim paper," Michel said.

"You put in the ad?"

"No, she did."

"What did she say?" Rumina asked. "I'm being nosey, aren't I?" She eyed him for a moment. "You don't have to tell us. Let me guess: Beautiful American Muslim – that's a BAM."

She laughed, and Michel said, "No. This is how it went, listen –" he closed his eyes, to recall, then recited, "– 'Muslimah, blue-eyed, slim, age thirty, looking for a good-looking Muslim man in thirties for possible marriage. . . .' I So I applied and we exchanged photographs and so on."

"Have you called her? Why don't you give her a call from here?"

"Maybe tomorrow. It's a little late now, there."

Ramji breathed out a sigh, watched Michel look gratefully at Rumina.

He had come to them like a spectre out of nowhere, or from TV-land, or the imagination. And his presence among them had grown. He was now a man with a past, and a photograph of someone he loved. He was one of them. It was not going to be easy to be rid of him.

8

*I*t was the middle of the night. Ramji sat up in bed. After a moment's hesitation, he slipped out and stepped quietly towards the bedroom door. He turned to glance behind him at Rumina; she had not stirred, was lying on her belly, one arm above her and over her pillow. Ramji went to the living room, turned on the light beside the couch, then from the bookshelf picked out a slim paperback book. It was K. Ali's *101 Letters* – its front and back covers a matte black, with no illustration, only bold white and red type, its spine green with black type. This little book, an argument in theology, history, and cultural freedom, had gone up like a missile and landed on a random target, the town of Ashfield, Michigan, causing disruption, taking three lives.

When news of the Phantom's book broke a few weeks ago, by the time Ramji arrived at Hooked on Print on Third Street to buy a copy it was sold out. There had not been many copies to begin with, Sam the manager told him. But – he put a hand under the counter, gave a shadow of a smile – he had saved "you guys" a copy. There was always a calm but knowing look on his face when dealing with people from the Company. A former radical perhaps.

Ramji had flipped through the book once, soon after acquiring it; he had been aware of some of its contents even before that, through Zayd's discussions at the office regarding the Phantom's letters. In his mind Ramji had always dismissed the author as some academic crank who had garnered undeserved attention. And yet Ramji had found himself in silent agreement with some of the opinions expressed. He would not have denied, though, that there were things said in the book that could offend some people. Rumina for one – she had been sitting with him when he first browsed through the book – had been offended by one passage in particular. Ramji turned the pages and found it, the Phantom's Letter 23 . . .

"Why don't you quote it?" Will asks.

Will Jones, the friendly federal inquisitor, who arrived one day with photographs of the bombed bookstore and said, "Tell me, how did the likes of *you* get involved in such an event?" and then became a regular visitor, presumably to record for his agency how a person like me – haunted by the ghosts of faraway places – ticks in its alien manner.

Thus he breaks into my narrative, barges in. But why deny him access, simply for the sake of narrative form? He's always been at hand – a gravitational force influencing my trajectory, though I've tried to keep a steady hand as I write my story. But now I've entered his own territory – the bookstore bombing and its aftermath, and the *seeming coincidence* (his term) of my involvement with a protagonist of this attack and with that of another twenty-five years ago.

Why my unwillingness to quote from the Phantom's book? It's a free country, as Will reminds me, you can say anything you want to here. I don't quite buy this; nowhere is free from those who, let us say, have strong feelings. But also, to be fair, if governments can put their scissors to compromising exposés, or lock up secrets for years – and they do, you know that, Will – then why not accept censorship from the guardians of the faith? If security of the state is a crucial consideration, then why not also security of the faith?

He doesn't buy this, of course.

Am I scared? you might ask, point-blank.

To which my answer: You bet I am.

I tell him so, he responds with a brief nod.

And so back to Ramji mulling over the book.

Ramji recalled the time a few years before, when a death sentence was pronounced on a certain internationally renowned author for his published writing. Ramji and a few others in the Chicago area and even in Detroit and Toronto felt compelled to *say* something. They were traumatized. Imagine: a judge in a faraway place that means little to you, its culture and way of religious practice alien to yours – a judge from such a distant place could decide that you – yes, you so-and-so – were a sinner and therefore should die!

And so they prepared an anthology of letters of protest against the death sentence and more generally against such grim religious dictates from afar: You cannot do this! You are simply terrorizing ordinary folks who turn off the lights every night on their innocent children, and in their loneliness confront their souls and their consciences and, yes, their faiths – but faiths their own to grapple with, not anyone else's to judge. Leave us alone.

But just before the collection went to press, they got cold feet. Ramji spent a sleepless night dreaming up all kinds of scenarios in which his children would be orphaned; or killed, leaving him childless. The project was shelved for another day that never came. Cowardice pure and simple, but necessary.

And so Letter 23, whose contents had offended Rumina, and which no doubt were repugnant to Michel, Ramji flipped by. He stopped at another letter, one he'd stopped at before, ruminated on its contents. As on the first occasion he had come across it, but more strongly now, it brought to mind an idea he didn't care to entertain, something quite outlandish: It reminded him of a scene at the "musical mosque" many years ago one Friday night in Cambridge.

Sona, who had been leader of the mosque, had a couple of detractors then, two new members of more orthodox beliefs who insisted that the congregation should face in the direction of Mecca. And Sona, outraged, had said, "I'll be damned if I face east." Everyone had looked aghast – surely this was not quite the way to say it.

Sona . . . who for the past twenty-five years had single-mindedly taken up a cause against encroaching orthodoxy among his people – tilting at windmills, it had always seemed to Ramji.

And Ramji wondered also, Why the *101* letters in this book? Surely a coincidence, that it was also the number so auspicious to us at home in Tanzania, this *prime* number . . .

I pray to God it's not you, Sona, who's responsible for this mad campaign, this Phantom. . . . I have Michel in the other room and I don't know what he's been up to. The last thing I need is to believe you responsible for this mischief.

Am I myself going crazy, seeing Phantoms everywhere?

We were a simple people with simple beliefs, unknown to the world. What has happened?

9

The next afternoon the interview continued in Ramji's apartment. Rumina was at work. Darcy arrived late, pleading phone calls at the office. Naseem dropped him off, and he came bearing a package which he asked to be put in the fridge. It was raining outside and first he went to the bathroom to dry himself with a towel. As on the previous day, he seemed maddeningly blasé about what was to Ramji a nerve-wracking development about which the Company – meaning mainly Darcy – had to reach some resolution. That morning Michel had been quiet and brooding and Ramji had felt sorry for him. Zayd had called from New York, much to Ramji's surprise, to ask how the interview was proceeding. Ramji hid his disappointment in Darcy. Michel had been delighted to speak with Zayd.

Darcy came into the living room, where the other two were waiting, and said genially: "So Michel, tell us more about your life as a counter-revolutionary!"

He ended his involvement with the Movement after three years, Michel said. He also quit his degree program and went to work in his uncle's pharmacy in East Lansing. His uncle was his father's younger brother, married with two children, both girls. Some months later he moved with his uncle's family to Ashfield, near Detroit. One day while on a visit to Toronto he ran across a former Movement acquaintance in a downtown street who asked him if he had any desire to visit East Africa. A free trip with tourist hotels was promised. It was an easy job, a demonstration in Dar es Salaam. They had to depart almost immediately. He thought this was a good opportunity for a free vacation; he also had some relations left in Dar, so he accepted the offer. The Movement had never sent him on an assignment out of the country before.

He was given barely a couple of days in which to return to Ashfield and prepare for his departure, which would be from New York. He flew with five other young men, first to Amsterdam and from there to Dar. They all had American passports but had been instructed to carry with them whatever former Iranian identification papers or passports they still possessed.

They arrived in Dar at night, were taken to a fancy new hotel away from town and a short stroll from the sea. In the morning some of them went to the beach. It was hot, the tide was coming in, and they decided to go for a swim. They were in the water maybe ten minutes when a Toyota cruiser drove down onto the sand and parked — their local liaison, the bearded Indian called Rehmat who had met them at the airport, stepped out and told them off for leaving the hotel. The driver, who was an American, then joined Rehmat and also started to speak to them. Hi, he said. You can call me Johnson. Consider this a holiday, for a week, except when you are required to be certain places. There's going to be a demonstration at two in the afternoon against the sale of pork in the city. You will be taken to a site where the demonstration will pass, and from there you should simply walk with the procession — but keep to the background, don't get involved in scuffles. When you talk to anyone, give the impression that you are from Iran, that should not be hard to do. Even if you are a non-believer, give the impression of an Islamic zealot, a fundamentalist. Address people as "Brother" or "Sister," and so on. Afterwards walk back to the point where you were dropped off.

Michel paused.

"And?" Darcy asked.

For the first time since Michel began his story the day before, there was a look of excitement on Darcy — a gleam in his eyes, his mouth set firm.

"We did as told."

"Do you recall any of the streets you passed through?"

Michel hesitated.

"Morogoro Road?"

"Yes . . . and the street behind it, with the big mosque."

There was a faraway look on Darcy's face. It occurred to Ramji that Darcy might have actually set eyes on Michel, looking down from his office on the demonstration passing in the street below.

That afternoon Michel spent with his relations in Dar, an uncle and his family, who lived in an apartment over their shop, in a two-storey building. He had told them he was on a holiday with friends, which was partly true. He was convinced to spend the night at their place, and while still there the next morning he read about Mr. Darcy's claims in the local papers. It seemed that when the demonstration passed by Mr. Darcy's building, his assistants had lured two of the Movement guys upstairs to his office and obtained the information from them that they had actually come from the U.S. Mr. Darcy went on to claim that the United States was using the Pork Riots in its campaign to discredit the Iranian government. Michel explained to his uncle that he and his friends had seen a demonstration downtown the day before, had asked what it was for, and then joined it.

Very shortly after that he got a phone call from one of his Movement companions telling him to mind what he said and to say his goodbyes that day, as they would be leaving for Mombasa, Kenya, that night or early next morning.

All his relations came to drop him off at the hotel later that afternoon, an occurrence that Rehmat thought was simply a godsend, because it lent an impression of innocence to Michel's presence in Dar, and by extension to the presence of those who had come with him. The two men who had allowed themselves to be lured by Mr. Darcy's assistants had been reprimanded, but nothing could be done about it. Late at night, after a party at Rehmat's opulent house in Oyster Bay, where a lot of food and drinks were served by servants, Michel and his Movement friends were whisked off to the airport and flown to Mombasa for a two-day holiday on the beach. After that they returned to the States.

Darcy asked with a twinkle in his eyes: "Is that all you did in the name of counter-revolution – a few demonstrations here and there? Just supply your body, and your voice?"

"Yes. There were more dangerous assignments, but I wasn't picked."

"Did you volunteer?"

"Yes," Michel said uneasily, as Ramji got up to answer the doorbell.

It was Ramji's landlord, Svend, the genial Swede, standing at the door with a grin on his face.

"Hullo there. Hi. Hi." He greeted everyone in turn, giving brief bows. "There was no answer on the telephone, and I was sure I heard sounds from below – what is this, an interview?" Svend had already met Michel a couple of times, once on the stairs outside, and once inside the apartment when he came to pick up misdirected mail, a common occurrence. "I won't disturb you," Svend said. "I just brought you some hardware." He placed a hinge and a few screws in Ramji's hand.

"Have some coffee before you go," Ramji offered.

Svend stayed awhile for the coffee, then left.

"Any mementos of your trip – tickets?" Darcy asked.

"Tickets, boarding passes, we had to hand everything over. But I have a few things."

He went inside to his room, returned with a valise. From it he extracted a few papers and some photographs. He handed the pictures over to Darcy. Ramji got up and went to stand behind Darcy's couch so he could look at them.

"Photographs!" Darcy exclaimed. "They let you take photographs?"

There were three, all of which had been taken at a beach. In one, a group of twelve in swimming trunks, standing in a huddle with arms around one another; in the next, vacant beach chairs and a thatched shed behind it; and finally –

"They were taken in Mombasa – where we were flown from Dar es Salaam."

"Who are they?" Ramji asked, indicating the two men walking in front of a coconut palm in the third photo.

"That's Johnson, with me."

Not a very good likeness of Michel, the photo was taken from a distance. Beside him was a short, stocky white man in a green tropical shirt and red shorts, the shirt hanging out and partly unbuttoned. Darcy stared long at the photograph, as if trying to recall if he had seen the man while he was in Dar. Michel, watching him, grinned, perhaps having called to mind some quirk of the American.

"He came to Mombasa to see us off," Michel said.

"And he very obligingly let someone take his picture . . ."

"He didn't know."

"I'll take these," Darcy said, gathering the photographs, "if that's all right."

Michel seemed to hesitate, eyed Ramji for a fleeting moment, then said sure.

"Anything else? What do you have there?"

A baggage tag and a boarding pass.

"Seems like you were having second thoughts about your friends . . ."

Michel shrugged.

"Well, young man," Darcy said, getting up, "at least you've corroborated my story. Who could have supposed that. I was made to look like a fool when I broke the story; but I stuck to my guns." He put a hand on Michel's shoulder. "But I'm not sure we can do much with it, it's water under the bridge."

Ramji drew a quick breath, said: "Except that it's connected to the events in Ashfield, so Michel says. Surely −" We should hear it out, he wanted to say, but Darcy interrupted, sounding annoyed.

"Yes, yes, of course, and we are getting to that." He looked sharply at Michel and asked: "And exactly how does it relate to Ashfield?"

In an even, low voice, Michel told him: "I believe the bombing in Ashfield to be the work of two people from the Movement."

By now Ramji had expected something of the sort; and so, obviously, had Darcy.

Darcy glared at Michel. "All right," he said. "This is what I suggest. There's no time for the full story now — all the hows and whys. You two get together and produce that written account, the complete story, from Michel's schooling in Lausanne to the bombing in Ashfield. Do it tomorrow, and early Friday we'll have a meeting at Inqalab to decide what's to be done."

There was nothing more to say. Michel looked deflated, his revelation having made no great impression. And Ramji wondered why they had proceeded — at Darcy's insistence — in so leisurely a fashion, as if Michel's information did not really matter, as if there was a desire to postpone the moment of decision.

There was a sound at the door: Rumina.

She arrived in the living room where the others were, and Darcy quickly went to give her a peck on the cheek before Ramji could quite reach her. Michel gave a small wave and she waved back.

"You're staying for dinner, I hope?" Rumina said to Darcy.

"Yes, my dear," he replied, "but the food is courtesy of Santa Monica Caterers today. I asked your man to keep it in the fridge."

She said, "Oh, wonderful. I bet it's something special," and went towards the awaiting Ramji.

Darcy headed off to the drinks cupboard in the kitchen, saying, "Meanwhile I'll have a little thirst-quencher."

After dinner Darcy sat on the floor reciting Persian poetry, drinking and telling the story of the love of his life, while Ramji, sitting across from him and also on the floor, found himself not listening but growing tired, and trying to pay attention to Michel helping Rumina with the dishes. *Why am I so stupidly jealous of him? Rumina loves me and no one else, I know that, and he is already engaged. . . .* This morning Ramji had watched from the window as Rumina got into her car, and saw that she had wrapped a scarf around her head. It wasn't until the middle of the day that the thought went searing through his mind: Was she beginning to cover her head *again*, in the traditional way? Had Shirin's photo last night struck a chord of guilt in her? *The path of the godless is lonely, Ramji, you knew that.* But when Rumina had come in the door that afternoon, her head was bare.

Darcy's demeanour was odd. Usually when he drank he was reflective, digressive, dryly ironical. But this occasion took him to a private, unshared memory, into those corridors he hadn't visited in a long time, in which resided his one-time love, because of whom he'd apparently suffered scorn and ostracism. As the evening drew on he entered into a long and bitter denunciation of the Community. Finally he said, "Saqi," speaking to an imaginary cup-bearer, the Persian poets' beloved bartender, "give this old propagandist his last draught and send him on his way into the moonless night. . . ." He received baklava and coffee instead.

Naaz and Amir came to pick him up, and seeing his state as he clambered unsteadily to his feet, she scolded, "Bapa, look at your-self, what kind of example are you setting?"

It seemed a most ridiculous statement, but she had just come from a morally uplifting and exorbitantly ticketed lecture-dinner. Her sari was blue-black and glittering.

Darcy responded, "My dear, my time for setting examples is long past."

The next morning, after Rumina had left, Ramji sat down with Michel and heard the rest of his story. Afterwards Michel kept mostly to himself, going out once for a short walk, and Ramji sat down at the computer and prepared a fair copy of the complete narrative.

Michel first explained why he had stopped working for the Movement (with the exception of that one trip he had taken to Dar). He had become bored with collecting signatures at subway stations and shopping malls; there didn't seem to be any end in sight to their campaign against Iran. After a while, he was not even sure of the authenticity of some of the photographs of torture victims that he showed. He just did as he was told. Sometimes there would be other people doing the same, from other organizations, or other countries. Meanwhile his family was very concerned. His brothers and sisters, and his parents, had all settled down where they were, and two of his nieces were grown up. He was thirty. And so he agreed to join his uncle's pharmacy in East Lansing, and then moved with his uncle to Ashfield, Michigan.

The community of Shamsi Muslims in Ashfield, Michel said,

was small and intimate, with seven families, who were originally from India, Pakistan, Uganda, and Tanzania. Three families, including that of Michel's uncle, had coordinated their move into the town in 1989, and there was at first some resentment among the townspeople against these "Muslems."

There was a little bit of harassment from town toughs, in the form of silly notes pinned to the mosque door, or hooting of truck horns during prayers. The Community people had to modify their ways, become discreet. During the Gulf War they displayed the usual tokens of patriotism – yellow ribbons on trees, photos in the display window of two local boys serving in the army. Some weeks later three men entered the mosque and quickly mooned the congregation before fleeing. Michel's uncle – who was rather hot-headed – went to Detroit and bought a Winchester rifle and a pistol. If this is how they want to play it, was the feeling among some of the men, then so be it. The situation improved, however, and the town's dignitaries came to the Community's festivities next time around, and all seemed well.

Then the Phantom affair broke.

The Book and Video Haven in Ashfield specialized in war, science fiction, and porn, with a bit of racial bigotry thrown in. One day, the display window of the store, usually filled with Rambo-type images, was laid out with copies of K. Ali's *101 Letters*, with a crude sign saying: THE HIDDEN TRUTH ABOUT ISLAM – AN INSIDER'S VIEW. Apparently Stokes, the bookstore owner, had himself crossed the border into Canada and purchased there a few hundred copies.

The Community at first protested and went to see Stokes. They were rudely turned away. They went to the town council and the police, all to no avail. Then, one Thursday, three days after the books first appeared in the store, a large demonstration took place. Three hundred people from nearby areas, including Detroit and Windsor, Canada, were present. Angry speeches were made, and there were a few calls to burn down the bookstore. An action committee was struck, which included Michel. It met once, the night of the protest, but nothing came of the meeting. At the demonstration, however, Michel met two of his comrades from the Movement, Roy and Pierre, both of whom had gone with him to Dar. It was an amazing coincidence, though Michel did not make much more of it then. They had come from Ann Arbor to observe the proceedings, they told him. They too apparently had left the Movement.

Then late Friday night the bookstore was bombed; events took a frightening turn against those who had spoken out at the demo. But Michel was certain now that Roy and Pierre's presence in town had been far from a coincidence; the Movement had to be behind the bombing, it was just the sort of thing it would do, to draw attention to Islamic extremism. When he called the number in Ann Arbor which the two men had given him, he found that it was not even in operation. Who would give heed to his suspicions? Not the government, surely. He was onto a hot story but was himself under suspicion. He took a plane to Los Angeles from Detroit to look for Mr. Darcy of *Inqalab*. It was Mr. Darcy, after all, who had exposed the Movement's activities in Dar once before.

"The activities in Dar es Salaam did not involve bombing or any such crimes," Ramji observed.

Michel, seated across from Ramji, looked down, shook his head. "But you don't know the Movement. Roy is no ordinary guy, I know that he used to go on the more active assignments."

"Which involved bombing places and so on?"

Michel nodded.

"Still, you have only a suspicion."

"That's why I came to *Inqalab*."

"What did you think it could do for you?"

"Publish my story. That's all. You don't have to do anything else for me — after that I'm on my own."

It was late. Michel had gone out for a long walk. Rumina was on the couch, absorbed with a recent preoccupation, writing in what she called her Swahili notebook. Ramji sat in front of his computer monitor screen, musing.

So finally this is the story. And we sit here in the silent night, hostage to the events it describes. Electron images on a screen, really, put there by the fingers of this man. . . . And Michel, whose story this is, is out strolling in the street, thinking what? I wish I knew. The first part of his story has the ring of truth to it, it corroborates Darcy's own version of the Pork Riots, and there's the plane ticket and other evidence. But the last, the crucial part, hangs together with the rest by the sighting of two people and a suspicion. If there was a truth to that suspicion, surely the authorities would pay heed and dig it out. And, if necessary, a story in our magazine would provide the incentive. Isn't that why he came to us, after all? I only wish all this was somewhere far away and not here in my own home.

But suppose if that last part of the story were a lie. . . . Michel had grown into the household. You wanted to help him if he was in trouble. How do you imagine such a person making a bomb, planting it outside a bookstore window, causing a blast that would kill three innocent people?

After the action committee in Ashfield have met, some of the younger members (three, for instance, is a good number) get together to form an even tighter group: outraged at the treatment of the Community and their faith by townsfolk, they will do something about it. They call upon Michel's boasts of assignments abroad with a secret organization, and he shows them how to make a bomb. Late one night, when the protests have died down and things appear to have gone back to normal, they plant their device outside the bookstore and await the results . . .

But then evidence of the bomb-making would be found, surely – some place where it would point a finger at him and his friends? He could always say it was planted there by the Movement . . .

Rumina appeared behind him, said, "You look sad," put her arms around him. "What is it?"

"I don't quite know . . . it'll go away." He took one hand and fondled it, kissed it. The idle screen in front of him, he noticed, was now showing a calming aquatic scene.

"Anything I can do to make it better?"

"I don't think so . . ."

"Oh?"

"I didn't mean it that way –"

She tried to pull her hand away, but he wouldn't release it. She tugged harder and their eyes met, hers flashing, his pleading. Don't change, his told her, don't become like that – and she thought the better of it and came closer, her face level with his.

"It's Michel's story, isn't it? Why have you kept it from me, and why is it so hush-hush?"

"It's almost finished — you'll be the first to read it when it's done. It's not hush-hush. It's just that I —"

"All right. I'll wait."

She eased herself gently from his hold and went away, and he stared after her, his heart pounding. Perhaps you've already guessed, he thought. Perhaps you already know.

10

*T*hey had failed to watch the news last night, and so a
headline in the morning paper's front page caught him with a jolt:

BOMBING SUSPECT DETAINED.

An FBI spokeswoman acknowledged Thursday that a male
suspect has been detained in Detroit for questioning in the
bookstore-bombing case. He was identified as Asif Lalji, a busi-
nessman, aged 25. Other suspects are expected to be named
soon, the spokeswoman said, adding that a nationwide net had
been cast for the perpetrators of the bombing on January 20,
which claimed three lives and destroyed approximately a third
of the bookstore. Several hundred people have been questioned by federal agents . . .

Ramji passed the paper over to Michel, across their breakfasts, with
the item of interest facing up, and Michel took his time reading it,
before looking up and saying quietly, "They haven't named me,"
then adding a little more strongly, "They're completely on the
wrong track. Asif only spoke out against the book."

And the right track? And Asif? Rumina was home, lounging in the living room taking in the gloss of *Good Morning America*, having promised Michel a sightseeing tour later in the day. Ramji had convinced himself not to misinterpret what was only a natural act of hospitality on her part towards their guest. So, telling Michel to be discreet and not draw too much attention to himself, and giving Rumina a look that implied the world (kissing in public had never been their way), he drove off to work.

Today was the day of decision, in the matter of Michel, though the outcome was far from certain. But, it seemed to Ramji, they had taken so long simply listening to Michel's story that *Inqalab* now owed it to him to publish it. After that, as Michel himself put it, he was on his own. But would Darcy go along with that? Michel's presence appeared to have unsettled him. He seemed uncharacteristically cynical, and even unpleasant towards Michel, when he should have welcomed the young man who had come to seek his help, drawn to him by his radical image, his sensational exposé in Dar, his magazine. To Ramji, even in his drunken form Darcy had seemed far from himself. Well, we'll see today what he comes up with . . .

As soon as he arrived at the office, Ramji handed copies of Michel's story to Darcy, Basu, and Zayd. The four of them got together in the conference room a couple of hours later, and a bitter quarrel ensued over the story's fate.

Darcy and Zayd had begun a heated argument in the latter's office, emerging from it still debating, pausing just long enough for Zayd to scowl and tell John and Sajjad to disappear until after lunch, before entering the conference room. Basu and Ramji were already seated across from each other; Basu had just invited Ramji to a wedding reception for a friend's daughter in Torrance on Saturday. Darcy sat as usual at the head of the table, Basu and Zayd further up on either side, and Ramji next to Zayd.

By Michel's own admission, Darcy argued, he had trained in the use of firearms; had even volunteered for, as he put it, more dangerous missions; and therefore had shown himself willing to damage property, do physical harm, perhaps even kill. He had expressed no qualms about misrepresenting himself as a religious zealot or fanatic, as he had done during his sojourn in East Africa. His views on the Phantom's book were unequivocal – he disliked it intensely, he had been part of a rally that had called for its burning. Perhaps he was not very bright and was easily duped. How could one be assured then of his innocence? Perhaps he had been deluded into thinking the Company had ways of hiding him, had contacts that could take care of him.

"We simply cannot publish it. It's too risky."

"But we've known of the risks all along, Mr. Darcy," Basu said. "We've never been afraid to take risks in the past – it's in the nature of our mission as journalists."

Darcy glared at Basu, then at Ramji. "There's a line to be drawn. We cannot afford to be associated with this – this – fanatical element," he said. "We cannot be seen to be abetting terrorists – or –"

"Please!" exclaimed Zayd.

Why did it take the old man three days to tell us this? Ramji wondered. What was he up to yesterday? Did he run any checks on the Movement, as he said he would? And since when has *he* been afraid of risk? He's been to jail for publishing his views, he's been beaten up for exposing people, he risked his visa application

to the U.S. for a controversial account of the Pork Riots in Dar. . . .
And now Michel's story about the Movement: one risk too many?

This business about Pierre and Roy, Darcy went on – unable to
hide a sneer at the mention of their names – surely that was a red
herring. How could any organization, let alone the Movement,
believe they could get away with a bombing in the United States
with such a far-fetched plan, implicating innocent citizens? He
didn't believe it.

"We need to find out more about those two, Roy and Pierre,"
Basu said. "But timing is of the essence. Much of the story is true
in any case, and if the rest isn't, we can retract; we're only journalists. This is our chance –"

"We wouldn't have to retract it," Ramji said. "We simply
publish it as the story told to us by a frightened young man from
Ashfield – the town where the bookstore was bombed. He came
to us because he trusted us to listen to it." For the briefest moment
he met Darcy's eye. "We owe that much to him – we led him on,
after all. We've always known his story ultimately had to do with
the bombing, he told us at the outset what his views were on that
book, and that he thought he might be named as a suspect." Ramji
paused, then finished: "And if any part of it is untrue, so be it, it's
his responsibility, he's out in the open and answerable."

To which Zayd said emphatically, "It's our opportunity for a
major story. We have a man in our hands who has a damning story
to tell about the hypocrisy of the U.S. government abroad. . . .
Look, Mr. Darcy," Zayd pleaded, "this is what we've always stood
for – the little guy, the powerless fellow. The poorest countries of
the world who are pawns of big governments, where children die
because they cannot afford a couple of Aspirins or a blanket . . .
you've stood for the same causes before –"

"Yes," answered Darcy tersely, "and for more than forty years now."

"Then let's publish this guy's story, for God's sake. Part of it you yourself were witness to, you wrote about it. The rest of it, true or not, can be our – our gift to him!"

"We don't give gifts to killers," said Darcy in the same cold voice.

"So now he is a killer!" Zayd shot back, losing his temper. "What happened to 'innocent until proven guilty'? Does he *look* like a killer? He is from *your* community! Ask Ramji, he's known the boy – Ramji, does he look like a killer to you?"

They all stopped to stare at Ramji, and he returned their look hesitantly: Zayd turned sideways to face him, impatient, ready to shake an answer out of him if need be; Basu, a sympathetic eyebrow raised, perhaps sensing his discomfiture; and Darcy, almost sinister with that thin cold smile, so different from the convivial guest of the other night, lovesick and nostalgic in his cups, spouting Persian poetry.

"I think by 'killer' we mean here someone who planted a bomb for a cause and in the process killed some people unintentionally," Ramji said, but didn't answer Zayd's question.

Darcy's smile turned triumphant, and Zayd looked away disgustedly.

Do we know what it means to kill? Ramji wondered. Do we see the death, the destruction, and the grief when we speak so glibly about it? Do we think of the survivors and what we owe to them, and to the memories of the innocent dead? . . . We owe it to them and to our own security, and to that of those we love, and to our commitment to make this society work, to hand over the guilty to punishment. . . . Perhaps these thoughts, or some of them, came only much later, when the time came to sit with himself and understand his actions, look at a shattered, legless torso of a woman and ask: How did *I* come into this picture?

Ramji went on, "But, to be absolutely fair, Mr. Darcy, we've not used terms like 'killer' and 'terrorist' so lightly in this office before."

"A wrong choice of words on my part then," Darcy said, reddening a bit. "In any case, I don't want to dredge up that pork incident now, unless it ties in to the bombing, which I am not convinced it does, as I've just explained. I know you people are disappointed, but this is where I stand."

He looked briefly across at each of the other three men in the room, both his hands on the table, as if ready to get up if there was no more argument. Boyish-looking Zayd, toying with his pen, eyes smouldering as he glared first at Ramji and then at Basu, couldn't resist the gauntlet. In a controlled voice that seemed to take him an effort to achieve, he said, "Forgive me for saying this, Mr. Darcy, but you don't seem to be the same man who took over *Inqalab* from Basu and me. And also, this is not the first time you have stood in the way of a crucial, unique, and groundbreaking story – there was that PLO interview . . ."

"I have not stood in the way of anything!" said Darcy sharply; a spray of spittle from the mouth, a drink of water, then a clearing of the throat. "All I have required is a rigorous editorial policy and less of this hot-headed radicalism simply for the pleasure of it!"

He carried the vote, by way of veto. The story could not go in.

Meanwhile what to do with Michel? He is not our responsibility, Darcy said, flatly – it's up to his family to help him. We *are* his family, in a manner of speaking, you and I, Ramji thought. If Michel calls his relatives in Ashfield now, Zayd said, the cops might be upon him and us like a pack of hounds. At this juncture Darcy got up and left the room. When he had gone, the rest of them felt free to discuss Michel's fate. Zayd volunteered to spend time with Michel the following day. Let me take him off your hands, he said to Ramji, at least for a day. I'll take him to meet my family, and on the way I will also discuss his options with him.

And he took it upon himself to verify, in the coming week, as much of Michel's story as was possible. The story was still there, he said, it hadn't gone away. There was only the question of what to do with it, and when.

Basu improved on Zayd's suggestion. Why not convince Michel to return to Ashfield in the meantime – that would create a good impression on the authorities there. It would also take Michel off their hands completely, though they did not voice that thought.

It was finally agreed that Zayd would pick up Michel from Ramji's home the next day and convince him to return to Ashfield, reassuring him that some of those at the Company would try to do whatever they could for him.

Following that meeting Ramji drove straight home. When he arrived, Rumina and Michel were not back yet. It was four o'clock and Ramji decided to go out for a walk. It was brilliant outside but gusty and he wore a sweatshirt over his shorts. He felt dismal; the quarrel earlier in the day at the office had been bitter and emotional; it had left echoes, many thoughts in the mind. Yet perhaps it had been inevitable. After all, Darcy was only human. It was he, Ramji, who since his childhood days had held him up in awe, a fiery knight fighting selflessly and with abandon for the causes of the downtrodden. And perhaps he had been some of that, once upon a time. But who could fault him, this late in life, for being too careful, for not taking the risks he might once have taken?

Ramji walked all the way to Manhattan Beach and back. When he returned, Rumina and Michel were not back yet. He made himself a drink and sat down in the living room. He wondered if it was time to cook, decided not yet. All of a sudden he found himself entertaining a thought which startled him. It would be so unlike me, he said to himself – yet it would be perfectly within my right to do what I am about to do. . . . He paused for sounds, in case that very moment Michel and Rumina had arrived and were on their way up. They weren't. Then, still a little nervous, he went over to Michel's room and looked for his guest's valise. It was on the desk, and he unzipped it open. He found the L.A.–Detroit return ticket, the incoming boarding pass, a dog-eared John Grisham novel; a copy of *Inqalab*, a couple of months old; a diary with assorted entries. Next, Ramji went through the clothes in the closet, found nothing interesting. So far so good, he thought; as it should be. He found the suitcase under the bed, pulled it out. There was a lock on it. Ramji knew all about these luggage pad-locks, they provided only placebal security. He went out to the kitchen, found a bunch of tiny keys in a cabinet drawer, and in two tries had the suitcase open. There was an attaché case inside, with a hefty feel to it, locked with a combination. Nothing else of significance. Stumped, angry – why couldn't this search end simply? – Ramji put the suitcase back as he found it. He went back to the valise, flipped through the diary. There were phone numbers and addresses, of friends, family members across the continent, the Company in L.A., and a few others, unfamiliar. And then two short, cryptic entries caught his eye, one below the other: each beginning with the letters LH, followed by three digits and then what seemed like dates and times, for the coming Sunday night, Monday night. Pulse racing, yet with cold purpose, he took the book to the kitchen, copied the lines on a piece of paper, returned to the bedroom, and put everything back, telling himself, Ramji you're imagining, this means nothing. But a locked attaché case in a locked suitcase? No proof, and you have his word. . . . *Word*? Can I simply depend on his word? You want an easy way out, admit it. . . . But what's the harm in making sure, one owes it to oneself, and to the girl who's naively showing the guest around?

He began to prepare dinner, engrossing himself completely in the task at hand. And soon the stew was on the stove and the *ugali* ready. He sat down before an old TV rerun, and as a short police chase began and ended on the screen with a gun battle, he picked up the portable phone and called up a nearby travel agency. LH? – yes, they told him, that meant Lufthansa, the numbers indicated flights leaving Los Angeles for Frankfurt Sunday night, and Frankfurt for Dar es Salaam the following night.

He heard Rumina's cheerful voice coming up the stairs, then the lock turning, and they walked in. She was in blue jeans, with a long white embroidered *kameez* covering her hips, and she was beaming, radiant. The attire is modest, he thought, according to the dictates of tradition. Am I imagining things?

"Guess where I took him!" she said gaily.

"Where?" Ramji replied, struggling to smile.

"All the way to Malibu Beach and back, a couple of hours at Universal Studios, and finally the Yoga Shrine," she said.

Like a child she forgets so easily, hurts so innocently. The shrine was *our* special retreat, where we made our confessions and dreamed of our future.

"I knew you wouldn't mind," she said, moving closer to him, and he gave her a squeeze. Michel watched them with an approving grin.

When she was out of hearing Ramji gave Michel his end of the news, that the Company had decided not to publish his story. He couldn't help feeling a shot of satisfaction in that look of disappointment, the face losing its glow, the shrug: "Not surprising, after all." Ramji told him Zayd would take him out for the day the next morning, and would talk to him about what would be best for him now.

After dinner the three of them sat down to a game of Bao, played with stones on a thick wooden board carved out with rows of bowl-shaped cavities. On his way to school in Dar, early in the morning, Ramji would see old men sitting outside the doorways of their homes playing the game. That's what Bao brought to mind, the long walk to school and the old men; Grandma waiting at home. Someone was actually marketing Bao in the U.S. now, in the museum stores.

They watched the late news, then went out for a walk along the beach. Rumina and Michel had discovered friends in common and she was yammering away at him about girls they had known, who had got married as teenagers and had turned into solemn, responsible wives, with children and a lot of money. Ramji walked on ahead, finding it difficult to accept his own feelings. He was jealous. Michel was younger and far more attractive and sympathetic. He felt left out in their presence. But he was being ridiculous, Rumina was utterly devoted to him, and Michel had a fiancé back home, Shirin, whom he looked forward to marrying. . . . And those Lufthansa flights? The flight numbers in the diary could mean anything. And the attaché case in the suitcase? Not a sign of guilt, surely, he could have brought a lot of money with him, for example. Still, when Michel leaves, that will be all for the better.

Rumina had crept up behind him and put her arm into his. His heart was pounding. He had a sudden sense of foreboding.

Sounds of TV applause filtered in from the living room and through their bedroom door; out there Michel was awake and restless, and in here very much on Ramji's mind. He wondered if Michel was on Rumina's too. They had got into bed tired, and now lay on their backs unable to sleep. The ceiling above them reflected the large window looking out. The last vehicle had driven past on the road down below, some time ago. They heard Michel go to his room, and return shortly to the living room; the groan of creaking pine from the armchair. That was a badly designed object, and lumpy too. Svend had promised to replace it, but was tarrying, and the new model in his catalogue was costly. There were other things too that needed attention about the place – a light switch, a leak in the ceiling near the kitchen. . . . All evidence of their ongoing life together; a life, a home that should be protected from all manner of threats and not be taken for granted as we are so easily prone to do.

He moved slightly and she turned over beside him and ran a hand across his forehead.

"Michel thinks the world of you . . . a man of your word is what he called you, someone you can absolutely trust."

Ramji wondered what to make of that.

"What did you and Michel talk about at the shrine?"

"This and that." She played with his hair, watched him. "He is quite deep in his own way," she said, and paused again. Then: "He believes in God."

They were quiet for a while, Ramji breathing deeply, trying to raise a thought, a response.

She asked: "Why didn't you tell me – about him?"

He turned on his side to face her in the semidarkness. "What?" he said.

"About him, the incident in his town . . ."

So she knows. He's told her.

He said: "I was afraid. I didn't want to worry you . . ."

"Oh." He saw the glint from her eyes, took her warm hand.

"Michel said we're lucky we have each other . . ."

"I know I'm lucky," Ramji replied. But my heart aches so, filled with the poison of jealousy and insecurity and possessiveness. What's in *your* heart, girl?

"Suppose he's guilty –" he began.

"But he's not! He told me and I believe him. And he knows that you believe him too."

He didn't know what to say to her. I'm in it, up to my neck, and sinking. Unless, pray God (for old times' sake at least, I did believe in You once), pray God he *is* innocent, happily, joyously so, and vindicated.

He told her of the day's events, of Darcy's doubts, and watched her look of dismay.

"It was Zayd and Basu who supported Michel. And we have decided that it would be best for Michel to return."

"Michel *is* innocent," she said. "I am convinced of it! I have already told him he can stay here as long as is . . . necessary."

The embrace, finally, was loose, and failed to calm the turmoil within them.

11

They had woken up in a warm, close embrace, opened their eyes and looked at each other, frightened, and amazed; fearful of having lost each other while sojourning in the world of dream and nightmare and sleep. And then hugged each other even tighter, with the certainty that they were each other's, absolutely and forever, nothing should come in the way.

And they made amends. Ramji said it was nice of her to have shown kindness to their guest, who was far from home and must surely also be frightened. Rumina admitted that perhaps she got too carried away last night, their home was *theirs*, and they should both talk to Michel later and convince him to return to Ashfield and speak to the government investigators. They then got up and had the coffee which Michel had already made, and shortly afterwards Zayd came and took Michel away for the day.

And so after a long time, he cannot recall how long, the love nest is devoid of alien presence . . .

He lies stretched out on his back on the floor, not touching it, he thinks, in bliss-filled suspension, like a mist, while somewhere inside she's humming along with the music and beautifying her lovely self . . .

Perhaps, he muses in this forgetful moment of abandon, a daughter; and I would like to call her Shanti, for peace . . . if we had a daughter, if we had a child, which she so much wants.

"We're making breakfast," she says, gliding past, leaving a whiff of – what? – lemony milk and spice, honey and musk, and everything nice . . . these Zanzibaris have always been adept with their seductive wiles.

"Wait – come," he bids.

"You get up and help," she retorts.

"No, come here," with a straight face, he, setting a love trap she knows all about yet comes to him all the same, and from the floor he watches her approach.

"Oh no, not now, and I've just had my bath."

"All the more, dear . . . to ravish you. Just stand there . . . come down, you –" he pulls the dress, the hand, she resists, relents – "here, here, let's have Zanzibari mango for starters . . ."

"Ramji! That was the only once – one freak time –"

"No argument – not now, my lovely . . ."

"Not all the way –"

She lowers herself onto him as he pulls off her white knickers. (Why not panties? Panties suggest TV ads and packaged underwear and sterile mannequins, that's how the mind is formed – it's knickers for me, suggesting the body the wearer the elastic the pulling-down-ability across the smooth cool behind.) He runs his fingers down her spine, her back, her buttocks, down the cleft, the raw roughness, up and down, raw and rough . . .

"Come on, Ramji . . ."

"Mango – *mawazo, alphonso* . . ."

"*Shindano?*" How can she resist. Everyone has a special taste in mangoes.

"Say *mrdngam* . . ."

"Mri – no –!"

"You're a lecher, Ramji –"

"Funny." They're lying on their backs now, side by side. "We think of the excesses of youth and the moderation of maturity – but youth can't hold a candle to middle-aged depravity, to which nothing is dirty or shocking or impossible. Isn't that so?"

He turns to look at her. *Do I deserve you? I don't care, but I will never let you go. No handsome stranger, no man of God or Devil, of any colour or race will take you away from me* . . .

"I don't know – I'm not that old, you know . . ."

They made a wonderful brunch for two. To start with, a whole coconut, split, the meat scraped off and squeezed for the milk. The onions chopped very fine; the white pigeon peas boiled and the creamy sauce prepared using crushed green chillies, coriander, smidgins of turmeric, garlic. That was *mbaazi*. Then the fried bread, from the yeasty dough prepared beforehand, some days earlier. *Mbaazi na maandazi*, Zanzibaris swore by it, at least the older ones, those not corrupted by the baseness of greasy chicken and chips, which, as Darcy said, had corrupted the cuisine back home. He would of course get a portion, not to do so would be unforgivable.

They were both reconciled to Darcy's display of caution

regarding Michel; it was natural for the old man to feel protective about the life he had now in California.

"But I still feel that somehow he misled me," Ramji said. "When he invited me to join him and after I arrived, he gave me the impression that he was still the same old warhorse."

"But he did hint to you once that he desired you to help him take the Company into more moderate directions, didn't he?"

"I guess so. But I was never sure what exactly he meant."

And about his sponsor, that mysterious organization called the Overland Foundation with its poetry-spouting director, let's not say another word and assume only the best possible motives.

"And he did bring us together."

Ramji agreed; for that they should be eternally grateful to Darcy.

Afterwards they sat in the living room, Rumina looking over the paper, throwing amused looks at Ramji as he watched the cartoons and chuckled away like a boy.

That night they were to go to the wedding party in Torrance, to which Basu had invited them, and so Rumina had gone off to the shops to look for a gift and get what else she needed for the outing. Alone, at home, Ramji puttered about at first, doing minor chores. He argued successfully against undertaking something time-consuming, such as changing the faulty light switch, and sat down by the phone.

Should he call the kids? No, they would be out now, Saturday noon (their time), at religious classes, and Sunday was when he usually called them . . . though tomorrow was the day of the Friendship Walk. . . . He thought for a while, wondered if he should call up Sona in Boston; they hadn't spoken in months. He argued against that too.

A little later the phone rang.

"Can I speak to Mehboob?" a voice said. An elderly voice, a scratchy, back-home paternal voice that draws you in familiarly.

"He's out for the moment," answered Ramji. "Can I take a message? Are you his uncle?"

Michel was not supposed to have broadcast his whereabouts. To how many people had he given this phone number?

"My name is Akbarali Aziz, I am his father. I am calling from Calgary. Please tell him that I called."

"I will," Ramji said. "Did Mehboob give you this number?"

"That he did. And you are? . . ."

Ramji gave his family particulars. *Aré*, yes, Mr. Aziz said of Ramji's grandmother, But I knew her *well*! And she had one daughter. Yes, my mother, Ramji told him. They discussed "prospects" in Canada and America for their Community; and they discussed the Friendship Walk which was scheduled for the following day in every city in North America where the Community had a presence. Are you walking? Ramji asked Mr. Aziz. The man said yes, he was walking with the Golden Club. And you? Yes, Uncle, Ramji said, I'll be walking. (Everyone at the office had been roped in for the event by the Naaz-Naseem duo.) And how are your own family, Mr. Aziz asked, your wife, children? They are fine, Ramji said. Finally the man said, "You'll see him off safely, won't you? My son is a decent, religious boy; he was only misled . . ."

When the man had rung off, Ramji remained sitting where he was, by the phone, tense with excitement. *You'll see him off, won't you?* And "Aziz"? That must be the new, more "Islamic" family name, for the New World.

The notepaper on which Ramji had copied out the airline flight details from Michel's diary was in his shirt pocket; it also had the number for Lufthansa. Ramji fished out the paper, he picked up the phone, slowly dialled the number for the airline: I don't know what to expect, but I'll just make sure. Sounding anxious, which he was, he pretended to be a passenger, a Mr. M. Aziz, confirming his prior bookings, and gave all the details of the flight. Tense with excitement, he awaited the answer. And then: Yes, Mr. Aziz, the friendly voice told him, all was confirmed on the flight to Frankfurt tomorrow night and thence onward to Dar.

So Michel had used the new family surname Aziz to book the flight.

He was only misled, his father had said; and he committed this one error and wanted to escape the consequences? You'll see him off safely, won't you? . . . an appeal to one of us. . . . But if he were innocent, wouldn't the family keep him close to them, and defend him if the need arose, instead of letting him sneak away?

The lock turned, the door rattled, then swung open, and Rumina came in, weighed down by a shopping bag in one hand and clothes from the dry cleaners in the other.

"Hi," she said. "I settled for a gift certificate in the end, is that all right? – from a kitchen store."

"Just great," he said.

Should he tell her what he's found out? Should he tell her now or later? . . . He doesn't know.

"I'm going to go take a nap," she said, standing at their bedroom door, her hands still full, "and later will you make the tea?"

"You can count on it," he said and watched her go in and close the door.

What to think of Michel now, what to do? Had Michel lied, had he taken part in the bombing after all? But surely by "he was misled" Mr. Aziz only meant that "the boy" had been influenced in the past into frittering away a good many years of his life with the Movement, and not that he had let himself get involved in the bombing of the bookstore . . .

But if he were innocent, why would he want to abscond, all that distance, to Dar es Salaam — away from all his close family, instead of staying around to defend himself? An escape would only confirm his guilt in the eyes of the law. It was certainly not what your father would go along with if you were innocent.

A long time ago pretty Lucy-Anne Miller had put him in a similar quandary, saying, I had nothing to do with it (or something like that), hide me for a few days. She too had an escape plan, in her case she was set to drive away to Canada. But deep down in his guts, Ramji thought now, he *must* have known that she had had something to do with "it." And if he had admitted to himself then that she had to have been involved in the bombing of the ISS building, what *should* he have done?

Advise her to give herself up to the police?

"You're broody," Rumina said later.

"A little, perhaps. I just want this whole affair to be over — then we can *live*, just for ourselves."

"Hmm," she murmured, nodding.

The doorbell sounded, she got up to answer it. It was Michel, back from his day out with Zayd. He came in, looking cheerful and holding in his hand what looked like a black globe.

"I bought a present for you," he said, giving the black object to Rumina, "and for Ramji, too, of course," he added quickly. He had found it in a junk shop downtown: a Makonde carving from Tanzania, with what appeared to be two heads, either human or monkey, in the centre, four smooth limbs emerging from each and intertwining to form a sphere of intricate latticework.

Rumina loved it, thanked Michel profusely; and, Yes, it's beautiful, Ramji said, with a nod at him. A token of friendship, a goodbye gift – or an omen?

12

*T*he bridegroom, in a yellow sparkling turban and silver-and-grey Indian suit, his face hidden behind a white veil of jasmine strings, was led into the wedding ceremony high upon a horse, a glistening brown and black genuine Arab thoroughbred, which was preceded by a wailing reed flute and tabla and a bevy of whirling dancing women and girls in colourful saris and boys in red-and-yellow silk costumes. Delhi Delight, said Basu, that's the name of the horse, it's won the Kentucky Derby, and the sire is the great Shen-shah from Ireland. It doesn't race anymore, of course, he added unnecessarily.

A section of the banquet hall had been reserved for the wedding ceremony, watched by about a couple of hundred people seated in rows. Basu was on one side of Ramji, Rumina was on the other, then Michel. Ramji felt intensely aware of Michel's presence. He took Rumina's hand.

The ceremony was officiated by a man in priestly garb; he was moonlighting, actually, as Basu explained. Like the horse, he was also on show – a mathematics professor from UCLA, reportedly the possessor of numerous patents, but now bare-chested and wearing a dhoti, sitting cross-legged on the floor. The bride and groom sat across the ceremonial fire from him.

When the groom's jasmine veil was finally lifted, a Caucasian face was revealed, with straight brown hair.

"He's an *American!*" said Basu to Ramji.

To which someone behind them muttered: "And the bride is not American?"

"Very apt," Ramji murmured to a red-faced Basu.

The ceremony over, the crowd stood up to mingle and search for refreshments. The bride and groom were escorted to a sofa in a reserved area of the hall covered with a blue oriental carpet and scatterings of rose petals, and on each side of them were enormous flower arrangements. Two cameras were on duty.

The groom appeared to be around twenty-five years old, the bride about the same age. He was of average height and muscular in build. The bride, attired in a traditional red sari and amply though tastefully bejewelled, her face pink with makeup and natural blush, looked breathtakingly lovely. Somehow at a wedding, Ramji observed to himself, the bride's handlers always managed to give her a look that was at once beautiful, innocent and virginal.

One reason why Basu had brought them to this wedding in Torrance was to show them an exotic, "multicultural" event – an American wedding that was also Indian, and Hindu. Because it was a controversial wedding, Basu said, many who should have come, friends of the family, had decided to give it a pass. And so bodies were needed, Indian bodies to lend an air of success to the affair.

Among the Indians he knew, Basu explained, there was always a competition, friendly and sometimes not so friendly, measured by the professional achievements of their children. A doctor or a lawyer counted high. There was a story about the "tragedy" of a couple whose only child secured a place in "only" (as they put it) engineering (instead of law or medicine) and had to move to Phoenix to hide their shame. The story was possibly exaggerated, but it had the ring of plausibility. The different Indian groups naturally preferred their children to marry among their own kind and class.

And so tonight's wedding was ill-attended by families with eligible children. It set just the wrong example, for instance, for a girl who was at that tender age when she was prone to get dreamy-eyed over, if not exactly an Arnold Schwarzenegger look-alike hulk from the college football team, then perhaps a Tom Cruise, or worse, an earnest poet, when she should be thinking of a fellow-Indian gynecologist or geriatrician who would become that stout Republican unit, a gilded pillar of immigrant society.

The bride's father, an acquaintance of Basu, came over. He was a Mr. Anand, a small thin man with a long face and high forehead, wearing a grey suit pinned with a red rose. He was an engineer working for a gyroscope manufacturer. "So nice you could come. Please eat. Please – come – and congratulate the couple." The happiness on his face looked somewhat under strain.

Ramji did as he was bid, followed Mr. Anand to meet the couple, who were now by themselves and looked revived. James, the groom, turned out to be a student of commerce. A definite strike against the marriage, if the game were not already lost.

"Super boy, simply great kid," Mr. Anand said to Ramji, when they had moved on to make way for other well-wishers of the couple.

"How did they meet?" Ramji asked. "Do they go to college together?"

"Yes." Mr. Anand eyed Ramji for a moment, found him fit to open his heart to. "You know, at first we were dead against the marriage. No way, we said. I'll lock you up in your room, I told her – not seriously, of course. And my wife, Mrs. Anand, you should meet her – she's not fluent in English, but she's very religious – she threatened to starve herself to death. When you bring up a daughter, you expect to be able to talk to her husband – speaking in English is not the same thing. Then Vinita said to us, At least find out more about Jim – that's his name – talk to his parents. I telephoned the parents and they invited us for dinner. After dinner they said to my wife and me, 'Mr. and Mrs. Anand, we have accepted your daughter Vini as our daughter, we have known her for over two years. We now ask you to accept our son James as yours.' They're an old family, very devout and respectable."

"How did they agree to their son becoming a Hindu?" Ramji asked Basu when Mr. Anand was out of earshot.

"Oh – he has not become Hindu. He simply agreed to the ceremony. And the Anands agreed to a church wedding, that's taking place tomorrow. It's a private affair, mostly with Jim's people."

A devout Christian family and an observant Hindu one. What happens to the children of that union?

Basu read his mind. "They've agreed that the children should be baptized."

"He doesn't seem very happy, does he?"

"Who – Anand? No. They are desperate for their son now, an Indian girl of the appropriate caste is being sought."

Basu's Lata had turned seventeen and was already thinking of university. Basu had on his hands two projects, saving money first for her college fees, and then for the girl's wedding. The first he and his wife could more or less manage. As for the second . . . sometimes eligible Indian boys expected gifts – a house or a car were not unusual demands, or wads of cash. What could a socialist editor of a radical newspaper manage for a decent gift?

Ramji saw a worried expression come over Basu's face; perhaps he was already regretting having come to this wedding, to be reminded of all the worries of having a daughter.

"Can you really control them?" Ramji asked, "they'll do exactly as they please, no?"

Basu had a hearty laugh at this. "There speaks the concerned father – admit it, now. The idea, as you know," he said, "is to restrict their options from the beginning – that is the way most parents do it. You can't lock them up, you and I know that. But you can let them think they choose their friends while you pick the area you live in and the school they go to, and the friends you associate with – and let's face it, the Indian lifestyle, with Indian people, is very attractive and loving for the children. The rest is luck."

Still, Ramji thought – watching Lata and Leila and Hanif and a couple of others meandering freely now among the crowd and chatting and laughing and feasting on Indian buffet – you can never quite say what they will be up to. The kids are a change of weather hovering in the background, waiting to happen.

Rumina and Michel had wandered off together. Ramji peered into the crowd, couldn't see them. He felt irritated, then a welling up of anger at Michel's thoughtlessness. And Rumina did seem to go overboard with her friendliness. He felt terribly unhappy and alone.

There was loud applause as the bride and groom were escorted to the door, and then showered with rice and flower petals. By this time the bride had changed into a dress. A white Rolls-Royce with chauffeur awaited to take them away to a life of connubial bliss. In American fashion the bride threw her bouquet of flowers over her shoulder; it didn't land in anyone's hands, but fell a few feet short of the crowd. There was a scrummage of young girls anxious to pick it up. For each one, hopefully, a doctor or lawyer awaited in the wings.

Then Rumina appeared, and she was pulling Michel by the hand. Ramji felt his face redden with scorching emotion, the more so as he was certain Lata and Leila had stopped in their tracks to watch him react. Finally he waved at Rumina and she came over with Michel.

Shortly afterwards Mr. Anand brought his wife to meet them. She was a well-built woman in her fifties wearing a purple sari, also pinned with a red rose, and they all shook hands and talked of what a wonderful event this was. It was hot, the husband and wife were sweaty, and their roses looked squashed.

On the drive back the talk was about the horse at the wedding.

"We went to look at Delhi Delight," Rumina said to Ramji. "It was quite grand and very solemn. Did you know that Michel is an expert on thoroughbred horses?"

"No, I never realized that," Ramji muttered.

"Hardly an expert," Michel said. "I used to follow racing news many years ago."

He went on to tell them, in some detail, about the kidnapping and killing of Shen-shah, Delhi Delight's sire, in Ireland in the eighties.

In bed later that night, Rumina said, "Michel was quite taken by the wedding ceremony . . . all the rituals and costumes and the music."

"Don't forget the horse."

"It *was* a magnificent sight, wasn't it?"

"You're *not* going to go on about the horse . . ."

"What have you against it?"

"Someone should talk about the bride and groom for a change, for Chrissakes."

"We hardly know anything about them."

"Precisely. If you hadn't been flirting with Michel you might have heard their story."

There, he spat it out, this venom he'd been harbouring.

"You should be ashamed. How could you say such a thing." A tone of voice, a verdict he'd never heard before, from her.

She turned away, on her side. Her eyes were open, he could tell, he could see one eyelash flickering. She was waiting, and he moved closer, put an arm around her, felt her heartbeat under the breast in his palm.

"I'm sorry." He wasn't; but he was terribly hurt and wasn't sure whose fault it was.

"I was thinking . . . ," she said after a while.

"Yes?"

"You know Dr. Weinstein wants me to go with him to Kenya and Tanzania?"

"Yes . . ."

Dr. Weinstein was one of her private students. For years he had watched African wildlife shows on TV and video, and finally he took it upon himself to learn Swahili to put some authenticity into his African experience. Rumina had been trying hard to convince him to go to East Africa himself, and he always told her he would go only if she accompanied him.

"If I went with him, it would be a great chance to go back — I've never been back —"

"By all means you should go," and perhaps meet up with Michel there? "And if I came along too?"

"That would be nice." Then, softly: "And what have we decided about Michel?"

"Let's wait till tomorrow," he told her, caressing her hair, tucking away a strand from her forehead.

He lay on his back, thinking. Soon he became aware of her deep breathing, and he turned onto his side and watched her.

After a while, when he couldn't sleep, he got out of bed to get a glass of milk, then went and stood looking out the window of the living room. Outside, the street was deserted, two rows of lamps led off to Pier Ave and beyond. In the background, if he paid attention, was the intermittent sound of traffic on Sepulveda a few blocks away; more mysterious, from the opposite direction, the crashing of waves, the constant drumming, endless. The sky was clear.

Staring out at the cavern of the black starry night, he thought that that was surely the resting place of what was constantly being lost, funnelled away from the world; it was the repository of lost time. And so nothing was really lost after all, one had only to be able to visit that world out there and look around. In that world lay all that had been in his life. He recalled walking along an empty street at 4 a.m. with his grandmother, on their way to early mosque for meditation. He would have been ten. Uhuru Street, with a watchman huddled in the shadows every few stores, lamppost lights dimly glowing, his chappals padding *flippety-flip* on the road, hers shuffling *shrr-shrr* along it. This was the world he left twenty-seven years ago, often dreaming of returning, never quite making it . . . a world always vivid in his mind, strongly beating in his heart. Africa.

Then there was Ginnie in America. That gorgeous night together, when he lost his virginity. I *loved* you, Ginnie, I loved you . . . in so many ways. My new-found land — remember that poem I sent you, highlighting the lines. How silly you thought I was, quite rightly so; and then that day, They've scooped me out, you said, but still cheerful in the hospital bed, puffed cheeks and bald head inside that wig, so close to death. *Go where your heart takes you, you said, we don't judge you, it is a joy simply seeing you make your way in the world.*

It was unfair, to have known her so briefly and lost her. They could have talked of so many things had she lived, and laughed whimsically about the past. She would have told him what he was like then — and she would have brought him back to earth now, said something like: Ramji, you don't owe anything to the world, except to those you love and who love you. . . . I wonder what she would make of my life now?

He walked towards Michel's door, paused there for a second. Slowly he opened it, and without a sound, stepped in. There was a light from the window that partially illuminated the room. Ramji stood beside the bed, watched the younger man's breath coming even and soft. He was in pyjama pants only, and lying on his back, one leg bent and resting sideways, the other drawn up forwards, its big toe, curiously, upturned. In his arms he embraced a pillow. The day's stubble on his chin, the mouth slightly open.

What dream, what man?

Michel opened his eyes, was staring back at him. "You want me to go from your life," he said.

Ramji took a long, deep breath, his silence implying assent; then he took a chair, sat down by the bed, and said quietly: "Your father called earlier today – just before you returned from your outing with Zayd. He asked me to tell you that."

"Oh," a soft expletive, and Michel continued staring abstractly at the ceiling.

There was a brief silence between them, a moment of anticipatory stillness, and then Ramji said, in the same tone of voice as before, "How many of you were involved in that bombing?"

Michel took a moment to reply, then said, "Three."

He turned his face and Ramji saw a look of helplessness on him.

The other two who were involved with him were Shahin and Sadru, university students in Detroit. Sadru's father owned a hardware store, through which they obtained the nitrites. And Michel had blasting caps, a timer, and other paraphernalia left over from an assignment he had undertaken during his Movement days.

"So," Ramji said, "you had set off a bomb before?"

"Yes. A pro-Iranian newspaper in Toronto."

"And casualties?"

"None, it was Sunday."

And the same thing for the bookstore bombing – Michel's voice rising in pitch: no casualties were intended, the dead woman – Jeanine Summer – worked at his uncle's store, she had taken the week off and was supposed to have gone on holiday with her boyfriend and child.

He was now sitting up in the bed, his voice earnest and pleading: "I swear – we didn't mean to kill . . . just to teach the town a lesson for its hatred." He was looking crumpled and very much defeated.

"You should give up your plans for escaping," Ramji said, "and turn yourself in. Your friends and family can then arrange a good defence. There's no escape in any case, you should know that – they'll find you wherever you go."

There was a pause, then Ramji said, "Rumina. She believes you're innocent."

"I know."

They discussed a course of action, sat together in silence in the partial darkness of the room. Afterwards Michel lay back in bed, eyes open. And some time later Ramji came to with a jerk of the head, realizing he had finally dozed off. Michel was stretched out full length on the bed, sleeping.

13

*A*nd then finally it was over. He would never be able
to say, later, if the conclusion could have possibly, by different
management, turned out better or worse. He had forced the
outcome, somewhat. Was it out of some belief in justice and
accountability; or plain common sense; or fear for himself and
those he held close; or the jealousy eating into him? In the most
important decisions, in matters that involved his innermost spirit,
Ramji had never been able to be unequivocal; his inner life had
always been steeped in ambiguity and doubt. He had never
belonged to any one place entirely, not stood behind a cause or
movement without reservations; when he left a judgemental,
jealous God for the cold thrill of reason, he still could not do
without portents and symbols, always yearned for moral certainty.
The upside to this nature was a partial immunity to betrayal and
failure. And so his friend Shawn's reversal, or Darcy's diminish-
ment from an awesome and principled god to a weak old man; the
realization that Lucy-Anne had lied to him in his room – all these
came with a sense of shock, yes, and pain, but sufficiently muted.
Only in his current love had he been able to become so totally

passionate and absorbed and hopeful. Events, nevertheless, plotted out its demise with the precision of a theorem.

※

It was the day of the Shamsi Friendship Walk, which had been organized with much anticipation and fanfare by the Community, to collect money for Third World causes. Some two thousand spectators had gathered at the Rose Bowl in Pasadena to watch the almost five hundred participants of the walk. There were people from as far away as Washington, D.C., and Vancouver – friends, well-wishers, Community leaders. On the green field, a stage had been set up for all manner of diversions: a middle-aged rock band playing hits of the sixties; the president of the national Community Council giving the V-sign with both hands, reminding one of Richard Nixon in his heyday, urging people to walk, walk, walk; a jokester; a group of bare-chested Indians dancing their version of African *ngoma*. Colourful outfits and brilliant track shoes dazzled the eye. Naseem guided her Golden Club with a baton from shade to sun, drinks to bathrooms, to keep them in fine form before the walk. Among the elderly Ramji noticed an obviously uncomfortable Darcy, perhaps itching for a scotch. And the press had once again stood up Naaz, and she was fuming, clipboard in one hand, a pen-whistle and a camera round her neck. She looked ravishing, and seemed to be getting into a number of jostles and tight squeezes, through no fault of her own; and men seemed to go out of their way to greet her, hoping presumably for cheek contact.

Ramji had come to the walk by himself. He did not think it wise for Michel to spend time at the festivities, where some people might recognize him. But he did not want to leave Michel alone, either, so he asked Rumina to stay with him. By this arrangement he was also making amends to her for his suspicions and his outburst of the previous evening. During their conversation in the night, Michel had agreed that Ramji would take him to a police station the next day, Monday, in the company of a lawyer. There were a few lawyers in the Community, and Naaz could be prevailed upon to use her influence in acquiring the services of one. Earlier in the morning, Michel's father had called. Ramji had picked up the phone and explained to him what had been decided. Mr. Aziz had sounded stunned: "Are you sure?"

"It's the only way, Uncle, believe me," Ramji told him.

Michel and his father had then spoken. Rumina had been out of earshot. Ramji had not yet told Rumina about that decision, or indeed about Michel's confession in the night. She was up early and he had not had a private moment with her after that. But he was sure that Michel would tell her, and that perhaps was best.

Ramji had obtained his yellow-and-black Friendship Walk T-shirt and was waiting with a crowd of people. The president announced over the loudspeaker the names of all the cities participating in this Friendship event for Third World aid. There was tumultuous applause, and he raised both hands to lead on the cheering to even greater intensity, before gesturing for silence. He thanked various organizations and individuals, and announced the figure he expected his constituents to raise during this walkathon. A health expert came to the microphone and advised the walkers on elementary precautions to take, such as monitoring their heart rates and drinking the recommended liquids. Finally, at a little past ten, a long whistle blew, and a mass of yellow-and-black T-shirts set off behind the president. People walked for themselves or for teams. For every round of the field completed they received a

rubber stamp on their numbered cards, from voluteers. Individual
and team prizes would be awarded at the end of the event.

Ramji walked alone for a while, elated by the experience even
though he was unable to keep away completely stray reminders of
the recent events. There was a common purpose and humour in
the day's proceedings that, he realized as he walked, had quite
touched him. When he had finished one round of the field, he
found himself joined by a chatty Hanif. A little later Leila and Lata
too came over, and the four of them set a brisk pace during which
they passed Basu and Zayd. After a couple of rounds the kids left
him, and Ramji settled down to a more easy pace by himself. He
had aimed to walk for at least two and a half hours that day.

A cloud covered the sun and a sudden chill blew in the air.
This, at least, was how he would remember it, that moment when
it seemed to him that there was also a sudden silence around him,
as if the sound had been somehow muted. And in the midst of
that muted scene he found himself being approached by Leila,
who caught him by the arm and said, "Come," and then, to his
befuddlement, added, "There's been an incident, my mother's
waiting –"

"Where? What's happened?" he asked.

"Rumina . . ."

She seemed to fly off, a figure in blue tights and long T-shirt,
and Ramji raced after her, desperately, through a crowd of walkers
and towards the exits, and the parking lot. *What happened? Is she all
right? What happened?*

He lost sight of Leila but ran straight into Naaz, who took
hold of him by the forearm and said, "Come with me. I am driving
you."

"But where?" he asked helplessly. "Is she all right?"

"To the hospital," she replied. "Come –"

A police officer had been standing beside her. By now Darcy had come up, as had Basu and Zayd, and Leila, Lata, and Hanif.

"She's all right," Naaz said, pulling Ramji by the arm. "The officers here received a radio call to find you here. She must have told the police where you were."

And Michel? he wondered in a daze. Has he been captured? This is what it's all about, isn't it? How did they find out where he was?

Naaz drove him in his car, straight to the hospital, and Darcy came along with them. Naaz seemed to have got wind that the event that was now unfolding had to do with the bombing of the bookstore in Ashfield. And so, despite her concern for Ramji and her taking command so effectively, she couldn't help grumbling and chiding: Well, we got the publicity we wanted – more than we needed; I always warned you, Bapa, about your reckless statements and that magazine. . . . We don't do such things, it's not *us*! How did a bombing suspect come to be one of us, and what was he doing in Ramji's apartment with Rumina?

The complete picture of what had happened was given to them only at the hospital. Following a lead, police had arrived in full force at the apartment in Hermosa Beach. Michel refused to surrender himself, claiming he had Rumina as his hostage. Police negotiators spoke to him through the apartment door and over the phone. They asked him to bring Rumina on the line. Michel refused at first, then relented. In a shaky voice Rumina told the cops that Michel had tied her to a table, and that he had a large knife and a gun. At this point Michel fired a shot through the front window. It went clean through to the house across the street. On the phone Michel sounded frightened, desperate, and confused. He

404 ◆ M. G. VASSANJI

asked for a flight out of the country, but couldn't decide where to. Later he asked for a press conference. He was told there wasn't enough time to arrange it then, but he could talk to the media later. The police arranged to have Michel's father and his fiancée Shirin speak to him. To Shirin he said, "You should marry someone else, if something happens to me." This alerted the cops to the possibility of suicide, and danger to Rumina. Michel thenceforth refused to speak to them. His family had arranged for someone from the Los Angeles Shamsi community to come and talk to him, but the police decided not to wait. As they attempted to crash through into the apartment, Michel fired one shot, at the door. Rumina screamed. Then he fired another shot, this time at his head, killing himself. The police suspected that Rumina had been faking her plight; she had been, if anything, a voluntary hostage. She was not tied when they got to her, but she kept on screaming. She was being treated for shock.

Her eyes were open when they went to see her, in a room by herself. She was lying on her back, her head raised on a pillow and turned just a little, to face the door. Ramji saw the grief, the weakness, the helpless look; he rushed towards her side, but before he got there she turned away.

I brought Rumina home the next day. Straight from the hospital we met Darcy, Naseem, and Naaz for lunch; I thought the conversation and the company would bring her out. But she hardly ate and spoke as much, and the situation was saved only thanks to the cheery spirits of the other two women. I told myself she was still in shock, she needed more time to recover; but the image of her turning away from me the previous afternoon gnawed at me without mercy. There had been something instinctive about the gesture, it seemed to carry a terrible meaning for me that I dreaded to entertain. When we got home, I asked Rumina, Can you talk about it – what happened? and she quickly said, No, not now. In the evening I took her out to eat and she picked at her food. I cannot recall what we spoke about. We returned, watched some television, then she went to bed, taking a prescription sedative. In the morning I suggested I stay home with her. She said quite forcefully that I should go to work, she would be all right, all she needed was some time. She smiled, sounded tantalizingly close to her normal self. But did I know her then? I left with a kiss and a warm glow in my heart. I have not seen her since.

When I returned in the afternoon I found a note on the dining table: "I'm going away. I need to be alone – at least for a while. Please forgive me for the pain I caused you." She had packed a suitcase. Frantically, incredulous at first, and with growing desperation,

I called up friends and hotels, to no avail. Weeks later I found out from Dr. Weinstein that she had been with him to East Africa and back; and a former colleague at the coffee shop where Rumina had worked, and which I'd begun desperately to frequent like a crazed being, informed me out of pity that Rumina had gone briefly to Michigan soon after she left me. Why would she go to Michigan, it had meant nothing in our life together; was it to see Michel's folks? And where was she now? Neither Dr. Weinstein nor the friend seemed to have any idea.

How do I explain what deep sorrow her loss has meant for me? She haunts my existence. Doubts and questions prey on me. Did she think that I betrayed Michel by convincing him to turn himself in rather than helping him to escape? If so, why this harsh judgement upon my motives? Unless Michel now meant more to her than I did. Or is it simply that the shock of seeing a friend shooting himself in the head was too much for her. Had she no feeling left for me, that she saw no need even to explain what troubled her so much? What of our love for each other, what of all those promises and plans we made together? Simply water under the bridge? She was never like that, I will never believe that of her. In that phrase "Please forgive me" lies my salvation. She must come back.

The culmination of the incident in Ashfield, Michel's refuge with me, his death by his own hand while under siege by the police, and the capture of his accomplices received national coverage in the news media. I received some notoriety as the person who had harboured one of the bookstore bombers, and photos of the house in which I had lived had also appeared in the news. It took little time therefore for Svend to put up a shingle bearing his innocent-sounding Swedish name outside the house, for the benefit of curious passersby and to placate seething neighbours, letting them know he was not associated with foreign extremists. It was clear to me that I had to vacate; and in any case, with Rumina gone, the place was a hell for me to live in. I stayed a few weeks with Naseem in Santa Monica, then found this little place a few blocks down from her on Moonlight Drive, a stone's throw from Venice, almost, in an arrangement very like the one Rumina and I had had with Svend.

I've had my share of well-wishers here. Darcy has been a steady though unobtrusive presence, calming. We go on walks or find a place to sit at a café or on a bench facing the beach. We do not speak, except obliquely, about the Michel episode. There's nothing much left to say about it. He has generously kept me on the payroll, until I've recovered, he says, though I don't anticipate going back to work for the Company. Its sponsors have decided to stop publication of the magazine, having been embarrassed by its attraction for the book-store bombers, and Zayd has found employment elsewhere. It is unlikely that his zealous quest for that elusive and now silent Phantom Author will ever be fulfilled. That's just as well.

Naaz has been a surprisingly persistent visitor. She's seen me as a challenge, broken by grief and therefore ripe material to be brought back into the fold of the Community. But I find her entertaining, delightfully decadent and quite happy with the con-tradictions of her life.

And Leila, Hanif, and Lata – that trio from the pampered generation – have taken it upon themselves to keep an eye on me while pretending to visit the beach around here.

What triggered the tragic event that fateful day of the Friendship Walk? From media accounts, which federal agents confirmed when they interrogated me, it seems that the chain of events was set off by my phone conversation with Michel's father. As soon as I had told him that it had been decided the best course of action was that Michel voluntarily talk to the police and turn himself in, federal authorities traced numerous calls made by Mr. Aziz, several of them to his brother in Ashfield. Michel's uncle had then desperately, and only once, tried to reach Michel in L.A. This was what the Feds, who had been monitoring telephone lines in Ashfield, needed to lead them to my doorstep. Michel had already been missed, and considered a suspect, for having left Ashfield. The police had hoped that withholding his name from the press would give him a sense of false security wherever he'd taken himself to, and that he might lead them ultimately to bigger fish. All they caught was me. An outcome not entirely unsatisfactory, according to Will Jones, the man who's been my regular if sporadic companion over these last few months. Disaffections lurk right beneath the surface of our democracy, he explains; grievances against history and fate threaten to tear at its fabric; these defects in our pluralist society have to be understood by the guardians of its security.

I think of Sona and myself, as we arrived wide-eyed upon these shores twenty-seven years ago on a hot and rainy August night; I think of how very very far we have come. I was thrilled by the discovery of the new, I rejoiced in breaking free of the old, in being on my own, enlightened, unfettered. But the djinni I released with me would nag at me in perpetuity, a feeling of betrayal and emptiness like a goad upon my conscience. And Sona? He would remain ever faithful to the truth of history, like a gallant but crazed knight he would fight vainly for the sanctity of his Clio. If he stumbled, if he fell, he would always have his cloister to return to, a cocoon of ideas to hide under. I exposed all, risked everything – and became a casualty, finally, of an anonymous "phantom" campaigner not unlike him in his obsessions.

Will and I have spent many days together, tentative at first, more cordial afterwards. We've talked and quarrelled, reminisced, gone out for walks, sat at my kitchen table or dining table over coffee and sandwiches, or on the porch with a bottle of wine. We've played tennis and thrown a football. All I know of him is that he's from Kentucky, his father was a baker, he's not married.

Now that I've come to the end of my story, it's time for him to leave me. On this final day he's brought me out on Sunset Boulevard for lunch, at a restaurant Rumina and I once went to, for an evening of jazz music.

Over a light lunch we talk of many things. He's off on a holiday to England, shortly, with a woman from the local FBI office. I'd love to go to Africa and all those exotic places, he says, but (he sounds contrite) I need the basic comforts of an American. Nothing wrong with that, I say. And no, I have no immediate plans to go anywhere. Just before we depart he picks up his attaché case from beside him on the floor, holds up a hand to make me stay, then brings the case up onto his lap and flips the lid open.

"One minute. I've got a present for you."

"Oh yes? What is that?"

"It's a letter, a very special letter."

The media coverage I have received has been sufficient to bring me unexpected mail, mostly hateful, from people I did not know, but there were a few pleasant surprises. One of these was from

Lyris Unger, who had introduced me a long time ago to the Divine
Anand Mission in Newton, Mass. "You might recall our friendship
in the early seventies . . . ," she wrote. Friendship! I wonder what
she looks like now. I recall the thin girl in leather boots and brown
corduroys sitting next to me in a Greyhound bus. She lives in
Boston and for the last fifteen years has been a disciple of a Divine
Mother in Pondicherry, India.

The letters have been sent to me either at the Company offices
or at the house in Hermosa Beach, and in the early stages of its
investigation the FBI duly scrutinized them before handing them
over. It has been a while since Will last brought any mail for me
and so this letter comes as a surprise.

It is from Lucy-Anne.

It's easy to say that there is a sense of unreality about it; I don't
quite know what I am thinking as I hold the envelope in my hand,
ready to open it. But my hand gives a slight tremble, my face is
flushed . . .

Dear Ramji –

I was so very happy to discover finally where you were. I
only wish the circumstances were better. I hope it all turns out
all right for you in the end. I cannot imagine you as a part of
anything bad. Whenever I have thought about the excesses
of my own past, your example of kindness and moderation has
always been a model for me. I cannot atone enough for my
errors of the past. Our cause was just and real, and it is too easy
to say at our age that we were young and in a hurry; but we
were rash, certainly, and thoughtless and cruel at times. . . . Do
you know that Ebrahim Abdulwahab is my husband? . . . I am

a teacher here in Denver, to a bunch of Russian, Mexican, and Hmong kids, among others, and I have a couple of my own in college now. . . . Any chance of your coming this way?

Love, Lucy-Anne

Two people. One who had believed in the destruction she caused, now free to atone and make good; and another, also destructive, but naive and not quite so sure of himself – and not so well connected either – washed away in the flood.

"Well . . . ," I say. He's watching me, curiously, and so I hand him the letter and he reads it. When he gives it back to me, with thanks, I think he knows what's going on in my mind. Such has become the nature of our relationship.

"We held it for a few weeks," he says, about the letter. "We were debating whether to read it – there's still a file on her." He smiles. "But as you see, we didn't read it – until now."

Instead of driving me straight back to Venice or letting me take a cab, he enters through the gate of the Yoga Shrine further along on Sunset Boulevard, saying, "This is one place I bet you haven't looked for your Rumina."

He's wrong, as he well knows it, but it's a good place to get off and we say our goodbyes. I stroll through this green haven in the midst of the city's concrete, I walk alongside the lake with its charming windmill, the ducks and swans paddling placidly on the waters, until I reach the spot, the bench I know so well. I sit there for a long time, an hour perhaps. I feel strangely depleted, after having recalled my life for Will over these weeks, and surely also for myself. There are raw spots now, exposed in the heart. There's a thrill to their warm throbbing, yet they are not to be pressed too hard. What remains now? what new beginning, what direction? And Will's remark about this being the one place I haven't looked for her – a provocative reminder of my, as yet, fruitless inquiries?

And so I pray for a miracle. It's another half hour before I see a figure approaching round the bend, from the direction of the entrance. Her head is covered with a scarf, and she has on a long dress – and that quick walk is surely familiar? I very much want her to be the woman I've lost.

April 28, 1995

Author's Note

This book is a work of fiction. All the characters described here, the institutions called the Tech and the ISS, and the towns of Runymede, Glenmore, and Ashfield are fictitious; also fictitious are various organizations, including Inqalab International, the Freedom Action Committee, the Third World Liberation Front, and the Restore Iran Movement. The events described in this novel are all imaginary, except for the obvious and acknowledged historical ones, of which, however, I have given my own renditions. I should add that I have altered the year and some other details of the "forced marriage" episode in Zanzibar.

I should like to thank Umesh and Anita Garg, Shahbanu and Edward Goldberg, Saleem and Yasmin Kassam, Razia Damji and Jalal Ebrahim for their hospitality in Indiana, Pennsylvania, and California, and for their generous responses to my questions; Pankaj and Kishan Singh, of Shimla, and Harish Narang and Neerja Chand, of New Delhi; Fatma Aloo for whispering a story in my ear, in Dar es Salaam; Frances and Robin Davidson-Arnott and Stella Sandahl for providing refuge in Toronto; Laila Visram for the same in Santa Monica; and William and Tekla Deverell for making available a beautiful green spot on Pender Island to disappear into; my agent, Jan Whitford, for her encouragement; Mohamed Alibhai for answering many queries and Amin Malak for his enthusiasm and for putting some of my fears at rest; John Oliver Perry for a last-minute and timely response regarding Newton (Massachusetts); the MIT archives (Cambridge) and the North York Public Library (Toronto) for kindly obtaining or making available much useful historical material; the Canada Council for the Arts, for a generous grant; and also the Indian Institute of Advanced Study and its director, Professor Mrinal Miri, for their hospitality in Shimla, India.

Finally I am grateful to my family, Nurjehan, Anil, and Kabir, for their tolerance; to McClelland & Stewart for keeping faith; to my editor, Ellen Seligman, for her patience and brilliant observations; to my copy editor, Charles Stuart, for his care and for his useful suggestions; and to Anita Chong for her always cheerful and helpful assistance.